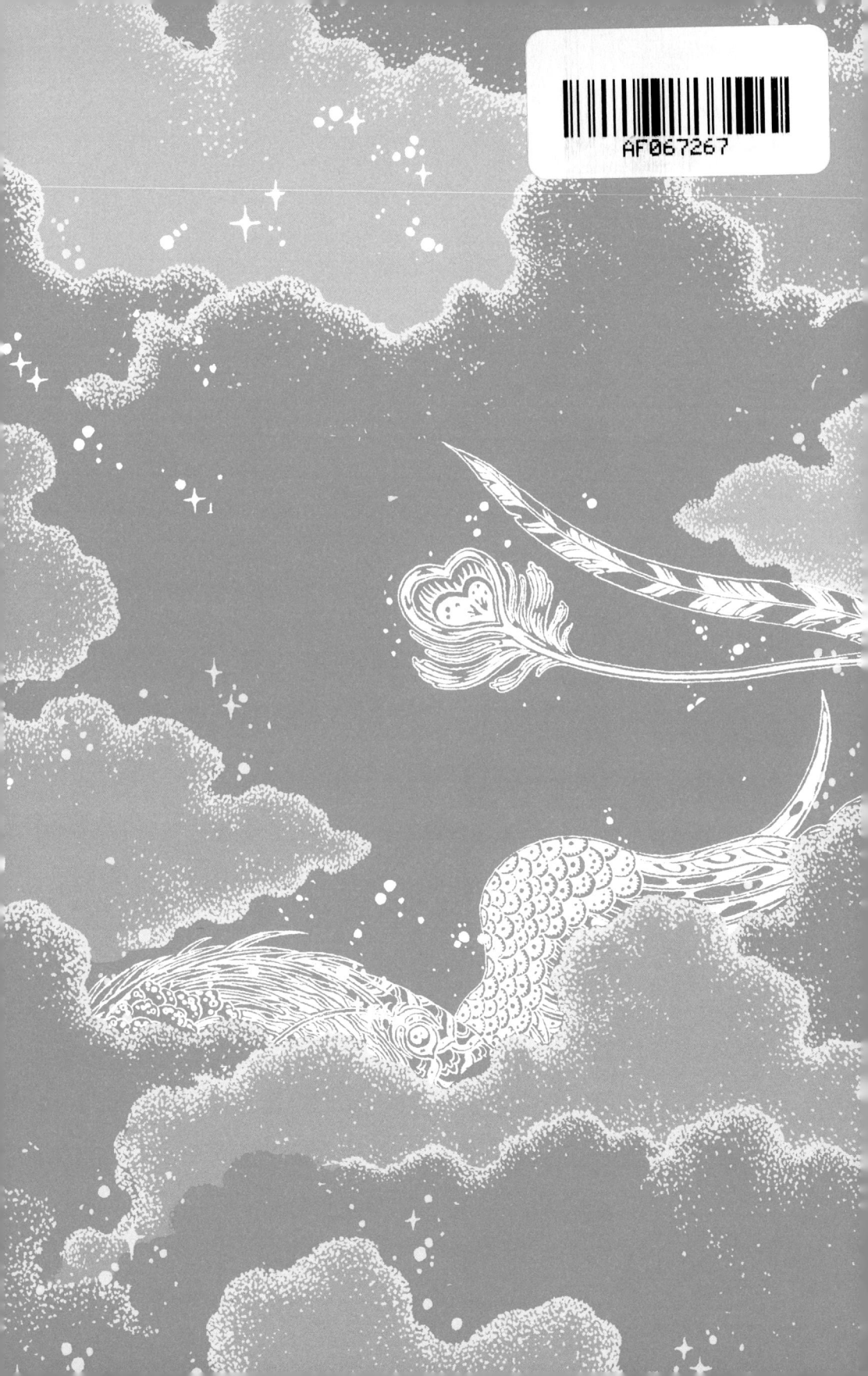

DAWN
OF THE
FIREBIRD

DAWN
OF THE
FIREBIRD

SARAH MUGHAL RANA

BLOOMSBURY ARCHER
LONDON · OXFORD · NEW YORK · NEW DELHI · SYDNEY

BLOOMSBURY ARCHER
Bloomsbury Publishing Plc
50 Bedford Square, London, WC1B 3DP, UK
Bloomsbury Publishing Ireland Limited,
29 Earlsfort Terrace, Dublin 2, D02 AY28, Ireland

BLOOMSBURY, BLOOMSBURY ARCHER and the Archer logo
are trademarks of Bloomsbury Publishing Plc

First published in Great Britain 2025

Copyright © Sarah Mughal Rana, 2025
Map © Nicolette Caven, 2025

Sarah Mughal Rana is identified as the author of this work in accordance with
the Copyright, Designs and Patents Act 1988

This is a work of fiction. Names and characters are the product of the author's
imagination and any resemblance to actual persons, living or dead, is entirely coincidental

All rights reserved. No part of this publication may be: i) reproduced or transmitted
in any form, electronic or mechanical, including photocopying, recording or by means
of any information storage or retrieval system without prior permission in writing
from the publishers; or ii) used or reproduced in any way for the training,
development or operation of artificial intelligence (AI) technologies, including
generative AI technologies. The rights holders expressly reserve this publication from
the text and data mining exception as per Article 4(3) of the Digital
Single Market Directive (EU) 2019/790

A catalogue record for this book is available from the British Library

ISBN: HB: 978-1-5266-7437-1; TPB: 978-1-5266-7438-8;
GOLDSBORO EDITION: 978-1-0372-0116-5; EBOOK: 978-1-5266-7436-4

2 4 6 8 10 9 7 5 3 1

Typeset by Integra Software Services Pvt. Ltd.
Printed and bound in Great Britain by Clays Ltd, Elcograf S.p.A

To find out more about our authors and books visit www.bloomsbury.com
and sign up for our newsletters
For product safety related questions contact productsafety@bloomsbury.com

To the children who look to the sky wishing to see stars but are only met with smoke and flames.

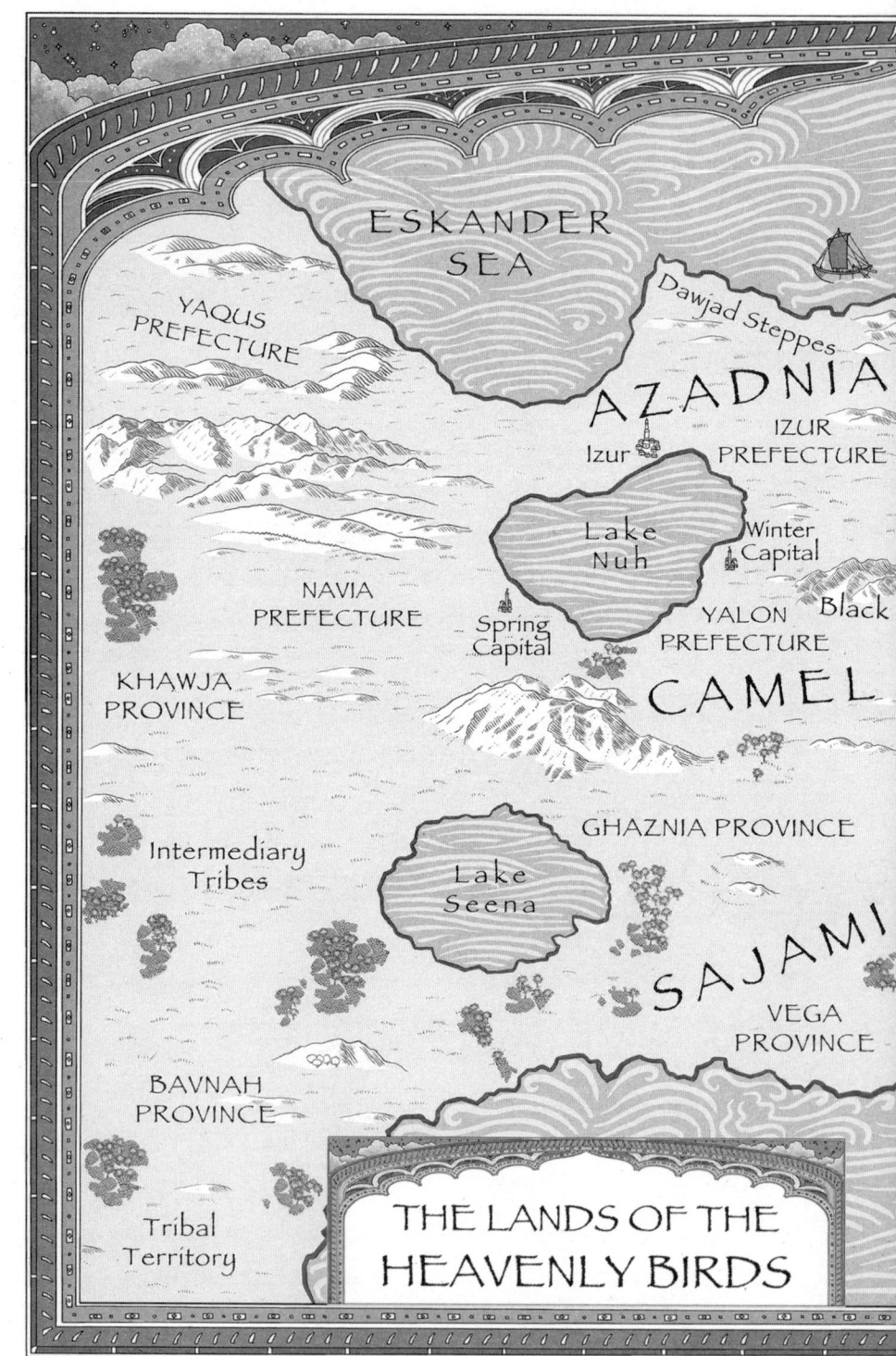

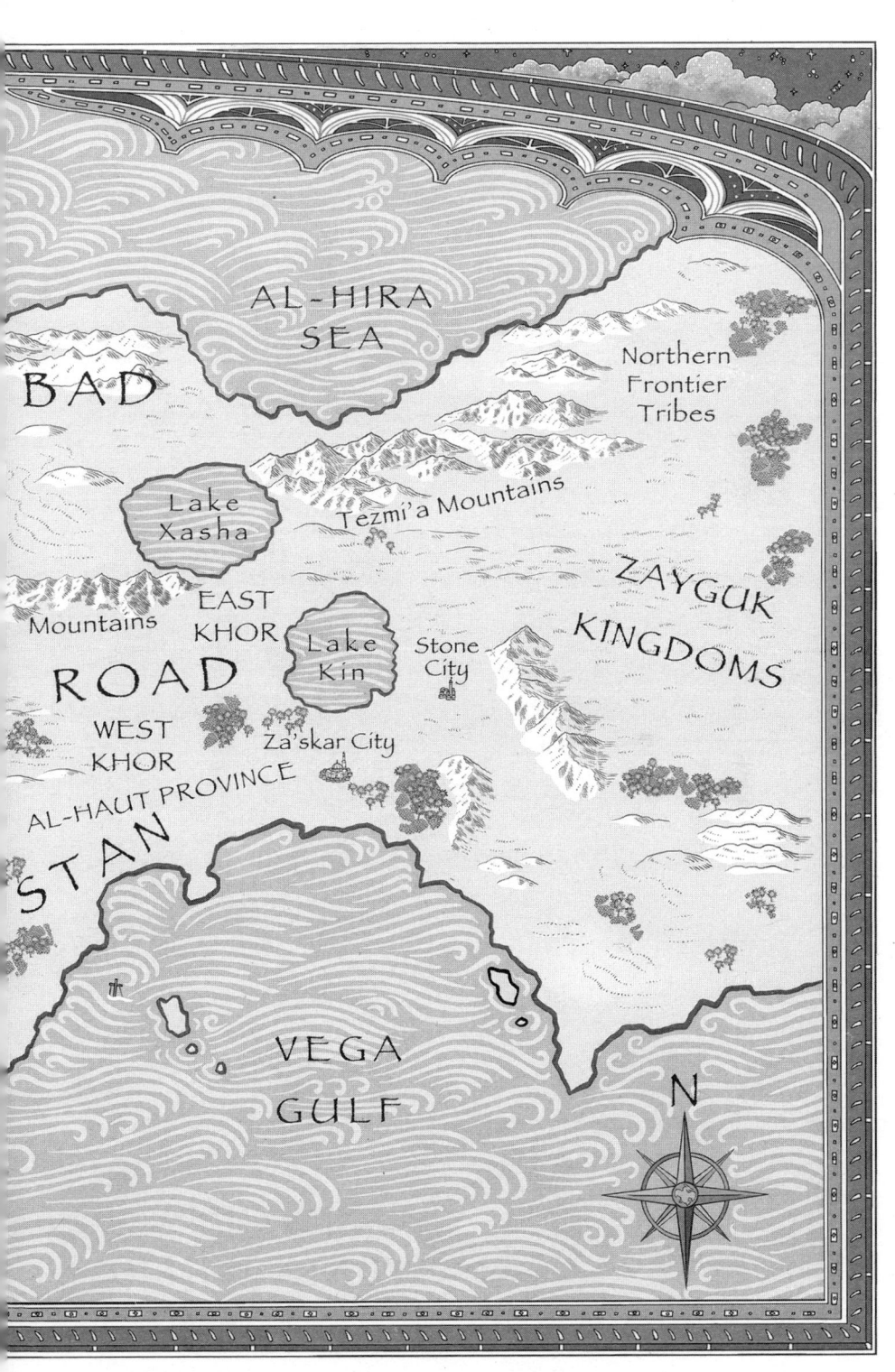

PART ONE

The Zahr Clan

The Divine Creator created us as so. Jinn are smokeless fire-beings of the Unseen world, concealed behind the Veil, blessed with physical might. Humans are the Children of Adam, moulded from clay, blessed with intellect. Jinn may perceive us, but we cannot perceive them.

We are the balance of the world. Woe to the humans who fall to the temptation of the jinn to practise black magick.

—ORAL TALES OF CHIEF FOLKTELLER
BABSHAH KHATUN, USUR CLAN, YEAR 500,
ERA OF THE HEAVENLY BIRDS

Before...

YEAR 495 AFTER NUH'S GREAT FLOOD, ERA OF THE HEAVENLY BIRDS

Tezmi'a Mountains, Azadniabad Empire

I would inherit the power of the Heavens, Uma had said so.

But my power was a curse, this she did not have to say. Like any great legend, my tale began with tragedy.

In the stories later recounted from my maternal uncle, my uma had a glad-tiding the night of my birth, as all mothers of gifted children did. It was near the winter solstice in the year 495, she dreamt of light emanating from my infant body, bathing her in a cool glow. She knew the Divine had shown the power I would come to inherit: nūr, cold Heavenly light, the same spiritual power that flows through the firebird.

But that night when I sprang free of Uma's womb, our chieftains dreamt of a world of darkness. War and destruction.

She is an omen, the tribe murmured, despite my uncle the khan reprimanding their frivolous superstitions. *Her mother refuses to name her, nor does her father, the Great Emperor, accept her. With his many wives and heirs, this child is but one of many.* But Uma knew in her heart that blessings came with a little suffering, that was the Divine's way. *My child is neither cursed nor omen. She has the affinity of light.* Uma liked her secrets. This one she tucked close to her chest.

In the spring pastures of our valley Tezmi'a, that year brought a drought that starved the lands, killing portions of herd. Other peculiar happenings sowed fear in the tribe: more raids, more deaths. When Uma suckled me, wild birds would encircle the yurt before flapping into the felt tents, spilling dried meat, spoiling the yak milk and provoking our hunting birds.

'The girl is cursed,' my clansmen argued.

'The girl is simply a girl. And we are God-fearing men,' my uncle would reprimand. 'We blame misfortune on no one but our own sins.'

'But the birds,' the tribe would insist, 'they surround the babe. She is unnatural!' It was true – wherever I was carried there was the sweep of wings above, and birdsong from the trees.

Swaddling me close, the khan's most favoured wife spoke. Babshah Khatun. To her, not one dared argue. 'Enough, you superstitious fools. She is a blessing who has brought forth more birds for hunting. She is unusual; but, unusual children bear the greatest gifts. However I hear your fear. The chief folkteller has the hearts of their kinsmen, for they carry the histories of our sorrows. As your folkteller, Divine as my witness, I will make this babe my apprentice. She will carry with her the tales of your greatest joys and fears until the end of her days.'

The stern lady, though young, never broke her oaths. In irony, her oath became my curse.

In the winter quarters, the best pastures were south of the alpine lake. That year, the khan's tribe erected their yurts and herded thousands of yaks, wild mares and lambs at the base of the harsh snow-capped mountains, amongst the rolling green alpine meadows, thin grass growing above cold dirt. From the lake, icy streams broke through the rocky grasslands of Tezmi'a.

It was my seventh Flood Festival, commemorating the day Nuh left the ark after the Great Flood. That morning, the children competed, to see whose prized hunting bird would find the keenest prey. Before long, the khan's favoured wife interrupted and led the children up the pastures until they reached the end of the settlement of tents, toward the thick woodland.

Some of the tribe's warriors, who'd escorted goods and cattle across the mountain pass for the emperor's merchants, rested against the boundary of trees, waxing their compound bows. Others sipped apricot tea to fling back the wet chill, nodding to us in greeting. The khan sat with them, my uma – his sister – beside him. When she spotted our group, Uma scowled and stalked toward us.

'O, Babshah, what senseless idea do you have now?'

Babshah Khatun merely smiled in silence. Uma placed a hand against my back, staring at the hunting birds cowing upon my shoulder. She warned, 'Do not go too south of the mountain pass. There are patrols from the enemy clans who snatch away children like her.'

Still Babshah Khatun continued deep into the womb of the valley, past protruding boulders, and clumps of elm, into the tall deep grasses that fattened the wild onagers. Trails where humans rarely ventured, and the jinn-folk still reigned. The wind whispered into the children's hair. The entombed roots of wizened trees sprawled through the woodlands, and whizzing sprites, those mischievous little apprentices to the long-passed fae of these lands, showered seeds to pollinate the flora. A deceivingly drowsy day for the violence that it promised. A place where the old ways still mattered and the Divine-made boundary between jinn-folk and human blurred.

Determined, I tripped along next to Babshah, resisting the urge to clasp the long end of her yak leather tunic, lest she think me not brave. Even my hunting buzzards on my shoulders canted their heads, curious.

Babshah sat squat and brushed her pale hand across the dirt. Her black hair swung with the wind, a dozen thin braids clasped in silver beads and an array of hawk feathers, not dissimilar to my own. The only difference was a camel-skin cord around her temple with a blue wooden block indicating her status as a wife of the khan.

'Today, we will do a new type of hunt,' Babshah declared. 'Hunting by folktelling.'

The children murmured amongst themselves, but Babshah did not elaborate. Instead, she latched on to my hand – 'Prepare yourself, my apprentice' – before continuing along the fir path.

When we stopped, and it came time for our hunting pairings, my milk-sibling Haj refused to take me as a partner. He was ten years old, only three years my senior, but the gap was large enough to fuel his arrogance. He took his complaints to Babshah.

'My uma says to stay away from her, else she will curse my bird's game! I train with a spotted sparrowhawk. The girl trains with a pair of sooty buzzards. Smaller and useless, just like her. With all the birds that follow her, she will scare away the prey.'

'I may be Ayşenör's only child, but I am not useless,' I muttered, keeping my lip from trembling.

Haj merely puffed his round cheeks and narrowed his blazing black eyes before snatching my arm. 'What did you say?'

At his intense words, my other clansmen eyed me curiously. Their parents had also warned them about the strange little girl who attracted the eccentric crows, the screeching hawks.

I held Haj's gaze. Babshah said if my tribe thought my very existence was cursed, I would prove nothing except through my actions.

'Enough, Haj.' Babshah wrenched him away. He stormed off.

I shrank behind Babshah's furred robes, but the woman was no longer my kinsman. Instead, her grey eyes reflected the anciency of a tradition spanning eons: the chief folkteller of the tribe. Yanking me out from her legs, she wagged a bony finger.

'O, young apprentice. Remember my teachings.'

'B-but they hate me, Babshah Khatun.'

She stooped to my height. 'A folkteller speaks truth through the lore of history. The people can love or curse you for it. A most severe task, not all can bear its burden. Your uma was to be the next folkteller, but she resisted and it fell to me. Foolish woman that she is, Ayşenör. *You will not fail my entrustment.*' This was the first time I'd been entrusted with anything. It felt precious. I nodded fiercely.

The children scattered into the forest to begin the hunt. Haj and I strapped our bows and arrows, to use if and only if our hawks failed in catching quarry.

We hunkered through the trails, musk deer mewing through the foliage. At the first clearing, a thin stream gusted the rocky terrain. The woodland swallowed any sunlight. My young buzzards curled on to my shoulders uneasily, digging into the furs of my tunic, a thin leather cord around one of their talons. Haj sneered at both birds. He was seasoned in his bird bondage. He didn't need a creance to tether his hawk.

Haj tied his bait to a hemp rope, recited a prayer and swung it in practised loops, his sparrowhawk flapping to and fro in powerful strokes.

Haj did not allow me to use my buzzards. Instead, his sparrowhawk caught chubby sage grouse and quails. I sat back against the trees, stroking the long necks of my birds. Gradually, I heard the voices of the other children growing louder.

'Older Brother, do you hear that yelling?' I asked.

'Who is yelling?' Haj turned. His sparrowhawk returned to his shoulder, talons empty. The bird curled its beak against his collar, shivering.

'Something is wrong, Older Brother.' I glanced about the forest.

'Of course you'd be scared,' he snapped with a frown.

The ground tremored, startling the rest of his words. The voices of the other children rose into shrill screams. Haj backed away so fast, his foot twisted against a stubborn root.

'Brother!' I clenched his arm to steady him as he fell heavy against me. My heart rattled and I brushed the bow and arrow strapped to my leather vest. 'We must go.'

He nodded. 'Your uma warned us from going south of the pass.'

We retraced our trail back toward the open pastures. The commotion reached us first. I saw the other children shoving forward out of the woodland, pointing to something behind them.

Haj gestured to his older sister Hawah. She was flushed and gasping for air as if she'd run the entire length of the valley. 'Brother, there's a beast! We must flee!'

'Flee? Where do you think you are going? My lesson is not yet finished.' Babshah swooped into the field as though appearing from nowhere, her robes flapping behind her. 'Do not run, little cowards.'

'B-Babshah Khatun. It's the same beast from your stories,' Hawah insisted.

'Which kind?'

Hawah paled. 'A great buffalo with deepest blue fur, and an enormous horn – the size of a small tree. As sharp as the khan's blades! But its eyes,' she paused, shivered and spoke, 'such red eyes like hellfire!'

'A karkadann. This is a rare blessing,' Babshah mused. 'The great horned beast from the jinn-folk roams wild in remote terrain. And, what of it?'

The children tittered in nervous laughter. *A karkadann*, the word spread. 'It will devour us,' Hawah insisted.

'Fear not, child. I have a young apprentice who will hunt it. A hunt through folktelling.'

Understanding dawned on me. I knew suddenly, as I knew to expect the rise and fall of the sun, she expected me to subdue the ancient beast. She'd brought the tribe's children as bait.

Babshah caught my gaze and her lips smirked up.

A roar split the air and the companion birds at our shoulders shrieked and cawed like a bad omen. Even a bright swarm of sprites flew past our shoulders. *Run!* I heard their high screams.

I scrambled away as a dark blur trampled through the pine trees, knocking down trunks like a child tossing clay dolls.

'Observe well, young tribesmen,' Babshah announced nonchalantly, but not before gripping my wrist hard. A forceful woman, she did as she pleased. 'Today, this *cursed* girl's training will be conveyed to the tribe. She will enchant the beast with her tongue before felling it with a single strike.'

My whole being trembled. 'I cannot,' I admitted.

The wind lashed against our backs, but the chief folkteller held steadfast against its punishment. From a cloth pouch dangling from her lambskin belts, she produced a stick of black powder and two masks. She smeared the black sormeh on the waterlines of my eyes, then strapped the wooden ceremonial mask engraved with wild wolfish features and crane feathers on to my face.

She smiled. 'You must, my apprentice. Together, we will use your training and defeat the beast with a story. Chin up. Arms long and strong. *Become* the words. Heed me, the creatures of jinn-folk are inept beings who fall for sweet words.'

My birds nuzzled into my shoulder. I stroked their beaks. 'At ease,' I croaked.

At that, the karkadann trampled forth into the field, tearing the hanging eaves of elm. A coat of fur, blue as a corpse, enclosed a thick muscular body. The beast roved in a large circle, horn casually piercing through fir trunks and slinging them away. Smoke huffed through its bloated nostrils, a silver blazing fire. The children sobbed and shrank, avoiding the sailing trees.

'Quit your warbling!' Babshah huffed at them, face suddenly serious. 'The beast scents the youngest virgin souls. Do not attract its attention.'

Before I could flee, she shoved me forward into the path of the karkadann. Only a thin glacial stream, from run-off sloping over the grass, lay between me and the beast. Its heavy hooves stomped through the icy water with such force, the water showered into a mist. Red eyes of fury tracked my careful movements. I crouched and circled it fast. It thrashed and twisted its body to follow me.

Using the diversion, I unwound my leather cord, swinging the rope. The birds at my shoulder answered, soaring rapidly over the karkadann.

Though Haj assumed my buzzards to be paltry and insignificant, Babshah boasted that twin buzzards are advantageous for size and speed, a deception paired in two.

Under my breath, I prayed to the Divine to keep me safe, for the humans, animals and jinn-folk are all under His creation. Then I ordered, 'Now,' and one buzzard dove into the karkadann's hide, its beak piercing fur. The karkadann bucked and roared, jabbing its long horn to swipe the bird. As the first buzzard, it distracted the beast.

My cord swung, and the other buzzard shot forward, raking its talons across the beast's thick neck. As the second bird, it gave the brunt of attack.

'Good, my apprentice. Now to enchant it with my story...' Babshah brushed her robes nonchalantly and drew her body straight, fixed on her mask and faced the karkadann. The chief folkteller began thus her tale.

'O, tribesmen and jinn, let me tell you a legend as old as the clay itself. Once the world was not so.'

The karkadann stilled.

'Before the Great Flood, before humans, before even Prophet Father Adam, there were the angels and the jinn.

'The One Great Divine, God of all creation, shaped the angels from the purest Heavenly light; created the jinn from the smokeless part of the flame; moulded humans from dirt and clay.

'Two creations: jinn of the smokeless fire, and humans of dirt, but both with souls and free will; and angels with none – made only to obey the Divine who created the Heavens.'

Stood beside Babshah, I scooped the wettest dirt, shaping it quickly into a human form, just as she'd taught me. Using the shadows of the trees against sunlight, I moved to the rhythm of Babshah's words. I stooped low and stalked around the karkadann, arms up, holding the earthen doll. The shadow of my form played against the ground, growing into a mean, black gangly outline of a make-believe jinn that plucked and devoured the clay doll.

My teeth gnashed with concentration. The karkadann, enchanted by my shadow, roared, swinging its horned head in response. My foot slid back. I matched its stance. Abruptly, it ceased its cry. Whether in wonder or confusion, I could not be sure.

Babshah nodded approvingly. For a second, her gaze on my shadow hesitated. *Something* in the shadow moved without me. I shook my head and continued to act out Babshah's tale, my movements becoming a dance to accompany her words.

'In a time when the desert winds whispered secrets beyond even the sea, when the only beings that dwelled were fire-imbued tribes, reigned the jinn. Those creatures of smokeless fire.

'Some were righteous, yet most harboured not love, but mischief, warring amongst themselves and spreading corruption across Brother-Nature.'

I stepped close to the karkadann, sending the children scurrying back. Their cries fell silent as it lowered its head.

When I placed my hand before the beast, my tribesmen gasped. I offered the beast my clay doll. Reflected in its red, intelligent eyes, I saw myself burning. But I wore a warrior mask, embodying a beast as well, and I stared back.

Attack me, beast, I imagined shouting.

Babshah continued her tale. 'With their powers, the jinn weaved illusions and deceit, shapeshifting to trick even their own kin. They traversed vast distances in the blink of an eye up to the cosmos; they eavesdropped on the murmurs of Heaven's affairs. Such arrogance invoked the wrath of the Divine. The angels were commanded to cast the jinn tribes into the hinterlands and oceans beyond mortal sight.'

Though its body was still, an icy white mist poured from the beast's mouth, like a river, and the cold of it stroked against my mask. Instead of fleeing, I bent my legs and leapt over the mist – as if a fire-being myself – so fast that I didn't feel the icy burn before dropping and rolling to my feet.

The crowd gasped at the trick. I unclasped my fur vest, flapping it with a whip of my arm like a crow's wing.

'Thus, the Veil between Seen and Unseen was drawn, hiding the jinn from human eyes, except when they shapeshifted into animals. Yet, they linger, tempting the hearts of humans with worldly desires away from Prophet Father Adam's and Nuh's teachings.'

I partitioned the vest like a Veil between the karkadann and myself before shrinking on to all fours.

'Shunned from the Seen world, many jinn reside in some matters of forgotten objects, from desolate mountains to needles, and under trees – from the demonic dîv to the accursed marid, to ghûls, sil'a and karkadann.'

Babshah's telling followed my silent crawl.

'Beware, young ones. Lest you fall prey to the beasts who devour souls. Or worse, the jinn's enchantments tempting humans into black magick, a type of forbidden power that does not use faith or the Heavens, but instead mischief and deceit. For once ensnared by the jinn, escape is a distant dream.'

I crawled behind the karkadann as it rumbled toward Babshah, bewitched by her tale. Had such a beast in its long existence ever heard a story spun from humans about its own jinn-kind?

I mouthed a prayer, by praising the Divine, into my hands. Then I blew across the karkadann's hide, and it writhed from the effect of the prayer, its hooves staggering before it turned around. It stamped a thick foot, readying to charge toward me.

Babshah held up one finger. *One chance*, she signalled.

I squared my shoulders and whistled for my buzzards. With a final loop of my cord, the two birds dove into the beast, swiping and raking talons. The karkadann swung its horn to swat them. With the beast's head lifted up, it charged at me.

I ran forward and propelled my foot off the nearest boulder for height. My body spun and, in the air, I notched the arrow above my shoulders, shooting backwards. The arrow buried itself into the soft underside of the beast's risen neck, which yielded until the shaft disappeared.

Babshah neared the end of her tale.

With a broken mew, the karkadann stilled and collapsed. Its body melted into the shadows, leaving only a curved, shimmering horn. According to Babshah's legends, a karkadann's horn, when ground and brewed, cured any illness.

I landed in a crouch. 'And,' I proclaimed the final words. The buzzards rose forward, and the other birds flocked into the pasture. They squawked a haunting harmony. 'Perhaps there is a jinn amongst us, sitting before the woodland.'

Without my realising, the tribe's older warriors had joined the gathering. I spotted Uma, her mouth parted in delighted shock, and the khan beside her, eyes crinkling. I couldn't recall my mother's happiness until now.

'Our jinn huntress,' the khan declared, lifting the horn relic and my hand.

'No, our folkteller,' Babshah Khatun corrected her husband.

Never had my kinsmen smiled at me. No one flinched at seeing the birds surround me.

'Sister!' Haj pulled me to his chest. My heart flapped wildly at the honorific. He lifted me on to his shoulders. 'Our folkteller,' he shouted. My milk-siblings swarmed us, echoing the chant, asking how I'd challenged the beast. My jaw ached from the urge to grin.

That day, with blood and story, I began to win the hearts of my tribe, and they mine. If only this peace had lasted.

The following year, every holy Friday after eventide prayers, I narrated stories with Babshah Khatun. As the years wore on, I grew taller than my uma. While training with Babshah, my tribesmen came to look forward to my tales, nameless though I was.

Every Flood Festival after we'd come of age to begin warrior duties, my milk-siblings engaged in the tradition of milk threading. I awoke on my thirteenth festival at dusk, peeking out from behind the folds of my tent to see my cousins lined up beside their fathers, holding thread dyed amber from mare milk, while chugging down honey-sweetened yak kumis.

Afterwards, Hawah came to our yurt, beaming with arms dyed in swirling gold, and a silver ornamental headdress woven with feathers over her braids. It struck me how her cheeks no longer wobbled; her square jaw was prominent; her tawny features sharpened out.

'Ayşenör's daughter, are you coming to play mountain polo with us? The local garrison guards are joining us,' she said.

My gaze lingered on the headdress. 'Is that a gift?'

'My dada traded for it,' she answered.

On her newly dyed arms, I saw symbols of feathers, the shape of Nuh's ark, and even seventy-seven swirls. Envy burned through my blood. Not for the first time, but with real fury, I wondered, why didn't I have a father to bestow gifts? To dye me? To name me?

'Are you coming?' Hawah asked, again.

'No,' I answered quietly.

When Hawah left, I stormed into my yurt. 'Uma,' I demanded not for the first time, 'Where is my dada? It's a holy day. He didn't thread me.'

Uma sighed and gathered a spool and needle. 'Give me your arm.'

I yanked it back. 'You dye my arms every Flood Festival, but now I wish for my dada to do it.'

Uma's brows furrowed, and even that appeared soft on her delicate features. Thin and long-necked, she was graceful like a crane. Her skin was between olive and fair, and her hair hung down to her hips in thick ebony braids woven through with buzzard feathers. She tutted her tongue. 'In all your thirteen years, have I or Babshah let you feel his absence?'

'Uma, if I answer honestly, will you be sad? You say the followers of Prophet Father Adam must always tell the truth.'

She paused. 'Nothing you say will ever sadden me.' She curved the gold thread, mixed in dye and mare milk, through my forearms, smiling to soften my hisses of pain, and that kept me from crying. The burn of it stung like salt rubbed in a cut: slow, persistent.

'If he cannot dye my arms or name me, so be it. But why have you not named me?'

Leaning over my arms, Uma shared the knowledge that was our greatest weapon: 'My daughter, you know your dada is the emperor of Azadniabad; he forbade me from naming you when I carried you in my womb. For that, one day, the emperor will give you a name.'

Azadniabad: a vast empire to the west that ruled our vassal lands. I knew why the elder chiefs worried about my existence, for I was the daughter of an emperor who'd rejected his child… it was as if I was kinless.

'The emperor must name me,' I declared.

But she shook her head, dozens of black braids bouncing wayward. 'He lives afar in his courts.'

'Then why did the emperor wed you? And when?'

'Powerful men sacrifice much for a greater purpose. The emperor sent his warriors through this mountain pass to ally with our tribe as a protectorate. In turn, our pastures would receive protection from his soldiers while we guard and escort caravan goods across these trade routes. He chose me to wed from amongst the khan's sisters and I agreed to it. I am not sure how old I was. We die so young out here, age becomes frivolous. I might've been fifteen years.'

'But if the emperor likes you, he could bring us to him.'

Uma's jade eyes darkened. 'One day we will go, God willing. But the Azadnian courts are unfit for tribes like ours.'

Uma's hand quivered against my arm, the needle bobbing deep into my skin. A dot of blood welled up and tears sprung to my eyes. Teeth clenched, I blinked them away.

'When you are powerful,' Uma murmured half to herself, 'he will accept you. Strength to an emperor is as a holy book to the worshipper. Power the only way to gain his favour.'

I stared down at my hands. What power did I have that would appease my dada, a grand emperor?

But Uma did not worry. I know now, she recalled the dream she had of my birth, the one of Heavenly light. She knew someday I'd wield the power of nūr.

'Ayşenör,' the khan interjected. We both turned as he entered the yurt. He'd been listening. Usur Khan was a stern yet young man, strong-boned and graceful like a snow leopard, with thick flushed skin that wobbled as he spoke and braided hair pulled into a rough knot.

I bowed my head. 'Peace unto you, Khan.'

'And you, niece.' He patted my cap, his beard scratching the wool. 'Indeed, the Azadnian emperor chose your uma as one of his wives. But she left out in her explanation that she charmed him with her beauty and storytelling, enrapturing him with a folktale. Cunning apprentice as she was!'

Uma ducked her head. 'Perhaps. Although he spoke admiringly of my folktelling before our wedding, it was only because his empire has lost such customs. He would not know a good telling if it told him so. After that, I vowed to never tell a tale again.'

The khan roared with laughter before facing me.

Carefully, he relieved Uma of the needle and mare milk. She stepped back, watching him curiously. He took my arm. 'Your dada is not here, but if he was, would he know how to thread you in the ways of our tribe?' he chided.

'O, Khan, we should teach him.'

'O, daughter of my sister, an emperor is on a throne to enslave the people to his desires, not for the slaves to inflict their desires on to him. An emperor cannot be taught. Certainly not by his vassals.'

My head reeled with all I did not know, could not imagine. 'But you are a khan. You are like an emperor too. At fifteen years old, you united the four clans between these mountains under your banner.'

'A khan of one tribe can hardly win against an empire. We are ants to them. When your uma married the emperor, she was shunned from his courts in a matter of weeks. His other wives and the Azadnian nobles could not bear a humble woman of the steppe-people in their lavish courts. They think us barbaric because we listen to the wind, and move with the herds, settling along the troughs of the valley and eating from the basins of the land, cultivating the little we have.'

I sank beneath his knowing gaze. 'With no dada, I do not belong here nor there. I've heard the chiefs' concerns about me.'

His finger tilted my chin. 'You are not lacking, but between two worlds. Perhaps one day your difference will be of great worth to us all.' He moved the thread, shaping intricate feathers on my reddened arms.

'Did you know,' he traced the glyphs, 'on your skin are the shapes of the Heavenly Crane. Centuries after the Great Flood, it was this ancient crane who freed Nuh's descendants, including our ancestors, from the jinn invaders. The Heavenly Crane belonged to the first Azadnian tribe. And now it's the symbol of your father's empire. When you yearn for him, look at the threading. A piece of his empire and history is upon your arms now.'

'What of you, Khan?'

He thumped his forehead against mine. 'You speak our language, tell our stories. You hold our history, and now,' he snipped the thread, 'I have threaded your arms. You carry a piece of my heart, daughter of my favoured sister.' He winked.

The wind rattled the wooden lattice of the tent, plastered by felt mats to brave against the cold stoles of daybreak. I shuddered with it. 'Then I will speak your stories with my entire soul, my Khan.'

He smiled and said, 'I traded this for you.' He handed me a pair of oxidised earrings, beaded with welded old coins and hawk feathers, engraved in swirls.

As he clipped them on, a deafening cry rang through the tents, shattering our peace, and my smile disappeared. The khan jumped to his feet. Outside, his apprentice, a young hunter of fifteen years, rode in on horseback, drenched in blood.

'A raid,' the boy gasped out. 'At the Tezmi'a gorge. They attacked the escorted caravan party and broke through the dam, flooding the northern pass.'

The khan was whisked away on to his red horse.

We followed the tribesmen into the centre of the pastures. Raids had always been common throughout the Camel Road – soldiers ravaging oasis city-states, empires vying for a slice of the trade routes. We had always been able to defend ourselves; I assumed the khan could thwart any invaders. But two more of our best archers poured into the settlement, carrying corpses. A lifeless boy was passed to one of my uncles, neck dangling back from the torso.

'Haj?' Uma cried as his father cradled his corpse.

'No.' I staggered forward but Uma yanked me back. *My hunting partner. My milk-brother.*

'And they've captured Hawah,' the archer spoke quietly. A disquiet rippled across the tents and grasslands, dispiriting even the mules.

It was not our first raid, but it was the only one whose consequences felled my closest kin. I was unable to look away. Then I was greeted with a sight even more terrifying than my cousin's body.

My stomach lurched and bile rose. 'U-Uma, what is that shadow?' I stuttered. For a darkness had sprouted from Haj's neck, writhing like spilled ink. It rose like a black serpent, and one milky white eye fixed upon me.

'Uma!' I cried out. The shadow frothed over his body like a swarm of locusts, turning in my direction.

Uma clenched my hand. 'Run inside our tent. Grab my blade. Do not come out.'

'What is that shadow?' I sobbed.

She covered my eyes. 'It's a body. You need not look.'

'But the demon, the jinn.'

'What demon? What jinn?' Uma shook her head. 'You are frightened. Run inside. And heed my words. Do *not* come out.'

Why didn't Uma see it? Why didn't Uma see the shadow atop the boy's corpse?

Belonging…

YEAR 508 AFTER NUH'S GREAT FLOOD, ERA OF THE HEAVENLY BIRDS

Hawah never returned. This was only the beginning. Raids steadily increased and with them, more bodies. Those who weren't killed were captured by enemy tribes, into marriage or servitude.

On the morning of the winter solstice, weeks after Haj's burial, Uma handed me her finest, thinnest dagger to hide down my breeches.

'If they take you, you will need this,' she explained.

I handled the needle-like blade, my heart buzzing. 'But I cannot win against older warriors. Besides, I am better with a bow and arrow. Or with my birds.'

She smiled bitterly. 'It's not to fight, foolish child. When they capture you, they will use you – as a servant, and a body. They've done it before, to plant fear in the rest of us. Our enemies are the bordering clans allied with the rival empire. They want to conquer these lands, so they conquer the people first, including their bodies. When they take you, grab this knife, my child.'

'And then what do I do, Uma?'

'Slice it right here,' she said, gentler and warmer to ease the cold suggestion, pointing at her own throat. 'It will end your life, and that is better. The enemy will never be able to keep you.'

I nodded, but a profounder thought hit me. Studying the sorrow lacing Uma's eyes, had the enemy once captured her?

Instead of asking, I accepted the blade.

Her words haunted me in the gloaming that evening as I was fastening rope around stone, my twin buzzards soaring in circles from my shoulders to the fir trees.

Babshah Khatun came beside me. 'Enough with this.' She pulled my hands aside. 'Today is a festive occasion, and our tribe is mourning. They need hope.'

I hesitated, glancing around. Because of the first raid, the flooded dam spoiled our pastures. A drought followed. With harvest diminished, trade with nearby villages at a loss, tributary taxes heightened, settlers from the west eating away at any good grasslands, and our herd thin… famine was becoming a mounting problem.

'Hope will not feed the animals nor line our stomachs.'

In response, Babshah kicked the stones, and the buzzards cawed above us.

'Babshah,' I protested. 'Uma says to prepare stones for the elders to tie around their stomachs, to stop hunger pangs.'

'Nonsense,' she said and stifled a yawn. She kicked at more rocks.

'Nonsense?' I gawked.

Earlier, I had caught Sheeth, my elder cousin, catching worms near the stream to fry. Without being able to trade for stalks of milled wheat, we dried grass and white mud to a powdery dough and used it to make dumplings. Two children died that night from hard stools. My stomach felt heavy, as if a rock protruded from my gut. Our only relief came from a flock of thin mares and pearl wheat cultivation around our river canals.

We'd always migrated in a circular pattern from southern winter to northern spring grasslands around Lake Xasha. The khan had discussed migrating further for better pasture, but the rival clans at the end of the pass would never let us settle further. Already they were hungry to conquer us, sniffing our weakened state.

'Why does the khan not ask my dada, the emperor, for help?'

Babshah stilled. 'Not that greedy fool.'

'The emperor cannot be a fool.'

'Gah.' She batted her hands. 'An overseer, a king – he could be God's chosen one and my words will not change. He needs us more than we need him. We're the important ones, guarding the routes here for his goods and tea trade, while fighting his enemies.'

'Do you hate him?'

She looked thoughtful. Her girlish lashes cast shadows beneath her eyes. 'No. As long as he leaves our tribe be after we pay him our tributaries. See, child, these emperors love our lands but are troubled at what to do with the people living on them. The seasons change, a new conqueror sweeps in, uses our trade, turns our clans against each other, tells us to attack for their sake and defend their borders, and when they're overthrown, the next overseer comes in and does the same. I've had enough of empires and soldiers.'

'You married a khan.'

She ducked her head, smiling behind a curtain of dark braids. 'I was thirteen years and he was as young too. But my khan swore he was an honourable boy and look at him now. Unlike the emperor, the khan's greed has limits. He is a good man.'

'The emperor must be a good man too. He's my dada.'

'Perhaps. I once reasoned with your uma to refuse to wed him, but if she hadn't wed him, would you be born?'

I couldn't understand much of her words at the time, about the politics of conquerors. I did understand though that only Babshah was daring enough to slander the most powerful man of our lands. I lifted my hands to hide my grin. 'I'm happy I was born.'

Babshah smiled wistfully. 'As am I. Now what of my idea, child? Let us feed the tribe hope with a story.'

'A story won't feed us,' I grumbled.

'Hope is its own sustenance,' she said softly. Her grey eyes, like weak milk-tea, warmed my soul. 'Tonight, we'll remind them about the tale of the Raven and the Crane.'

I sighed and flattened my hand on my chest. 'Order me, Babshah Khatun.'

That eventide, night struck like thunder, quick and loud – a storm cloud sweeping aside the light. I called out to my cousins from the centre of the yurts. Many of the older tribesmen trickled forward, keen on a tale to sweeten a bitter black winter's night, for Babshah was to tell a story.

The clouds hung low, a thin rime to the air that stung my eyes. The youngest clumped together before the blaze, fur shawls wrapped around their leathers. I grabbed my beryl chador, a gift from Babshah's girlhood, laying the veil atop my yak-wool cap, which clinked with beaded coins above my ceremonial mask.

Babshah too veiled herself before the tribes-people, as many chief folktellers did. A blue scarf was knotted at the top, resting down her back; red beads and hawk feathers fringed down her forehead and a silver stone necklace nestled against her throat. She sat herself at the front. Her heavy fur robes, worn and frayed, brought a comfort that eased the shoulders of the people. The black sormeh around her eyes, the only feature outside the veil, made for a chilling stare. It demanded the presence of even the wind, which sat and sighed for the tale.

My stomach dropped at seeing our tribe's dwindled numbers. Once, humans lived as long as the people of Nuh, to over five hundred years. But in these days, people only lived to two hundred. With the famine and harsh alpine pastures, our tribe would be fortunate to make it past forty.

I stood beside Babshah on the frozen dirt. She extended her arms. 'In a time when the world was a babe and the Heavens spoke to mortals, there lived a great messenger named Prophet Nuh. With a heart as vast as the ocean and a voice that echoed through the ages, for ten centuries but fifty years less, he warned his nation of impending doom. Alas, they turned deaf ears. Do you know what came next?'

'A Heavenly punishment!' I sang.

'Indeed,' Babshah agreed, in a deceptively light voice. 'The Divine opened the floodgates of Heaven and the sky sobbed upon the world. Even the clay vomited forth floodwaters, a mighty torrent that swept away humanity. Only Prophet Nuh and his faithful boarded the ark, sailing through waves that cleansed the world of its corruption. But few remember who else was on that ark. Show us, young daughter.'

I swung my arms. My gold-threading flashed before the firelight. My buzzard answered the call, shrilling as it flew around my head, its feathers drifting to the yellow grass. I hid my satisfaction.

The crowd leant in.

'On Nuh's ark were three birds sent by the Divine: a Heavenly Three-Headed Raven and a Heavenly Crane,' I spoke. 'Yet the third bird, the mighty Simorgh, wise beyond measure, soared above the ark, following its own path like us nomads, only to descend at the end of... of an era—' Something in my chest lurched, and my practised words stumbled. I grabbed my throat, hoping the crowd didn't notice.

Babshah continued, saving my mistake. 'For centuries the ark drifted, until the floodwaters receded, and the clay emerged from the depths. The Heavenly Birds sighted land, and humanity on the ark settled upon the world again. For generations, the Heavenly Raven and the Heavenly Crane accompanied a clan from amongst Nuh's virtuous descendants. Using their Heavens-bestowed abilities, the birds defended the growing kingdoms, healing wounded, battling jinn-folk and black magick invaders. But as prophets came and went, darkness crept once again into the hearts of men.'

I fell and swooped and twirled with the hawk, our shadows against the firelight re-enacting the ancient battles. When the buzzard flapped over my head, I plucked loose a feather.

'One day,' Babshah said, 'there was a monk who always fasted and paid alms-tax. His name was Eajīz. He was not privy to the matters of worldly men. But as humanity learnt black magick, and worshipped jinn-folk, naming them as deities, darkness spread. The Jinn Wars began. When his tribe was threatened, Eajīz, the monk, felt a calling to safeguard them. He prayed and recited the Divine's seventy-seven names. In answer, the Heavenly Crane and the Heavenly Raven each gifted a feather to that righteous monk. But it was more than a humble gift, for the feather bestowed seventy-seven gold bonds that connected the monk's body to the Heavens. These bonds fed him an extraordinary power tied to a Heavenly virtue. Strong enough to rival even the jinn.

'Soon other clans learned of this. Greed swept across the people. For every battle fought in the Jinn Wars, warriors plucked a feather from one of the two Heavenly Birds, granting them the same seventy-seven bonds to Heaven, the same Heavenly Energy. But each stolen feather in turn stole the strength of the birds. Such warriors, gifted with power from the birds of Heaven, were each named Eajīz after the monk, but they shared none of his righteousness.'

I drew back my hand and the buzzard descended to the grassy plain.

'After these Eajīz warriors had plucked and stolen seventy-seven feathers from each bird, alas, the two Heavenly creatures could no longer fly. They were left alive but drained by human greed. For centuries, the warriors' descendants spread across the continent, forming their own tribes and loyalties and kingdoms. That was long ago. Now the Divine chooses an Eajīz from each generation of the warriors' descendants to bear one of the seventy-seven affinities. The lines of succession are lost in the mists of time; the revelation of each new Eajīz is a gift that is unpredictable but Heavenly sent,' Babshah said.

For my next trick, I lifted my finger, directing the buzzard to fly upwards, but the bird didn't follow the action. Disgruntled, I tried again. Suddenly, it flapped away. It was not alone.

The fir trees gasped out a flurry of hawks. No one else seemed to notice the creatures fleeing, attention fixed upon Babshah.

Babshah quelled her kin with an eye. 'It has been over two centuries since our tribe has had an Eajīz in our midst. As kingdoms around us swell with Eajīz warriors, we in the grasslands are alone, attacked and starved. On this eve, glance about you. There are no prophets nor revelations in our era. Heaven has stopped speaking to us mortals caught between war. The birds and righteous Eajīz have passed away into legend. Only we, the descendants, remain, bearing their legacy. A reminder of our shared ancestry and a test of our will when given power.'

She flung out an arm. 'We must be like the third Heavenly Bird, the mighty Simorgh, who chose to fly above Nuh's ark, from one era to the next, refusing to align nor side with any war. We belong to this firebird, swaying from one settlement to the next in the cuts of the mountains. We may not be Eajīz; nor are we jinn. We are humans. We are better—'

Her voice hitched. The fire's shadows playing against the ground grew odd.

Now it was my turn to save Babshah. 'We are like the firebird. And the best of Nuh's descendants,' I concluded. The tribesmen stood and hooted in awe.

But Babshah did not move. It hit me – Babshah had never made a mistake in telling a story.

'Babshah Khatun?' I gently enquired, sniffing the wet from my nose.

Her mouth parted. A strange breeze rustled the valley, a whining sound. The people's laughter snuffed like frost against flame.

'Babshah!'

If not for the redness spreading across Babshah's stomach, I would marvel at her perfect stillness, as if winter's affair had simply frozen her in place.

Then her body tipped forward, face smashing on the hard-packed dirt. Crimson pooled around her twitching body. Behind her, the night stretched open like a dark, gaping mouth. I thought I saw flying stars across the sky.

No. Whistling fire arrows.

I had no time to run. The next two arrows clunked into my left shin and thigh. Pain ripped through me. The world blurred. I smelled smoke. I heard yells.

Arrows rained from the heavens. Someone threw me back. I saw the blurry outline of my cousin Sheeth. He crouched over me as arrows buried into his back. My mouth opened to scream. His body collapsed upon me.

Sheeth. I couldn't move. *Run!* My ears rang.

'Run!' Uma screamed, her face swimming above me.

She pulled me up and carried me toward the red horses, the youngest and elderly already there. Our tribe's warriors, donning their wooden crane-feathered masks, rode toward the raiders.

Uma's hands slipped along my waist, slick in my blood. She lifted me on to the horse before swinging on. One hand held me while the other gripped her bow and arrow.

We galloped across the grasslands toward the west of the valley, through the narrow pass.

'We must go down the mountain then west,' Uma explained breathlessly in my ear over the pounding of hooves. 'There is an Azadnian border garrison. The warlordess and her warriors will send aid; they are loyal to our emperor.'

From my left, enemies streamed out of the dark dressed in finer furs than our own, hemmed in red and black raven feathers, and on their faces were tawny animal masks with crimson beads. The raiders captured the youngest and elderly tribesmen who were riding in a group ahead of us before retreating. I couldn't let my mind dwell on what would be done to them as prisoners. I thought about the knife shoved down my breeches.

Uma's voice quavered behind me. 'We'll circle around.' But we didn't make it that far.

A row of horses streamed out from the woodlands, hindering our path. Their riders' wolf masks, decorated in raven feathers, absorbed the firelight.

'Uma,' I breathed heavily. 'G-grab the reins. Give me your bow.' Sweat collided with the salt of my tears. I took her bow and arrow. My thighs didn't possess the strength to grip the horse for the both of us. But my hands still worked. For our tribesmen, wielding the bow was as natural as breathing.

Uma guided the horse in a fast loop until the raiding horsemen were behind us.

'Now!' I heard their commander cry. Fiery arrows arced over the valley, plummeting toward us. The horse threatened to buck, head swaying.

Biting my tongue, I forced my feet through the stirrups to stand, putting the weight on my right leg instead of my left. My body was narrow; my balance still steady. *It's like hunting*, I reminded myself.

Notching an arrow, I twisted my body back. The string snapped and the arrow went flying behind. A scream seized the air.

'Again!' Uma cried and the other children ahead of us fired as well. Our warriors engaged the bulk of the raiders, but hundreds flooded the plains, overwhelming escape paths. Arrow after arrow I sank into the enemy, but it was no use.

A raider leapt from her horse and lunged across our path, sword slicing through the horse's legs. I went flying, landing hard on the grassland. Another blade shallowly carved down my lower back and, instead of air, I gurgled blood and flipped on to my side, curling up.

A hand seized my ankle, dragging me across pebbled dirt that scraped against my cheeks. Soil filled my mouth. I hacked dirt, and shrieked to throw off the enemy, my fist connecting with a rock-hard jaw.

'Animals,' I heard someone above me spit before a clog stomped hard on my wrist. I gasped out, eyes flitting upwards. The enemy climbed on top of me, pinning me in place with a sword to my neck. On the wolfish mask, the raven feathers swung with his momentum; his grey eyes reflected the fires blazing around us – and the terror on my expression.

Uma's warnings had come true. Nausea roiled through me. I dug my heels into the dirt for momentum but my wounds made it impossible. My soul warbled. My vision darkened. I felt myself float away, watching from afar.

'A cornered deer,' the raider murmured, dragging his sword feather-light down my torso, tearing into cloth and skin. 'Look at you thrash and panic.'

'No!' Uma screamed. She crawled through the grass to shield me, but another raider dragged her away.

Her scream disturbed my terror. *Her blade.* My soul slammed back into my body. With my only good hand, I fumbled for the blade against my waistband just as the raider grabbed my hips. Without thinking, my blade jammed into his belly. The force reverberated up my arms. The blade rebounded off a rib but I slammed it again. And again.

Eventually he slumped against me. His blood ran down my body as I shoved his corpse away and crawled on to all fours, then pulled the arrows out of my left leg.

The other raider, further now, hadn't noticed her dead comrade. Instead, she dragged Uma by the hair toward a tree stump. She cocked her head, her tawny mask of raven feathers gleaming under the starlight. But her dark stare, as she gazed down at Uma, showed not pity, not empathy. What had we done to make her despise us so?

'So even beasts are capable of love?' she simply asked, poising the sword above Uma.

The world slowed. Below the raider, a shadow formed. Something from the empty blackness stared at me. I think I stopped breathing. I wondered if death was supposed to look this frightening, even to a child: a ghoulish shadow. My nails clawed into the dirt. I couldn't suck in a breath.

The shadow slithered along the grass, twitching before settling on my chest. *Take me*, I mentally screamed to it. That would be better than to die beneath the enemy's sword. The shadow dove into my chest, chewing at my heart.

I gasped. My eyes flooded with tears. But my neck craned, grasping for one last look at Uma. She shuddered on the ground beneath her attacker, an arrow protruding from her shoulder. I needed to *live* to protect her.

I begged, *O, Divine, I am not ready to die, but if I do, do not let it be in vain. Save Uma. Save this tribe.*

The shadow disappeared into me. My chest unclenched, the pressure releasing until I inhaled air, the pain across my body growing. Then… thin gold lines rose up like malleable threads from my arms, legs, chest, tongue. They shot upwards as if to the Heavens. Pulsing, shaking – they were an entity of Divine making.

More pain lanced through my body and I howled. The warrior glanced in my direction before refocusing on Uma. *She cannot see the gold lines around my body*, I realised.

The threads shuddered, as if *something* from the Heavens flowed through it, into my body. A white wave of light erupted. Everything turned *bright* like the night retiring to dawn.

To my shock, the cold brightness emanated from *me*. It pulsed densely before shooting forward and cleaving the warrior like a white blade to churned butter. There was nothing left of her body but a spread of limbs, scattered.

Heavenly light, like in Babshah's stories: the power of nūr.

The other raiders turned at the display. The nūr rose in me like a torrential wave as I limped to my feet.

What struck me most in that moment was not the death I dealt out, but rather the sheer awe brimming in Uma's gaze – fear and satisfaction warring against each other. I turned to the other raiders with a strange calm, reaching into my own pain. The Heavenly light answered, cutting down soldiers until reinforcements arrived from the Azadnian village.

My fingers curled around the holy affinity, basking in its immensity. Through the carnage I felt like a stranger looking down upon myself, mind clear. *I can save them*, I thought. Like Babshah's tales, my tribe will hail me as a Heavenly warrior, a way to reclaim the glory of our steppes.

Once, the people thought I was a curse. Now I can be a blessing.

How wrong I was. When the affinity faded and my body collapsed, I looked up. I'd been too late. Our tribesmen were already dead. The dusty wasteland spread before me, the cracked ground resembling the textured underbelly of a rattlesnake. Destruction was all that was left across the grasslands, and a Heavenly power that saved no one. It breathed its cursed air, wreaking havoc until no tent, human nor beast went untouched.

As reinforcements trickled through the settlement, Uma and I stumbled back to the central pastures, sighting our burned yurts in the middle of the Tezmi'a valley.

The khan's decapitated head was staked upon a broken spear. Eyes open and suspended in death, the khan stared solemnly at the image of our own destruction as if spinning a story now in the realm of souls, taking the tribe's legends with him.

More lifeless bodies populated our settlement than any survivors. And many more must have been captured. I couldn't discern Babshah from the other bodies, all a mangle of blood. From our tribe of over two thousand, barely three hundred survived.

Eventually that day was called the Night of Tezmi'a by my people. A night of ruin.

It was the beginning of my curse: I had potential for strength, but without death I could never reach its peak.

Becoming…

Babshah Khatun, Usur Khan, Hawah, Haj, Sheeth, Mehmet, Ayslan, Habil—

The names blurred in my mind along with memories: of arriving in darkness after endless days of walking; the exchange of murmured words between my uma and a figure at a garrison; a dry room and a bowl of poultices. After days of travel with Uma, I had risen in a daze – barely registering the horses, or arriving at a gated city – before a swarm of guards led us to a quiet room of gold walls, the calm suddenly shattered by a partition sliding open, a voice from a servant announcing, 'His Blessed awaits you.'

'Get up,' Uma hissed. I rocked on the kilim rug, gazing at the gold-threading dyed along my forearms.

Babshah Khatun, Usur Khan, Hawah, Haj, Sheeth, Mehmet, Ayslan, Habil—

'Up now, child.' Uma's calloused hands gripped me.

I suddenly remembered to breathe. 'Help me,' I gasped out and my words careened through the small room. 'My head, it hurts. W-who will tell their stories, Uma? I cannot forget the names of the dead. Please, I can hear their voices, their stories – I-I must go to Babshah. To finish the folktale—'

Uma wretched me upwards in a bruising grip. Her glassy eyes like knobs of jade mirrored my own. '*Enough.* You are stronger than the dead.'

I pressed my palms to my cheeks. 'No, no, Uma, I'm not. We must return to Tezmi'a! Babshah Khatun is waiting!'

Her fingers dug harder. 'Babshah is dead! The lands of the Camel Road are not our home! *Not anymore.*'

I stilled. Behind her, a palace servant watched us stiffly from the entrance of the small administrative room.

'We have journeyed too far into the heart of Azadniabad to turn back. We will have one chance,' her voice wavered, 'for the emperor is never in the business of mercy to give more. The emperor does not know about your affinity gifted from the Heavens. But when he does, he will give us refuge. Please.' Her voice hitched. 'You have yearned to meet your dada. Today he can finally name you.'

From the doorway, the servant cleared her throat.

We followed her down a long corridor. At any other time, I would have marvelled at the illuminated floral paintings, the walls of blue silk tapestries woven through with shimmering garlands, the crane carvings on stelae, the embellished copper lanterns holding firelight, but I could not conjure any feeling, numb like frost.

Dragging my leg behind me, my braids hung like black straw around my face. We passed through a light blue marble archway with a dome at the top, painted cranes at the borders. Inside it were wide copper inner gates that guards swung open into a grand hall.

I fixated on the honey-gold mosaic tiling, smooth beneath my broken clogs otherwise accustomed to uneven mountain terrain. Two courtly-looking men flanked a circular dais, dressed in extravagant robes the colour of dried clay, with intricate teal threads and brocade waist-sashes. I'd never seen clothes like this. At the centre of the dais, a man sat cross-legged atop crimson floor cushions with gold tassels. Incense puffed smoke from the corners.

I stumbled back at seeing the man. He looked... like me. His back rested against an odd throne, as if the ivory was a living, breathing creature – vines and flora sprouted from between the niches and carvings, a creation from nature. A marble slab, dahlia flowers decorating the borders, connected the low throne to the ceiling, carved with stelae commemorating Nuh's ark. Blue domes formed a great circumference, gleaming in gold calligraphy. A carved crane's head bowed from the middle; the rest of the circle was etched in motifs of humans riding horned karkadann.

'Look at me, child,' the man's low voice ordered.

You are... between two worlds. Perhaps one day your difference will be of great worth to us all. The khan's words returned at once. Tears finally pattered down my cheeks.

Slowly, I shifted my eyes to his. *Dada*, I mouthed, but dared not say.

The emperor was a tall slender man with a cold face, neither kind nor cruel. His deep onyx eyes studied me alike. My head tilted. I had assumed I was Uma's mirror but I saw little pieces of myself in him – the tall slope of our eyes, the curliness of our hair, the angular face, the hunger in our gazes.

The emperor rested his chin atop his palm, elbow balanced on his knee. He wore a long honey qaftan and felted waist-sash with floral embroidery, its scented oil wafting through the room. The ceremonial khanjar strapped to his side was bejewelled in sapphire, while a blue outer robe pooled around his folded ankles. Crane feathers were stitched across his drooping sleeves. Covering his temple was a low indigo turban, his short black-blue curls blending into the shadows of the throne room, escaping the headwrap. His sleeves were rolled up, arms decorated with dyes in blue-threading depicting Nuh's ark and the crane upon a lotus.

Beside his dais, flurrying in a wide brass cage upon a cushioned divan, were all kinds of birds – black kites, hawks and, finally, four cranes.

The emperor sighed loudly. 'Ayşenör, let us settle this pragmatically.'

Uma stiffened at the mention of her name but did not lift her head.

'Though you've petitioned my court, asking to be sheltered in my palaces, I have decided it's best to send you to my garrison near Tezmi'a. Your people were my vassals, so it's better you return to the mountains. The garrison will be better for your...' He pursed his lips. 'Your lifestyle, your ways. Worry not, my estate is well kept, the warlordess under my thumb. If you remain here, your daughter won't survive my courts.'

My head snapped to him. *Your daughter*. Dada did not claim me as his own.

'If you wish for anything else, speak now.'

I nudged Uma but she merely stared at the mosaic tiles. 'Your Blessed, I have not returned to your capital for myself. I return for my daughter. Our enemies at the border grow stronger. The Sajamistan Empire sends their frontier clans on melees. There is nothing in the lands of the Camel Road for us anymore. Here, we can be of help.'

'Help?' He perched forward, uncrossing his legs and standing. 'I wish for your safety, but I will not tolerate foolish suggestions. My servants will escort you to the women's inner palace. Tomorrow, you depart for my garrison.'

Uma did not move. 'Look at your daughter.'

His eyes grew impossibly dark. 'You dare order me?' He stepped down but I moved in front of Uma, provoking his gaze. Visibly, he reeled back his anger, swallowing hard. 'Who are you, child, to stand before me? You shouldn't even be alive after your soul—' He paused and shook his head. 'Leave. The days your uma lived here, she nearly died. It's for your own good.'

'But—'

He turned away and swept a hand. A guard tugged at Uma.

'Don't touch her!' I cried out.

'And what will you do?' The guard appraised me.

As I did the day of the raid, I reached into the well of pain inside my heart; I begged the Divine to bestow the affinity once more. My chest unclenched. A gold line sprung out from my palm, and white light expanded through it. It shone around me, making the guard stumble away from us.

The guard lifted her mask. The nūr's light was reflected in the black of her gaze. She turned to the equally stunned emperor.

'The girl is an Eajīz,' the emperor murmured. It was not a question.

I clenched my fist and, with difficulty, the light sputtered and dispersed. Uma's gaze found the emperor, finally pinning him in place on the dais.

'You see?' she said quietly. 'I returned for her.'

Oh. Uma had bided her time, for this.

Only at her side, could I feel her trembling body.

The emperor's keen gaze tracked the remnants of light. 'No, you've both returned for *me*. Come forward, child. Show the nūr.'

Sweat beaded down my face. With difficulty, I churned the light but it sparked listlessly and disappeared, my weak control evident.

He cupped his chin once more and glanced at the second guard, who I realised was not a guard at all but a courtly adviser. He swept forward. He was young, hair shorn close to his scalp. He leant toward the emperor and glanced at me, and then, oddly, gestured toward the cage of birds beside the dais. At last, the adviser stepped back and the emperor bent a stern gaze upon me.

'I have three wives who I've treated equally, bearing me a dozen heirs. I have seven children much older than you, formidable warriors, with my eldest daughter at twenty years old preparing to progress my clan. But you wandering thing… you are not raised in our ways. You do not understand my people. And you speak the court's dialect with difficulty, I hear in your rough accent. You are merely thirteen years old. What do *you* offer me?'

My brows knitted. Out of the corner of my eyes, the darkness of the room stirred, the fabric of space inhaling. Gooseflesh puckered down my arms. The shadow I witnessed on the cusp of death appeared behind the emperor, waiting as it had by the grave.

I did not wish to die. But a persistent keenness kneaded through me, an urge that made me feel as if I was observing the microcosm of this moment from afar. Somehow, from the shadow's presence, I knew that if I made the wrong move, I would be killed. I was afraid to even blink.

'I-I can learn,' I said, daring to look at the emperor.

'Anyone can learn.'

I had nūr, and that made me valuable. But perhaps the emperor would find a child he could not control as equal a threat as the foes at his borders. Perhaps he feared one day I might turn against him. What did he want?

'I am nothing,' I answered, kneeling. 'I am unlearned. I do not know my letters. I am blank. But a blank canvas can be written according to its scriber. My destiny is in the hands of the Divine who has led me back to you. So write me as you please, Dada.'

He inclined his head, satisfied. 'Tell me how the raid on your tribe made you feel?'

'Helpless,' I spoke softly. 'I thought the khan was mighty, but he fell quickly, like a struck boar, and they impaled his skull on a stake. We were surrounded.'

It hurt to say. Though recently there had been raids, famine – ill mares, elders scooping tough stool from our bottoms, mouths that tasted of ash – there had also been the quietude of the valley, our steady drowsy movements through the gorges, the hunting birds, the stories of Babshah, the gold-threading from Uma and the khan. There was a miserable kind of happiness in those memories. I missed it.

Tears spilled down my cheeks. Dada brushed a thumb under my eye and examined the moisture impassively. 'You weep.'

'Yes. I-I am remembering.'

He crouched until we were level. 'You must forget. These memories, they will weigh against you, as a sin burdens the soul.'

'Forget? But Babshah... Usur Khan, milk-brother Haj... the dead? Babshah said a folkteller must carry the history and sorrows of our home—'

'Home?' He swept away the tears. 'This is your home. You were a Zahr from birth.'

'A Zahr?'

'My clan,' he explained plainly. 'Now it is *our* clan. Just as the original Azadnian clan united clansmen into a circle under the throne, swearing to protect these lands... we, the Zahrs, now rule and protect Azadniabad. From enemies like the ones who raided you. We carry the Heavenly Crane's mandate.'

'How many enemies?' I choked out.

'Other kingdoms exist, other empires, other rulers. Sajamistan Empire is encroaching at our borderlands, but they are one of many. Do you wish to be protected?'

Without a doubt.

He pulled me close and the shock of the embrace heaved a gasp through my lips. 'I can protect you. But you must forget the past.'

Forget, I heard the whisper. *Yes, I can forget.*

'Forgo your tribe. Their reminder will bring you pain. Here, you will no longer be alone. My monks will train you as an Eajīz. But you must never breathe a word about your nūr to anyone else – not your cousins, not the clan. That you wield nūr is a threat to my wives and heirs' power in the courts. When you are older – stronger – *then* we will reveal your Heavenly affinity,' the emperor explained. 'The only ones who will know are my advisers here: one is my eldest son, and the other is my brother – your uncle Hyat.' He swept a hand to the young adviser, and then the older-looking man flanking his low throne. 'This is our secret. Can you keep a secret? It's my first task for you.'

I nodded feebly.

'I ask in return that you must swear to protect Azadniabad just as I shall protect you.' He pulled back. 'Here you will bring glory to our clan.'

Without my dada, I would be nothing. I would be made to return to the steppes, and Uma and I would die as nothing, alone. Worse than death was living without a legacy to carve upon the world. Bowing my head, I vowed to gain his approval.

The emperor raised his palm.

'Last night, I dreamt my court's crane flew to my fist, looking to the Heavens with its right eye. My Chief Dream-Interpreter,' the emperor pointed to his son, 'is a monk. He interpreted that when an emperor has a dream of his courtly bird in such a way, it presages a disturbance in the realm's affairs: a good or bad omen. It's no coincidence that you arrived at my doorsteps the very next day. You are the fulfilment of that dream. Let us see what you prove to be.'

Behind him, a crane fluttered in the brass gilded cage, creaking a broken tune.

The emperor held out his hand to me. 'When I strike my sword, what shall you be?'

'Your blade,' I answered.

This would be the only time my dada smiled upon me, for once not an emperor, but a father pleased with his child.

I

YEAR 508 AFTER NUH'S GREAT FLOOD, ERA OF THE HEAVENLY BIRDS

Yalon, Winter Capital of Azadniabad

The glow of dusk spills through the stained-glass portrait towering over the throne room as the emperor of Azadniabad sits cross-legged on the circular throne with a blade gripped across his lap.

Once, Uma told me that a story can be found on the palms of one's hands. Are the hands soft and supple like a naïve sparrow bird soaring high on its first flight? Or are the hands rough and scarred like a hawk set on seizing its prey?

Studying the emperor's marred hands as he unsheathes his dagger, I think, *hawk*.

I stand behind a wooden divider that partitions me in the women's quarters behind the throne room. In the three days since our arrival to Azadniabad, I've been stowed inside the royal monastery, under the monk's care.

Today, the emperor will declare my existence to his courts. I wonder if he will give me a name.

I watch him through the latticed partition, as he lifts his khanjar blade to his temple.

Before him, seated in a honeycomb formation, is the Zahr clan in their entirety. My mouth dries as I lean to get a better look at my new clansmen in such neat, fine attire. Warriors garbed in heavy dark blue and gold qaftans with sewn crane feathers, pale felt capes dragging at their heels and thick bronze velvet waist-sashes, stoop below the throne dais. With a fisted hand at the torso, they incline their heads. Amongst them are young women with their curly hair loose, or in half topknots, pinned with crane feathers – not at all the thin, long braids of the girls I grew up with. Even their peculiar jewellery is made up of flower garlands woven intricately into bangles, dangly earrings and head ornaments. And there are some shrouded in headdresses and veils – the oldest and wedded court women, it seems.

Every clansman, from young to old, bears an ivory-hilted blade strapped on to their right arm. Even from a distance, I see a flash of blue-threading dyed along their skin: cranes, arks and lotuses, in the designs of this empire.

'Forged by blood, bound by duty, I offer my soul by the white blade,' the clan chants, pressing their blades to their foreheads.

'… Slave to the Zahr clan,' the emperor finishes before folding his hand over his fist, circling it above his belly: a greeting of peace in Azadniabad. It is strange to me how these customs mimicked the movements of the Heavenly Crane, who represented a circle of life according to the monks.

As the emperor proceeds with his session of court, I step back from the partition, wincing at my tight shoes. Moccasins of delicately beaded leather and woven crane feathers; strange and beautiful, and yet much too small for me.

'Must I wear these– ?'

'Hush.' Uma stands before a wide mosaic mirror in the chamber, tightening the knot of her modest headdress. 'Look and learn, if you wish to be a part of your dada's court,' she orders me. 'Soon you will have a Zahr blade.'

'If the emperor does not have her head first,' my attendant bemoans quietly from behind us, catching our gazes in the mirror.

'Nonsense, Andaleeb,' Uma says with a scowl.

'Have a look at her and tell me she isn't a disgrace.' My attendant glances at my attire. She had buttoned me into a qaftan of indigo linen falling in frills to my ankles; white puffed sleeves were adorned with floral embroidery. Around my ribs, she fastened a velvet waist-sash entwined with lotus patterns.

I ripped much of it off.

With a pleading look at Uma, Andaleeb waves her hand. 'We have time, still. Let me change your daughter before she offends the great martial clans. I begged her to wear the Zahr clan's clothes, but no. The girl's braids are like your steppe-tribe; she covers our qaftan with *your* tribe's leathery vest; there's even a stain of blood on it! Worse, she wears her khan's hat.' Andaleeb glares up at the tetragram-shaped yak wool, the last symbol of the khan's reign. She snatches it off me. 'Wear the Azadnian one.'

She holds out a conical cap with a singular crane feather. To my grief, she even touches my silver earrings gifted by the khan. 'And you must remove these. They are crooked and cheap; they do not belong to the floral jewellery of the capital.'

'You are wrong. I wear your garb. But I also wear pieces of my tribe.' My hand grazes the lotus shawl of this empire, tucked under my vest of yak and camel skins. 'My clothes are a marriage of both worlds.'

'Why so stubborn?' Andaleeb studies me in disbelief.

I glance into the mirror, gnawing at my lip to keep the tremble stiff. How could I explain this to her? That, despite my promise to the emperor, I cling on to my past as much as my future. I should not have survived the raid. Do I deserve to live? No. But I vowed to carry the stories of the khan and their ways. Babshah would say to forget would be a betrayal.

'She is a stubborn one,' Uma agrees, less concerned.

'You are encouraging her?'

'Not at all,' Uma says, but she purses her lips and I know she is lying. She wants me like this, as if the parts she'd left behind in the Camel Road are in me now.

My attendant shakes her head with a perpetual frown that, in the three days of being here, always seems to deepen at the sight of my presence. 'This will cost you, girl,' she warns me. 'The different branches of the Azadnian courts are protective of their own. And in the eyes of the great clans, you are a foreigner, a barbarian from the pastoralists. You must *earn* your clan's loyalty. Not open yourself to attacks. And if they try to kill you along the way,' her lips curve down, 'then you must thwart their threats before they strike.'

'My own half-siblings would hurt me?' I glance through the partition in disbelief.

'These are Azadnian clans. They use the bounties of nature and clay – both in healing and in weapons – like flora, herbs, plants… *poisons*. The

Divine only knows how many times the emperor's siblings attempted to assassinate him when his mother favoured him for the throne. Seeing how you act now… his wives would not hesitate to kill you.'

A faint nausea takes hold of me. This is normal to them all. Death. Deception. My chest clenches, a fierce longing for the routine under Babshah—

I tear myself from the thoughts. 'Worry not,' I tell my attendant. 'In these three days, the emperor trained me himself in poison tests. He told me it's the weapon of his courts.'

Without replying, the attendant turns toward the lattice gaps in the partition, watching the court procession. It passes long and slow. A weekly ritual, which many nobility join for. I struggle to make sense of it, grasping only that subjects from far and wide petition the Zahr clan's elders, the emperor's being the highest court for the most pressing petitions. He waits and listens, and his scribes write furiously into bunches of rolled papyrus. It ends with a long prayer and the court gates shut behind the last subject with a creak.

At last, the emperor orders, 'My Zahrs, at attention.'

The attendant drags us from around the partition, toward another light blue archway into the throne room, so low, in fact, it forces people to bow their heads as they enter. The attendant informs me this was intentional on the emperor's part – and in case of an attack.

We walk toward the centre of the court, into a gathering of women who are wearing nearly identical clothing to Uma. These must be the emperor's other wives.

Now out from behind the partition, I see the familiar throne room. Unlike felt yurts, the surroundings are hard walls. Above us, looping cobalt domes refract dapples of waning sunlight. Below the ceiling are thatches of thorned vines and blue wildflowers that crawl along the cupola niches of the great hall's ivory walls toward the throne, as if the plants are living creatures.

Dark shapes move against the branches. *Birds.* Diminutive chirping blue tits, fluttering black francolins and ivory myna, and delicate halcyon birds perched upon the branches of olive trees breaking from the brambly throne. I do not see a source of dirt nor water, as if magick courses from the crane throne to the quivering roots.

The court is filled with the gathering of notables, lounging on rich white felt rugs and divans under the olive trees, drinking rose tea from palm-sized glasses. Some hold long sticks of lavish hand fans, fashioned from blue parchment decorated in coins; and others speak with scribes, small doves perched on their shoulders.

The interior flings rays of setting sunlight. My reflection refracts in the stained glass, the radiant blue like a vast lake from Nuh's flood, and my lips curve up.

Gooseflesh rises up my arm, for in my reflection my lips do not move. In the reflection looking back at me, my eyes grow darker and, I swear to the Divine I see a familiar shadow behind me. At once, I move back, tripping over my feet.

'D-did you see that?' I hurry toward my attendant.

'Pay attention,' Andaleeb snaps, turning me to face the throne.

The emperor steps around a divan supporting a cage of courtly cranes. In the reflection of the emperor's heavy black eyes, the trees and flora around the dais shimmer.

'Peace unto the daughter of my fourth wife, third child of the Usur tribe, who has returned to Azadniabad at my order. After thwarting Sajamistani invaders at the Tezmi'a pastures, and protecting our borderlands, the child has proven worthy of the Zahrs.' The emperor turns to appraise me and pauses in disbelief. Murmurs spread amongst the court.

'One of us?' speaks a grasping woman standing beside Uma. 'The girl is dressed like her people instead.' Another voice to my left asks, 'Might she be confused about her loyalties? Her place?'

The emperor's eyes, like sodden ink, stare at me. 'She knows her place well, Dunya.' But his gaze sweeps over the animal-skin vest, then my hawk-feathered braids before settling on my face in a silent rage.

I must appear so odd to the clan ruling these palaces, a creature who does not belong. In the cold pastures of the Camel Road, our stitches were simply the product of our hunts, and a lesson in necessity. Whatever staved off frostbite the best, whatever was best suited for hunting – dyed camel skin stuffed with feathers, humble leathers, tawny and crimson hides. Here and there, we'd trade for textiles, but not as bright or fine as even the garb of these palace servants.

Looking back at the cool stares of the court, I do not flinch, accepting my pathetic effort.

A woman steps forward and the other wives part to allow her. The emperor called her Dunya. She appears as pure and pale clothed as a crane. Her face is concealed by a white veil and a headdress covers her hair trimmed by teal glass beads. A velvet sash is tight around her round waist.

She lifts her sleeves to her face, and laughs behind them, the sound devoid of warmth. Beside her, Uma shoots me a warning.

Dunya beckons me forward. From her arm, she unsheathes an ivory blade and uses the edge to tap my hat. 'There's no need for the fur hat of the khan's tribe,' a subtle tap at the threading upon my arms, 'and you bear the gold-threading of the steppe-peoples. It's charming, but conflicting loyalties in an emperor's daughter are a dangerous thing,' a tap at my braids, 'and you do not look like a Zahr. Even your hair bears the scent of the pastures. In fact, you might as well be one of our enemies from Sajamistan with the way you reject the symbols of your father's empire. Child, were you forced upon us?'

I glance at the emperor but he remains quiet. Uma is silent too. My body flushes as the clan stares ahead blankly. At the back, head bowed, my attendant has a knowing glimmer to her eyes, sending more heat shooting through me. The khan once declared I am between two worlds. *I must make a choice*, I realise.

'To celebrate this daughter's arrival,' Dunya declares, 'we will feast after the fast is broken.' The clan murmurs in agreement, and at the wave of her hand, stands. As the court disperses, Dunya tugs at my sleeve. 'Go to my daughter Zhasna. You will eat in our circle tonight.' Her smile of triumph is not directed toward me, but at Uma.

The dining quarters are a strange affair. The room is long with several circular low-tables. All the nobility are sat at different circles, with my father at the far end. Zhasna, who had introduced herself after her uma's invitation, guides me to the centre of the carpeted room, to a low-table layered in extravagant red linens. I pass by the cross-legged forms of other clansmen. Zhasna points out cousins and half-siblings. There's Yun, the second-eldest son of Dunya; Azra, another heir; then cousins upon cousins. Jirjis, Nahid and Belzzar. I lose count.

Zhasna waves at a row of advisers, and a visiting warlord from a western prefecture. I recognise Hyat Uncle. The advisers glance at me curiously. But the warlord seems to stare and stare.

'Why does he look at me like that?' I shiver.

Zhasna glances at him quickly, lips twisted in distaste. 'It's best you avoid that warlord. He is Akashun, Wolf of the Khajak prefecture.'

Then Zhasna pulls me to a floor cushion across from Uma and Dunya. I learn Zhasna is older than me by two years, with a sweet voice, and more forthcoming than her cold mother. She's shorter, rounder and healthier than me, with light brown eyes like brewed cinnamon-bark tea.

'Peace,' Dunya says to Uma and me. 'We break fast here every eventide and dawn.'

Despite my nerves, my eyes widen at the delicacies arranged on the circular tables. Servants carry brass trays and long meat skewers. There are mounds of ghee-greased mutton sprinkled with rose petals and crumbled pistachio, and blue-patterned ceramic bowls of steaming pilaf, the rice spiced with saffron and turmeric and lamb yakhni broth, garnished in bursting apricots and fat, oozing sultanas.

Baskets upon baskets of long, ribbed crescent-shaped flatbread the length of my torso, dusted in black and white sesame seeds, are placed on woven reed mats. I touch the braided wheat on the edge… the lines resembles feathers. And at the centre of the flatbread, a stamp of a firelotus carved by rooster quill, unlike the rounder flatbreads we'd traded for in the Camel Road. Servants follow it with tall copper saucers steaming with green tea.

Zhasna places before me a small plate which smells like medicinal apricot seed and bitter berries. Then Dunya heaps slivers of the mutton kebab, rice and a red stinging buttery sauce on to my plate, along with the crescent-shaped flatbread.

'Is all of this for me?' I say, thinking it impossible.

Dunya smirks. 'Your kind was reduced to what they hunted or traded for. In Azadniabad, we've the bounties of our prefectures. The capital imports its mares and lamb from the shepherds of the steppes. The flatbread is from here, the breadbasket of our empire. The western wetlands grow our rice…'

I hardly pay attention to her long-winded answer as I tear off a piece of bread, ghee melting into my hand. I pray and blow thrice on the bread and pass it forward to Uma. But Zhasna grabs my hand as other clansmen begin to stare.

'This is not your tribe in Tezmi'a anymore,' Zhasna says quietly. 'My uma told me of your strange traditions out there, high up the mountains. You bless the food thrice and pass it forward to your kin. And you eat seated before the hearth.'

My lips break into a smile, hearing Zhasna describe the familiar customs. She meets my eye, and her gaze softens. Her next words are hesitant. 'Here, we allow the eldest mother to eat the first bite, as a sign of respect. *We* do not break the bread first.'

'Why?'

'We follow the crane's ways. Once, the bird clans – like humanity – nested in solitude. Then the Heavenly Crane called other cranes into families of circles under their Bird King. Even in battle, the cranes, the most graceful of birds, attack in intricate circle manoeuvres. So we learn from them: we eat and drink, together in a circle with other clans.'

'All of this is… confusing,' I admit only for her ears.

Something wavers on her face. 'It must be,' she agrees. But behind her, there is a dark expression in Dunya as she watches our exchange. Like an omen.

At each table, the eldest women break the flatbread with a short prayer. Even at the emperor's circle, surrounded by his officers, he awaits an old-looking crone, more ancient-appearing than even the spirits of Babshah's tales.

After Dunya breaks the fast in our circle, people begin conversing and eating. I stare at the excess of food on my plate. 'This is too much.'

'It's all for you.' Again a hesitation in Zhasna's expression. *Something is wrong*, my instincts heckle.

Across from me, Uma wraps a flatbread around a shaved sliver of mutton, and dips it into the shared sauce bowl. She holds it out for me. But Zhasna swipes it away.

'Mmmm, there is nothing tastier than what an uma hand feeds us, right?' She winks.

'She does not need her uma's hand to thrive,' Dunya interjects, biting into a thick hunk of kebab. 'Eat, child.'

It sounds like an order. I clench my jaw and scoop the raisins and meat into the bread. Just as I am about to bite into it, Zhasna bats the food from my hand and it spills across the table.

'Zhasna!' Dunya scolds, glaring at her daughter. 'Eat,' she repeats to me.

This time, I scoop the food fast, chew and swallow. Zhasna does not meet my eyes, though an uneasy expression crosses her face.

'How do you like our food?' Dunya asks.

'Good, Second-Uma.' It is finer, less greasy than what I'm used to in the grasslands. After a moment, my heart races and I double over.

'But you look unwell,' Dunya presses.

My stomach turns again but I wash it down with piping tea. The nausea does not subside. Bile floods my throat but I swallow that down as well. My heart kicks up faster and faster like a restless horse.

I stand hastily, the room swaying. My palpitating heart, the urge to vomit my stomach's contents, the black dotting my vision, the muscles in my torso spasming...

I turn to discover Dunya staring baldly like a hawk. Zhasna leans against her, eyes blank. Though we've dined from the same trays of food...

The truth scratches at me. *It's my plate*, I weakly piece together. The poison must have been swiped across my plate before Zhasna placed it in front of me.

My knees shake. I fall over.

'Emperor!' Uma shrieks. The chatter of the hall dampens. The emperor stands and servants rush forward.

My head lolls backwards on the felt mats. Cries erupt around me. I stare unblinkingly at the lucent domed ceiling. The carving of a hunched crane seems to smile lovingly down at me. My hands convulse, and I raise them. A spiderweb of blue spreads between my fingers. I wheeze, but my throat constricts. Something grows at the base of my mouth, like a stubborn rock. I squeeze and scratch at my own throat, nails tearing into thin skin. The thing in my mouth grows, blocking any air and my eyes widen. I need to breathe.

Servants flip me on to my side, pounding my back.

The emperor stands above me, a grave frown stitched across his lips. I expect anything but the utter mortification spreading across his person. He is embarrassed.

The daughter he proudly introduced to his imperial court – to his clan – was dressed like a barbarian, was poisoned easily, was dead before she finished her first meal, I imagine Dunya exclaiming.

Tears press at my eyes. Time seems to still. I feel, in horror, my heart ebbing.

A dark shadow emerges from my chest, spilling on to the carpet, the same milky apparition I saw on the night of my tribe's slaughter. The shadow's face is featureless, save for its eye: white and forlorn like a full moon. It points at my heart. *I want to live*, I scream, but in this odd in-between state of life and death, I am soundless.

The dark shadow dives back into my chest. A warmth spreads through my limbs and air slowly trickles back into my mouth. My senses return briefly.

Servants are carrying me into the apothecary quarters. I am laid on a floor-bed. The emperor speaks to a healer but I cannot make out the words.

The emperor shoves two fingers into my mouth. Something black and chalky, like the clay dumplings I would scavenge and boil in hunger, makes its way down my throat. My eyes twitch and images float before me.

I am no longer in the apothecary. I lie in a felt yurt, shivering in front of a circular hearth, a warm hand against my temple. From the flames, long shadows dance against the woollen mats beneath me.

Hope is its own sustenance, little warrior. A voice echoes, belonging to a young woman with grey eyes and a sharp tongue. *Live to tell our hopes, folkteller.*

My tribe is alive. They are nursing me to health.

'I will,' I vow to her.

'You will what?' a harsh voice breaks the poison-induced imaginings.

I blink hard and return to the cold chambers of the apothecary, the stinging scent of herbs in my nose and the pale gold arches above me crawling with vines.

The emperor swims before my vision. His back is turned to me. 'You were poisoned by someone in my court. You will have more such enemies,' he explains calmly. 'I thought you were clever. I even trained you in poisons in private.'

'But... we trained for only three days,' I stammer out. I wish he would face me – embrace me like a dada should.

'Repeat this.' He turns, and what I thought would be concern is in fact a stewing anger. 'Three days? Three days is enough time to be clever. I trained you myself. I warned you of our customs. And still you fell for an obvious trick before my entire court. My other children are not so foolish to trust a stranger's hand that feeds them. They self-study; they anticipate their enemies. In Azadniabad, we are the deception of the

Heavenly Crane, mastering nature's offerings in healing, and weapons through its *poisons*.'

I try to sit up and grasp his hand, but the emperor moves back.

'You've mortified me. You are no Zahr-zad. I took pity on you because you are an Eajīz who defended our borderlands against the Sajamistan Empire. My mistake. I cannot promise you more of my attention, nor training. I have warlords who pay fealty; petitioners, notables and prefectures to keep in check. You will leave at once and reside in my eastern garrison until you are older, wiser.' His words crawl into my fears.

We both know who poisoned me, I wish to scream. Instead, the charcoal makes me vomit into my own lap.

'M-mercy, my Emperor,' I wheeze out.

His smile is a knife edge. 'The charcoal and clay suction I fed you will not be enough for such a fast-acting poison.' The emperor lifts a stub of arak root and begins chewing on it. 'In a few minutes' time, your limbs will be paralysed. Try moving now, daughter. You cannot.'

His hand reaches beneath his velvet waist-sash, and retrieves a small pot, dangling it. 'Fortunately, the apothecarist examined your food dish and identified the poison. This pot is the antidote.'

'Antidote,' I repeat, willing my fingers to grab it, but my senses do not obey. I want Uma here but I am alone. There is only the emperor and his will. 'Please, Dada.' My eyes reach toward him. He is my dada, for that I trust him. He will save me. He will not inflict pain—

'Strength,' he says quietly. 'You ache for the balm? You must know the poison. You have three tries to guess how you were poisoned.' His eyes reflect the night. Sweat dampens his forehead. He wipes it. 'I warned you, daughter. I told you to forget, to destroy your past life and make yourself anew, for me. For the clan. Yet you presented yourself to my court like… like the barbarians who know not structure, order. Our way of living. And despite our poison training, you've fallen to its weapon so quickly.'

In my panic, I swallow my saliva instead of regurgitating it, choking again. But the emperor simply stands and watches, chewing on an arak root dangling crookedly from his mouth, hardly concerned that his child is being strangled by the poison below him, clawing at her neck, begging for the balm.

Think. I recall the smell from my plate, of apricot and… *Why hadn't I connected it?*

Somehow I gasp out, *Buckleberry juice with ground apricot seed,* but the toll of the poison makes my words a knobbed jumble.

The emperor slumps forward, a faint relief in his outward breath as he holds out the pot.

'Correct.'

2

The first wife of the emperor is a wretched, hard woman. The next day, she wastes no time in seeking me out in the apothecary quarters where I recover on a floor-bed. It's the sombre grey hour before sunrise, when other mortals bend forward in prayer and plead for mercy in the sacred dusk. But she must find that beneath her.

Dunya perches on a divan near my floor-bed, observing my recovery with thinly veiled interest. She orders away the palace physicians and tells them to let me suffer.

I am ready for her. I did not rest. In the long terrible night, as the winds screeched through the palace grounds, and my heart alongside it, I curled into myself, holding on to the mortal body I had almost left behind that day. *Make yourself anew.* That I could do.

I'd imagined cleaving parts of my soul, wedging the memories of my childhood on the steppes, into the darkest abyss of my being. I'd lifted a finger and channelled my affinity. Using my anguish, harnessing it, I stroked a flicker of nūr that arose from my hand.

Then I turned my affinity against my heart, for it had become clear that in order to survive I had to be my own enemy. I instructed that cold cosmic light to shatter all that I knew of my past life – the bloodied memories, the painful folktales of the tribe and Babshah that haunted me.

And now, before dawn, I glance at the brass mirror on the wall opposite. I lift my hand and tear off my last reminder of my tribe: the tetragram-shaped cap. With that, I rip out all that made me who I was before.

For a second, my reflection in the mirror changes. For the barest moment, something plays into a shadow behind me. I place my hand down. My reflection in the mirror delays the movement, staring amusingly at me.

I jolt and my reflection is normal again. I unwind the dozen braids of my hair, reminding myself: I am not the daughter of the khan's sister, apprentice of the chief folkteller.

I am a warrior of Azadniabad, Empire of the Heavenly Crane, eighth child of the Great Emperor Fatih, child of his fourth wife Ayşenör.

And so, instead of cowering beneath Dunya, I match the gaze of the first wife of the emperor. Clench the waver from my jaw. Fist my shaking fingers tight.

'Second-Uma.' The title tastes as wrong as her black soul. 'The emperor must know it was you and Zhasna behind the poison. I will not bow beneath you. Poison as you must. I swallowed it. I live.'

She waves her hand. 'Stupid child, you cannot even walk properly from your wounds. I did you a favour.'

I grip the hem of my qaftan, nails tearing a hole in the blue mulberry cloth. Behind her, the brass mirror reflects our positions, her on one end and I on the other.

'Azadniabad is the symbol of the Heavenly Crane – we are one with our sibling, Brother-Nature. Even in violence, we act as the crane, deceptive but with grace.' She smiles with teeth. 'So you see, the poison wouldn't have killed you. If I wanted to be done with you quickly, I'd have used a faster-acting venom. My dear little bird, this was a warning. The opportunity to run. Take this as a sign to flee back to the snivelling shepherds who grasp the horses, walk with your nature and speak to the wind. Listen to how you talk in that brutish accent; you butcher the refinement of our tones. The emperor is mortified by your presence, so much so, he had you stowed for three days in the monastery with the senile old monks. An empire is not fit for the likes of your wild kind.'

'Second-Uma, what of your kind then, the type to poison unsuspecting girls?'

'Yes.' She is brazen. She stands and paces the length of the apothecary, her silver earrings, woven with white jasmine flowers, swinging with the momentum, incense billowing around her. Her fingers brush veins of plants crawling along the patterned niches of the marbled wall, juniper and cherry puckering the stems. The tang of medicinal herbs with fruit makes my head hurt.

'You've already wasted your chance in gaining the emperor's favour. It's best you return to whatever remains of your uma's tribe. Or do you want another taste of my poisons?'

It's the easiest answer yet. This is *my* father's court, not Dunya's. I refuse to lose another home – another family. I will choose a clan and it will be this one. I've seen worse monsters than a mere poison.

After Dunya departs, I retch into a clay pot, my stomach spasming from the remnants of the poison. I wonder if I've truly lost my only chance to call this palace my home. I place down the pot. *No.*

Waving down a passing attendant, I order them to bring me the clothes of the Zahr clansmen, for I have the emperor to convince in my favour.

With the attendant's aid, I prepare myself. Under a conical wool cap, my curly hair is loose and oiled, one thin plait woven with tassels of crane feathers and jasmine flowers. My raw silk qaftan is buttoned, the hem embroidered in gold flora, matching the younger clansmen. I tighten a bronze velvet waist-sash, a pale cape falling down my back.

I stalk from the apothecary into the palace corridors, roiling with cold-faced guards and slaving officers barking orders. I find a hall of steep ivory cloisters winding up to the administrative complex of the palace. On each side, carved openings bestow great views of the palace grounds below me.

The capital is a series of fertile lowlands ribbed by the carcasses of green mountains, bringing a clash of chilling wet and fog. Rising from the clouds, the ziggurats are closely set within the palace grounds, constructed of limestone bricks, painted in blue embossed glyphs that trail in whorled circles, portraying Azadnian history: battles of ancient beasts, angels flying to aid humanity, and the Heavenly Crane leading the first Azadnian tribes to thwart malicious jinn.

Two aži, the winged serpents, slumber inside deep moats surrounding the imperial quarters. Open sehans bisect the pomegranate and poppy gardens, surrounded by towering geometric walls, with a blue axis pond at the centre of each private courtyard. Even in the far distance, the sun beams down on the city interface of tightly stacked sandstone homes, unlike the scarce stone villages of the Camel Road.

At last, I reach a pair of inner gates under a vaulted dome, with an inscription of silver calligraphy across the blue tiling, as if the cosmos were laid bare above me. I do not know my letters. I ask the guards if this entrance leads to the throne room.

'Yes, Master Zahr.' They bow, and I shift uncomfortably at the action.

'This is the holy eighth gate of obedience, in the Central Ziggurat, reserved for attendants and bureaucrats,' a female guard explains before nodding me in.

Inside, on the left side of the corridor, the emperor is before the gates of the throne room, walking in with his advisers.

'Dada,' I call out, tripping over the cape of my qaftan.

He pauses at the low entrance but does not face me.

'My Emperor, please. Bless me with another chance.' I reach for his hand but he bats it away.

'You broke your first promise. Why should I believe you?'

'I did not understand before. But I understand now.'

Poison was the court's weapon. Yet there were more frightful things than envious children and sadistic wives. I recall the enemy's sword poised above Uma. The raider pinning me to the dirt, pawing his hands all over me. The famine that dwindled us into a shell of our glory. The aftermath of a pillaged tribe. I shake those reminders away.

'Test me, my Emperor,' I croak. 'I made myself anew.'

His head inclines slightly, taking in my clan attire.

Without pause, the emperor turns and summons the attendants for food from the palace kitchens. They return with a tray of soups, and flatbreads stuffed to the brim with minced meat and potato. It smells enticing. A test.

Inside the throne room, we bow and fold on to kilim, the brass tray of food between us on the rug. A cage of cranes rustles behind the emperor.

On the tray, his calloused hands slice the crescent-shaped flatbread into fourths. He passes me one piece.

Poison. This is a better, kinder enemy, I accept. So I take the bread.

My tongue prods at it before I have a bite. Chewing, I study the emperor. His brows are drawn together with crease lines on his sandy skin, earned from years of rule. The tense posture of his body is a taut bow, eager for release. I roll the bread over my tongue, reducing it to mush, recalling the poisons I'd studied for three days under the emperor.

His patience worn thin with my silence, he opens his mouth.

'Wait!' I plead. 'I think I've figured it out.'

Clenching his jaw, his gaze touches mine briefly. 'You think, or you know?'

His words are a test. I must choose my next ones carefully. 'I know, Emperor.'

Bending forward on the kilim, the frayed sunburst of threads providing a slight buffer against the cold stone of the floor, he assesses me. An unmasking gaze chipping away at any strength.

'Choose as if it's a matter of life or death, daughter.'

Choice, a fickle concept; an illusion served on a golden platter. Sweat pools against my neck despite the chill. Thin slivers of red, raised skin from raking my nails across my skin are etched against the column of my neck.

Blood trickling down your chest; bile searing your tongue mixed with buckleberry poison, your limbs slackening—

My neck quivers at the memory. My fingers ache to itch my scabs. But no victory is achieved without pain, I know this well.

'Choose,' the emperor snaps, the past and present winding into his tone.

I spit the bread on to the tray. 'There is barley, millet and rock salt.' I pause.

He waits.

'But there is also knapweed ground with red scorpion poison.'

Outside the wind roars, rattling the throne room, as if Brother-Nature is warning me not to provoke the emperor's wrath. For a tense moment, he stares, aloof. His obsidian eyes suck any courage from my soul. He's watching for any hesitation – any weakness – to reprimand. A heartbeat passes before his face suddenly breaks.

'Correct.'

Before relief can kick in, he passes me a bowl of yakhni, then another flatbread and a stuffed pastry. I chew and regurgitate it all. I stammer through naming the poisons laced in the food, the same ones he had me study in my first days after arriving. It's a simple circumstance. A small mercy. He *wants* to bestow me another chance.

Eventually, the throbbing ache in my head dulls. The emperor's tests end. He reclines back on his cushion, considering me in a new light. His voice drops tartly. 'Do you finally understand the consequences of failing?'

'I would die.'

'By whose hand?' He raises a brow.

My second hesitation. 'Y-your enemies.'

'No. *Your* enemies.' He drums his fingers against the tray. 'Tell me, who poisoned you?'

'What?'

Now his brows furrow. 'Last evening. Do you recall who poisoned you?'

My mind recedes into the jaws of that memory, while my body remains in his grip, panic in my heart. It returns in fragments. Amongst it, wisps of Zhasna beside me, warm. And that is it. The emperor ordered me to make myself anew. All the gruesomeness, gone in a second. I think I'm forgetting how it felt to be poisoned by my own kin.

I... I do not remember. And I am relieved.

'I cannot remember. And that is better.' I bow my head.

'You truly do not recall? Perhaps it's the effect of the poison. Though I've never seen this happen.' He pinches and lifts my chin, exposing my thin pale throat, veined and bruised. His finger brushes the scabs tenderly. 'My suspicion is Dunya and Zhasna. I have no proof. We all ate from the same platters of food, tasted by the poison testers.'

'Does Dunya suspect...' my voice lowers, 'that I'm an Eajīz... and wield nūr?'

'Let us pray not. Or else, she wouldn't hesitate to outright kill you, as many of our kin have done to others out of jealousy.' His shoulders shake at the musings as if it is all one great jest. 'If you are to survive my courts, you must gain Dunya's affection. She is my first wife; my children with her are my best warriors. Our eldest daughter is a powerful governess in the south-east, groomed to be my heir. You will suffer as Dunya's enemy. But as her ally, you will live blissfully.' He brushes his hand against my cheek. 'But you also have mightier enemies to contend with.'

'Like who?' I say thickly.

'The clans who raided your uma's tribe. They are loyal to Sajamistan, the Empire of the Heavenly Raven. Sajamistan has many armies. But their most powerful military is an Eajīz battalion, recruits trained by their oldest martial arts schools. An entire elite army of warriors like you, blessed by the Heavens. Leading them is the strongest Eajīz: the Sepāhbad-vizier, a general of generals.' His eyes recede as if gazing out at the future. 'That is who you will train to be. Not equal to our enemy. Instead, more powerful.'

'I vow it.' I drop my head.

'Go rest. Tomorrow begins your real training – constant training. I've not the time to teach you. But the monks will. Remember what I've said. You must earn this clan's loyalty.'

He dismisses me. I loosen my clenched fingers and press my hands to my face. As the memories of the poisoned meal come howling back, I wonder: do children in this palace swallow poisons as I must?

3

I return shortly to the apothecary and a physician cleanses me of any residual poisons. Before long, a familiar monk enters and I recognise him as the Chief Dream-Interpreter. And the emperor's eldest son.

At seventeen years old, he is a tall young man of blunt features and a hard jaw covered in a thin shadow of a beard, with shorn hair like raven-feathers as dark as his stark eyes. His white and mustard-yellow robes flow to bony ankles, the sleeves hemmed with delicate silver lotus embroidery. A pale girded waist-sash yanks tight around his long-limbed frame. A strange brightness exudes from his light brown skin, like Heavenly light. A sign of piety and fasting.

'Peace, Younger Sister,' he greets, a circled fist above his belly. I return it. 'Forgiveness for my uma. She likes her cruelty as much as she favours her poisons.'

I pause halfway in my bow. 'Y-you are Dunya's son?'

'Well, I was her eldest. But as a warrior monk, son to the faith and student to the 1000 Wings of Crane Monastic School, I've forgone all material relations of this temporal world. Now, I remain only the Chief Dream-Interpreter of the court.' He bends at the waist slightly, with a grin. 'And good riddance. Having Dunya as a mother is inviting cruelty.'

I glance around, wondering what ears in the palace will convey his insults. 'She will hear you.'

'Let her!'

I decide I like this half-brother of mine. 'Well, she is cruel,' I agree carefully.

'The emperor instructed me to train you in poisons and in your...' he lowers his voice, '*affinity* as an Eajīz. But be careful now, little bird. This palace is a vulture ready to swallow its prey. Fear not. I know Dunya and her tricks well.'

'I thought I'd train with warriors. But you're... a monk.'

He raises a brow and before I can blink, he's behind me. A khanjar blade that I hadn't seen him unsheathe digs into my back. 'I'll have you know I was the clan's most promising martial artist before I abdicated. Besides, the senior monks are great warriors.'

'Dunya says the senior monks are senile and old,' I say quietly.

'Have you no respect for your elders?' he gasps.

'N-no, I mean, yes! I respect all elders,' I protest before I feel his body shake against me in silent laughter.

'Try to fight back.' He prods the dagger harder until my back aches. Instinctively, my hand raises, and I fall into the well of pain resonating from my back, going deeper until I find the hurt, the grief – the fear of losing another place to belong. My hand shudders before a wisp of nūr materialises at my fingertips. The silver light hardly flickers.

Older Brother chuckles. 'At least summon the affinity. You cannot even threaten me properly.' He releases his blade.

'Even if you know the martial arts, you aren't an Eajīz. What do you know of affinities?' I retort.

'Well, I hadn't anticipated our first lesson starting so soon. By God, you're greedy.'

'First lesson?'

He crosses the room and takes an agarwood incense stick from the burning fumer. Before I can react, he shoves the incense close to my mouth and I choke, ashy smoke clogging my throat, puffing out of my nostrils in a seething burn. Just as quickly, he retracts it.

'Lift your hand,' he orders calmly. 'Breathe the incense inwardly and say any prayer.'

My throat and eyes sting through the smoke. 'Mad monk, I-I think *you* need the prayer.' I cough and sputter.

'The prayer is not necessary, but for a novice Eajīz like yourself, prayer will focus your attention. Any prayer to the Heavens will suffice; it could be spoken or said silently in your heart. It could be stories, poetry, odes about holy warriors, the Divine's seventy-seven names or any remembrance of faith.' He shrugs.

'I cannot say a prayer; I can hardly think through this smoke,' I wheeze out. Instead, I reach desperately into the pain – the fear quickly rising – and my nūr sputters from my fingers.

'No.' Older Brother seems to read through my efforts. 'You are reaching instinctually into pain, *again*. That's an unreliable method to summon your affinity, it corrupts the soul. Think of the Heavenly Crane. To summon, you must nurture your relationship with the Heavens through humility and prayer. Repeat this simple prayer in your head: *Most Abundant, Most Merciful, strengthen my affinity's bonds with the Heavens.*'

He waits. Reluctantly, my eyes shut. Through the cloud of incense, I obey him.

A pinch in my finger forces my gaze to reopen, revealing a small burst of white Heavenly light: nūr.

I gawk. Then, unexpectedly, a gold line rises out of my finger into a thin shimmering rod. The gold line lifts upwards like a stem, plunging into the apothecary's ceiling and disappearing, as if immaterial. It seems separate from the nūr.

Everything vanishes – the pain pressing against my throat, the fear, the tightness in my chest, the loudness of my thoughts. It loosens. A strange quietness engulfs my senses like I am beneath water. My hand jerks but the gold line remains above my finger.

'How do you feel?' Older Brother asks, almost in wonder at the nūr.

'Like… like my soul is no longer in pain,' I gasp out, my nerves thrumming as if the Heavens were plucking at the strings of my heart.

'With prayer, your attention is honed and your emotions at peace, strengthening your Heavenly bonds. That's how you summon your Eajīz affinity,' he says. 'Think of a seed planted in the dirt, it sprouts roots upon roots. Roots carry nutrients to the stem. For every Eajīz, your roots are your bonds with Heaven. The bond carries energy from the Heavens to your soul to summon the affinity. Without bonds, you are not an Eajīz. This is your Heavenly Contract.'

Sweat breaks against my neck from maintaining the nūr. 'I'm confused. Why did you shove incense down my throat?'

Older Brother gives a secretive smile. 'You doubted my ability to teach you. Incense and meditation are other forms of prayer to help a novice expand their Heavenly bonds. And I wanted an excuse to poke you with a stick.'

'Mad monk,' I mutter.

'Your affinity is nūr: cosmic light,' he continues. 'Every Eajīz has their own affinity, different from each other, depending on how Heaven chooses to bless them. There are seventy-seven total affinities.

Every affinity comes from the feathers of the Heavenly Birds, creatures connected to the Heavens. And thus, as an Eajīz, you are bonded to the Heavens and the blessed birds, and therefore to nature.' He glances at my hand and then away. 'I wish I could see your Heavenly bonds. I've only read ancient codexes, accounting the earliest affinities of Eajīz monks.'

I reach out to graze the thin gold line, but my fingers pass through the incorporeal bond. Older Brother watches the light on my palm, and a glint – of awe, maybe envy – flashes in his gaze.

'You cannot see this gold line above my hand?' I ask.

'Which line?' A frown pulls at his lips and his next words come out quickly. 'Is it your Heavenly bond?'

I close my fist and the white nūr disappears. 'Nothing.' I cough out more incense through a glare. He could see my nūr but he cannot see the bond above my hand. Perhaps only other Eajīz can see them.

He does not push the matter and instead whisks the incense stick against my hand, once and twice, sure and fast, as if to remind himself that I am real. Then with a shake of his head: 'An Eajīz in the flesh. And she is my sister. The Heavens have truly blessed me.' His grin seems to grow. He might be happier about my affinity than I.

Then he crosses his arms, smug even. 'Still believe the monks are senile fools?'

'I never said that,' I mumble. 'Perhaps they know a little bit.'

His eyes widen along with his smile. 'Stubborn! I think I like you, Younger Sister. The monks here are the only ones you can trust, for they've taken a Heavenly Oath to keep your affinity a secret. If they break it, their souls are condemned in this life and the next. And the monks have the ancient texts on the Heavenly Birds memorised. For instance, if you'd lived here, I would have long ago seen the signs that you are an Eajīz for myself.'

'Which signs? I know sometimes birds followed me. And the tribe's chiefs had strange dreams about my birth. Some thought I was a curse.'

He nods. 'You aren't cursed and those signs aren't special. Many Eajīz were born with birds flapping about them, trees speaking or the stars reading peace. It's a glad-tiding from the Divine. After a few years, the signs cease. If you'd been raised here in Azadniabad,' his voice drops with a softness that sounds regretful, 'the monks would have known quickly. Your maternal tribe didn't know better… they can't have had an Eajīz for over two centuries. And now they're gone.'

I flinch but Older Brother does not notice. 'You are in good hands here. Several Eajīz warriors have trained under the senior monks.'

'There are other Eajīz here?' A sprout of hope blossoms in my chest.

He scratches his head. 'Well, there are only a handful in our entire empire. Unfortunately, most Eajīz reside in the bordering land of Sajamistan, our fiercest enemies. I know the eldest monk in our spring capital is an Eajīz, long retired from battle almost a century ago. But no, there are none presently here in the winter palace.'

'A century ago,' I breathe.

He leads me out of the apothecary as I mull over this information. I ask, 'Did you tell Dunya about my affinity? Is that why she hates me?'

He bends down until we are level. 'I haven't. She doesn't hate *you*. She hates what you are. She quickly realised a new daughter of the emperor who is related to a khan is a threat. A child raised in the harshest alpine valleys, who learnt to hunt before she could speak, from a tribe that thwarts the threats at our borderlands… you could be a formidable martial artist under the right guidance. Poison was her way to test your resilience. But how you respond matters more than your past.'

'How shall we respond, Older Brother?'

'In kind.' He smiles with confidence before rolling up the velvet sleeves of his white and amber robe. 'With poisons, little bird.'

'More poisons,' I say reluctantly. We enter the main corridors and I struggle not to step on his robes.

'I've been informed you do not have a name?'

I shrink away. 'I am waiting for Dada to name me.'

'I can name you. Steppe-buzzard seems fitting.' His eyes twinkle.

'No. I've waited years for Dada to do it.'

'Very well. The emperor wanted to name me Fatih, after himself. But Dunya refused and took me after her dada. Eliyas.'

'Eliyas.' I taste it. 'I like your name.' He tucks my hand close into his arm and I wonder if this is what it's like having a real sibling.

He pauses abruptly in the corridor. 'Come out. Enough hiding.' From the stone pillars garnished in white-dotted dahlia, a familiar girl squeaks, then peers through the flora. Zhasna.

I startle back but Eliyas holds firmly. 'Do not run, little bird. I will not let her hurt you again. I ought to lash her for her cruel actions.'

Zhasna draws straight, addressing me. 'I-I tried to stop Uma. I didn't mean to poison you.' The girl's eyes are wet, and she wrings her hands into the pleats of her milky qaftan.

'Yes, you did,' Eliyas snorts before he scruffs at his thin beard. 'Dunya is like that, using her children instead of dirtying her own hands.'

Suddenly the girl's tear-stained face, coupled with memories of the previous night and the soreness of my poisoned stomach, brings me up short. My hands form into fists. Zhasna is probably lying. I was naïve to think I would find friends amongst the other young clansmen. They only see me as an outsider – a threat. 'If Dunya wanted to poison me, she should've used a faster one. Maybe the bristles of a yellow-spotted caterpillar.'

Zhasna opens her mouth and closes it. 'You are strange.'

'You are the stranger for poisoning your sibling.'

Wordlessly, Zhasna turns away down the corridor. Eliyas glances between us and sighs long. Watching her flee, my heart twinges in what feels almost like remorse.

Eliyas takes me to Uma who awaits us at the monastery between the outer and inner palace gates. The inner palaces are inside a circle-shaped wall, and outside that are the outer grounds with the paymaster, storehouse and scribe offices, eventually leading to hilly paths toward the central capital.

Behind the stone-bricked walls, an expanse of trimmed gardens holds delicate shrubs of glittering berry bushes and gnarled frankincense trees. On our way, Eliyas points out the polished stone of floral-themed stelae. Marbled monuments contest for space with honey-amber and blue geometric tiling.

I pause, recognising one, and Eliyas runs his hand against it. 'The art of our winter capital is a homage to the creatures of the Unseen world – the jinn-folk – because this prefecture borders Sajamistan, and their architects were obsessed with the jinn. This stone relief is a karkadann. The first Azadnian tribes rode out on the beasts, to battle invaders during the Jinn Wars. Finding a karkadann in the hinterlands is rare. It takes months to tame—'

'I know about karkadann,' I interrupt without thinking.

Eliyas pauses. 'How?'

I try to cling to the sudden memory, but a fog descends in my mind, the images cloudy. 'Never mind,' I mutter, and we continue along.

Other statues we pass depict tall, winged warriors with large pointed ears – the Heavens-condemned parî, creatures of fae and mischief. The path continues into a meadow of lush pink-golden deciduous and pomegranate trees drooping under the weight of their own bounties, arils crunching beneath my white moccasins. The hills reveal a monastery built into the centre of the spindly mountains.

We climb up the wet stone steps, and I almost slip but Eliyas catches my arm. At my right, a thin stream dribbles down the bedrock, into a pond with blights of pink and blue fish, buried under white firelotuses.

The sunlight catches the seven gold-burnished arches staggered against one another, rising from the bedrock, shaped into small complexes, like the round stalks of a…

'White lotus,' I breathe out, wondering why I hadn't noticed it before.

Eliyas points upwards. 'The lotus monastery is a timeless relic built when the founding Azadnian clan began their rule. Here the monks started the 1000 Wings of Crane School. They mastered the relationship between Brother-Nature and Heaven, using nature's bounties, to prepare their fight against the magicians and jinn who'd invaded centuries after the Great Flood.'

'Magicians?'

He winks and pulls me up the final step. 'Another time. Let's go. Your uma is waiting.'

We remove our moccasins and cross long halls; the wooden flooring teemed with designs portraying an idyllic scene: olive rugs with threads knotted into ducks in a stream, with floral banks and with the three Heavenly Birds soaring in the sky. The women's quarters lay on the opposite side of a partition.

Uma is inside our room. She sets me out from her, inspects my limbs and neck. 'Oh, child.'

'Do not call me child.'

'It is who you are to me.'

'I do not feel like one.' Hollowly, I touch the scabs at my collar.

Uma glances at Eliyas. 'Thank you. The emperor forbade me from going to the apothecary.'

He bows. 'Of course, Ayşenör. You were once my Second-Uma.' He departs with a promise to return at dusk for training.

When he's gone, Uma pours chai from a copper-enamelled saucer before handing me two dark sugar cubes to place under my tongue. After passing the cardamom and saffron-scented drink, she tilts her gaze to the domed ceiling, the dark blue veil of her headdress dragging on the ground.

'Sometimes I wonder if our enemies here are greater than out there. What would Babshah think?'

My brows furrow. 'Who is Babshah?'

'Is this an attempt at humour?' Uma's voice trails away at my blank expression. She studies me as if seeing something that I do not. 'Impossible.'

A dull ache begins in my head, and I clench my fingers into fists. 'Uma, all day I've remembered pieces of our tribe like a dream. But am I horrible if I do not want to remember the rest? Who is this Babshah?'

After a long moment where her eyes are hard and unreadable, she places a hand upon my chest. 'I was selfish to encourage you to dress like our tribe. People are cruel but simple creatures. Under a royal clan, we cannot exist between worlds. We must choose one. In this empire, you are told to act, dress, eat and speak differently, to forgo your tribe's ways. Listen to them, then. Forgetting your pains might be a disguised blessing.'

'You do not resent me for forgetting?'

'I do,' she says honestly. 'But if you truly love your people, they make up parts of your soul. When you ache for your tribe but cannot place who and why – they are here.' She curls her fingers against my bosom. 'Etched in your heart, they rest. Even if you forget, your soul will not, and your heart beats on. The greatest gift is to live for them. The ones you love *are* your soul.'

My shoulders drop, relieving the pinch in my chest.

Uma straightens. 'Dunya has forbidden the other clansmen from allowing us to dine in their meal circles. For now, we're to stay here with the monks. But at night, the emperor has ordered me to a room in the women's inner palace.' She swallows uneasily, fingers knotting the stray threads of her headdress.

My head bows. 'I vow, Uma, we will dine with the clan tomorrow on the holy Friday. Watch.'

Pushing past my uma, I hurry left then right, down the winding corridors of the monastery. Spilling out of the illuminated archway on to the top of the stone steps, I catch sight of Eliyas. He stands below with some monks in medicinal gardens of blue poppy and balchar.

'Older Brother!' I shout. He ceases his talk and turns. I descend the steps. 'I cannot wait until tomorrow. I want to show the clan, show Dunya – show all of the Azadnian court – that I too belong in the circles of the Heavenly Crane. I choose this path.'

He indulges my anger with a mulling look. 'Little bird, do you have the willingness to train? For victory requires guile, and suffering. That is the true warrior's way.'

'Yes.'

The next evening, I keep to my promise.

With Uma, I arrive at the dining hall, to Dunya's great displeasure. But still showing she is expecting me in her circle from the way she gestures to the silver cushion across from her, nodding at my qaftan, velvet waist-sash and crane feathers, identical to the other young Zahrs.

'Peace be unto you.' Dunya lifts her heavily draped blue sleeves, a thin strip of silver fur at the hem. Her fingers are adorned with rings and bracelets stamped in the design of a firelotus, with petals woven around the band, glittering under the copper lanterns. She smiles politely behind her sleeves. I only see the stark outline of black sormeh around her eyes.

I lift my sleeves to circle my fist. 'And you, Second-Uma. Please, break the fast.' Behind her, Eliyas nods, reassuring me. He sits cross-legged beside the senior officers of the emperor's court. He informed me the emperor would not be at the meal, busy in the throne room meeting a delegation.

Dunya bends down to her daughter, hissing orders. Zhasna scurries away, only to return with a tray of elaborate small dishes – quivering pots of oiled lamb dumplings, skewers of red quail. One bowl contains yakhni and root vegetables, another shorpa from lamb organs. A long plate balances a fried flat, spiced saffron kebab, glistening with jiggly marrow. The last plate has semolina with nuts, a halva dish.

'You offended me at the last meal,' Dunya says coolly. 'A Zahr dines from beginning to end with the clan.' *You will eat all of it*, is her silent order.

Very well. Beside me, Uma hesitantly dips the flatbread into the shorpa, bringing it to her mouth. Just as it grazes her lips, I grab her hand. I use my tongue to prod at the spicy broth colliding with a thin film of...

Boeki scorpion slime. Boeki poison.

I meet Dunya's gaze and say, 'Uma, I wish to eat all of the food. A Zahr must not refuse their clansman's invitation.'

Before Uma or Dunya can protest, I push the entire bite into my mouth and swallow.

Dunya grips the reed mat, leaning forward. 'What is the meaning of this?' At her thunderous words, the hall hushes. Other clansmen incline their heads in interest.

'I am eating your food.' I shovel quail down my throat. 'It's tasty.'

'Are you mad?' Suddenly, Uma swats away the breadbasket.

But my brother quickly strides through the circular tables, reaching Uma. Eliyas winds an arm around her waist, pulling back as Uma struggles against him. She jabs a finger at Dunya.

'I thought your cruelty would dull with age but I was wrong! You've edged sharper at my return. Poisoning a mere child younger than your own, someone who hasn't tasted life until now. You would steal another clan from her out of envy!'

'Uma, enough,' I choke out. Eliyas drags her out of the hall as I make my way through the lamb dumplings. *Swallow*, I think to myself.

Dunya blinks hard. 'Stop that.'

'It was your invitation to break fast, Second-Uma.' I chew more. 'I taste boeki. Not to worry. The emperor had me study this poison well.' I lift a round kebab and pause through a surge of nausea. 'Bristles of a yellow-spotted caterpillar. Nicely done. But it would be more effective to use this poison in the dumplings, as the ground lamb and onion would conceal it well.'

Dunya grips my wrist. 'You were not raised as a proper Azadnian, so you hardly know poisons or healing antidotes. If you continue, you will die. Or have you revealed your nature? As mad as the masochistic death-worshippers of Sajamistan?'

A sharp voice speaks over her. 'Uma, if this child from the barbarians insists on understanding our ways, let her continue. She is killing herself. Or perhaps she won't break so easily.' I make out the familiar face of Zhasna. Her eyes glint at the promise of bloodshed. Slowly, the other clan elders, advisers and the visiting warlord abandon their food to surround our table and watch me devour the poisoned meal. Why eat, when even away from battle, their bloodlust hungers for a different type of meal: an act of violence waiting to happen.

My hand stuffs food down my throat faster. I hardly chew. I plop a salt cube under my tongue and wash it down with sheer chai from a copper-enamelled saucer of cardamom- and saffron-spiced black and green tea.

Eliyas returns and his steady eyes urge me on.

'You do not fear death, child?' Dunya asks in a measured tone, but her eyes are black slits. Now she thought me a child?

To diminish my standing. My gaze narrows and I snap a flatbread in half.

While Dunya had thought me recovering, with my brother's help, I prepared to suffer. He diluted my stomach in a watery white clay and charcoal suction. Then we placed bitter prunus cherries under my tongue, for Eliyas said that would help my stomach produce more bile. We made a gamble. *Ingest the food hastily and then pray. I know my uma's favoured poisons*, Eliyas ordered.

'Corpses no longer scare me,' I finally answer. Life was large but its skin so fragile, and so were its dreams. I dreamt of belonging here, but Dunya's killing of that dream I find more frightening than death. I know I have felt belonging once before – before Sajamistan's death-obsessed masochists destroyed my tribe – but that memory buried itself in the grave when the emperor ordered me to build myself anew. For some reason, there is only the here and now. The past receding with every passing moment, every bite of poison.

'Every soul fears death. You lie like a fumbling child,' Dunya objects. Her arm reaches out, floral bangles, bejewelled like the red of a crane's eye, winking beneath the firelight of the copper lanterns strung above us. She swipes sweat slipping down my chin, wetting the table. 'We smell your fear,' she coos.

I glance up at the watching clansmen; she-warriors with loose hair adorned in crane feathers, and eyes curious; the men with long silver felt capes and velvet waist-sashes, ivory daggers tucked underneath, glinting mockingly. I see the blurring outline of my half-siblings whose names I hardly remember as poison bleeds through my veins. The scent of sesame flatbread clashes with the sharp tang of the black juniper and blue poppies crawling along the walls. I want to vomit. But I cannot fail before their expectant gazes.

Gritting my teeth, I raise my finger shakily. My words begin slurring from the poison. 'L-let us see if you fear it too, Second-Uma. Eliyas, may you pass my halva plate?'

Dunya glares at her son as he nudges forward the only food I have not touched: cubed halva, shaved rose sprinkled across the glistening ghee pooling at the top. I scrape the wet semolina into my hands. 'Here, Second-Uma. You said a Zahr dines from beginning to end with the clan. However, we have broken the most important Azadnian custom: the eldest woman in the circle must break bread first. I have eaten all the flatbread. But I have not touched my halva. You must eat it, or would you refuse a clansman's food?'

She stills.

I scoop a rosy morsel into my swollen mouth. 'Y-you've gifted me this meal. It *cannot* be poisoned, for I've eaten all of it and I-I am fine.'

Her fingers dig into the wooden slab of table, nails tearing into the reed mat. She understands the position I have put her in before the court. My hand extends again. 'Take your halva and complete the custom.'

She parts her lips closer to the sugared semolina. Her temple glistens with sweat beneath the firelight. Beside her, Zhasna is bleached bone-pale in fear.

'Uma, don't eat it!' Her daughter tries to snatch away the morsel.

But Dunya is not one to fall back from an open challenge. 'Half-daughter of mine, I will have your halva.' The cold acknowledgement sends a rush through me. Dunya swallows it from my hand.

Her lips twist, throat swallowing with visible effort. But she compacts her expression through sheer will.

There is quiet in the hall, then.

I stand. My fist circles once in the Azadnian greeting. 'Forged by blood, bound by duty, I offer my soul by the white blade,' I speak quietly, but it rends upon the air like a knife.

'Slave to the Zahr clan,' Dunya finishes and unsheathes the ivory blade at her trembling arm, pressing the flat end to her forehead in a sign of reluctant acceptance.

'Let us dine together as a clan next eve. Peace unto you.' I push back, and bow my head, heavy sleeves risen to hide my shaking face.

I turn away. My limbs feel heavy. My tongue is bloated. I taste metallic blood against my teeth. The muscles around my throat convulse from an impending vomit. I do not make it one step more. My knees buckle and I am about to fall, when a hand latches on to my upper arm.

'Keep walking,' Zhasna says through gritted teeth. 'Do not weaken now, young warrior. You must go on, alone.' Another hand joins her; one of my older half-siblings. Together, they shove me onward. From the corner of my eye, I spot Uma straining against one of my clansmen.

I stagger and pass Eliyas, too, who curls his hands, conflicted as he wishes to help. But Zhasna is correct. I must leave dignified, and alone, as a show of strength. I press forward, drenched in my own sweat.

Around me, the elder clansmen no longer eye me in distaste, but with another expression more difficult to discern. Different viziers nod their acknowledgement, which sends a rush of warmth through me. Every empire has eight viziers: left-hands, in charge of martial and economic affairs, and right-hands, in charge of social and the court's judiciary affairs.

'Well done,' someone hums. My head turns right; the voice belongs to an imposing figure, a curved kilij blade strapped to his leather waistband. He wears a blue and emerald qaftan, but with a crane-feathered turban slung around his forehead, his long black hair tied above the opening. Sormeh darkens his wide brown eyes; a trimmed beard skims along his prominent, square jaw, and his features are long, as if chiselled with a blade. It's the visiting warlord from the western jade mountains. A small dove curls on his shoulder, flapping restlessly. *Akashun, Wolf of the Khajak prefecture*, I recall Zhasna saying.

'I will see you again,' Warlord Akashun promises quietly.

But it's not his words that still me. My gaze is taken by what is behind him. Something dark stretches across the amber-fretted tapestries of the wall. A bloated figure, black and woolly. My senses seize. A bone-white eye observes me hungrily.

No one notices the shadowy figure. *It is not real. It is the poison*, I convince myself. With great difficulty, I pass it.

I duck through the low threshold of the dining hall and limp past gilded teal corridors, straight to the apothecary. The apothecarist's eyes widen at my shaking form.

'A-antidotes,' I rasp. Eliyas and I had prepared four antidotes, based on his predictions of Dunya's poisons.

After twisting the glass toppers of each decanter, the apothecarist pours all four down my throat. 'I take it, you coming here like this will be a routine happening,' she notes.

'Yes.'

Eliyas comes inside, grinning. 'You bested Dunya.'

I stagger forward, collapse into his arms and vomit all over his robes. Behind him, Zhasna enters the room but recoils. More Zahr cousins press at their backs too, watching incredulously.

The next hours I come in and out of consciousness. I hear voices arguing above me. At one point, Zhasna glances down at my cold shivering body.

'Will she even survive?' Zhasna prods Eliyas, who presses a tangy herb-steeped cloth to my forehead.

'Helpful you both were, not stopping Dunya,' another girl snaps, facing Eliyas and Zhasna.

'Well, the girl had to prove herself,' a gruff voice supplies, belonging to an older boy resembling Eliyas.

'Yun is correct. A Zahr does not soften oneself for a stranger.' Zhasna crosses her arms.

'Shut it,' Eliyas scolds and pushes them back like the eldest he is. 'As if you didn't enjoy this affair, bloodthirsty ghûls.' He lifts my body, cradling me to his chest despite the vomit staining his white robes.

'Sorry, Older Brother.' I smile weakly. Eliyas soothes my hair back, presses a kiss to my temple, and I gasp out. No one had ever done so to me.

'Take rest, little bird; you did well. I'm here. And your clansmen accept you into their home.'

4

YEARS 508–510 AFTER NUH'S GREAT FLOOD, ERA OF THE HEAVENLY BIRDS

Training comes as swift as a storm in a summer pasture: a moment of peace before an onslaught that drenches me in the sweat of chores, tasks, lectures and lashings under stern senior monks.

It begins when I am almost fully recovered from the poisons. Eliyas helps me climb up the monastery steps, warning me what is to come in my training.

'—and the monks do not take tardiness lightly, unless you wish to have your meals withheld, back lashed –' At the entrance, Eliyas pauses, eyes catching above. A trinity of ravens curls on to the seventh archway, black forms silent, still, as if in mourning.

Eliyas raises a palm, muttering names of the Divine. 'As a dream-interpreter, I learnt that sleep is the twin of death, and to understand death, I must study the living. Ravens can be an omen of living death.'

My heart is a flighty thing. 'But whose death?'

He shakes his head. 'Do not worry. We do not dislike ravens, nor do we revere them.'

'So you fear them.'

'Think of the story of Prophet Father Adam. The raven directed Adam's sinful son to bury his brother – the first murder of mankind. It's human instinct to fear these creatures, for who wishes to be obtusely reminded of their own mortality? Worse, ravens are the symbol of Sajamistan: masochists obsessed with death, tombs, jinn-folk. Was it not clans of Sajamistan's borderland who massacred your tribe?'

My head pounds and a flash of images penetrates my mind: raven-feathered masks and arrows. I taste copper, the blood of that night seeping into the present. Clumsily, I imitate Eliyas, silently praying to the Divine to protect me from a dishonourable death, but the ravens simply shriek in protest.

'I cannot fear that which I must defeat.'

Eliyas wears a bitter smile as he steps into the monastery. 'Indeed.'

With that, my lessons begin. Due to the crane's contemplative relationship with nature, I spend my dawns in the monastic gardens, beside Eliyas, meditating on olive orchards and black juniper or blue poppy – all kinds of flower beds, to unify my relationship with Brother-Nature.

I don't know if the emperor learnt of my victory against Dunya, but beneath his strict aspect, I detect pride, or perhaps, simply relief. It becomes custom that Uma and I are invited to dine in the circle of his closest clansmen.

Poisons are no longer a weapon to threaten me, but a keen art for the clan to observe each other's resolve. There are eight great courtly clans in Azadniabad's court – each specialised in the wealth and cultivation of particular plants, herbs and stones, trading these wares to merchants, monasteries and kingdoms across the continent.

I learn poison is commonplace in court, that it happens all over the palace as a means of manoeuvring alliances. In the first months, at the end of the meal, clans across the lower courts presented me gifts of delicacies from their fiefdoms. As the new daughter of the emperor, I had no choice but to accept them.

'Taste it,' they'd urge without deception.

After the first gift, I quickly learnt it's a game of poisons to satisfy their intrigue after Dunya's challenge.

Healing and poisons are the realm of the Azadnian courts, but I couldn't forget the first time I was poisoned, the sensation of paralysis, my body at a plant's mercy. I never wish to feel so weak again. I begin to master poisons under Eliyas, not to simply identify their properties but to build a slow resistance, to surpass the masters in the royal courts. I find that, past the pain, most rewarding.

As time passes, I learn more about my siblings.

Yun, my older half-brother, is crueller than the others, but for that, less guarded. After I recover, he invites me to train with the younger Zahrs. Outside the monastery, in the courtyards, we practise under the royal temples' senior martial artists. Yun shares a striking resemblance to Eliyas; they would be as twins, if in another life the older brother hadn't renounced his ranking in the clan and shorn off his hair. Younger than Eliyas by a year, with trimmed curls, identical coppery eyes and sharp features cut from stone, Yun is a hard reflection to Eliyas's softer nature, as a prodigy martial artist, and he knows it.

Azra is the daughter of the emperor's second wife, and quiet but disciplined in her martial routine; she's a regular sparring partner for Yun, and the monks' favoured student.

And Zhasna… I learn is a court poet. A strategy to charm the notables in favour of the Zahr clan. The emperor's weapons aren't always poisons, daggers and sharp words, I've come to realise. At court, melodiously charming, Zhasna recites odes about the Divine mandate after the Great Flood, and the parable of the Zahrs' righteous authority to rule. Most mornings, she attends her apprenticeship under the tutelage of the Chief Court Poet.

Eventually, I enter the circle of the Zahr clan, receiving a new-found respect. In the summers, the emperor sends me with Yun to prefectures across Azadniabad, to acquaint myself with the trades, histories and tribes of the empire – even the mystic monastic schools within the remotest northern caves. As my siblings grow older, they depart and return after spring campaigns to defend our borderlands against Sajamistan in the south, and reconquer lands from warlord fiefdoms in the east and west. Some of my cousins have taken on roles of governorship in the prefectures.

For me, the emperor says my time is best spent in the capital, alongside him, as his future left-hand vizier. Whenever I return to the spring or winter capital, I continue classes on martial history, strategy and training my affinity with Eliyas, who reads from ancient manuscripts about Eajīz warriors, or the strategy of conquerors like Eskander.

Through Eliyas's lessons, I learn about other Eajīz affinities – warriors long dead, or living in the Sajamistan Empire – though a part of me still longs to meet another Eajīz. Eliyas orders me to recite odes about holy warriors – another form of faith – to strengthen my Heavenly bonds.

'In the heart of the Mist Mountains where the cosmos sleep, the Simorgh, the third sagely bird, guards Heaven's secrets, bestowing wisdom to worthy warriors and guiding the presage of a great new era,' I recite back one morning. We hang upside down on the branches of olive trees, meditating on nature.

Eliyas nods at me. 'As you recite about the firebird, contemplate your seventy-seven bonds; they represent your contract with Heaven. The Heavenly bonds come from the Unseen, the spiritual world, and— *Do not stop praying!*' he snaps.

'Sorry,' I wheeze out, the blood rushing to my head making this difficult. Through my recitation, slowly, gold lines, as thin and weak as a strand of mule hair, rise from different points on my body, upwards to the Heavens, flowing with Heavenly Energy.

Eliyas cannot see the Heavenly bonds because they are separate from an affinity; every Eajīz has seventy-seven bonds used to summon Heavenly Energy, which feeds their power.

Eliyas suddenly points at the white nūr flashing from my feet. 'Your bonds are growing; you can summon nūr through your feet as well. This will increase as your affinity is manifested through the different bonds on your body.'

I glance up at my hanging legs. 'Where else?'

He waves at the length of me. 'You have bonds concentrated around your womb, arms and legs that store Heavenly Energy. There are Heavenly bonds even in each eye and the tongue, but those are nearly impossible to use. In fact, the best Eajīz can perhaps utilise only half of their seventy-seven bonds throughout their life,' he explains.

I find myself enjoying lessons on Eajīzi more than any other class.

Eventually, I move from the monastery to a communal room in the women's inner palace with Uma. Many nights, she disappears, summoned by the emperor. Some months, I catch Uma gripping her stomach, but she assures me she is only ill and I trust her – wrapped up in my new life.

I lean into the tight embrace of it, the time before Azadniabad becoming more like the dark shadow of a nightmare. Something I glimpse looking back at me in the mirror, if I linger too long. But there is assurance in even that reminder; better a shadow to remind me that at any moment, this life – this home – can be taken from me too.

YEAR 510 AFTER NUH'S GREAT FLOOD, ERA OF THE HEAVENLY BIRDS

Navia, Spring Capital of Azadniabad

'You've found a better teacher,' Eliyas says one morning before our lessons. We are cross-legged below the hills leading into the juniper and orchard meadows outside the outer palace walls, playing the strategy game of saktab, the board strewn between us on a kilim. It's a few days past the spring solstice. We reside in the north-western spring capital of Navia, hedged on a hill overlooking its luminous freshwater lake from Nuh's Great Flood. Eliyas told me Navia – a settlement famous for its stone masonry – is the indigenous city of the Zahrs before they overthrew their Azad clan cousins almost 200 years ago and seized rule.

'Who said so?'

'Yun told me you prefer his training,' Eliyas accuses me mildly, rearranging his legs in front of me. Recently Yun has begun imparting lessons of the secret Zahr martial arts system called the Seven Gentle Paths of Dawjad – something he'd learnt on his travels to the northern prefecture of Izur and brought back to me.

'N-no,' I reply with a quick smile. 'No one is a greater mentor than you, Older Brother.'

'Ah, you suck-up. You say that not to wound my heart.' He leans his head against a stela, entombed with flood runes, before pushing his brass piece across the sandblasted gameboard. 'I concede,' he declares.

My grin disappears when I glance down. 'You ignored my last opening, and let me win.'

'The fact that you noticed shows your tact. Remember, some battles are worth losing for the greater war. I like conceding to you, little bird.' He winks before pulling me to my feet but his words perturb me.

'What war?'

A breeze sweeps fast, a gust of dirt and damp before it scatters. With it, I hear shouts. I turn toward the beaten paths winding into the meadow. A group of monks runs past the beekeeper huts, shouting at each other in a hurry.

'Why are the monks running?' I ask. A flurry of black kites swoops past us and... *buzzards.*

A distant memory slams into my head, hard. *Sooty buzzards curl against my neck. I fasten a leather creance to their talons before the hunt. A folkteller carries the histories of our sorrows, a woman tells me sadly.*

Caught in the memory, I find myself standing up, running after the birds.

'Don't go!' Eliyas protests.

The birds soar toward the orchards and I chase after them. I realise how far I've run only when I catch up to them.

The birds surround a young woman leaning against a juniper tree, panting. Initially I think her clothed in a fine lace, but as I go nearer, I see her brown skin is webbed by black veins with a thick jumble of red scars between her breasts. Her pupils swallow her eyes, pitching them black. As she stumbles and trembles, the birds descend to peck at her neck, and she shouts unintelligibly.

Eliyas yanks me behind him, eyes widening at the woman. 'You have to go,' he instructs me.

'But this woman needs help and clothes. She's naked!' The woman turns at the sound of my voice and Eliyas covers my eyes. I jab my elbow into his gut. 'I know you are looking, deceitful monk.'

'This is not a time for humour.'

I push him away. 'What's wrong with her?'

He thins his lips. 'I must summon the monks. This woman is under their care. Nothing for you to be concerned about.'

The woman's nose raises, and she sniffs like a beast prowling its prey. She catches my eyes and her lips twitch, teeth and nails coated in red. Blood.

Eliyas shoves me away, but the woman bounds forward, so fast it cannot be humanly possible.

Her hands curl around my arms and she wrenches me from Older Brother. 'M-Mitra,' she rasps. Spittle lands in my eye as she throttles my shoulders. 'B-by the Divine – the bond – in the Unseen,' she cries in a strange dialect.

I lift my hand, instinctively muttering a prayer, and a flicker of white nūr dances on the tip of my finger. Summoning has become easier.

But as I summon my nūr, the woman's eyes latch on to the two gold bonds rising from my hand. The only thought that crosses my mind is, *if she can see the Heavenly bonds, she must be an Eajīz*, before the woman throws me down on to rough bramble, knocking the breath out of my lungs.

Eliyas lunges forward, foot twisting, his leather moccasin slamming into the woman's sternum. She goes flying into a cluster of wild orchard bushes.

'By the Divine,' Eliyas commands, and reaches into his belt, spinning a small red jade pot over his hand. His corded muscles bulge beneath his robes as he leaps forward, reminding me that he is as much warrior as he is monk. His fingers dip into the pot, and I smell the potency: blessed Navian olive oil. Clawing together his fingers, he rakes it down the woman's forehead in a criss-cross motion, and she convulses and screeches. He yanks his finger across her throat, and slams the butt of his palm into her collarbone while reciting something low and fast before blowing across her. She crumples and does not move.

Eliyas helps me up, scowling. 'What were you doing? Never summon your affinity against anyone on the palace grounds. There are eyes and ears waiting to sell any information against you!'

'B-but she attacked me.'

'You don't need an affinity to defend yourself against a young woman, when you've been training—' As he crouches before the unconscious woman, slathering her arms in olive oil, he goes on in a lecture. He yanks off his robes, shrouding her naked body. When he tires of berating me, he leans against the juniper tree, shaking his head, the covered woman now in his tremoring arms.

Any objection dies on my tongue. Exorcising the woman must have drained him of energy. But I do not need him to protect me. Training my affinity in secret over the past two years has grown my Heavenly bonds. I should be allowed to use it.

'Older Brother, it's my affinity. Subduing the nūr is like cleaving half of myself from the other. I want to train openly, without fear of the Zahrs targeting me in envy. Surely they wouldn't now.'

His eyes darken. 'You would not be the first sibling murdered in envy despite being our kin.'

My mind drifts to last evening. After incense and remembrance, I questioned the most senior monk if there was more to Eajīz training. He quietly admitted that monasteries in Azadniabad were finite in their knowledge about Eajīzi. Not even our most remote monasteries could be of help, because ancient Eajīz texts were all horded in enemy lands: the Sajamistan Empire and their army. Begrudgingly, in my weakest moments, I wondered about the Eajīz schools in Sajamistan.

Eliyas's deceptively pleasant voice returns me to the present. 'If you're desperate to train in the open, perhaps we should send you away again, to the remote north. I heard the mystic schools are smaller, but if you're so eager…'

'Not again,' I yelp.

'I thought so.' Eliyas begins to trudge forward with the unconscious woman in his arms. 'Did she hurt you?'

I follow at his heels; my gaze flits to the old scars ribboning her collarbone. 'I'm fine. But is she dead?'

'No. The oil only burns the jinn inside her. My hand against her neck is a spiritual strike to behead the jinn, but it inflicts very little mortal damage.'

'She's possessed?'

'Yes, by foul jinn, a shai'tan like the ifrit. Only the wickedest jinn-folk can possess a human like that and damage their soul. She is under the monks' care. They perform exorcisms, but the possessing jinn makes the mortal flee rampant.'

In the monastery, I'd seen possessed persons seeking a priest's help, but never someone like her, as if their insides had been thoroughly blackened.

'The woman saw my Heavenly bonds. She must be an Eajīz,' I say.

'She is?' Eliyas asks – but without intonation. He must already know this.

'She saw the Heavenly bonds from the points on my hands,' I say firmly. 'Only another Eajīz can see them. She *is* an Eajīz.'

'*Was,*' he says quietly.

I recall Eliyas's first lesson, that an affinity's bonds represent a contract with Heaven. It occurs to me… can an Eajīz break their Heavenly Contract?

'Eajīz are still mortal,' he speaks shortly. 'Any mortal, as the story of Adam shows, can fall to temptation. When an Eajīz becomes unfaithful to the Divine – if they summon their affinity from the Hells instead of the Heavens, by turning to the worst jinn – they no longer practise as an Eajīzi. They become no better than a magician.' Eliyas warns me with a long look. 'Magicians are people who seek refuge in jinn-folk to practise black magick. Not long after the Great Flood, magicians rose from a Sajam city-state and subjugated this continent, beginning the Jinn Wars. If it was not for the Divine gifting us the Heavenly Birds, and through them, the gift of Eajīzi, we would have been annihilated. You must never break your bonds with Heaven.'

A shiver courses down my back. 'Magicians sound like the clans of Sajamistan – obsessed with jinn-folk and death. If this woman is an Eajīz… and she is possessed by jinn, does that mean jinn can hurt me too?'

He pauses at the steps of the monastery. 'I will not let them. Fear not, you have the monks to guide you.'

'If what you say is true, she broke her Heavenly Contract,' I point out, heart still hammering from her attack. 'If she's corrupted, she's like the Sajamistanis. You should kill her.'

He jumps at this, nearly dropping the woman. 'Killing should not be your first instinct.'

I pull away from him. 'I've killed before. Uma says I killed many Sajamistani invaders in Tezmi'a. Though in truth, I do not remember much of it.'

'That was different.' He seems troubled at my casual tone. 'Preserve life when you can, promise?'

I place my hand on my heart. In his presence, I feel abashed. My chest loosens, the heat inside me dispersing. 'Of course, Older Brother.'

I follow Eliyas up the stone steps, but ahead of me, he suddenly gasps. I smell it before I see it. A metallic tang carried in the wind. From the archway, a gathering of monks shouts for the emperor.

'What is it?' I draw up the steps before my brother can order me away.

Two bodies with necks bent at odd angles are strewn across the entryway. Their heads hang limp by a string of sinews on the cusp of snapping, connected to a stump, spine bone peeking through. Blue robes are bunched around the corpses, belonging to young monks.

I fall to my knees. The corpses' chests are open as if long nails ripped the tawny skin down the middle. In the gaping cavities, black locusts chitter inside, thin legs crawling over each other in an eager lump to chew at quivering organs.

My eyes snag on a purplish organ, tossed on the steps, that was once a heart but now is a mesh of muscle and blood. I wince. I should look away, but a quiet curiosity compels me instead. The heart appears as if some creature chewed and spat it out.

In a daze, I glance at the unconscious woman in Eliyas's arms, her lips coated red. He seems to come to the same conclusion, quickly dropping her into a monk's arms to take to the exorcism ward.

Then Eliyas rakes his fingers through the stubbly strands of his hair. 'I must find the emperor—' He pales, looking behind me, and for the first time, I hear him curse. 'What in the Eight Gates of Hells?'

I turn. Three figures approach the monastery across the dirt paths.

'Peace, Chief Dream-Interpreter,' a voice calls out at the bottom of the steps, and I rush down for a better look.

'Warlord Akashun?' I recognise him. Again, a small dove perches on his shoulder, neck coiled against his head. Two warriors linger behind him. A tall, graceful woman, in a tawny qaftan, with a headdress decorated in white jasmine flowers, and a boy who looks to be around sixteen years old.

My gaze snags on the seal stitched over their outer garments. Eight crane wings. These are allied warlords in the Council of the Eight Cranes, from other prefectures.

Suddenly, Eliyas is in front of me, half obscuring them from view. He bows, his stare somewhere between contempt and worry. 'Warlord of Khajak. Warlord of Izur. And Warlordess of Yaqus.' His fingers wrap around my wrist, and I stiffen.

The young warlord of Izur catches my gaze; a boy admired in court whispers. The emperor spoke of him as a boy who, at fifteen years, ruthlessly conquered the northern mountains. Izur is a natural fortress against the raids of steppe-tribes in the Camel Road. This boy betrayed his own kin by allying with the emperor before executing his father, and calling himself warlord *and* khagan, to rule both steppe-peoples in the region and the sedentary townships.

The boyish warlord's light eyes study me, but with a cruel smile that does not match his youth.

Warlord Akashun returns Eliyas's greeting. 'We were summoned for the war council. We'll be taking our leave soon.' He looks up at the towering monastery. 'I trust the possessed woman is well?'

'She's been subdued.' Eliyas's grip digs into my wrist. 'And I trust you to leave the affairs of the Unseen to the monastery. Including the woman.'

'Of course, but you remember why this woman is known to me,' Warlord Akashun responds ominously. His eyes turn to me, running from my face to my feet. 'A blessing to see you, nameless *little bird*. That is what your clansmen call you.' Eliyas tightens his fingers into my arm in warning. I stifle a wince. Akashun strokes the neck of his dove but watches Eliyas. 'I bid my peace. And I await your letters.'

What letters? I notice Akashun's calculated look. Has he mentioned them in front of me intentionally?

Eliyas releases my wrist and wipes his damp hand against his robes, tilting his head slightly.

After Akashun leaves, the warlordess of Yaqus lingers. 'So this is the one who's taken to mastering poisons? A young steppe-girl? A nameless daughter?'

This time I do not let Eliyas stop me. 'Nameless though I am, I am a warrior for the Zahr clan.'

'Be silent,' Eliyas orders.

The warlordess flashes her teeth in a version of a smile. 'Which fighting style?'

My chin raises. 'A Zahr system. With techniques adopted from the Seven Gentle Paths of Dawjad, to find the pathways of Brother-Nature.'

The warlordess turns to address the boy warlord. 'This martial art originates from your lands, the historic clans in Izur. Perhaps you can help train her.'

'Even that the Zahrs steal from us,' he mutters.

I ignore him. 'I will serve the emperor. By poison or blade.'

'Ambitious,' the warlordess answers smoothly. 'But your ivory blade is such a small thing. Like your will.'

My hand goes to the khanjar on my left arm. A symbol of Zahr. As Uma said, I no longer have to shove a blade down my trousers. I have a different blade as my entrustment.

'If she possessed any of the strength of the ancient clans, she wouldn't be her father's dog,' the warlord boy laughs.

'I'm not a dog.'

'And all she has are empty words.' For all his youth, he is equally blunt.

The warlordess bows her head. 'Eliyas, I trust this child won't be misled under your care.' Her brown eyes spark at me. 'Think sensibly. What clan is there to serve when it's clinging to its last dregs of power? And there is no point in power when you have nothing left to rule.'

That night, in a private study, the emperor questions Eliyas and me about the ordeal. Hyat Uncle sits behind him.

Eliyas speaks for me, but oddly, in his recounting, he does not inform the emperor about the treasonous exchange of words with the warlords.

'Did Akashun see the possessed woman? Or the corpses?' Hyat prods.

'Hardly,' Eliyas lies smoothly, and I blanch.

'Good.' The emperor notices my questioning look and says, 'Warlord Akashun is the Wolf of Khajak. If you encounter Akashun again, go to the inner palaces. You must stay away from him.'

'Is he remaining in the capital much longer?' I ask.

Eliyas juts in. 'Akashun negotiated a prisoner exchange between us and our enemies in the Sajamistan Empire.'

'We should refuse his help.' Hyat Uncle shakes his head.

The emperor must be swallowing his own venom from the way he grimaces. 'Sometimes men do one good act, with the hope to get in exchange another. Long ago, Akashun was an ally of Sajamistan's western garrison clans before aligning to me. Now he has used that influence to negotiate a prisoner exchange to buy goodwill in my court. And I am in no position to refuse it, though I wish I could. Of the prisoners, one is a powerful daughter of the eight great clans, caught as a spy when she infiltrated Sajamistan's armies—'

I remember from my lessons that the eight clans are the oldest, most influential in Azadniabad's courts, including the Zahrs.

'– if I refuse Akashun's help, we risk losing that clan's good favour.' The emperor clenches his jaw. 'But by conceding to his help, he has also gained their good favour.'

A chill cleaves down my spine.

'And I also suspect it was one of Akashun's allies in the monastery who freed the possessed woman, to attack you.'

I sit up. 'Why would he do that?'

'To provoke you. He has suspicions about your true nature.' The emperor pauses. 'There was also the warlord from Izur. What did you make of him?'

'The boy is cruel,' I put simply.

The emperor glances down at his parchments. 'I proposed marrying him to you, to secure an alliance.'

Eliyas stiffens beside me. I brace my hand against the spruce desk, blinking once, twice.

'Marriage?'

'It's a diplomatic strategy I used for my eldest daughter Bavsag. I married her to the prefect of Arsduq, in the south-east. Over four years, she poisoned her husband slowly, until he was bedridden, so she became governess. With the warlords coming under Akashun's influence, they are all attempting to defy me. Bavsag is not strong enough yet to turn against seven other prefectures for my sake. For that, we need Izur to consolidate our eastern prefectures – the bulk of trade routes out of Azadniabad.'

I draw forward on the cushion. It's not a terrible strategy. Still, my chest thumps like a restless steed. I ask carefully, 'Does he have another wife?'

'We will set the condition that he dismisses his other wives. I know you; you would be able to do away with him and take over Izur's affairs.'

'What about my affinity? He is not a fool. He is young. Hungry. He is a snake who murdered his father for power. He called me your dog. We…' I falter at the emperor's darkening expression. The ominous warning isn't missed, snapping me into place. Behind him stirs the blackness of the room's corners, and there, like always, a shadow stares at me. As it smiles, I spot jagged teeth.

Hyat Uncle simply sighs from behind my father before reaching across the desk and grabbing my elbow.

'Reconsider, my Emperor.' He rattles my arm. 'She is the first Eajīz from amongst your children; an unprecedented opportunity to infiltrate Sajamistan's military institute through a kinsman you can trust. That is better for us than a marriage alliance.'

My head snaps to my uncle. 'Me? Spy in Sajamistan?'

The emperor glares at him and their words lull to a back and forth too low for my ears. With a firm shake of his head, the emperor affirms, 'No,' without looking at me. 'I've decided to wed her, in due time. For now, we need her resistant. To this.' The emperor withdraws a white nephrite pot from beneath the low-table, a finger-span wide. He faces me again. 'Eliyas will use this in your poison training.'

'What is that?'

'Jinn-poison. These are substances from the Unseen world, different from human poisons.' The emperor lifts the lid of the pot, a greyish, pungent powder appearing like little more than rot inside. 'There are thousands of jinn-poisons harvested from Sajamistani monks in the jinn city of Za'skar. This particular poison, when injected, allows the youngest of jinn to possess your throat. They control your tongue, slur your speech and command your thoughts. If the monks do not exorcise it with an antidote, eventually it causes you to rip out your own throat.'

Eliyas pales. Beneath the low-table, he reaches for my hand, squeezing it tight. I do not understand his concern.

'My poison testers have been unable to master jinn-poisons as fast as I'd like. But you are young; you've grown resistant to human poisons. As an Eajīz, your soul has a relationship with the Unseen world, so you can master jinn-poisons. You will train slowly. Will you do this for me, child?'

'Of course, my Emperor,' I say eagerly.

He looks to my brother. 'Eliyas, you will train her, secretly, as you have trained her mind and body. Harder than ever before. And you must bring drops of her blood in the monastery, to measure her resistance. I will await your reports.'

After we are dismissed, the emperor stops me by replacing Hyat's grip on my elbow. Leaning down, his voice is harsh in my ear. 'Do not defy my decision again.'

'Yes.' I hurriedly bow, my shawl sagging against my shoulders as if broken down, too, under his glare. But an ache plumbs through my chest; it's like his long cold fingers clutch my heart instead of my arm.

5

YEARS 510–512 AFTER NUH'S GREAT FLOOD, ERA OF THE HEAVENLY BIRDS

In the mornings, I drink diluted doses of the slow-acting jinn-poison. The first type consists of the bones of horned beasts. Eliyas takes the powder provided by the emperor: ground karkadann hooves.

By the end of morning lessons, Eliyas scribes any effects of the jinn-poison. At noon, he raises the potency by brewing it in tea. I taste my way through breads and broths and more teas.

By eve, the jinn-poison fully kicks in, racking me in sweats and hearing strange whispers. Some nights I perceive a familiar shadow at the corner of my floor-bed, a pair of milky eyes watching me. Eliyas exorcises the poison through a bath of blessed olive oil. He questions me about my symptoms and collects blood drops. I tell him everything except about the strange shadow, since I had seen it before I began mastering jinn-poisons. *It is not real*, I always chant to myself.

With more poison exposure, my symptoms lessen over time until the night terrors disappear, though the shadow does not.

But the shadow is not the only strange happening.

In the next eighteen months, the emperor becomes absent; he spends his resources fighting melees across the northern and western prefectures. He recalls his kin from the autumn and winter capital Yalon, returning them to his stronghold in Navia. I am rarely permitted to leave the palace grounds. With scarce cattle from the steppe-borderlands raided by Sajamistan, and the shortage of white wheat from Yalon due to border incursions, Eliyas becomes more creative in diluting poisons in my meals.

During one morning of jinn-poison training, Eliyas holds out a clay bowl.

My tongue dips into the yakhni stewed from a skinny rooster. The backs of my feet are blistered from endless scratching. With a practised motion, I heave the poison out of my body into an empty clay pot. We've moved on to poisons derived from the feathers of aži.

'No more,' I whisper. Eliyas takes the bowl with a troubled look. I take note of a smattering of bruises under his jaw as he helps me lay on the floor-bed. He forces rosehip tea down my throat with a dollop of walnut oil and whisks me with cedar branches to return feeling to my limbs.

As I begin to drift off, I hear the emperor ask, 'How is she?', from the entrance of the apothecary. I keep my eyes closed, my breathing slow and sleep-like.

Eliyas answers as though a clenched jaw. 'This is the third time she's been bedridden this month alone. You promised one jinn-poison every lunar month, but you've forced her to ingest three in the past week. You rarely let her leave the apothecary now. It's her prison. She's hardly done being a child.'

'She's sixteen,' the emperor snaps. 'Her people from her uma's tribe would marry and rule their tribe long before this age.'

'Your Blessed, she's under your clan and is your child. Not your weapon. Her soul cannot handle such poisons much longer,' Eliyas continues in a tight voice.

Our father sounds bitter. 'Know your place as my adviser, not a clansman. You ceded that right.'

Silence.

Eliyas's voice turns to cold steel. 'My Emperor, I am still your adviser. You hope to harvest the strengths of jinn-poison, to use it in your armies – to counter the Eajīz from Sajamistan, and your dissenting warlords. But it's no use if *the girl dies.*'

I hold my breath, unaccustomed to hearing someone defy the emperor like so.

'*Please*, Dada,' Eliyas insists more gently. The rare use of the honorific thaws the emperor before he releases a heavy sigh.

'I ought to throw you out for your disrespect.'

'Ah, but you could never forgo your favoured son.'

I half squint as the emperor clasps Eliyas's shoulder. There's a strange clench in my chest watching the familiar ease at which they push and pull in their exchange. My father has never done this with me.

'Understand, my son, that I have no choice but to use these jinn-poisons.' The emperor turns toward me and crouches, hand cold against my head. 'Daughter, tell me, did you not beg for a name? And to join my clan?'

I stir, blinking my eyes open fully, avoiding Eliyas. 'Of course,' I say, my voice hoarse.

'You have yet to fully earn it. I do not want to test you like this.' He caresses my cheek. A strange sensation rises in me. 'But sometimes…'

Swallowing hard, I finish his sentence. 'Sometimes pain is necessary for control.'

'You will remain here until you've conquered the poison.'

After the emperor has left, Eliyas scowls at me. 'He is worse. Paranoid, and desperate.'

'He is backed into a corner.' I watch Eliyas wring a wet cloth, bringing it to my forehead.

'And that is his fault,' he says.

It might be the fever raging in my head, but for a second, Eliyas's lips turn down, defiant. My eyes narrow. 'Do not speak of our dada like so.'

'You defend him even when he hurts you; even when you are ill because of him – *and nameless* because he refuses to acknowledge you? Now he uses your body for these jinn-poisons.'

I startle and my hands grip the blanket tighter. 'He does not hurt me.' My tone is like ice.

'He does.' But Eliyas pauses as if reading something in me, that I cannot.

'The emperor *will* acknowledge me.'

Eliyas places the clay pot down with a thud. 'Foolish little bird,' he sighs. 'The warlords are not wrong. Look at what I feed you. If we don't have bread in the palaces, we certainly have none for our subjects. The emperor couldn't defend our border from the raids or control the buffer tribes from taking the wheat trade in Yalon, so we all suffer. The famine out east is his doing.'

'Which warlord?' I demand, fearing the answer.

But Eliyas has already turned away, his pale robes brushing against my blistered skin. The clang of the pot is the only sign of his cold anger.

Nameless, he said. The emperor *will* name me. I know the language he speaks, one of values and bargains.

At night, in the apothecary, I rummage through the poison manuscripts that the emperor had given to Eliyas, made of cotton-stuffed camel skin. There are also salt tablet copies, hieroglyphs etched in the red baked clay, and newer manuscripts written in standard cuneiform logo script. It's rudimentary Adamic, derived from the original children of Adam.

I hold the first text, called *Za'skar City, the Magicians' Study of Jinn-Poisons*. These are texts on the Unseen world of the jinn and on the oldest human civilisations before those nations were destroyed by the Divine in the Great Flood.

I skim through the parchment, covered in faded symbols. *Aged olive oil, two azhdahak winged serpent's feathers, a drop of goat's blood, ground apricot seeds, Black Mountain snake scales…*

Bile sears my throat. This poison causes limb paralysis before changing the human skin into the scales of an azhdahak. Then you die miserably. There is also an antidote. *Aged olive oil, black cumin blessed with the Divine's seventy-seven names, the soot of frankincense…*

More bile. I swallow it. 'Perfect,' I breathe.

In the apothecary, after grinding the ingredients in a coppery mortar, I extract a fraction of the poison's amount to begin exposure.

I lift my right hand and mentally recite a remembrance of the Divine, manifesting a Heavenly bond from my finger. On it, nūr splinters like gold glass through the room's copper lanterns. Using its pale light, I kneel on the divan, wind chill pricking my skin from the slightly ajar window shutters. Gritting my teeth, I use my left hand to drag the tip of my ivory khanjar down my right forearm. The skin peels back like a ripened pear, crimson pooling into the cup containing the poison. It takes six counts before the blood blackens. For this first taste, it's a test of exposure, not ingestion.

I arrange the extracted poison on the brass tray beside kumis; the fermented lamb milk will help my mouth hold in the poison. After I bless the antidote, I lay out my indigo shawl to muffle any sounds.

Sloshing the clay cup, I contemplate which method to use to take it. Will it be too bitter to gargle? Or shall I swish it around inside my cheeks to make note of its taste?

I settle on the latter and braid my hair back with a tassel.

Nameless. The emperor's sneer penetrates my mind his obsidian gaze coating my thoughts in black. Lifting the cup, I throw back the poison, holding it in my mouth. A burnt bitter flavour bursts on to my tongue, stinging my gums before the kumis soothes the pain. I shove the shawl over my mouth, stray tawny threads piercing my flaky lips.

Immediately, a blinding pain spears my gut. A choked sound gets wrangled in my mouth. A drop of the poison slides down my throat and I panic.

The spasms reverberate up my spine, and I struggle to remain upright. Cold sweat drenches my qaftan, but the heat slithering through my blood makes it feel as if my body is boiling.

The heat rises and I cry out into the shawl, hoping the noise doesn't rouse any attendants. At my feet, the shadow that has always followed at my heels grows into a crooked shape, staring hungrily at me.

My skin intensifies from pink to a red hue, and I spit out the poison, my shawl absorbing it. My fingernails claw into the rugs as I grope around for the antidote, but my vision blurs.

I blink furiously. I cannot see. *You will die here, the product of your own failures. The emperor will find your body, black and red with feathers, blood clogged into tar—*

My limbs numb to a prickly sensation. I collapse face first into the tray, spilling the contents. *O, Divine*, I beg. Desperately, my mouth opens, and I dip my tongue into the spilled antidote.

The spicy tang of black cumin revives my senses and I swallow, a wheeze creaking through my lips. The antidote works sluggishly through my body. I do not know how long I lie there until movement returns to my limbs.

Greased in a film of my own sweat, I gulp down more kumis. Somehow, I am alive. From the success, a laugh bubbles in my chest – that is, until vomit erupts from my mouth.

Eliyas is wrong. I am an emperor's daughter. I *am* worthy. I am his claws. Except I do not scream the words aloud, I swaddle them close to my chest, for the emperor prefers it when I keep my protests silent; when I keep myself cold and sharp.

Then I do it again.

The next day, after circles of knowledge under my grandmasters, I resolve to follow Eliyas, to find out his connection to the warlords after his nearly treasonous words.

Between my poison training, for the first few days, I slip into an old repository dug beside the meditation quarters, watching through the lattice partition between dusty rolled-up kilim rugs. I observe Eliyas entering the meditation room in the evenings, teaching classes to peasants, secluding himself in remembrance or distributing charity with novice monks.

Finally, on Thursday, when Eliyas enters the meditation room after sunset, as he always does, he burns barks of oud to perfume the room.

'Peace,' I hear a familiar voice mutter as the gates of the room swing open.

Warlord Akashun enters silently, sitting cross-legged beside Eliyas.

They exchange rapid murmurs and I press my ear to the partition to discern their words.

Eliyas's tone is harsh. 'My report of the poisons will be sent via the messenger. But I've summoned you here to question your intentions with me. What game are you playing? Why risk mentioning our letters to my sister? I see the suspicion in her eyes.'

'Your reluctance to tell her has forced my hand. Fear not. Your sister has been raised under your care; she is loyal to you more than anyone else in your accursed clan.'

Eliyas stares at the kilim lining the ground, impassive. 'She has a will of her own.'

'She is nameless; she has no soul nor will, except what you mould of her.'

'Her namelessness may be her curse. But she has defied it and made her own soul. I've advised the emperor about her name.'

The warlord sighs. 'So be it.' A knock interrupts Akashun's next words. He hesitates and places his hand on Eliyas's shoulder, as paternal as our emperor. 'The delegation is here. Remember why we do this. Our subjects deserve better.' He bows his head and walks toward the gated entrance.

My legs quiver and I shove a fist into my mouth to stop a strangled cry from emitting. I do not understand much of what they said but I do know one truth: Eliyas is a spy informing Warlord Akashun about my jinn-poisons. I do not know why the poisons are important. But Eliyas has deceived me.

The gates gasp open like a hung jaw. A tension weighs down the air; sweat pools at my back.

I attempt to move, to lift my feet. But try as I must, my senses do not obey. Something claws over my heart. *Fear.* The marrow-deep kind.

'Peace of death,' a new voice greets as the delegation enters the room.

Somehow, my fingers cling to the wooden engravings of the partition. I manage to peer closer. And I wish I had not. There are three people distinguished as warriors by their martial attire and sharpened khanjars.

Two masked men wear pale beaded tunics with unfamiliar embroidery and baggy dark trousers fitted at the ankle, the waist tied by hemp cords. They walk with a silent grace on leathery clogs, washed crimson shawls, with raven feathers, tied under their shoulders, down to their hips. The garb is harsh lines and high collars with odd jewellery of lamb horns and bones, which I've never seen before.

A short, sinewy woman, who appears to be the leader, wears layered white linen with drooping sleeves. The bodice is beaded in silver coins, tucked into baggy trousers. Instead of a cap or floral jewellery, she has donned a simple head ornament of curved yak-tail bones and oxidised silver.

She tilts her head and her long braid brushes against her hip, corded by eaves of raven feathers. In a hushed voice, she begins speaking with Akashun, making it difficult to hear anything. A strange marking stands out on her forehead, a black and red line. Around her neck is a pale wolfish mask, adorned with feathers. Unmistakably so their masks—

– of raven feathers reflect the fires blazing around us – the terror on my expression. Uma screams but the raider drags her away. My apprentice, an old voice murmurs. *She will carry with her the tales of your greatest joys and fears until the end of her days.* I yank myself from the memories, envisioning nūr dissipating it.

These are warriors of the Sajamistan Empire. Our enemies. Why is Eliyas meeting them?

A strangled cry starts to wrench from my throat but I lift my shawl to muffle it. The coursing memories are a flood, breaking past any dam I have built. I touch my cheek under the shawl. I do not recall the last time I ever shed a tear.

At the slight sound, Eliyas pauses mid word and glances toward the partition. Only from knowing him for so long can I read the worry betrayed on his face.

One of the Sajamistani warriors follows this movement; his mask hides his features, except his short black hair and narrowed eyes.

His leader calls out to him. 'Stay on guard, outside,' she orders him in a varied dialect.

Pulse thundering, I crawl out of the depository room, stumbling down servant corridors to the outer monastic gardens before running to a cluster of thorny olive and vomiting into the plants. I remain there for a long moment.

'Little bird?'

I glance up to see Eliyas, rushing down the steps toward me.

'You shouldn't be here. Are you mad?' he snaps quietly, dropping into a crouch.

His betrayal is swept from my mind. 'E-Eliyas,' I blubber. 'I-I saw t-the raven masks… m-my tribe… I-I c-cannot move—'

His eyes widen. He has never seen me like this: cowering, afraid. He's never heard me speak of my past. Self-disgust surges against my fear.

Eliyas takes my hands, pressing them to his lips. 'Breathe. You must leave before anyone sees you. Please. I'll find you in the eve, when we go to the bazaar.'

He re-tugs the shawl across my face. I stand shakily and step away. My eyes lift.

The young warrior is there at the entrance of the monastery. He stares at us a beat longer, with a studied interest, despite the rest of the Sajamistani delegation remaining inside. Heart in my throat, I turn my veiled face away, fleeing across the courtyard like the coward I am.

6

The next day, Eliyas cuts our poison tests short. The emperor is permitting Yun and Eliyas to take the youngest clansmen to the bazaar in celebration of the prisoner exchange with Sajamistan.

'– and tonight is a special evening,' my father tells me before presenting a pair of silver floral earrings, which piques my memories. 'Your uma once told me that as a young girl, you wished for a gift during your tribe's festivals. Instead, as a token for your obedience, I pass on this heirloom as my entrustment, daughter. For this eve, the sky-interpreters foretell that the Heavens will burn with shooting stars.'

He reaches out to rest his hand on my head. My throat tightens. Even seeing his warmth, I'm unable to meet the emperor in the eye. Unable to parse my revelation that his favoured son is a spy, I've felt numb all morning.

Or perhaps Eliyas is the one truly deceiving Warlord Akashun, pretending to be an ally, for the sake of the emperor?

The foul feeling only grows when we head to the bazaar, a bittersweet affair, in the eastern quarters of the spring capital, surrounding the marshes near the palace walls. Yun leads us down dirt-paved paths along the wetlands. We walk against a startling wind, dour with such wetness that my cheeks feel damp, the din of trade coalescing the air.

After reaching the main quarters – and half-heartedly eating halva – I break away from the rest of my clansmen to search for Eliyas. It isn't until I turn the corner that I spot him at a distance. Old habit kicks in. My lips part open to call out before halting. His strides are hasty, moving away from the bazaar. My insides prickle in foreboding. I watch him trudge up the path, the end of his robes disappearing around a stall corner.

Once again, I follow Eliyas.

He walks most of the way to the eastern gates of the bazaar before swerving suddenly along the shell-rock walls. Navia City differs from the winter capital: here the bazaar is surrounded by seven great gates. Eliyas takes another turn next to one of the gates, ducking into an arch outside a small temple looming like a dim creature at the end of the market. I crouch nearby against a closed shop and creep forward.

Eliyas circles the temple entrance, tucking a piece of tied parchment behind a loose wooden panel below a frieze of an ark. My brows knit as he glances up as if muttering a prayer, and then steps back. He moves in a practised way, as if he's done this many times – as if he's been doing it for years.

The sweet tang of sugar in my mouth becomes bitter. After Eliyas disappears, I jump forward, loosen the panel and snatch the scroll of parchment. I unravel the hemp rope.

His words are a scratch of indiscernible glyphs, in a code I do not recognise. He's a scholar, more well read than I. But one symbol stands out to me, a glyph for the huma feather, and then the seal for Warlord Akashun. My fingers tremble. He must be reporting to Akashun on the jinn-poisons I train against.

How do I protect my clan when it's our very own who threatens them? Am I capable of betraying *him*?

My grip against the papyrus causes the edges to tear. I search the other panels but find no other letters. The temple walls are engraved in friezes that show a circle of Zahr thrones below the Heavenly Crane. My eyes widen at the jagged lines where locals have scratched out the imperial seal.

I back away, tucking the parchment into my velvet waist-sash. Ducking my head, I shoulder through the crowds of the bazaar, searching for my siblings.

'Little bird!' Yun's voice breaks through my daze. He stands between Azra and a threader, gesturing me over.

If Eliyas could be a traitor, does that mean Yun is next?

Reluctantly, I follow them through alleyways brimming with shouting sellers competing for buyers, in densely pressed-together stalls draped in beryl and yellow curtains, lit by oil lamps. Perfumed ash drifts with the current. But there are only half the number of merchants than I normally see. Artisans grab at my arms, insistent on inking henna. Yun bats them away and orders the threader to add more blue-threading to our arms in spheres of cranes. I cannot muster any feeling nor smile, even as the blue overlays some of my old gold-threading.

Just as I wonder how to confront Eliyas, a hand encircles my arm, wrenching me from Zhasna, Azra and Yun and throwing me up as if I am a little girl once again.

'Eliyas?'

He braces my weight easily on to his back. *Older Brother*, I remind myself, wrapping my arms around his warm neck, the sensation easing the stiffness in my chest. If I tell Yun or Zhasna about Eliyas, am I betraying my own brother?

'Try to catch up,' Eliyas calls out to our brethren.

'Wait a moment—' Yun protests.

'Go!' Zhasna bellows.

'Hold on tight.' Eliyas sprints forward, robes flapping behind him, carrying me along as though I am the child he first met years ago. But in this, he is wrong. Perhaps that is why he has not confided in me. To him, I will always be a little bird.

Eliyas dodges merchants balancing stacks of millet breads atop their head, shouting about special deals.

'Watch it,' one yelps.

I bow my chin in greeting as Eliyas barrels past familiar monks, and merchants with all kinds of wares, even leaping over drops of manure left by grunting cattle led by shepherds.

'There,' Eliyas gasps out when we face the central quarters filled with families, dressed-up children giggling. He finally drops me. 'We made it in time for the travelling poets.'

Is this another scheme? To use the cover of night to hide his deception? I wonder if visiting the bazaar with his siblings was simply an excuse.

An older man passes around a pouch filled with gold sultanas, dried figs and sugared pistachios to snack on. Robed poets stand upon large stones. As I sit, the crowd begins to gasp at the Heavens, fiery stars streaking violently across the sky.

'Praise be to the Creator of the Heavens and clay!' the poets begin. 'He who alights the sky in celestial light. It's the constellation of the Simorgh. A rare sight, and an omen.'

My other siblings catch up to us. Yun is too stunned at the display above to berate Eliyas. The burning stars smatter in the shape of a white firebird. It's as if the bird is corporeal, shining in nūr. The poets use the opportunity to begin a rapid ode about Azadnian folk-heroes.

'In the heart of the Mist Mountains rested a mighty firebird, the Simorgh – the third Heavenly Bird – training the warrior clans for a great era,' one begins.

I recall this tale from my lessons.

But the tale makes me think how our own empire is fracturing apart, no longer powerful.

Secession from the warlords is leading to the emperor's slipping influence, Eliyas explained once, as if he played no role in it.

'Little bird?' Eliyas breaks my reverie. 'I thought I'd distracted you. Yesterday, I've never seen you cry like that. You don't speak of your uma's tribe.'

I stiffen. 'Why speak of those I cannot remember.'

He leans forward. 'You don't remember many things, I've noticed.' My brows knit but he waves his hand.

'Who were those Sajamistani delegates in the emperor's court?' I muster the courage to ask.

'Eajīz.'

My mouth hangs open. 'Those were Eajīz? Like... ?' *Me.*

A darker question rises in me. Warlord Akashun and Eliyas met with the Sajamistani delegation before the official prisoner exchange. What does this mean?

My brother's eyes flit to Azra and Yun before he nods subtly. 'The highest-ranked Eajīz from Sajamistan, bred in martial arts schools. Their leader led the prisoner exchange: the Sepāhbad-vizier, a general of generals.'

'And a monster,' Yun interjects without glancing away from the poets. 'Death-worshippers. Masochists. The Sepāhbad trains her army to have an obsession with death. We've tried to send informants to spy in their armies and even their courts. The Sepāhbad sent their organs back with a messenger for us to use in a mockery of a burial.'

'The Sepāhbad was the woman with the marking on her forehead,' I say, piecing things together. If I am to be the emperor's left-hand vizier, that means the Sepāhbad would be my direct rival.

'I hear she won't be the Sepāhbad for much longer.'

'How does Sajamistan have an Eajīz army, but we don't?'

Eliyas's eyes fall past me. 'Our empire is not unified. When the Heavenly Birds sighted land for Nuh's ark, the birds chose a city that became the birthplace of magick. Today, that is Sajamistan's capital Za'skar. It is the reason why many Eajīz are born in Sajamistan; it's the resting place of the Heavenly Birds, and who knows how many prophets. Eajīz power is closely tied to land. For that, Sajamistan has all and every text on Eajīzi.'

I study Eliyas wearily. He sounds almost wistful, and I think back to his conversation with Warlord Akashun.

'Sajamistanis cannot be human, but animals. I've seen how their clans massacre our own.' I am careful that my voice does not break.

He pokes his tongue between his teeth in quiet thought. 'They are strange,' he agrees. 'Their customs, language, even the way they eat, very strange. We follow the Heavenly Crane, and they mimic the values of the Heavenly Three-Headed Raven. They call us heretics, and blame us for the deaths of the Heavenly Birds. But in truth, I think we all are more similar than we lead ourselves to believe. Are we all not descendants of Adam?'

Suddenly his betrayal, and the distance between us, comes screaming back into my mind and my manner turns cold. 'You answer like a monk. Have you tired of your preaching, Older Brother?'

'You look pale,' he notes instead.

'I am unwell,' I agree.

He presses a hand against my temple. 'It must be the jinn-poisons,' he murmurs.

An anger loosens my lips. 'Strange, this bond between us. You care for me, yet you are my poisoner.'

Eliyas pauses. 'Against my will.'

'Which part?' I smile bitterly.

The poets begin a new performance, about the Great Emperor. It takes me a moment to see that it's a mocking ode about his rule. Some onlookers laugh, and others shout in favour of the emperor.

Yun shoots to his feet. 'Such blasphemy against our own clan. They dare speak ill of—'

Azra stamps on his foot. 'Don't start a scene.'

'We've stayed past our time.' Yun hastens us away. But I notice Eliyas lingering. He raises his head to the dimming sky, the Simorgh constellation a white inferno against the dark vista, while around us the crowd demand another performance about ancient warriors.

'Perhaps it's a new era. Sometimes, I think we are still in need of heroes,' Eliyas says grimly.

7

In the early dusk, as the emperor tests my resistance to the poisons of aži creatures, my fingers brush against Eliyas's letter, tucked in my waist-sash.

'Three poisons conquered in only two weeks,' the emperor murmurs, as if to himself. If only he knew of how I trained by myself to master them. A coldness seeps into his onyx eyes. 'But I need more.'

'More?' My voice scrapes through a dry, swollen tongue.

'Do you doubt me?'

I sit on my folded legs, pressing the ivory blade to my forehead, and bow. 'Never.'

His smile is a scar in the dwindling firelight. 'Rise, young Zahr. Your sacrifices will be rewarded.' His next words stun me. 'I've decided... you will be named.'

I drop the blade. It clatters once and falls silent.

'A name,' I breathe.

'There was an Eajīz whom the Adamic legends tell of, for she met the firebird, the third bird who flew above Nuh's ark but never landed, choosing to never interfere directly in mankind's affairs. At the height of the Jinn Wars, she ventured to the Mist Mountains to tame the wild wisdom of the Heavenly Simorgh, returning alive at black winter to tell the tale. For your loyalty, you will bear her name. At dawn, you are born anew, and I will be your master.'

The shadow behind the emperor seems to leer at me. The letter burns against my ribs. *Loyalty.* If I do not tell the emperor about Eliyas, will I lose my name, my clan — another home?

I stoop so low, my back curves as a babe tucked in the womb. To serve as though I'm laid under the executioner's blade, squealing like a bald rooster stripped of its feathers beneath a butcher. My life is simply a mistake in the cosmos. It was made for sacrifice.

In the monks' teachings, they say prayers make everything better, they make the bad go away. But as I recite prayers, I only feel sick. Those prayers are for a girl with dreams.

But I can have none of those.

As the emperor opens his mouth to announce my name, I croak out, 'Wait.'

His brows bunch together.

My hands lift, grazing the gifted earrings. An heirloom of this clan. I remind myself that Eliyas is the emperor's favoured son. The clan would not kill him. I see it in the softness of our emperor's eyes; in the way he addresses him. Even when Eliyas left the clan, the emperor was lenient in maintaining his son's courtly status.

Yes. I must do this. Slowly, I retrieve the letter from my waist-sash.

I tell him about Eliyas's betrayal.

I cannot wear the emperor's new name as a liar.

When I am done, the emperor's silence is long, heavy, until I tremble beneath its weight.

'Khamilla Nūr-e-Sûltana,' he rasps before reaching out and taking the tremoring letter. 'That is the name of the warrior which belongs to you. I do not know who to trust. But you… you have proven that you are an emperor's sword.'

My gaze flits up; his voice is grief-stricken before he blinks hard. He stands, crumpling the letter. As he takes a step forward, a breathless Yun barrels into the apothecary.

My brother grasps my shoulder before yanking his hand back. 'You're burning in fever!'

'Emperor,' Hyat Uncle says from behind him. 'A page from the winter palace has arrived.'

With their gazes as bleak as midwinter, I ask, 'What is it?'

Now Hyat's words tumble over one another. 'Yalon is lost. Sajamistan took advantage of the dissenting warlords and invaded. Yalon's prefect allied to Sajamistan, allowing their army to reconquer over half of the winter capital. And then the Arsduq prefecture was next. Our informants informed me that last eve, Sajamistani garrisons broke in and started a melee against Arsduq, wounding your daughter. I do not know if Governess Bavsag is alive.'

I'm reeling from Hyat's words, barely able to take in the disarray of his robes, the wild sheen in his eyes.

'How?' I sputter. 'The winter capital is gone?'

'It's that bastard,' Yun says, seething. 'I advised against the prisoner exchange. It was part of Warlord Akashun's strategy. He used Sajamistan's delegation to covertly negotiate and cut a deal, encouraging them to invade Yalon, while our warlords turned against the Zahrs, undermining your rule, Dada.'

The emperor brushes his hand against my hair, strangely tender. But his hard eyes are on his son. 'You leave tomorrow, to help your sister in the Arsduq campaign. Do not fail me.'

Yun bows his head. 'Of course.'

The emperor turns to me. 'As for the traitor in our midst…'

A sudden shout from the hall rends the air and a guard rushes into the chamber. She bows. 'There's been a breach at the walls – a riot—'

The emperor rises swiftly. Hyat and Yun follow at his heels. My eyes drop to the letter left discarded on the floor.

I scoop up the parchment and hurry out into the corridor, a haze of smoke shrouding the air, making me cough.

In the chaos of the corridors, servants spill to the gates leading outside, escorting notables to the safety of the inner palaces. In the sehan, the palace guards run in the opposite direction toward thick smoke wafting from the outer walls, barking orders, scimitars flashing in their hands.

In their midst, a familiar monk stands before the entryway of the women's quarters, pulling elders inside.

'Eliyas!' I yell out, running toward him.

'Little bird.' Eliyas grabs my arm when I reach him. 'There was an attack at the walls. You must flee into the inner palace as a precaution—'

I gulp hard and pull him into the trees, eucalyptus swaying against the stone walls in the dusk, their ominous shadows growing at my feet. 'Older Brother. Do not act as if you did not know about this attack.' I unfold my hand, revealing the letter from the temple.

Eliyas stares at it, his expression hard.

'Well?' I demand.

'I suspected you knew for a long time,' he simply says. 'I love my family, and I love our people beyond this city-state. It is from this love that I know we do not deserve to rule them.'

My fingers curl in and I struggle to speak through the sheet of smoke now clouding the air and my shaking voice. 'It's because of your betrayal, that you've encouraged – *no, helped* – the warlords to turn against Zahr rule! Look around you; is this attack what you wished for? What of Bavsag? Your own sister wounded – possibly killed – in Arsduq!'

'Bavsag,' his voice turns into venom, 'is as cruel as our dada. Besides, it's just as well – violence has already occurred outside these walls. Good that it has finally caught up to us. If a man does not value his own daughter, how can he value his subjects? The emperor has always failed in keeping the warlords in check. He grants his clan authority above all else, giving kinsmen priority for governorship in prefectures instead of the local tribes, while antagonising our borderlands, leading to raids. The famine racking our lands is on him.' Eliyas explains his treason calmly, even with the shouting around us, and that angers me.

'Warlord Akashun is no better!'

'Akashun is the better of two poisons. The other warlords fear him. He believes in unifying Azadniabad outside tribalism. And,' Eliyas's eyes darken, 'he understands Sajamistan. He's less stubborn, and open to new alliances, to exchange scholarship. He's curious about Eajīzi and the jinn-folk of the Unseen world, and for that he values the ancient ways.'

I stumble backwards at that revelation. 'Is that why you've trained me? Have I always been a study to you? You were intrigued because of my affinity; you betrayed our entire clan for... for what? The promise of more knowledge, to quench your thirst? Even if it means allying with our enemies across the border and inside our own court?'

His gaze narrows. 'Do you have such a low opinion of me? I did this out of belief. Our clan has lost its morals. We were once a clan that defended these lands fearlessly; we patroned the monasteries in this capital and valued the local tribes and monks. Now... look around you at the emperor's men desperate to protect the people inside these palace walls instead of the people outside of them.' And reluctantly, I follow his gaze peering into the smoke. 'The way the emperor pins our own clansmen against each other. I will not apologise for my actions, but I will always regret that I never took you into my confidence sooner. That I could never save you from *him*.'

'I don't need saving,' I say, but weakly. 'I will not lose another clan nor home. I am a Zahr-zad. I only wished for my Older Brother at my side. I wonder, did you see me as a sister, or a well of information for Akashun?'

That makes him snap. He clenches my arms. 'Do you dare? What more must I show you? I've raised you in my care!'

I shiver, whether with rage or fear, I cannot tell. 'You spied, for his sake.'

His lips pull down. 'I was shielding you, from our enemies, from the way Dada uses and hurts you, from our clan. If not me, someone else would have trained you in poisons – trained you into the *grave*. You cannot understand now. But I ask you to wait. To put your trust in your Older Brother. You deserve a clan where you could be free to practise your affinity. To not hide away your birth out of fear. If I could, I would tear you away from empires and clans. I would take you far, far away. I would return you to the lands of your uma's clan if I could.'

'They are dead. And the ones who slew them are dead too, by my hands.' I laugh quietly, the threat not lost on him.

Eliyas shifts forward, shoulders squared. Out of instinct, I move too. My foot slides into a low horse-stance, my finger hooking through my ivory blade. But Eliyas simply loops his arm around my neck, burying my face in his chest.

My eyes are forward, my head unable to move. Dimly I am aware of Zhasna and Uma behind him, spotting us from the gates and shouting, but Eliyas's voice in my ear is all I hear clearly.

'You're a little bird. I'd rather flay my skin than ever hurt you, Younger Sister. Please, I need you to wait. Wait before you report to the emperor,' he murmurs.

My trembling mouth opens. I whisper, 'I am sorry.'

From behind us, the emperor and three guards surge forward from the garden.

Before Eliyas could flee to Warlord Akashun, I kept him here, for the emperor.

The emperor comes to Eliyas wearing a detached expression, but a fire burns in those eyes. I know there is anguish there – I know the emperor feels the pain keenly in himself, for this is his prized son, the prodigal warrior.

Eliyas's mouth parts, his expression changing as he glances between us. Surprise, betrayal, and finally disappointment.

Eliyas gave me a choice. And before he could take me in with his sweet words, I chose.

'To think my own kin,' the emperor spits.

Eliyas stands to his full height and brushes his indigo robes, a smile in place. 'I don't deny it, Dada. Do as you please.'

The emperor raises a hand and before I can blink, smacks Eliyas hard. His back slams against the eucalyptus tree. The emperor tugs him up, another fist to his face, and another, and another. With every squelch of bone against flesh, the ground trembles.

'Eliyas!'

I sink to the ground, covering my ears. I've seen Older Brother spar faster than any clansman. Here, he does not raise a hand to defend himself against the emperor. For once I do not see him as a powerful adviser, a warrior monk. He seems a young man. A son who cannot raise a hand against his dada. He takes each fist, as if he'd endured this violence from him before.

The revelation of this makes it feel both familiar and worse.

A bloodied Eliyas grips the trunk, somehow shakily back on his feet. The emperor raises his hand again.

Without thinking, I lunge forward; his knuckles connect against my left cheekbone instead.

My head snaps into Eliyas's chest.

The emperor's eyes pin me in place before he snarls. Instead of continuing, he turns and shouts orders to the guards.

Eliyas cradles me to his chest, his back against the trunk. 'You f-fool,' he coughs out, tone wet.

'I-I had to tell him,' I say as he lifts his hand, touching my swelling cheek.

'No, you are a fool for taking his fist. You are not my shield. I am yours, little bird,' he says thickly.

'You are supposed to despise me. I didn't wait. I told—'

'Quiet,' he soothes. 'I expected it. Akashun assured me you would ally with us, but I know you better. Your heart is with your clan, a violent bond of love.'

'Love,' I echo. 'What is that? I don't know anything of it. If I loved you, why did I betray your trust?'

'I betrayed yours. We are both horrid at it,' he laughs melancholy. 'We don't have time before the guards take me.' He grips my chin. His head presses against mine in earnest, his voice a murmur. 'I dreamt long ago of the emperor's courtly birds. The bird of a king reflects the nature of their rule. Sometimes I see you as the bird. But in one terror, I saw his crane fighting with another on the divan. It's a sign, a new enemy will arise for the empire. I knew it was Akashun. I knew I would support him, if only to take another enemy out... our father.'

He pauses and shuts his eyes. 'Whatever comes next, I do not hate you. You, who've been misled and used, by Dada, our umas, our elders – by me – still I know you and I trust my upbringing of you. I've seen and interpreted my dreams. You are the most resilient girl. You will be powerful, even on a path of solitude. One day you will pave your own way, with your own power. I'm sorry, little bird. I could not save you from the emperor, from any of them, from what is to happen to you, and I could not give you the family you deserve. I could not even save myself. But you are strong. You do not realise it, but, on the Divine, this court is not fit for the likes of you, to be caged inside its walls. It's not the ways of your true tribe, for you are still your uma's daughter. The people you were born from; the ones who walk with the winds of Brother-Nature. Sooner or later, even a caged bird is let free.'

'Why do you speak like this, Eliyas? Dada will lash you; he might even imprison you, to halt your doings. But I will convince him to release you, even if it takes years!'

He kisses each cheek gently. 'That is not the way of honour in our clan, little bird.'

'But—'

He kisses my temple then. 'Beware of our father. The danger in ignoring your pain for so long is that the more you experience it, the more you become accustomed to it. Until you trick yourself into thinking you deserve it. You are better. I was not, but I'm honoured to leave as a martyr. Peace on you, I will see you in the next life, in Paradise.'

A forceful hand rips me away from Eliyas, dragging me across the courtyard. At the commotion, clansmen gather in the gardens; I spot Uma, Dunya, the other wives, my cousins and elders.

The emperor observes them all, calm. 'The clans will witness the cost of defiance.' He speaks low, but the words make me flinch.

Yun and Azra run from the outer walls, huge-eyed at the blood on Eliyas.

'Older Brother!' Yun starts, before spinning on the emperor, 'You cannot do this. It will ruin us—'

The emperor lifts his hand and Yun flinches. 'Do you wish to join him?'

'It's all my fault,' I cry.

'Do not look away, little sister.' Yun, who I've never seen shed a tear, has wet eyes. 'You must watch.'

A crowd of senior monks shoves through the gardens before a horde of palace guards thwarts them.

'This is injustice!' one of the monks yells, but he too is silenced.

Amidst the chaos, at the emperor's orders, Eliyas is dragged to the front of the courtyard.

The horror of what I've caused sets in.

Uma reaches my side. The air lingers with a haze of smoke, half of the guards at the outer walls subduing the breach, with another sizeable number fending off the angered monks and priests. Something slithers in the air… as if the wind itself is holding its breath.

Despite the yells and clanks of fighting, at the emperor's order, the notables of the eight great clans are forced to bow cross-legged in the courtyard, ivory blades pressed to their foreheads. A guard pushes me to sit between Azra and Yun.

Seeing Eliyas kicked down like a beaten dog, my vision blurs. I cannot sense anything, as if my soul is watching from afar. I see myself stand. I must go to him. *Older Brother*, my lips shape, but Yun hooks a finger into my collar.

'If the emperor sees even a tear on your face, you will be next,' he warns before tucking an arm around my waist. 'Take my hand; squeeze it,' he orders. 'The urge to cry will disappear.'

The sky lightens above us. It's a bloodied dawn, the stained-glass domes of the palaces reflecting the violent sky. The grounds shudder below the angered gusts of a grieving wind.

'She lied!' Dunya's shrill cry breaks through the clans. 'She is deceiving us!'

Quickly, a guard grasps a great axe, while holding the familiar cage of courtly cranes. They are executed first, a symbol of Eliyas's status as Chief Dream-Interpreter. Their bloodied heads fall in a sombre manner, the white stumps of their long necks twitching in a final cry, but at least in death, they've been freed from their cage. At them, Eliyas labours forward, struggling against the guards. His lips move in a prayer, more concerned with the dead birds than his own well-being.

He's struck in the face by a guard as if he was never the son of the emperor. I force back a cry. Eliyas is splayed down and laid out like a lamb to be butchered. He cranes his neck and our eyes lock. Even caked in blood, Older Brother looks calm – serene.

Life has been unkind to me, but with him, there were the sweeter moments. Past the betrayals, the warlords, the clans… he *is* my brother. I wish to see him smile again; to carry me on his back; to feed me halva; to hold my hand and guide it through martial stances; to tighten my shawl and tuck it beneath my chin.

As the tide of sorrow washes upon me, I remember that I am responsible for this, and it ceases. I keep my eyes steady upon him; I do not falter.

From Eliyas's feet, a familiar black shadow rises that no one can perceive but I. Wispy tendrils grow into knobbed, crooked limbs, and white eyes. A gap carved into its face reveals pointy teeth. The shadow droops, sniffing Eliyas in fascination. My being trembles. The shadow pauses, glancing at me in question.

More smoke cloaks us like a dark burial shroud. In the row to one side, Uma's expression urges: *you can stop this*. My fingers clench and I imagine nūr shielding Eliyas. It would only take a moment.

Eliyas mouths something, and I know it is the prayer that all the faithful do before their end: the Oneness of the Divine. Still looking at me, a bittersweet smile graces him. As if he's always known who I would choose. My hand clamps to my lips.

Behind him, and eager, the shadow's arm dives into Eliyas's chest, tugging out a sinewy red organ. Its teeth tear into the pulsing heart. I watch on, numb.

I must save Older Brother. My fingers point up, flickering with a Heavenly bond.

I halt. The emperor is watching me.

I have power. Why must I sit here quiet? Why am I not using it?

The emperor blinks slowly.

I curl into myself. I do not move again.

Because a different power ensnares you, more poignant and dangerous than any blessing from the Heavens: the deception of bonds. You are chained to it, my mind taunts me, as all I do is watch.

The emperor does not give me time to come to a decision. The executioner's axe crashes down and blood splatters the entire first row of our clan. A streak tracks down my cheek like a red tear.

Eliyas's head rolls off into the grass.

Then the screaming begins.

The crimson flesh of his twitching neck is all that is left of the young monk. The older monks yell. It was so quick. My nails have punctured Yun's arm from squeezing so hard.

This is not real, I chant.

'My son!' Dunya wails out, long, listless. For once, I do not take pleasure in her pain.

'He's ruined the only good person of this clan.' Yun bows his head. 'The emperor has ruined us.'

Uma once warned me, the purest flowers die, never the weeds. Because I like to ruin beautiful things. I will never unite with Eliyas in the next life of Paradise, for I do not deserve it.

The emperor's solemn victory is cut short. An uproar from the monks splits the imperial guards. Suddenly, I see other monks descending the paths of the monastery. More and more, turning against the guards. But there's another clash, drawing in from the outer palace walls.

'Warrior monks?' Yun lurches up.

My nose twitches and a haze of grey fog swirls through the grounds. The scent of sulphur permeates the air. I see the guards clashing with…

Those are raven masks, I realise in dread.

'They've surrounded the gates!'

As if they'd been waiting for this.

I jump to my feet. A siege of our own capital? *The breach was never a breach at all. It was a ruse… for the real attack was from inside the palace walls, with the help of forces from—*

'Sajamistan,' I say faintly.

And I can think of no one else but Warlord Akashun who would capitalise on Eliyas's execution.

'Azra!' a scream pierces through the scuffle. Yun lunges forward but he is too late. My elder sister falls to her knees, an arrow protruding from her chest. Beside her, Belzzar is motionless, dead, on the ground; two of the emperor's wives are cut down next by a monk; and then more elders are surrounded by raven-masked soldiers.

A mix of forces pours into the palace grounds, some with an emblem on their crisp tunics. Gold embroidery sewn in lines like Heavenly bonds. A small three-headed raven embellished across the breast of slit-sleeved, sable-furred cloaks. Hard masks in a shape between wolf and raven sculpt their countenances through the pale husks of painted bones, a terrifying animation that causes even the shadows to sulk at their feet.

Sajamistani soldiers.

'Go!' Yun pushes me away before he runs forward with palace guards. Across from me, I see Dunya, unmoving and stunned, before an attendant wrenches her up, and toward the gates.

An attendant lifts me to my feet.

'Where is Uma?' I spin around. But the palace grounds are overwhelmed with Warlord Akashun's forces joined with Sajamistan.

The attendant suddenly trips into me, her fingers brushing against my waist-sash before she flees.

The force makes me stumble back, but a new hand catches my elbow.

'Come quickly,' the emperor barks out. He tugs me to the eastern boundary of the courtyard, which descends to the meadow and stone huts of the beekeepers.

'Wait! Uma!' My heels dig into the cold dirt, but he does not stop. 'We must find her!'

'We have no time,' the emperor says, but his cold exterior wavers as he pushes me forward, a cluster of orchard trees obscuring us from view. 'We must make our escape below the hills, through the forest to the stone huts of the beekeepers, where my soldiers await to take us to Arsduq and Izur prefectures. Yun and Hyat will meet us there with the other clansmen.'

'What are you saying?' I hiss, a terrifying anger drifting through me. 'We are fleeing without her?'

He emits a sound of disgust.

This is my *uma*. This is his *wife*.

'You fool,' he sneers. 'You would risk us all to save *one* life? We were betrayed by one of our own; we must escape. Look above us, do you see them? To oust me, Warlord Akashun has allies from Sajamistan, *including the Sepāhbad.*'

'But—'

'We will salvage this. In Arsduq, I will send a page to the Izuri warlord. By wedding him to you, we will have our alliance, enough for the Zahrs to maintain a stronghold in the north-east before we retake our capital—'

A cry sounds behind us, a voice I recognise. *Uma.* Hasn't my purpose been for Uma, to pave a path to a new home? I thought power only mattered if our clan lived and I could be her shelter, her home.

But the emperor grips me, hard. For once, the chill that once sank into my bones cannot dampen my anger. I'm unable to think or feel. I cannot see anything.

Except that my mother was never protected.

'What of Uma?' I snap. 'Dunya? Eliyas? Sajamistanis crawl with the warlords, so how many of our own will you sacrifice?'

'I would sacrifice another if needed. This is simply your uma's fate,' he answers before releasing me, his eyes a glassy abyss. 'We must go, *now*. Remember why I do this. For our home. A warrior is incomplete without his sword; you are my blade, Khamilla. I need you. To gain Izur's support—'

'Another warlord?' I cannot control the redness that wells in my vision like an open wound. I wonder whose fate my fallen emperor would determine next.

Shaking all over, I turn around.

'Where are you going?' he demands, wrenching me back.

With my head pounding, I raise my pinky, a Heavenly bond from that finger opening into a thin gold line. The Heavenly bond shoots a hair-width of flashing white nūr into the emperor's side, forcing him back before I realise I am stumbling up the hill, away from him. The redness engulfs me entirely. I trip over a stone, but I cannot see in front of me. I only feel a blade against a neck. I see a smile of blood on a torn throat. I only see Eliyas's dead body. I imagine who of my clan will be dead next, like him. My legs straighten. *Keep moving*, I chant to myself.

'I refuse to abandon Uma,' I whisper.

Desperate, I reach the top of the hill and start running across the field toward the courtyards, where Sajamistani soldiers clash against palace guards.

There, I see her. Uma. But the hope slithers out of me. Raising my palm to angle my nūr across the grounds, I find it is no use. As always, I am an instant too late.

Uma is on the other side, in the trampled gardens. My range is not that far.

Everything slows. A sickness swells in me. Surrounded by Sajamistani soldiers, Uma fearlessly presses her khanjar against her throat before the soldiers realise what she is doing.

But I know, finally, Uma is finishing her own story. Rewriting it to its own fitting end, for what tale had Uma controlled in her miserable life before this moment?

She slits her own neck. The steel carves swiftly through her skin. Her body sways, her head wobbling as if wishing to caper off her frame. Her body collapses.

I sag against the ground behind a citrus tree.

'By the devil Shaytaan,' soldiers cry out, the wind carrying the curse.

My vision blurs, sharp grass stabbing into my legs as I kneel. Vomit fills my mouth, and I hurl into the dirt.

'Uma,' I gasp out, glancing back around the tree. Her body burns into the depths of my mind, and will curse me with its gory reminder until the end of my days. Even from here, the crimson is stark against the flora, remnants of henna-stained hair strewn against the ground. The skies open, as if the clouds rumble their outcries, as if Brother-Nature recognises the malice of the act and wishes to wash away the stain of sin.

'A pity,' a cold, familiar voice says. I glance over to see the masked Sajamistani soldier with dark hair kneel beside Uma's corpse. The one I spied from the delegation. 'It seems their kind might be more obsessed with death than our own.'

'A pity indeed, my Alif warrior,' a woman replies, coming beside him.

In disbelief, my hand curls around the trunk to steady my swaying feet. It's her. The leader of the delegation – the Sepāhbad-vizier, a general of generals in Sajamistan.

That is my uma they stand over. No. That *was* my uma. This is just as she'd promised.

A venomous taste lingers in the atmosphere. I cannot understand it. I cannot understand anything. After all we'd endured, Uma told me death was a better fate than to be captured by Sajamistan again. I thought we could beat this fate. I thought I'd beat it for her.

The air escapes my lungs and I curl into the tree to breathe but the smoke lingering in the wind makes it impossible.

'The emperor has fallen,' a cry goes out as a haggle of soldiers marches up the hill, dragging an indiscernible body. 'He's fallen!'

They throw a corpse down into the clearing. The eyes are dark and upturned, vanquish written across his bloodied features as if screaming the unjustness of his predicament to the Heavens. The body is covered in severe wounds.

Warlord Akashun's men are there, surrounding it. Seeing the corpse provokes a sudden incessant dizziness. I want to scream. I want to weep. But I can only stare. *That cannot be.* I stumble back. *That cannot be him.*

As the palace guards yell and begin retreating in to the chaos of bodies, I quickly recede through the bramble into the meadow. I run down rocky alluvium, relying on instinctive memory from training – paths that soldiers and their stallions would never risk embarking.

The emperor is alive. He fled to the huts. He is with Hyat Uncle, I assure myself.

As the sky morphs to the pale sheen of dawn, I loop around south, then down toward the stone huts.

'She's here,' a watchwoman cries out.

As soon as I cross the meadow, familiar clansmen turn from their steeds. Hyat rushes forward. I notice, then, the emperor is not with him. I stagger back and sink to my knees.

'He is not here?' I choke out. Hyat's eyes widen. My last hope winks out.

A weak wail escapes my throat. Uma warned me about Sajamistan. They capture and torture us. They cut us apart.

'Where is the emperor?' Hyat demands.

Behind him, all I make out is a great, familiar shadow. It steps forward, eagerly into Hyat, as I speak weakly to my uncle through its gangly face.

'The... the emperor is dead.'

The surviving Zahr clansmen begin shouting while Yun stares ahead blankly, Zhasna quiet beside him, pale as a sheet of ice.

My aunt Zunaykha whirls around, jabbing a finger toward me. 'This is her fault! There was no evidence of the monk-boy's crimes. For all we know, the girl could have planned his execution with Warlord Akashun!'

'Uma warned us.' Zhasna grips her khanjar to her chest. 'Dunya is never wrong. This is no sister of mine. She is the Qabil of our era, a traitorous son of Adam betraying her own kin.'

I begin backing away as their arguing persists amongst themselves. My hand wrings my waist-sash, brushing against parchment tucked there.

With tremoring hands, I peel open the letter. In disbelief I jam my fist into my mouth, biting hard. I scream.

It's him. He deceived Eliyas by encouraging him to confide in me, always knowing I would choose the emperor over my brother. He waited for this. He knew my actions would lead to Eliyas's execution, and capitalised on it to attain the throne.

My thoughts unbalance. The memories of Eliyas's beheading and then Uma's death constrict my lungs.

I wait for tears to fall but I know what the emperor forbade from me: my own sorrow. I am never allowed to weep.

I back away into the nearest hut, alone inside. My trembling palms raise, and as I did after the raid that massacred my uma's tribe, when the emperor ordered me to, I beg to wipe my memory. *Make me anew. Make me forget him.*

A stroke of nūr flickers out from my hand. I press it to my mouth, swallowing the light. I envision it gliding along the tangled skeins of my soul, delving into a cavern of memories, eviscerating every good thing I knew of Eliyas. *This is his fault. He was a traitor and now your clansmen are lost.* My mind recedes.

I evaporate the letter with a flash of the white cosmic light but its words echo mockingly.

You acted exactly like I wished. Through and through, you are a loyal dog to the Zahr clan, little bird. Thank you for ridding me of that foolishly idealistic monk, as if a Zahr with a soul as pure as his has a place in any Azadnian court. May the boy rest in a grave of nūr before judgement by the Divine. Now watch your clan crumble as swiftly as your Older Brother.

Let us meet in the dawn of this new era.

Your Blessing,
The Wolf of Khajak

PART TWO

City of Za'skar

The bond to Heaven is forged in war.

—ANNALS OF ZA'SKAR CITY, QABL SAGE ESKANDER ZA'SKAR ON THE METAPHYSICS OF EAJĪZI, SAJAMISTAN EMPIRE, YEAR 80, ERA OF THE GREAT FLOOD

8

YEAR 512 AFTER NUH'S GREAT FLOOD, ERA OF THE HEAVENLY BIRDS

My name came too late for me to use it.

The palace breach was meant as no more than a warning for the Zahr clan. After the riot from the lotus monastery, which Warlord Akashun was waiting for, he laid siege and took the Azadnian throne with the backing of Sajamistani forces.

That night, six of the eight great courtly clans switched allegiance to Akashun and six prefectures followed, in a tenuous alliance. The emperor had underestimated the loyalty of the monasteries, and the love of the common people for Eliyas. Outcries spread across the spring capital. *The beloved, pious monk of the Zahr clan executed unjustly without trial*, the people bellowed.

We flee Navia, heading to Arsduq prefecture, the last Zahr stronghold, taking momentary refuge in an elder's landholding.

In a servant's room there, I do not move for hours. The shadow rests opposite me, curling into the corner of the hearth, staring at my palms as if they are still coated in blood.

The partition shudders open, and Hyat Uncle enters the chambers. He is severe as he stirs the hearth, forcing me to sit below its niche for warmth. My insides are brisk, and no amount of fire will thaw them.

'Drink this, child.'

I am no child. But my uncle calls me that anyway. He forces my fingers around a teacup of piping kahvah and I hiss from the sudden heat. That strange sensation returns, the one that refused to yield when I was a girl at my tribe's slaughter; the one I felt as I held poison to my lips: the feeling of wanting to live, cruel as it is, unable to slip past my fingertips. It screams at me to act.

'The other clansmen are leaving.' Hyat says, and I rouse at those words.

From my uncle, I learn the surviving Zahrs are splitting off between Izur and Arsduq prefectures. On the condition of wedding a Zahr, the Izuri warlord did not side with Akashun, just yet. Dunya was left behind in the Navia capital so Zhasna will protect her by remaining in Warlord Akashun's new court – and as our eyes. Later we find that Dunya did not flee the chaos of the invasion but chose to embrace it, saying her marriage was to the emperor, not the man.

Hyat also informs me that, to appear compliant in this new era of his rule, Akashun has ordered the eldest Zahr clansmen to remain in his court and proposes marriage and clemency to the leftover wives of my father, instead of execution.

Governess Bavsag survived the earlier melee by the Sajamistani. My brother Yun is to go to Arsduq prefecture, to our sister the governess's stronghold, which controls the bulk of caravan trade to the Camel Road, making her nearly untouchable to the Azadnian warlords.

I glance down at my hands around the cup of kahvah, wondering where I am to go.

Hyat Uncle meets my blank gaze. Suddenly, his suggestion to the emperor from long ago returns at once: *She is the first Eajiz from amongst your children; an unprecedented opportunity to infiltrate Sajamistan's military institute through a kinsman you can trust.*

I remember which clan I am a part of: one made to die by the white blade.

And then the thought rises, slow but persistent, reverberating through my limbs as if travelling through a copse of blood and bones: Sajamistan has destroyed my future. But I could reclaim it.

At last, my stiff lips move. 'I am going.'

Hyat's head rises with a start. 'To Arsduq? Or to Izur?'

A mirthless sound bubbles from my throat, and I realise it's a laugh. 'Absolutely not.'

Izur prefecture should be my course of action – Uncle could agree to the marriage alliance on my behalf, and I would be stowed in the prefecture at the mercy of a rogue warlord, in exchange for giving him the knowledge of jinn-poisons. The Zahrs, led by Hyat, would use the alliance to slowly defy Warlord Akashun while I… would be discarded — somehow, someway.

But I'd miscalculated so much in this game of empires. My entire life has begun and ended with Sajamistan, from the deaths of my tribe in Tezmi'a to now, my Zahr clan.

'Then where?' Hyat prods, but his eyes are narrowed, and he seems to know my answer. An easy realisation. Has this not been what I've grovelled for years for — the chance to cut down our enemies? I blink hard.

My world rearranges itself until I see *myself* versus *the other*. The monsters clad in human skin.

'I will go to Sajamistan's great army,' I spit out. 'To infiltrate the ranks of our enemies. Had you not proposed it? But now I choose it. I will enlist in their Eajīz battalion.'

'You mean to go to the city Za'skar, where they breed their strategists, generals and martial warriors.' It is not a question. A light flickers in Hyat's eyes, undeniably satisfaction. But he tests me further. 'You might be discovered as a Zahr.'

'I am already dead. So for that, there is nothing that Sajamistan has not already destroyed of me.' My voice almost breaks but I clamp hard on that waver. 'To win at all costs. Burn down everything they've built. I will not forgive those death-worshippers until I've paid them in kind. But Hyat Uncle, you must work to turn the great clans in our favour. The Zahrs are fractured without the emperor. My own clan does not trust me. But the only thing that brings our warlords together is unification against our common enemy. It may take years but I must do this. For…' My voice trails, a bitter emotion choking the words. *The emperor. Uma. The Zahrs.* Purpose soothes the threat of grief.

I was taught by my clan about retaliation, vengeance, war. In Azadniabad, the monks claimed that corruption spread in Brother-Nature through the escalation of violence, one vile act begetting another, destroying the lands. Countless times I've wondered how to reconcile the preaching of warfare with the teachings of my childhood. Violence is used not only to gain power but to keep it. The fool that I was found those teachings jarring but now—

My jaw hardens. I stare at the shadow against the hearth and for a second it morphs into my Older Brother, *that monk*. My spirit burns with a seismic anger, and finally I feel warm.

Preserve life when you can, promise? Older Brother once asked of me. I am forcing myself not to remember him anymore, but I do remember that oath.

Pious folk like his kind in the monasteries always preached to break violence, to deter the thirst for revenge. But that piety is naïve. They do not understand. They do not understand what it is like to always have your future torn from you like a dagger through a tapestry. To never have a home to belong to.

Shall I turn the other cheek? I cannot. I may be a follower of Prophet Nuh and the lost scriptures, but to find forgiveness in me, well, that can only happen after my enemies are dead. Then I will happily forgive Sajamistan.

'We've sent spies before. Only two returned from an exchange with the Sepāhbad,' Hyat adds. 'Sajamistan's soldiers are paranoid about any Azadnian; they will sabotage you so you remain in the lowest ranks of their army. Your words, your accent and the symbols upon your arms will all make clear that you descend from an Azadnian clan. But you are a smart girl, a quality your father might have neglected to use, but finally you can.'

'Will I be the only Azadnian in their army?'

'No. There are others – very few though. Sajamistan accepts Eajīz from almost any clan because Eajīz are far between and few in number. But that does not mean your masters in that army will be kind. The Sepāhbad will be doubtful of you – but do not thwart the suspicion. Accept it boldly and then replace it.'

'The Sepāhbad.' I taste my enemy's title. The only sign of my rage is in the rattle of my teacup. 'It was the Sepāhbad that allied with Warlord Akashun, murdered the emperor and caused the death of Uma.'

Hyat lowers his teacup and dark kahvah sloshes over the rim. 'Yes. But her right-hand soldier has challenged her. Our informants tell us he has become the new Sepāhbad-vizier. He is young, ruthless and deeply distrustful,' my uncle warns as my mind flashes to the masked warrior with dark hair, 'dismissing almost every high-ranked warrior, who they call the Alif, under the former Sepāhbad. If we still ruled, you would have trained to be the Sepāhbad's rival and equal in all as a martial-vizier. Ironic that fate has given you another chance to seize it.' He pauses. 'Enlistment will not be an easy task. The tests are gruelling and you will have to prove yourself. Prepare yourself to journey to the borderlands of Sajamistan.'

'So be it. I have never made any decision of my own choosing, but in this, I am firm. I refuse to return without intelligence against our enemies.' My body shakes. For Hyat, this is about gathering leverage against the empire. For me, only revenge. One leads to the other, with the same end: Sajamistan's demise. 'I will show you. By the Divine, I vow to kill them. *Every single one in their armies will die.*'

Hyat Uncle's brown eyes look grim. And I remember, he, too, has lost a brother. He shifts on to his knees. 'Let us bow, left-hand of the fallen emperor.'

The wizened warrior of Zahr bows and presses the flat of his blade against his temple. The shadow gapes behind him as I lift my ivory dagger to my own head. It nicks my skin but the blood dribbling down my face tastes sweet against my lips.

After that, things move quickly. That same eve, fearful of more informants in our ranks, we decide against telling the Zahrs about the plan.

'She will be at my side in exile, in Izur,' my uncle lies to my brother.

A look of panic crosses Yun's face before he yanks me behind him. 'My sister must stay with me in Arsduq; it's safest. Azra is dead; I've lost Zhasna to Akashun's court; I cannot lose another too.'

'I'm having you return to another sister. After the attack on Arsduq, your elder sister has feigned neutrality, as she recovers from her wounds, but of course Akashun will never trust her. She cannot risk sheltering me. That would be an open declaration of war, but you – her brother – she can,' Hyat explains calmly. 'I need an heir's eyes in that prefecture.'

Yun's lips tug into a snarl before reproaching me. 'You are silent, tongueless girl.' But I do not move. 'Tell him not to separate us.'

My uncle approves of my silence. 'She has hardly spoken. She has lost the clan's trust.'

To that, my brother simply places a hand on my head. He says no farewell, or peace, nor kind words, but when he leans his head forward, his harsh words are only for my ears. 'You will be isolated from the clan, with no one to shield you. Be wary. Like the emperor, do not be alone with Hyat for long.'

I glance behind Yun. I do not see my brother. I see only a spindly shadow gawking at me from his heels. At last, I speak. 'I am forever the emperor's blade. A blade does not leave its holder's side. Wherever he walks, he will know I always follow.'

9

YEAR 514 AFTER NUH'S GREAT FLOOD, ERA OF
THE HEAVENLY BIRDS

Ghaznia Province, Sajamistan Empire

Prepare yourself, my uncle had said. Prepare we do, for my enlistment. Anger wraps around my heart like gold-threading. It smoulders in me through the long journey to Sajamistan; through stowing myself in Hyat's hovel in the mountainside; through throwing myself into his training of manuscripts and dialects, until the days bleed together and two years pass in a blink. But that is my anger; it robs one of time and sorrow. It throws my body into dark paths of fury – where I am at its mercy to accept it, of course.

Until finally, the week arrives for my enlistment in Sajamistan's army.

On that day, the black winter drops sudden, a marrow-deep damp that steals the breath of its inhabitants in cold huffs and lays a dusting of bone-white, virgin frost. As the wind whistles through the mountains of Ghaznia province tucked in the northern borderlands of Sajamistan, I shiver in my furs, watching my uncle in the dimly lit tearoom of our stone hovel.

He tests me about our story, front and backward, one last time. 'Your papers are ready,' he says, reclining against the divan of sheepskin. 'Tomorrow you will enlist in the army. Sajamistan's capital will be strange and different to you, but if there is anything the emperor and Eliyas trained you well in, it is your resilience.'

At hearing this mention, I ground my palms into the frozen floorboards, and they groan beneath me. I shut my eyes. 'Not that monk,' I force out.

'But then there is this weakness of yours to consider: your memory.' My uncle sighs. 'When I mention a word of your traitorous brother, your maternal tribe – anything of your past – your mind dissolves. You twist dates and time and memories.'

'I will be fine,' I mutter, but doubt creeps through my thoughts. Hyat calls them time-blanks. At first, I thought my uncle was lying to instil self-doubt, but I soon realised my memory *does* twist time in roundabout ways, mixing events. I assumed it to be the effects of poison training – but the memorisation required of me during my studies has not been poor. All the while, my subconscious laughs in glee. Hyat claims my mixing of memories must have slowly begun when I'd made myself forget memories of my uma's tribe. But in truth, the time-blanks have progressed since the execution of my traitorous brother.

He tuts his tongue. 'I must go to retrieve your parchments. Remember your cover. Shepherd the cattle down the mountain. Pretend to be an Azadnian servant buying salve for your ill master. We must maintain this routine. This is your last day before you walk into the arms of the enemy.'

Nodding, I draw forward, my shaky breaths fanning white in the cold air, laboured out like birth itself. Outside the wooden shutters, our mountain yaks and goats sound deep grunts, chewing on wisps of stubble and winter fodder.

'And remember to wrap your arms.'

'Already done.' I lift my forearms; my wrapping covers the gold-threading. And there is blue-threading of the crane symbols that I'd done with my half-siblings. Quickly, I blink away those memories.

'Be discreet. Wealthy clans in these parts of Sajamistan have Azadnian servants, stolen from raids. Worse, there are snatchers around these parts, with villagers disappearing.'

Though other Azadnians live in the Ghaznian borderland, like my uncle – some even venturing here to Sajamistan for richer trade, better pasture – it's always a risk to wander. It's common for tribes to be divided in their loyalties to each empire, or simply uncaring of empire affairs, tucked away in their small villages to survive yet another black winter. But the garrison soldiers lurk through the borderlands, and they are who I must watch out for.

I stand, wrapping my woollen shawl around my head. The shadow untucks itself from the corner of the room, following at my side.

'Do you have your blade?'

I tap my waistband, the khanjar tucked down my baggy trousers. Touching it evokes a pang in my chest. 'Of course.'

The journey to the peripheral hamlet is an hour down the mountainside, in the damp, bitter air of midday, chill puckering my skin in gooseflesh. The air is rough, freezing the goo in my nostrils so I can no longer inhale. Deep in the brambles of the blue expanse, cold fingers tickle my spine like that of an old witch woman, the air reeking with warning. Using my wooden crook, I bat along the goat and yak flock, pointing their henna-dyed heads down as the thick conifer forest unravels and twists.

Eventually, I reach a settlement sprawled down the steep slopes of the mountains, alluvial paths cutting into the rock side, overlooking rooftops of stony hovels and glacial river gorges. The central bazaar is on the edge of a lake, hosting all sorts of textiles traded from the Camel Road, but also smuggled goods from border townships. Knots of sleepy husbandry grunt outside the caravanserai, as shepherdesses break fast on sweet halva.

A priest greets the midday crowd at a temple's gates. He places a lamb bone into an offering pile, making me grimace.

Sajamistan's odd obsession with death is still as jarring as the first time I saw it. It's a custom – animal bones are collected in baskets every eve for the jinn-folk to feast on, though the Unseen creatures are imperceptible to our eyes. Even the temples are constructed from bone-stone, a masonry chipped from animal bone.

Shivering, I weave my herd past the priest, toward the stalls in front of the three-gated monastery.

A merchant manning one bellows to the crowd, 'We have pure water from the fiery wells of the Unseen world, said to be used by the jinn's ancient prophets millennia ago!' She waves the jar; shards of bone-pendants and raven feathers woven through her thick braid jingle with her movements. A sable cap holds her hair in place. All the embellishments to improve a nondescript face.

After securing my animal herd at the nearest apricot tree, I sell yak cheese to a baker for six meagre ingots. Then I wait at the apothecary stall behind a tall cloaked man. He trades for musk before stepping aside to make room for me.

The merchant greets me in the Ghaznian dialect. 'My sister, may the peace of death be upon you.'

Even speaking with a Sajamistani, a familiar rage presses against my ribs, but I swallow it down. 'And you,' I answer.

Two black cats purr around the clustered stall, jewelled and glittering in rich velvets and bone jewellery. Before the furred creatures, I glance at my peasant garb, a silk kerchief tied around my curls reeking of black seed oil. The thick calico of my robes, the colour of a weak winter-orange sun, is stained with poisons, and from the way the merchant purses her lips, she notices.

I tighten my shawl to shield my face before lying to the seller: 'My master is ill and requires preserved black seed in honey.'

'Ah, yes! Brewed into a tea of phoenix wings, a great salve for longevity—'

'Just honey,' I cut in impatiently. Her cats begin to hiss at one of my wayward goats, and I nudge it back toward my flock.

The merchant shakes her head. 'I insist, our phoenix wings for a discount.'

'No.'

'We have the best prices, sister!'

'I don't care.'

Beside me, I note the cloaked man's lips curving into a small smile. The merchant busies herself, wrenching open a glass jar, splashing in black seed oil and raw honey.

I hand the merchant the copper ingots, but she clicks her tongue upon weighing them. 'This won't do, sister. This is only three idriq, a third of the price.'

I frown. 'You must be overselling.'

She grins. 'No bargaining.'

'But this is overpriced!'

'And *I* want more riches, but we all are hopeless against higher powers, aren't we,' she retorts smartly. 'Border raids! Blame them for the steep price of harvesting honey.'

'A thief in common clothes,' I spit, and unfasten my satchel. Arguing would be reckless. She must hear my clumsy Ghaznian accent; knows I am a foreigner, frugal with her master's coin. Sajamistan's many dialects have several unvoiced consonants and glottal stops that I've yet to master.

As I'm turning, her cats suddenly leap from the stall toward my flock. Instinct alone makes my arms raise, intercepting them. Their talons rip into the white bandages around my right forearm, so quickly I hardly feel the pain, but the force makes me stumble back. It isn't until a pair of arms catch around my waist that I regain my footing.

'Are you well?' a cool voice asks into my ear.

It's the cloaked man who traded for musk. Ignoring the sting in my forearm, I quickly straighten away.

The mountain yak hardly arouse at the commotion but my goats skitter toward me on the wet path, splashing dirt which streaks across my cheek. I use my crook to bat my flock back into place before glaring at the merchant.

'Control your feline ruts,' I snap at the merchant.

Her eyes are curious as they survey my arm. 'My cats rarely provoke patrons unless they sense you are trouble. If you do not wish to pay, leave, *Azadnian*.' She is no longer warm. Unlike my cheeks that heat with fervour.

Scowling, I go to close my satchel—

A hand hovers above my exposed wrist, halting my movements.

'Will this do, sister?' the man offers softly. The merchant's eyes widen at the sight of two silver ingots, as do mine. From my shawl, I steal a glance at his features, making out a hard jaw over his collar, the rest indiscernible for the sheep furs matted around the hood of his cloak.

The merchant snatches at the silver. 'A wise bargain, my friend.' She hands him the honey and turns to the next client to cheat.

I stare at the silver and remember to bow, though more for the performativity of gratitude. 'Is it wise to brandish silver ingots? You will be a target for thieves.'

'Thieves,' he repeats before offering me the salve. 'You are not a native.'

Tension bristles up my neck as he glances at my right forearm. Unmistakably, the peeking of gold- and blue-threading of circular cranes is a clear mark of the empire I hail from.

His voice is cold but contemplative. 'In these mountains, the land's offerings are considered a gift from the Divine. The tribes say blessings cannot be owned, they must be shared, so thievery is rare from such community. I am only extending their generosity, *Azadnian*.'

A faint nausea floods my throat. My voice unsticks, and I make it as small as possible. 'I… am only a servant.'

The young man considers me and pushes down his hood. 'There is no need to fear me.'

But that makes it worse; better for the violence to be crude and blunt than the threat to be soft, hidden. I glance about, wary. 'Then I am in your debt.'

'Consider this to be my charity toll. It's Friday, the blessed day of Prophet Adam's death.' His small smile is almost self-deprecating as his hand reaches down, scruffing the neck of my wandering goat. 'And I admire shepherds.'

I blink at the soft words. There is no beard on his clean-shaven jaw, nor even long hair or a felt cap to stave frostbite. Instead, his raven black hair is a short crop of curls. With his tranquil words and bare face, I realise he is from the monastery.

'Very well. You have my prayers, monk.'

He turns fully, hazel eyes falling upon me. He is tall; my head comes to the height of his chin. His angular features are symmetrical and cold, eyes framed by lashes so thick, one would mistake them for sormeh. His skin is light, the apples of his cheeks faintly flushed, not unlike the local tribes exposed to the cold altitude. He could be the sole product of the Divine architect, whereby when He divided mercy into one hundred parts, and bestowed a slice to this world – leaving seventy-seven – a portion had been sculpted upon this monk, leaving the infinitesimal leftovers to the rest of humanity.

He is Sajamistani, I marvel, but he is still a monk, and I find monks more tolerable, in their quiet empathy, than any other person.

'It has been a long while since anyone has prayed for me. I welcome your prayers, shepherd girl.' His smile grows.

Before my mind can finish the thought, *he is a beautiful monk then*, the reminder that he is Sajamistani is louder, and the anger dampens the marvel.

He inclines his head and disappears into the bazaar toward a white gelding. A raven soars to his shoulder, making snug against his neck. For a wavering instant, my mind recedes into a sharp valley that tastes of wet and grasslands, of hunting buzzards cooing against my neck, but I shake loose the memory.

Then I am back to the present where the late crowd presses against me from all sides like a pilgrimage, the sweet aroma of fresh barley porridge and apricot-oiled flatbreads tempting me forward. My stomach growls but my hands turn over the jar.

There are no prayers in the business of deception. All I have is the blood oath I made to my clan. I hope it's enough.

10

The next day, at dusk, my uncle leads me to the Ghaznian citadel to enlist. The journey to the border of the central village feels short with the heat of fear pressing against my breastbone. The cold is merely a nip against my skin, time a blink, before we catch sight of thick, intricately curved walls of mud brick and bone-stone. The shadow follows at our heels, so silent and steady that I almost convince myself it truly is the blackness of my own shadow.

'The Sepāhbad-vizier of their army is no fool. Every action of his is a test. A paranoid bastard,' Hyat reminds me. Then he speaks more about our training; about my false cover as a servant. He reminds me of the information to search for if I successfully enlist: their battalions, their spies and finally, their knowledge of the Unseen world and jinn-folk.

At last, we slow.

We do not say farewell. Hyat simply lifts his Zahr khanjar and draws a line across his temple until blood weeps down his face. At my waistband, I pat my curved blade. Hyat melted the ivory crane-stamped hilt in the hearth, and struck a great iron crook against it, chipping away the Zahr welding until the pale sheen is no more than a stub encased above a silver blade.

'Remember your oath to the Heavens, little bird.' Hyat points up at the sky. The wind rattles through the eve like the cough of a sick child; the sky is a deep feverish blue lit by the firebird constellation scarring the sky.

Uneasiness fists my stomach. Once, my uma had claimed the Simorgh is a blessing, but each time I'd sighted it, there had been only cruelty in its wake. I know one truth, which is that I'd been weak in that past: someone incapable of saving my tribe, my clan or my uma.

A profound conclusion tangles within me. This constellation and I are one and the same, aren't we? That of an omen disguised as a blessing of light, perfectly content with its deception.

'I always will,' I answer quietly, digging my nails into my thigh.

After my uncle disappears through the conifer trees, I march on to the citadel. It's a defensive barricade above the river gorge, with looming turrets atop more turrets, of bone-stone engraved in gold cuneiforms of three-headed ravens.

Upon reaching the copper gates, I expect more fear, nerves, even anger, but strangely I am empty when I meet the gaze of the first guard.

'State your business,' she says flatly.

I hold my palm parallel to my chin, knuckles forward in their customary greeting. 'I am here to enlist at your citadel.' I speak slowly but her eyes narrow. Even two years of practising the uniform dialect of Sajamistan is futile. A native speaker will always weed out an imposter.

'Enlistment? Into what?'

'Into an army of Sajamistan.'

She blinks, taking in my peasant garb, my gaunt looks. 'Take her scrolls. Search her before she goes in,' she orders her comrade.

I cede the scroll which is a contract to a clan-master's house in the Ghaznian village, prepared by my uncle. Except for my pathetic dagger, I have no other belongings, but the guards are forced to pat along my limbs and back anyway. They roll up my sleeves, so it does not take them long to notice the crane symbols marring my forearms.

'Is this black humour? You're from Azadniabad?' the guard demands, her grip tight on my wrist.

'I am, as my papers indicate. The merchants here will recognise me as a local servant for years. I was captured in a raid from Tezmi'a and taken as a servant to be a shepherd for my master. But he died of an illness only last eve. With my master gone, and no land or wealth to my name, his will ended my contract, and I want to enlist in the Eajīz battalion.' I say this part quickly, but it only infuriates the guard further.

She twists her foot, and in a blink, my arm is wrenched low against my back. I gasp out from the tearing of my shoulder.

'Your kind dares,' she breathes against my ear, 'enter one of our armies?'

My teeth grit as she pulls harder, but I force out the words, 'Bring me to an administrator. I am an Eajīz, and I can very well prove—'

She throws me on to the cold dirt, but my arms cushion the fall. I lift on to one knee and breathe out a prayer before my right hand flicks forward, the Heavenly bonds along my knuckles splintering open. Heavenly Energy surges through the bonds, summoning my affinity. With a white splash, cold light manifests into a seductive amber, goading the worst of people to leap into its wrath.

As the nūr whooshes upwards between the guard and me – her eyes are owl-wide, making me conclude she must be a regular mortal, not an Eajīz – the air grows heavy and wet. Stunned, I touch my jaw at the sudden dampness.

The cold air pulls into a strange suction. It must be another affinity just arriving. My ears pop before water erupts from the density, dousing my nūr.

'What—' I stammer, but icy coldness streams into my mouth, eyes, ears, filling my lungs until the crack of my ribs makes me curl into myself. I cry out, fighting for air.

I expected to be attacked, beaten, but not killed instantly without a chance to finagle my way in.

Blindly, my hand clenches the frost-ridden ground, and I push on to my feet. Then a voice whispers from behind my ear, 'Not fast enough.' A blurred figure ducks under my arm and faces me.

My gaze locks on to illuminated eyes, and something inhuman stills me. I try to move but for that split second, my vision is overtaken by the gold of a thick Heavenly bond. It shoots out of the pupils of those eyes, wrapping around my neck, keeping me rooted in place.

This Eajīz is using eye bonds.

'Wait—' But the world blurs.

The Eajīz's hand curls into a claw, each finger jabbing into different points on my sternum, throat, torso, and when my wrist juts up to parry, they are somehow behind me, a finger pressed in the coiled spot between my shoulder blades.

The pain is not physical; it's spiritual, as if my soul has been ruptured from its corporeal roots. Even though I'm desperately mouthing the Divine's seventy-seven names, my soul can no longer sense my Heavenly bonds, the connection severed. Any Heavenly Energy within me thins like a frayed thread.

I need to run, or I will die—

The Eajīz reads my intent. 'Be still now.' His hand comes to a rest atop my head.

My vision begins clearing, enough for me to see that though his gaze is trained on me, he is addressing the two guards at the gates. 'She might run. Make it clean and healable.'

One guard grasps my left leg.

'No, I—'

She snaps it, a crack splitting the air. A stifled scream tears from my throat, salty saliva stinging the skin of my lip. The Eajīz catches me with his right arm. My head spins and vomit crawls up the back of my throat, leaving me no choice but to empty chunks of half-digested flatbread over the lambswool of his coat. He does not flinch.

He speaks, unfazed, his breath a puff of smoke. 'She won't be running now.' His voice is casual, like what he's done is nothing but a passing occurrence.

I am an animal cornered beneath them.

My mouth opens and blood spills out, dribbling down my chin. 'M-my soul, my bonds.' I panic.

'A shame. Even with power at your hands, you are reduced to this, crawling beneath someone else's feet. So tell me, foolish girl, why you have attacked this citadel?'

He lifts his hand and a small pictogram engraved in black-threading rests at the centre of his left palm. The dye is an indent of a black and red line. A singular Alif of the Adamic language. Small but prominent, and I recognise such a pictogram. I'd seen that marking years ago. It's the mark of the Sepāhbad-vizier.

I take in the warrior's pale mask, a blend of wolf and raven, in disbelief at the odds, before recalling Hyat's grim warning.

This must be the new Sepāhbad that my uncle referred to. This is that dark-haired right-hand warrior I saw, when the previous Sepāhbad invaded our capital and killed the emperor and provoked my uma's death.

This is the warrior who helped slaughter my clansmen.

A raven soars above the Sepāhbad before perching upon his shoulder. From my peripheral vision, I spot other soldiers who look like they've just arrived from the village. The Sepāhbad turns his head slightly and gestures once. The soldiers disperse into the citadel until it is only us and the guards positioned at the gates.

'You have not answered my question.' Under his mask, I make out hard hazel eyes.

Through the pain from my left, I force out, 'I-I did not attack first and... I never had any intention of... r-running.' I brush hair from my face. 'I came to enlist.'

The Sepāhbad pauses and stares at my features. Above his mask, a wrinkle forms between his brows. He unpeels his mask, letting it dangle around his neck.

'Shepherd girl,' the Sepāhbad says wryly, and I still.

'Monk?' I whisper in dread. It's the young man who had bartered for honey on my behalf.

His lips twist up, but I am the fool because I'd wrongly assumed him to be a monk. He'd never claimed to be one. How can someone who appeared so generous – so in tune to spirituality – be the Sepāhbad, applauded for his brutality?

The Sepāhbad releases me and I stagger on to my good leg. With his mask hanging from his neck, his features are clearer. Like in the bazaar, one might call him unnaturally beautiful. The black and gold embroidery of his tunic ripples in the dark. A three-pointed bone-stone pendant rests against his collarbone. He looks only a few years older than me, but Eajīz bear the long, cursed lifespan of jinn. The truth lies in the Sepāhbad's gaze, hinting at a wisdom far exceeding human proportions.

But whatever kindness he had worn in our first encounter is extinct. His gaze is sharpened by a dark keenness, such that if he were to peer into one's eyes, he could discover their griefs, angers, dreams, the very anchors of their soul, before crushing them between his fingers.

'You are a shepherdess but also an Eajīz,' he remarks while, on his shoulder, the raven cocks its head. He faces the guards. 'What have you learned?'

Imagine the ice-tonged paths of Ghaznia. Cold, and so still. It works. The heat within me recedes, leaving only cool anger. My uncle warned me if I fail the Sepāhbad's questions, I must accept death.

'After a raid, she was sold as a servant to this village. Her master was ill and died. She is free of her contract and wishes to enlist,' the guard explains.

'I see,' the Sepāhbad says to her, though now he is observing me. 'Is that all?' I nod carefully. He glances at my injury. 'Would you like your leg set?'

I hesitate, recalling my uncle's warnings about the nature of the Sepāhbad. He sounds coaxing, perhaps a comforting friend. This is a test. 'No. I came for a simple purpose.'

'Ah,' he says almost pleasantly. 'Would you like more honey?'

A jab about our encounter. I realise he cares little about these answers. My eyes burn but I blink hard. 'I would only like to enlist in your army. I-I have nothing left for me.'

The Sepāhbad doesn't loosen his gaze. 'What is your name?'

'Khamilla.'

'Clan.'

'Usur. Khamilla Usur-Khan.' It is difficult to hear him as my blood roars behind my ears.

'Khamilla,' he repeats as if tasting it. He must be piecing together that Usur-Khan was the nearly annihilated tribe from the Tezmi'a pastures between Azadniabad and Sajamistan. 'You are born in an Azadnian tribe.'

'Yes.'

The Sepāhbad turns away, hand gesturing to the guards in the way a shah might signal the execution of a paltry subject. *Even with my affinity, the Sepāhbad perceives no use in me. I am Azadnian; he will kill me as he killed my clansmen; he thinks me futile, pathetic.* My throat closes and I struggle to take my next breath.

'Wait!' I beg without shame as the guard steps forward, her scimitar unsheathed.

Despite my broken leg, I kneel until my knees imprint into the frozen dirt. I must discard everything for my purpose. I imagine I am speaking about my clan instead of an enemy.

'You are wrong. I know how to serve.' I speak not to him but to my life before this.

The Sepāhbad pauses. 'To live is to bow your head a little. If I let you live, will it bow to me?'

'Watch me.' I bring my head down to sell the lie. 'I have served masters dutifully my entire life. By the Creator, *I can serve you.*'

'Serving even a child can do.' He glances at the bone-stone mounds elevating the citadel. 'I care not for blood purity or even the name of an empire carved on your skin. I calculate only one's loyalty. Soldiers are the currency of war – and what they do to bring us to a position of strength. Tell me, what is your value?'

'My affinity is nūr. Before the Heavens, it is still power,' I insist. 'The mercy you showed me in the bazaar, I beg for it now.'

'But there is no mercy in my army.' He looks a little amused. 'Power kneels before me at my lever and command. Do not speak absurd notions of what power you may promise.'

A stillness sits heavily between us after his breezily uttered words, the kind of deceptive peace before the first drop of snow. I stare at the gates, even as he kneels before me so we are level.

Carefully, the Sepāhbad lifts my hand like a loved one to a loved one. A bout of nausea coils in my throat, but his grip tightens. He examines the mangled skin, the protruding veins, the awkward angles of broken bones that never healed right from years of training.

'This,' he soothes his finger over a nail, and I wince, 'could be torn off in one blink. Would you like that?'

'No.'

'Are you certain?'

'Yes.'

'We will check your master's contract,' he says, and I nod my head.

'You have been abandoned by your bloodline, empire and master. If you wish to serve me, you must have something you live for, vagabond.'

My tongue tastes the smoke from that day; I hear the clank of blades when our guards clashed against Warlord Akashun's forces; I see the raven feathers of Sajamistani warriors there to help him. My blood hums from the urge to do *something*.

I live to destroy you, I promise to myself, again, and again, as if it could soothe me.

Biting my tongue, I return to the present.

'As an Azadnian in this village, I will die.' My voice breaks.

From leather girdles around his waist, the Sepāhbad unsheathes a curved blade. With the other hand, he reaches toward my belt and pulls out my Zahr khanjar. Half melted and ugly.

'If it is death that you fear, then you cannot serve me. You might die in my army. You might die here. I see no point in this selfish desire of survival. That is not how my army functions.' His voice lowers. 'Every being serves a higher purpose, even the great shahs. But those who serve nothing have no direction. Serving can be slavery, it can be imprisoning, but it's also in our nature. In my army, you serve your superiors, your comrades, and nothing else.'

My blood curdles at his poisonous words. They strike so wrongly, but rooted beneath the pain is hard reasoning, a revelation I cannot refute.

He continues, 'Some beings are consumed by greed, coin; they serve for nothing but their own indulgence. An unworthy direction, but still it's *their* direction. You – you have none after your master's death, not anymore; or perhaps you had none to begin with. In you I see a girl never brave enough to return to her own empire. Bowing her head to her master, following the shepherd's path at a sheep's hide. A cowardice inherited by blood. It's hard to fight poison when that poison is a part of you.'

'*Not poison,*' I deny, but behind him, the shadow simpers closer, canting its head.

'You never returned to your true lands in Tezmi'a, and look where it's brought you, under the edge of my sword. Better your hands than mine.' The Sepāhbad's tone is spun silk, but it doesn't lessen the cruelty. He teases the Zahr blade in my direction.

We both stare at it. My neck strains to quell the shaking inside my body.

But I recall that sensation – the one of pure unadulterated life – pulsing and pounding behind my ribs. The will that craved a sense of belonging in my clan.

The choice is clear.

With trembling hands, I push away my khanjar. The Sepāhbad nods and flicks his blade in my direction, which clatters almost righteously at my knees. The gold-threaded handle glimmers. I reach out and press the flat of his blade to my forehead in acknowledgement.

Pride runs dry, but I never held any to begin with. Not when I was the emperor's daughter.

'We both know my decision,' I whisper, anger swelling in the rifts of my heart.

He considers me for a long moment. 'And what would that be?'

He's forcing me to proclaim my new allegiance. 'Sajamistan.' The utterance fills me with disgust. They ask me to cast aside my clan, my name. To become them.

'Have her leg set and bring her to the infirmary,' he orders the guards before standing. His gaze drops to the empty space between us, as if that chasm holds something that I cannot perceive. But that is fate, an empty space on a tablet scribed by the Divine to thread together two souls. In another life – if I'd become Azadniabad's vizier – I've no doubt this Sepāhbad-vizier and I were destined to meet like this anyway, an empty space between us as we stand on opposing sides.

He bows low in surprising sincerity before turning away. 'You have traded death to become an initiate. You will go to Za'skar, the city within a city where jinn and humans live together as one and Eajīz train to become their masters. I wish you well, initiate. Keep my blade as a reminder. If your oath is broken, your last duty ends with this blade and your blood running through your fingertips. Remember, there is no worth in one possessing no purpose.'

My kneeling legs buckle and I land on my hands, looking down at snow tainted by blood and vomit. My lips curve up, a panicked laugh caught in my throat. On the heels of relief, misgiving: this was too easy and I would be unwise to think he does not harbour suspicions about my intentions.

In the split moment before he disappears through the gates, I glance at his hands. His knuckles are calloused, gilded with faint scars.

Uma would deem him a hawk.

II

Za'skar City, Al-Haut port, Al-Haut Province, Sajamistan Empire

In the cramped, miserable caravan pulled by donkeys, I cling to the edge nearly falling out. The shadow is beside me, watching the passing scenery. My fingers graze my left earring, hanging uselessly at my lobe. We ride to the royal port capital Al-Haut in Sajamistan, home of the scholarly city of Za'skar.

As we cross the capital walls, the caravan jostles and shudders to a stop. A head pops through the camel-skin tent, belonging to a lithe young man, perhaps in his late twenties, who springs on to the cart, frightening the other voyagers with his rippling grace.

His coppery brown eyes are lined in sormeh; he has narrow features and the dusky red skin of desert inhabitants. His clothes have the typical sharp lines of Sajamistani attire: a high-collared pale tunic of fine linen with amber buttons, hemmed by stitches made of raven feathers, pale baggy trousers tight at his ankles, and a shawl crafted from tawny feathers tossed around his chest.

His curly hair is tied into a topknot, the tail of black muslin strewn around his head in a casual turban to shield the gales of gritty sand. The shadow of a beard bristles along his square jaw. On his arms, raven motifs gild his skin in the dye of blue- and black-threading. Even his earring is a bleached yak-tail bone in the lobe.

From his neck dangles a martial mask of bone-stone. His eyes begin to survey the passengers until they land on me, lighting up. My fingers dig into the tent of the caravan. Breathing hard. He must be an Eajīz from Za'skar.

Under the monks, I once wondered if I'd meet other Eajīz. But not like this. Never like this.

'May death be a peace upon you, new initiate,' he greets me. His dialect is the Sajamistani court vernacular, purged of the accents found in the other provinces.

'Who are you?' I ask.

'Unfortunately, your trifecta overseer, Yabghu of Squadron One, rukh.'

'Rukh?' I echo.

'Like the bird, *rukh*. We call low-ranks rukh. In this army, each initiate is placed within a trifecta: a group of three low-ranks mentored by a higher ranked warrior — an overseer.' Yabghu explains impatiently. 'Name?'

'Khamilla of the Usur-Khan tribe in the Tezmi'a steppes.'

'Wrong answer, Azadnian steppe-girl. A rukh has no name. Clan, tribal lands, these become insignificant in the Eajīz military. Your only identity is your rank — of course until you prove yourself.'

'I see,' I say warily.

'Bloodline?'

'None.'

'Good answer.' He slaps me lightly on the shoulder but the sheer strength behind this Eajīz warrior has stunned me, almost toppling me out of the caravan. Behind his easy smile, there is a tightness, and I squirm back on to my seat.

'Move,' Overseer Yabghu says to one of the passengers before squeezing into the caravan on my left side. He props his feet on the wooden ledge across, leather sandals nudging against a seated merchant who scowls at the offence. Yabghu merely smirks with the look of a man who knows he is superior to other mortals. I fight a wave of disgust. But I must get accustomed to this — touching and speaking with Sajamistanis.

'Rukh, look around you. It's not every day that an Azadnian witnesses the glory of our desert capital,' Yabghu tells me.

Before I can answer, the squawks of birds reach me.

During my long journey from the north, I was helpless against the envy that rose in me as I drank in Sajamistan's fat prosperity, evident by its provinces in the mountainous north and lush rolling hills; I felt it again on this journey, passing the desert valleys of bustling oasis cities fed at the expense of raids against us. The bone-stone masonry wealthier than any Azadnian craftsmanship. But I hadn't thought more of it.

Due to the growing shrieks of birds, and the glimmer in Yabghu's eye, I frown and lean my head out of the caravan.

Around us the rocky geography is a roughly patched quilt of landscapes, from the thrust of sand dunes and the saturation of blue salt craters to the occasional bursting streams. Not far ahead, I spot the bone-stone walls surrounding the ancient city-state. Clouds hang low so that flocks of birds appear to gasp out of them: ebony ravens, russet myna, fiery huma, and other abstract winged creatures I'd only read about in the legends found in the oldest tablets. The birds circle the blessed city with great warbles as if completing a pilgrimage.

My tongue is unable to formulate enough words. 'This city cannot be crafted by…'

'Human hands.' Yabghu finishes my thoughts. 'It is both. Jinn who gifted their labour to our architects.'

We pass through the gates. The sand-packed alleyways are flanked by winding eaves strung with smokeless copper lanterns embedded with gems, opals and rare pearls, a barely imperceptible liquid inside.

'This city is a legacy of riches from the bottom, darkest part of the ocean, retrieved by marid and jinn who once ruled here eons ago,' Yabghu explains.

In the royal quarters, bedrock supports a trifecta of palaces, at a strategic elevation, glittering with bulbous domes of crimson, gold and glass, shimmering like sunlight. Somehow the glass keeps clear despite the currents of nature. Copper bridges painted with raven glyphs weave one palace to the other, as if floating in the air of pluming clouds.

These are a people ruling the skies. And the creatures with it, not only land.

All of it should be impossible. But this is Sajamistan, an empire of tribes entwined with the Unseen world of jinn-folk and death. My eyes dart across the royal quarters over smooth glass palaces, paved somehow beside oasis ponds fed by the Vega Gulf's narrow seaside that gilds the south, shaped from the remnants of Nuh's Great Flood. Citadel fortress walls cut crosswise in double defensive rows, sectioning the city into quarters.

Predawn morning bakeries cough smoke while fishmongers set out the morning's catch. Greetings of death from milling city folk ring through the air of the Grand Bazaar, which reeks with cosmopolitanism and mercantile trades. My nose itches from stale animal-bone offerings. Scholars head to elaborate brass-gilded schools, and monks with tall conical caps begin their preaching in monasteries festooned with stained-glass mosaics. On the outskirts, sunlight glares against clusters of sunburnt clay villages amongst lush citrus gardens.

The caravan passes the city centre. Many people pull their shawls over their heads as they walk past a round, wooden structure, necks bowed, as if fearful.

'That cannot be *the* ark,' I stammer out.

Nuh's ark, in its humble half-eroded wood, outmatches any riches around it.

'A reminder of our end,' Yabghu says and I glance away. The contrast is clear – in Azadniabad, we meditated on being one with the life of nature – but in Sajamistan, they insist on being one with death, reminders of it all around.

We near a pair of inner gates, and Yabghu jumps out of the cart, dragging me with him. He turns and whistles up at the guards stationed on turrets.

The heat of the desert hits me like a slap and I cough through hot air and oud melting together. Before the caravan turns a corner, the dark shadow leaps out and crawls over to my feet, as always.

'Here it is, Za'skar City.' Yabghu gaze searches beyond. I follow his eyes, looking skyward. Slowly, the copper gates yawning up into the Heavens shake and tremble, seamed into the bedrock, separating the two worlds of teeming summer capital and scholarly city.

Yabghu's skin flushes in excitement. 'Look carefully, rukh.' He flourishes his arms. The gates finish opening and my eyes widen.

'*This* is the army?'

'Not only the army,' Yabghu corrects rather pridefully. 'The city within a city, an epicentre of jinn-folk, scholars and Eajīz. It is the birthplace of civilisation and magick, where the first jinn monarchs established courts before the Divine decreed punishment and the angels swept the smokeless fire-beings into the oceans; where Adam and Nuh came and went.'

Yabghu mistakes my fear for awe and crosses his arms.

'By the Divine, this is Za'skar: where the first standing army in the history of the world rose and resisted their conquerors.' His lips pull back into a sneer. 'Not a place for mundane mortals.'

Mist rolls from the abrupt collision of oases and hot air, tickling my skin like the strokes of an ink brush. Za'skar pulses like night and day, one end alive with wild gardens and monuments, and the other a blue salt desert, a sand-dappled vista, buckling beneath the sun's zenith. The city breathes power…

For an empire so undeserving.

Yabghu begins to tell me small facts about the city as we walk through the gate. 'Za'skar possesses an elite force of almost thirty thousand Eajīz. At any given moment, ten thousand reside here in the city; the rest are stationed in outposts. Some are advisers and senior officers, or generals employed under powerful clanhouses, not counting retired warriors. We're a small battalion but efficient—'

A sudden bell tolls through the air, ringing seven times, and Yabghu's pride bleeds away.

'That signal.' His voice tightens.

'What signal?'

Without answering, he pulls at my sleeve. The dark shadow follows in my direction. Around us, flurrying warriors rush down dunes and through fig gardens.

'You will see,' he replies grimly but his eyes catch on my forearm. 'Cover your threading.' He hastens his pace until we are running.

My eyes try to fill in my surroundings, but cries of orders and rough voices overtake the air.

'Keep up,' Yabghu barks as we delve into a maze of sandy avenues and quarters surrounded by pale sandstone and sandblasted complexes. Glistening ochre domes and stained-glass mausoleums with polygonal chambers decorated in green-hued geometrics lead to a bone-stone cemetery of martyrs.

'There,' Yabghu says, pointing to a tall amphitheatre enclosing a deep sand pit, adjacent to the cemetery.

'Lines!' officers yell and soldiers kneel in trios, forming long rows on the hard-packed balconies of the amphitheatre.

My gaze returns forward and—

I slam into a hard chest. A firm hand steadies my shoulder. 'At ease,' a smooth voice says from above. I glance up at an imposing warrior, dressed in a tunic identical to Yabghu's but ochre and crimson. His features are elegant from a hard jaw, sharp grey eyes and narrow nose – all of it pleasingly symmetrical.

He steps back and crosses his bulging arms, revealing gold-threading like mine along his sandy skin, a custom from the nomadic borderlands. But of course, the symbols are motifs of ravens; his tribe from

Sajamistan's slice of the Camel Road. His dark hair is tied into a small top-knot with raven feathers, a tawny shawl tied around his chest, like Yabghu. When we lock gazes, he cants his head as if unsure what to make of me before his eyes drop to my arms.

'Who is this?' A girl steps from behind him.

'This is the Azadnian initiate.' Overseer Yabghu waves them toward me, while using his other hand to yank down my sleeves. 'Surround her. Do not let the others see her yet.'

'But why—' I start, finding my voice again.

'Quiet,' Yabghu orders in a low snap, 'unless you have a death wish before you've become a proper initiate.' He faces the two warriors. 'Move quickly, Katayoun and Cemil.'

Katayoun must be the girl. She's shorter than me, but her muscles are thicker and corded, her skin a rich, dark brown. Her henna-stained copper hair is pulled into a braid at her waist, tasselled by bone-pendants. She wears a similar tunic to Yabghu's — except hers flows to her calves — and is fitted under a russet vest embroidered in gold swirls akin to Heavenly bonds. Her joints are covered in močpič martial wrappings. At her collar, a necklace of raven feathers and lamb-horn bones glistens in the sunlight.

'Is it wise to shield an Azadnian?' Cemil presses.

Yabghu uses his dagger to scratch at his neck. 'I hope you are not so arrogant as to question an overseer's orders.' His calm tone is enough to silence Cemil. 'Might I remind you, she is a comrade. In our trifecta.' He pauses with his dagger in his grip. 'Flank her. Now.'

The young warriors jump and hustle to either side of me. Still, Cemil's lips peel back. 'Coddling a rukh on her first day. Her accent and dialect are a dead giveaway.'

'Enough,' Katayoun hisses at him.

Yabghu gestures to the three of us but looks only at me, now using his khanjar to scratch his dark turban. 'Our last rukh died — rather tragic — but we have you to replace her.'

I just stare at him. Their last recruit died?

'An accident, really. Exhaustion from the rukhs' classes at the institute made her slip up during squadron training and a blunt arrow found its home in her eye. Anyway,' he claps, 'in our trifecta, Cemil has been in the army for almost two years, Katayoun only one, and you have none. Each trifecta is balanced this way, like the Three-Headed

Raven.' Overseer Yabghu then kneels, taking his spot in front of us, facing forward. 'Do not speak. Watch below.'

Two senior officers enter through a narrow sand-packed tunnel into the pit, dragging two chained bodies to the centre. Instinctively I look away, but Yabghu smacks my head.

'Eyes forward – *no, stop flinching*,' he snaps.

My world blurs, studying the tortured bodies.

'Of course she would flinch. These are her people, after all,' Cemil says carelessly.

A hush ripples through the crowd of thousands enclosing the amphitheatre.

A figure descends into the steps, the gold embroidery of his dark tunic beaming in the dawn, the raven curled upon his shoulder. The crowd bow their heads, lifting their clawed knuckles parallel to their chin, and I follow the salutation sluggishly. My breaths rattle in my throat; my eyes sting. My shoulders hunch as I press my knees harder into the sand to remind myself not to flee.

The Sepāhbad nods at the officers to string up the tortured bodies by their feet, upturned in the sand-rimmed pit. Two date palms growing on the perimeter, surrounded by pointy cacti, have been tied together at the top by a flax rope, and the men's legs are suspended at each end.

It happens quickly. They snap the rope, using sheer force to tear the bodies in two, red remains scattering among the jagged cacti below. Planks of flesh slew off in sloppy chunks, immediately attracting red wasps.

The Sepāhbad's inflection is gentle, but it carries firmly across the flanks. '*Live for the dead but bring death to the living*. That is what it means to be a Za'skar warrior to our enemies. Here, two spies from our own ranks dared sell intelligence to an Azadnian governess, costing the lives of garrison soldiers at another Arsduq melee. We have no mercy thus, for traitors.' His gaze roams through the onlookers. Impossibly – kneeling so far from him – for half a beat, our eyes meet: his cold, and mine shaken, my fears unspooled between his fingers. I reach toward my waistband, brushing the blade he bestowed me and then my melted Zahr blade.

Young warriors enter the pit, carrying baskets of food scraps. They unceremoniously dump them upon the corpses. Worms and fat maggots wiggle through the decay; more red wasps dive in, the meat of the dead in the happy bellies of the creatures. Rot unfurls in acidic fumes under the heat, stinging my eyes.

Everything blurs and the scattered corpses are no longer faceless but terrible imaginings. The emperor's onyx eyes stare lifelessly at me from a torn face. My throat clenches with the urge to vomit. On the other corpse, I see henna-stained hair strewn around a face gnawed on by crows; sorrow reflecting in her green eyes so like my own.

Uma, my lips mouth, but I stab my nails into the dirt. The corpses return to being merely corpses.

Then I take in the calm, almost eager, eyes of the surrounding warriors. Another violence stirs amongst the army. Their violence to defend this empire and mine to destroy it.

The Sepāhbad bows, and the ranks are dismissed.

Now I look not at the corpses, but at the black shadow that bounds down the amphitheatre pillars and crawls eagerly into the pile of decay, nibbling at entrails with a hunger that makes my own stomach echo strangely in answer.

Yabghu stands and brushes his trousers of dirt, grim-faced. 'Not the first day I imagined for you, rukh, but welcome to Za'skar.'

Despite the morning heat, a cold sweat breaks along my neck. Thousands of Za'skar warriors stamp their feet of sand and return to their assignments, with murmurs about the spies and Azadniabad flying between the ranks. Ignoring the shadow, I rub at my forearms as Yabghu leads our trifecta out of the sand pits.

'Hiding fresh blood, Fourth-Slash,' a razor-sharp voice mocks across the dispersing crowd.

'And what of it, Negar?' Yabghu doesn't spare a glance back.

A young woman who must be Negar steps forward with a dark glare, long russet hair swinging with bone-pendants. Her clothes are like Katayoun's except in pale shades of linen. Appraising me with a long look, Negar raises a marbled blade with four slashes by way of a greeting. At her heels, three other low-ranks study me in equally matched curiosity. They must be her trifecta.

'More like tainted blood,' another voice adds with a rough laugh. It belongs to a tall, burly woman – another overseer, perhaps, judging from the low-ranks behind her. Other trifectas pause at this, but my overseer yanks me away roughly, toward sandstone tunnels.

'If you value your life, keep walking,' Yabghu hisses.

'You cannot hide her forever, my overseer. The captain must have told them.' Cemil shakes his head.

Yabghu ignores him and leads us toward a patch of courtyards behind a cluster of illuminated crypts and ochre stone mausoleums.

When we're a safe distance away from the amphitheatre, I say, 'Surely in this city, I'm not the only,' my voice drops, '*Azadnian*. There must be other warriors descending from its clans.'

'Yes, perhaps a dozen here; the others are stationed at outposts in our provincial garrisons. There could be more who've lived in Sajamistan for over a generation and assimilated quietly and neatly.' He slows as we approach a garden of fountains. 'Outside of the forces supplied from clanhouses, Sajamistan's monarchy controls three standing armies of normal mortals. There is only *one* battalion for Eajīz. For that, Za'skar City looks past clans and tribes in its recruits.'

A flutter interrupts his explanation, as a large, white-feathered wing sweeps past my face. I stumble back into Cemil. Unfazed, Yabghu continues, 'Beware of the Heavenly ababil birds; they linger here in the Little Paradise gardens. On that note, look at the trees full of all kinds of berries. The bounties are forbidden to eat, the reddest berries descended from the Eden.'

Cemil looks slightly amused before shoving me away with the hidden strength of a Za'skar warrior. I straighten with a scowl. He will be a problem.

'Roughhousing a rukh on her first day. I taught you better than that.' Yabghu whacks Cemil.

Before us, little jewels of crisp oases, perhaps once fed from the Great Flood, spread across cracked sediment, rich fig and orange trees surrounding the glassy waters. Geometric fountains trail through the glistening foliage, emerald vines climbing wayward up pristine stone reliefs of jinn kings and ancient serpent beasts. Horned beasts slumber between the shrubs. Cheetahs prowl and human-headed peacocks splash water with their talons. Desert monkeys shriek through the poplars around the ponds.

Yabghu points at a walled crypt. 'The tombs of Prophet Adam and Hawah, his wife. Because of that, many jinn-folk and beasts are attracted here to greet them in peace. But the karkadann grow bored and well… ramming their horns into our sides is their version of play. For the monkeys, yanking your hair clean from your scalp is another. I suggest you carry incense with you, and a tongue full of prayers.'

'And this is natural, that jinn-folk live side by side with man?' I swallow uneasily, a memory pricking my thoughts. Something about the karkadann… but I will it away.

On the other side of Little Paradise, I sight children spilling out from a three-tiered sandstone structure carved out from the rose-gold bedrock. Yabghu follows my questioning gaze.

'Children live here?'

'They are young Eajīz, below the age of puberty – some orphaned, some from elite clanhouses. They study in fundamental pazktab schools sponsored by the sultana to control their affinity. For discipline, they do the chores in our kitchens. When they come of age, they enlist or are patroned under clanhouses of the royal courts. Cemil here was brought up in a pazktab school.' Yabghu nudges him and he rolls his eyes. 'And despite being an unpleasant ass, because of his time in the pazktab, he rose in the ranks quickly. In this city, many Eajīz hail from martial clans, trained first in pazktab schools to excel in Za'skar.'

I fight a grimace, understanding that I am against Eajīz initiates who've prepared for this their entire childhoods.

We near the apothecary quarters, a long ceramic pathway of ark statues, toward sun-brazen gold temples with prayer niches across the courtyards, though monks had beaten rows into the dirt from many prostrations. We pass two hammam used once a week; the baths are the only luxury afforded to warriors who otherwise bathe in partitioned rivers.

Yabghu shows me the training valleys, where squadrons practise battle simulations while terse officers scribe their formations on salt tablets. On sand fields, martial artists trade blows. Dunes tower high, unyielding in their might, concealing snakes, scorpions and perhaps the fossils of ancient beginnings lost beneath motes of sand. Uma once proclaimed deserts exist as warnings to the arrogant, punishing the curious by tempting them nearer. But in Za'skar, such warnings go unheeded by warriors who bury their fears in its terrain as they spar and roll before getting up and dusting off their tunics.

Yabghu explains that Za'skar follows a trifecta principle – unlike Azadniabad, halqas are not circles but a sacred trinity, where knowledge is studied in clans of three.

'In a matter of time, you will be fighting like them.' Yabghu nods forward. 'From a pathetic son of Adam's tribe to a knife-fighting warrior.' He unsheathes his khanjar. I realise every warrior possesses a sleek blade on their arm, the blue marbled hilt marked with slashes.

'See this?' His thumb guides my sight to the four white lines. 'Six years of training has made me a Fourth-Slash. Most do not surpass Fifth. This is the ranking system in the army. When you achieve four slashes, you graduate from the institute unless you wish to specialise under the scholars. Or you partake in larger military assignments. You have seasonal rotations at outposts, and the other half is off duty, or in Za'skar, as an overseer. If you receive the highest rank – Seventh-Slash – you've reached the standing of a Qabl master in the spiritual arts, and perhaps might even become part of the Sepāhbad's elite Alif. There are only thirteen active Seventh-Slash warriors.'

'Thirteen,' I echo.

The overseer smirks as though he can sense my greed. 'We wear the blades proudly to our knife fights, but you, trifle initiate, are a journey's time from holding one. You must *graduate* from your training blades. As a rukh, you begin at Zero-Slash.'

I seize this information. 'How long does it take for an initiate to climb rankings?'

He laughs like the question is from a child. 'It's cumulative. The scholars' assessments at the school; military simulations with our captain; your duels in Duxzam; how much one sucks up to a superior. These factor into reports to rank officers unless you are a genius – a rarity, really.'

Years is what he does not utter. Time I do not have. And being from Azadniabad… my breath rattles inside my chest.

I glance at Katayoun, who bears no slashes yet on her blade. And Cemil… he has two.

Before I could ask more questions, Yabghu holds out an arm. 'Understand the trifecta schedule at once. Every Friday and Saturday, we have no training and rukhs receive rationed waterskins to last seven days. You become sun sick, no one will help you. You fail examinations, do not whine to me or, Adam's sin, by offending a superior, you will beg the Divine for the jinn to curse you. You skip a class at the school or monastery, you are flogged. Every fifth day is tongue- and dry-fasting, no speaking sunrise until sundown. If caught breaking the rules, another bloody flogging. See the watchtowers,' he points to the city walls, 'one step outside past curfew, well… I will laugh over your dead body the next day when I find the arrows embedded in your heart. And remember, on the last day of each month, you receive a stipend. If you climb the ranks, you receive land or even an estate from clanhouses.

'The schedule is simple: twice a week, low-ranks have classes at the school. The other days, you will spend at the Qabl monastery to strengthen your Heavenly bonds. In the early mornings, each trifecta trains in martial arts. On Sundays, trifectas train with their squadron led by a mock captain to practise battle simulations in the tagmata – a regiment. Three squadrons form a tagmata. Za'skar is old. But behind it is blood, death and sacrifice. You wish to become a Heavenly warrior, to win Heaven's favour? You want this?'

My teeth grind together. 'Yes.' I force myself to bow my head.

'Then you must live and breathe her behemoth until Za'skar becomes a part of you. When one asks what your clan is, you say not lineage but Za'skar. When you embrace her wisdom, she will embrace you back. In the time of war, we dare not bow our heads and become fodder. Allow the unblessed mortals of the royal citadels to do that. We protect our empire. If you're here to become a mere foot soldier…' His lips pull down. 'Get lost.'

12

Before trifecta training begins, Yabghu hands me a pearl and crimson martial mask and takes me to the eastern quarters accessed by the outer brass gates. The mud-brick communes vary according to status; the lowest-ranked warriors are in segregated groups of fifteen while the Fourth-Slashes get rooms of two. A bone-stone wall partitions off the western quarters of Za'skar; a separate fortified enclave housing a taxonomy of retired warriors, senior officers, scholars, the Sepāhbad, his Alif warriors and the most senior Fifth-Slashes.

With a tight chest, in my communal room, I change into martial uniform, the same linen clothes as Katayoun: an ochre tunic, a sleeveless embroidered amber vest and dark baggy trousers with a raven-feathered hem, and a tawny shawl kept at the hip, to don for the hottest days. There are outer robes only required in classes.

A part of me is in disbelief that I am here, in the empire's capital. Through quivering hands, it takes two tries to tie my mask on my waist cord. The mask, hanging limply on the hemp string, reflects their lore; Sajamistanis claim the third face of their Heavenly Three-Headed Raven was in fact a she-wolf. Evident by a blend of wolfish and raven features on the mask.

A tremor brushes up my spine. Surrounded by enemies, I must do this alone.

'You are not alone.'

I jump and glance around the room, empty of other initiates. My stomach spools a thread of knots. Then I see *it*. Inside the hearth, the black shadow rests.

From years of observing it, fear does not race through me. That is, until the shadow shifts, from a gangly form into – impossibly – a ghoulish young... *girl?*

'Peace upon you,' she greets.

She has a white, bloodless face with pupil-less eyes. Her body is thin, translucent skin stretched over knobby skeletal bone, webbed in black lines like cracked porcelain. Her eyelids carved in blood red gawk at me. Her mouth parts, a tongue flickering out to wet her thin lips.

'You spoke,' I say in disbelief. The shadow that has accompanied me my entire life has never spoken.

'Peace,' she repeats. 'Upon. You.'

I flinch but her voice is cool, like crystalline river water. I must be going mad. This thing cannot speak. It should not speak.

'I can,' she puts in, as if hearing my thoughts.

This could be a jinn. *The Divine save me*, I mentally pray. *I seek refuge in you from the Unseen.*

'Stop that,' the shadow snaps. My pulse is a moth's tremor. Her voice is light, but unwanted, tangible and too powerful to ignore. No prayer can fling such a thing away.

'Am I cursed?' I grip the khanjar, hard enough that my fingers strain. 'I've seen it all my life and it has never once spoken.'

'I speak now because you've decided to need me, only at this moment,' the thing retorts.

This is my end, I realise. I wish I could believe that she is an angel but I doubt angels look as sickly as she does, nor do angels have the free will with which she moves.

'Perhaps this form is bad.' She glances down at herself. 'But I cannot change myself. I only took a form because is this not how one greets a companion?'

'*Companion?*'

'Yes, a companion of what you fear, desire and lust after. I'm you and you are me. I'm nothing and everything. Corporeal and spiritually immaterial.' She shrugs. 'You decide.'

My head begins aching at the nonsensical words like I'm reading sutras. Like my time-blanking.

'All living things have names. If you are real, you should have a name,' I speak slowly and my voice is uneven.

The shadow stiffens. 'I am not a living thing. What is my name?' She speaks like a child and with that, a sliver of my fear disappears.

The emperor once told me names hold power, for they grant one an identity, make one no longer a possession. My father resisted naming me. He'd stopped others from bestowing a name on me because no one should have power over me separate from his own.

This girl-creature does not need an identity. She does not need power. She is simply a manifestation of my madness.

When I meet the creature's expectant stare, I put force into my words. 'You are a creature of *no name*. And that is it. *You are nothing and no one. Only a curse.*'

She watches, so childlike. 'You've named me No-Name?'

I blink. 'What? No, that's not a name—'

'No-Name,' she repeats and smiles. 'A fitting name.'

'Usur-Khan?' Katayoun's voice breaches the room.

'Coming!' I tie my robe, strap on both of my khanjars and flee past No-Name as she grins.

13

It's a disorienting feeling having all your fears laid bare before you. I glance around at the city, then my overseer and the two low-ranks of our trifecta; enemies who, in a blink, would torture and hang me like the corpses in the amphitheatre, if they knew of my true identity. My hands raise and I curl them inwards, reminding myself of my dead clansmen, my slain parents. There is no point in resenting my reality – only bitter acceptance that I have walked into this pit of my own will.

Yabghu begins to take our trifecta up Za'skar's seven-tiered monastery, fitted with protruding red domes. The winds lash our raven-feathered robes in a flurry of leaves, mist and dirt.

'Catch up.' My overseer waves his hand before bounding at a graceful speed up the sandstone steps. Jammed into the belly of the mountains, the stairs stretch toward the Heavens, floating in the clouds. It's a winding staircase that sections off to different tiers and cloisters within the monastery, leading to the highest slanted roof.

'And remember, do not fall, little rukh,' Yabghu barks unhelpfully, already perched at the top, as I struggle not to trip over my flapping robes. The shadow of No-Name trails at my heels, as irrelevant but as eerie as the mountains displaying their jagged shadows against the clay.

The other two arrive at the roof first, and as I reach the last step, Cemil is standing off with Yabghu, his face stony, spine rigid below his long neck.

'—but, Overseer, you are his lieutenant.'

'And?'

'If anyone can convince the captain to draft me for the Marka, it's *you*.'

I slow, catching on to the word. *Marka*.

'Earn it first, underling.' Yabghu pats his shoulder before spotting me. 'That took you long enough, rukh.' The bang of a large daf – a drum – thunders through the monastery, the bone-stone domes amplifying the sound until the entire structure shudders. No-Name crawls to the corner of the roof, huddled against a cupola.

'Meditative rotations, for the monks,' Yabghu explains.

'We train here?' I ask.

Yabghu nods. 'On Mondays, we have classes inside with Grandmaster Umairah, an old warrior. Outside of that, trifectas are permitted to train anywhere. I prefer this roof or Little Paradise gardens.'

'To scare us.' Katayoun scowls at him.

He shrugs. 'If you fall off the roof, may the Divine be pleased with you in the next life. The most fundamental relationship for an Eajīz to gain strength is simple and linear – the more pain you suffer, the stronger your bonds to the Heavens.'

'Correct,' a hard voice peals out. A man detaches himself from a wooden entryway connected to one of the tiled domes. He glances over me, grunting, 'This is the piss of a girl?'

'Yes.' Yabghu lifts his curled hand before glancing at me. 'Greet your captain, Fayez of Squadron One.'

'May death be a peace upon you.' I bow and take in Fayez, a formidable man with a rock-blade shaven head, smooth light skin blue-threaded with ababil and raven motifs, and a pale shawl tied under his bulging armpits. He has the meandering look of an eroded riverbank, scarred skin and a lumpy nose carved out. His blade displays five proud lines – a Fifth-Slash.

At my bow, the smile touching Captain Fayez's features doesn't falter. 'I do not need your greeting of peace, but you will need mine, Azadnian.' His dark sandalled feet step up on to a slanted dome until he is above me. He plays with the clasp of a diminutive bone-pendant around his throat, nimble fingers knotting and unknotting with both hands, dextrous like mine. Like every high-rank here, I note.

'Remember this, rukh – if you have any hope to climb the rankings of this city, it's through my approval, worth its weight in gold.'

'Does this include the Marka?' I risk an ask and Cemil's narrow gaze darts to me.

Captain Fayez raises a brow. 'She knows about the Marka?'

Cemil steps between me and the captain. 'He would never draft an Azadnian for the Marka.'

'You speak as if I pose a threat to you.' I calmly meet Cemil's cold gaze. 'I do not even know what it is.'

A beat of silence settles, as loud as the knell of the monastic drums. Captain Fayez stares between us, a muscle twitching along his jaw before his expressions flattens. 'Very well.' He points far into the distance, at the blue craters within the salt desert, swarming with herons.

'Low-ranks are recruited into squadrons for the Marka of Za'skar, a sacred tournament dating back to the Jinn Era, when jinn tribes competed for territory like a game of polo. These days, we have remade this tradition. Anyone of Za'skar can choose their own squadron. In each squadron, only a total of thirty rukhs can compete with a captain and their overseers. The Marka is a strategy simulation. On the winter solstice, the recruited squadrons battle for territory. The best low-ranks within each squadron are guaranteed a rank shift, moving up one slash.' Captain Fayez points to the five ivory lines on the hilt of his khanjar. As if sensing my hunger, his lips curve up. 'That's how I received my first rank.'

I latch on to this revelation. If Captain Fayez drafts me instead of either Cemil or Katayoun for his squadron, I would jump to the next ranking, First-Slash, in less than a year.

'– but you are a new rukh. Undisciplined. Selfish. Greedy, disrupting the command chain. Uniformity is achieved in three ways.' Fayez points with his bone-stone pendant. 'Obedience. Command codes. And restraint. Qualities that you've yet to gain.' He waves his hand down. 'Summon your affinity.'

I flick Heavenly nūr on to my palm, using the method of the Azadnian monks: breathe meditatively into one of my bonds, send a prayer to the Divine and permit the affinity to channel forth from Heaven.

'Rukh, not only are your bonds thin, you summon using the wrong value system. Look at this ignorance. It's as if you are a child, using only prayers. The best Eajīz meditate every morning and night on a relationship with death, until prayers are hardly required for your bonds to have Heavenly Energy.'

I snuff the nūr. 'What?'

'But... you have potential.' Then Fayez is glaring daggers at Cemil. 'And you, swallow your arrogance. You might finally have competition.'

I only calculate one's power and strength. I could very well pick her for the Marka over you.'

My interest piques at this, wondering about Cemil's affinity. He clenches his fingers. 'Yes, Captain.'

'I've seen enough.' The captain bows to our overseer, throws a look of disgust at the trifecta and departs. Katayoun shares his scowl, watching Cemil and me.

Yabghu orders Katayoun and Cemil to warm their blood through stance training while he runs to the corner of the roof. He roves right through the huddled form of No-Name, making me flinch. She does not react to this, staring at our trifecta in silence.

Yabghu returns shortly with a wooden staff in hand and…

'Is that a bird's corpse?'

He raises a pile of animal bones and severed wings. 'These ababil birds passed naturally. But they left relics of their corpses— *no, stop gagging.*' But my horror is difficult to tuck away, the disgrace of it all.

'Because she's incapable of leaving behind what she knows of Azadniabad,' Cemil says, lifting a skeletal wing indifferently between his stances.

I take the severed wings. 'No, I can do this.'

Yabghu rakes his gaze unforgivingly over me. 'In knife fighting, we ease you into mastering the foundational nine stances. We meditate on the remembrance of death, for an Eajīz is a twin to the grave. Our connection to Heaven means we have one step in the psychospiritual world and one step in the temporal, mortal world. To die in battle is the highest honour.'

Cemil and Katayoun hold marble khanjars while Yabghu shoves a palm-sized onyx training knife aggressively into my hand as if I'm a babe. I almost curse at the insult of it.

Yabghu chuckles. 'O rukh, whatever clan you crawled from, they knew nothing of the marriage between true Eajīzi and martial arts. And you,' he examines me, 'look frail. What use is building on a weak foundation? Now repeat my stances.'

My scowl deepens, prompting another of his laughs, but at least he is no Cemil nor Captain Fayez. He is patient with me as we stoop low in the stance and breathe and recite the names of the Divine while contemplating death over the ababil corpse, the rancid scent making me gag again. Eventually, after the first exercise, it settles into my bones.

A smaller, darker thought wanders into my contemplations. If death is a mangle of bones and rot, is this what Uma preferred to become – primed to take her own life at a moment's notice?

'What else had she lived for,' No-Name says from behind my stance, startling me. Her pale bony body crawls across the glistening tiles – stooping to run the hole that is supposed to be her nose along the bird.

'Stop that,' I hiss at her.

'Stop what?' Yabghu lifts his staff. 'Have you quit meditating so soon?' In a blink, he strikes my swelling left leg, the weaker one, and I topple sideways, sliding down the slanted terrace. The tiles scrape sharply against my cheek before my fingers manage to scrape for purchase.

'Careful, rukh,' Yabghu dares to warn while I crawl to regain my spot.

'You did that on purpose,' I accuse, but his staff swings to my shoulder. My legs brace for it, stance balanced.

'I did?' He feigns.

I grit out another remembrance before saying, 'I am not the only rukh.'

'Of course.' The bastard thwacks Katayoun before he grins. Meanwhile, Cemil eases into each stance without trouble, the Second-Slash that he is.

Eventually, like in any meditative state, my seventy-seven bonds materialise through points on my body, gold lines stretching to the Heavens. With each breath, they thicken like shimmering roots, pulsing with Heavenly Energy.

'At each remembrance, focus on your Heavenly bonds like a muscle. Only then can you strengthen the spiritual muscle of your soul, called the ruh, and each bond within it. Breathe conservatively, to gather kinetic energy and transmit it in small doses, until, outside of training, you subconsciously save energy even while sleeping. A true Za'skar martial artist masters how to move merely by shifting their weight rather than using muscles that are not needed; the best fighters never lift their feet.'

Yabghu's hands move like the soft aches of the breeze, pushing upwards to the Heavens before clasping downwards at the end. Some are variations of common martial stances even in Azadniabad, and others are new... and strange. Like an awkward-limbed child, I follow along while breathing in the reeking, stale bird bones.

Yabghu cocks his head. 'You are not a complete novice.' I straighten at his thin compliment and note Cemil's watchful gaze on me. 'What is this style?' He puts down the staff. 'Like water flowing through roots.'

The blood drains from my cheeks. It's the Seven Gentle Paths of Dawjad.

'You've trained in martial arts for how long?'

Hyat Uncle advised me to accept any suspicions boldly. Better to speak less; only liars speak often. 'For years. It's common for servants to learn with the children of their masters.'

He unties the black muslin of his turban, wiping sweat from his temple. 'Here, we follow Eajīz arts. We'll improve how you summon Heavenly bonds in due time.'

Throughout the day, my muscles quiver and when I pause to catch my breath, Yabghu slams his foot into my back, sneering, 'I did not order rest. Repeat it, twice as long.'

He circles us, his staff batting Katayoun, Cemil and me if we dare slouch. Until midday, we sweep our arms and recite the sound, channelling into the movement of our forward-facing palms. We carve X shapes in the air, or trace loops. We do nothing else but this – five hundred, six hundred, seven hundred – almost eight hundred times.

After two hours of aching movements, he assigns stretches to practise in the evenings, for no martial artist is adept without flexibility. With an amused expression, he hands me an iron whisk to beat myself morning and night.

'This will develop your corporeal form into the martial phenomenon of *iron-bone*. Tap lightly but rapidly in striking motions.' He points to Katayoun, who demonstrates by brushing a whisk across the length of her arm in an upwards motion. 'Emphasise the collarbone because it's the easiest bone to break but the hardest to heal. The iron whisk bruises skin and raises welts, but it causes the body's tissue to become dense without increasing muscle mass. Your bones will be as tough as iron. *It will hurt*. But pain yields great reward.'

Experimentally, I tap my knuckle and wince.

'Today were principal breaths. Tomorrow, we begin Stratum training to supplement the forms. I don't expect a rukh to memorise the nine stances today.' Before relief kicks in, he grins smugly. 'I expect you to memorise their order by tomorrow. Cemil and Katayoun will help you.'

Once, the young girl in me was curious about the true nature of Eajīzi. Now it feels like the cost of fulfilling that desire was my clan. That part of me should stay dead.

'You truly think the captain would draft you in his Marka squadron? He despises Azadnians,' Cemil asks me, as we stamp away sand and remove our leathery clogs to break for evening fast.

After a long silence – filled with the clanks of thousands of warriors drinking tea, when we have taken our seats on floor cushions – I take Cemil in slowly. 'The captain said he looks at power. So it depends on if I prove my worth over you. And I will. But I wonder, do you feel threatened by a mere novice?'

Across from me, his fingers tighten over a ceramic teacup before his lips turn up. He grabs a copper jug, and pours rose kahvah into his cup. 'Time will tell. For now, let us drink tea, rukh.'

The pavilion is a long hall of slanting roofs carved with red embossed calligraphy; filigreed lanterns with raven carvings and coloured glass, blown by jinn, throw out smokeless fire in a haze of copper, courtesy of what I assume to be the jinn-folk's energy. Scents of fresh flatbread, smoky incense, stale bones and rose permeate the air in a strange blend.

Marbled low-tables for the trifectas, with hemp mats and rose cushions, stretch over bone-stone flooring layered in thick crimson kilim rugs. The geometric vaulting shines in hues of greens and golds, with strange paintings of ichor-wilted flora growing along tombs of martyrs, francolins dancing along the edges as if at any moment they might soar free from their cages.

Older pazktab children carry large platters as they dart between low-tables at the instruction of their masters. The furthest end of the pavilion is divided off by a great latticed partition with a stunning array of divans for higher ranks and visiting bureaucrats with courtly ravens perched on their shoulders. At the edge of the room is a marbled slab with carved niches, into which many pazktab children scrape piles of picked meat bones and food scraps.

'The local jinn-folk dine on bones and leftovers,' Yabghu had said when we entered. No-Name delights in this tradition, her shadow curled into a niche as she pokes her tongue into the jinns' scrapings, while I sit with my trifecta.

Eventually, Overseer Yabghu speaks up, 'Careful, underlings, I could have the captain pick Katayoun over you for the Marka,' which sends Cemil choking on his tea. Katayoun, as I've noticed, remains silent, merely observing our exchange with an inscrutable look.

Before Cemil can reply, a sea of trifectas filters into the pavilion, many staring at me. Word must have got around. I watch a familiar woman sit to our left.

'Overseer Negar,' Yabghu greets. Another crouches to his right, the same from the amphitheatre. 'Captain Madj.'

Pazktab children rush forward, serving rationed food of turmeric and saffron pilaf simmered in lamb yakhni, a spiced lentil stew, and a long black-sesame-coated flatbread with a quill-stamped raven symbol carved into the centre. It's smeared with aged garlic so sharp it stings my nose. After a prayer by a priest, and bones picked from the lamb pilaf into the offering piles, warriors begin to break flatbread into a spiced stew of lentils, barley and fenugreek. I pick at the bread, prodding my tongue into clay-oven-charred bits.

'What are you doing?' Cemil interjects and I drop the bread, realising that I'm instinctually checking for poisons.

'Losing her head,' Overseer Negar says from my left, resting her head on her palm. 'The poor girl's starved; she's never seen food like this before.'

'I agree, I've seen better.'

Negar's voice stays pleasant. 'Watch your mouth, rukh.'

Yabghu clears his throat. His glare tells me, enough. Making enemies like this is rash. Foolish of me.

I bow my head, wondering how to navigate this. If I concede, I appear like easy prey; if I speak hastily, I incur the wrath of my superior.

'The rukh's teacup is empty. She needs fresh kahvah. Give it to her.' Captain Madj plops a dark sugar cube under her tongue before raising her cup. 'We have a new initiate. Seems appropriate to drink kahvah to *it*.'

I ignore that jab. 'Yes,' I say hastily. This breaks the tension.

As I pour new tea, she waves down our long communal table. I learn she's captain of Squadron Three, and – I quietly note – probably Fayez's rival. I tuck that information away for later. She introduces a mix of low-ranks and high-ranks, whose names I hardly remember – Aizere, Yima, Sharra, and more and more – who hail from across the empire in various tribes and shades, and who pass clay pots containing fennel and mint bitters before the meal. How dare they act as a clan... like *my* clan.

Though it would be well for me to greet them, no words come forth; I've never spoken with students, especially an Eajīz of my age. Hyat Uncle prepared me for many things regarding war and violence, but nurturing relations – even basic civility – this, my clan could not teach me.

From the corner of my eye, I catch Yabghu frowning at my lack of effort.

My mood darkens and I lift my teacup of kahvah. As the rim grazes my lips, instinct tells me to look down.

Cemil's eyes darken. 'Wait.' Before I can react, he lunges across the table and knocks the cup from my hand. It flies backward, shattering against the wall beside Overseer Negar.

The pavilion dampens, nearby conversations falling into silence. From my right, Yabghu lifts my plate, cursing. Red scorpions skitter under it. Near the wall, my shattered teacup scurries with tawny beetles blending into the same shade as the tea.

At the commotion, No-Name leaves the jinns' offerings and rushes to the low-table, staring at the scorpions.

Cemil calmly recrosses his legs on his seat and sips his kahvah. 'Do not be surprised, Overseer. Of course she has enemies.'

'Those are poisonous,' Yabghu snaps. 'The pazktab children must have tainted her dishes while serving her meal.'

'See it as a gift,' a gruff voice says with a chuckle. I turn and an old crone of a man in scholarly robes leans against the teak partition, lips turned up mockingly. 'The pazktab students are simply welcoming her to our city with what her kind prefers – to be one with Brother-Nature.'

Laughter threatens to spill from my throat, to tell the scholar that this is *nothing* to the threats of the eight great clans of Azadniabad. I built resistance to red scorpion poison at the age of fourteen. Instead, I push back from the table and stand, the nearby soldiers and overseers staring up at me. My neck prickles from the weight of them. No-Name comes to my side.

'I will go,' I tell Overseer Yabghu, but privately, there is a quiet relief. Now I have another reason to cling on to my anger.

14

After a night of beating myself with an iron whisk, as per Yabghu's orders, I walk toward Little Paradise gardens for trifecta training. It is early, before the dim blue of dawn when the birds have not chirped, but the sun has started to awaken. At my side, No-Name steps tentatively through foliage fed from an oasis, picking through tall tulips and purplish saffron.

A weening light shines upon baby-horned bulls slumbering atop the fountain tiles, musk-scented water pouring through long qanat systems. Red sparrows warble quietly inside the azure bowls, clustered little babes yearning for a lick of Paradise waters. I am careful not to disturb the creatures as I make my way to a crop of almond and poplar trees, my waterskin filled with freshly brewed kahvah.

After climbing a low-hanging branch, I unsheathe my onyx. No-Name crouches against the base of the tree, and I try not to look at her.

'What is that?' she asks, pointing toward the fountains. Ignoring her, I balance on the limb through the nine stances with my training knife.

'What is that?' she repeats.

'What is what?' I snap just as a hoarse yell breaks through the clearing. Below the branches, I recognise dark blue tunics and loose, ill-fitting trousers with gold hemp cords yanked tight at the waist. It's Eajīz from the pazktab school.

I watch as three of the students surround another against the fountain.

A small boy with a swollen cheek and bloodied teeth shoves away the fists of a lanky girl. Before long, his satchel is ripped open as the girl tosses out his parchments and calligraphy set. She digs around furiously and proudly produces his bundle of apples, slivers of melon and dried lamb meat inside palm leaves.

Behind the bloodied boy, an even younger boy wails at the sight of his friend's demise. 'By the Divine, don't hurt him!' he yells through a broken lip.

'A brat barely done milking is ordering me what to do,' the lanky girl sneers.

'What is that?' No-Name asks again, half in shadows, eyes pitched black.

'*Who*, you mean. Those are pazktab children beating a boy,' I tell her. 'Will you help him?'

'No,' I decide, 'the pazktab children put scorpions in my tea.'

But the boy's cry has me peeking again. The leader clenches him by the collar, her knuckles digging into his fleshy neck.

'I am taking all of this,' she says, as her companions stuff the scraps of food in their satchels. 'But to be polite, we're leaving behind an apple. We have manners in stealing.'

I open my waterskin, knowing I should keep practising my nine stances before training, but somehow unable to look away from the children.

'What if he runs to the Qabl monks?' a student points out.

The girl scratches her kerchief. 'Okay.' Then she gives the boy a half-measured kick in the legs. He cries out, cradling it. 'Taken care of.'

I sip from my kahvah, marvelling at the pragmatism.

But the little one with the swollen lip staggers to his feet and pounces on the girl. She rears back into my tree. The force jostles the branch, knocking over my onyx knife and kahvah before I can blink.

What in the Gates of Hells. After scrambling down, I stride over and grab my waterskin.

The girl looks startled by both the falling objects and my sudden presence. 'Where did you come from?'

'Your...' I search for the appropriate word, '*training* knocked into my tree.'

'Who are you?'

'No one.' I glance at her fist and the boy who had the satchel. 'Please, continue on. But away from me. This is my trifecta's training grounds.'

'Training grounds?' The pazktab girl seethes.

The injured boy whimpers. I scoop up my onyx, ignoring that whimper. 'Besides, if you are going to thieve food from this boy, at least finish the job with dignity. You want to kick his leg? Smash his kneecaps instead. One quick blow. He won't be able to walk.'

'Why would I cripple him so violently? I have *some* morals.' The girl drops her fist and takes in the gold-threading below the sleeves of my tunic; recognition settles in that gaze. 'It's the Azadnian recruit from last eve.'

My gaze, too, narrows. 'Was it you who poisoned my meal?'

Without replying, she charges me with her companions hooting behind her. My eyes widen. I duck from her wild hook, spin and send a quick palm strike to her kidney. There was little force but it sends her crashing into the poplars. She does not stand again.

Her companions stare at me. 'It is true. Azadnians are child killers,' one mutters. They haul up the girl between their arms and run off, the apples and melons all but forgotten in their haste.

The target of those children scrambles to his feet. He's a stout boy and sun-browned, thick curls grazing his head.

'How did you do that to Arezu?' he breathes, limping toward me. 'Your movements... are like water.'

The other little boy, sporting a broken lip, merely watches us wide-eyed.

'It was simple, really. Even Azadnian arts have palm strikes, and combined with iron-bone training, it hurts.'

The boy throws himself at my feet. 'O master, I've read of iron-bone only in the martial tales.'

I blink down. 'What are you doing?'

'You went like *this*, and she went flying like *ahhh!* And she did not get back up!'

I retreat toward my almond tree, but he follows. I grimace. 'Please, get away before my overseer sees me with you – *you pudgy thing.*'

'You must teach me, esteemed Azadnian master—'

I nearly sputter out my tea. I am as far as one can be from a master. The opposite, actually.

'– *please*, I need your help. Pazktab schools are made up of martial clans, and the children without a clan or its protection are the rats. I know I am young but I hear the Sepāhbad was recruited at only thirteen years. His youth never hindered him. Train me!'

'No.'

'Please!'

'No.'

He decides on flattery. 'With your unpredictable style, the others will envy me. If you train me, I will do your bidding. You are Azadnian; I can ensure the others do not spoil your meals again!'

My cheeks heat at the thought of allying myself with a pazktab child, as if I am that desperate. He steps forward but I shove him back.

'You are simply confused. In fact, if they thrashed you black and blue, I'd have watched from my tree, content. I want nothing to do with disgusting *bone-reeking* pazktab children in Sajamistan. Pester another recruit to train you.'

With that, I retreat to the opposite end of the fountains until my trifecta arrives.

Throughout sunrise, as we train, I catch the same young boy peeking through the gardens, observing our stances.

Yabghu allots me a week of curricula to memorise before I join other unranked rukhs in the Easkaria institute. The scholars teach subjects ranging from arithmetic and old Adamic linguistics to theories of Eajīzi and martial history. But like the meal in the pavilion, my first week of classes becomes its own torturous trial.

'To be on time is to arrive early,' Yabghu advises me at midday, pointing to a school of bone-stone masonry of hexagonal patterns that glows above Za'skar City. Mist clings around its trifecta of bronze domes atop tall pillars like a white shroud, with a topiary of sweet lemon trees at its gates.

'This was the first school in the history of mankind, patronised by the wives of royal clan leaders long after Adam, containing centuries' worth of knowledge. A fine education but really every initiate's place of torture,' he warns me.

I follow Katayoun to the Easkaria institute for our halqa on martial history and strategy, while Cemil splits off for his Second-Slash classes.

Inside the musty, intimate chambers, the flooring is tiled in ivory shielded by embroidered rugs and silk cushions stuffed behind teak book rests called rahle. Cedar walls are plastered with camel-skin maps. The smog of myrrh incense fills the room, tickling my nostrils.

As we enter, Katayoun turns to me, her tawny eyes flat as always. 'I will say this once. Speak as little as possible to Scholar Mufasa.'

A leathery scholar sits cross-legged on a tall cushion at the front. I stop short. The same one who openly mocked me during the evening meal.

Scholar Mufasa has beady dark eyes, a stern mouth and severely clipped grey hair. Over his pale tunic, a pleated emerald robe bears a white pattern, the overgarment stretching to his ankles, slit sides slit, and girded by an embroidered belt. Stretching across his forehead is a black-threaded pictogram of an indented line with a teardrop – an esteemed symbol indicating his scholarly status. Behind him sit two apprentices on floor cushions.

'A quarter of an hour,' Scholar Mufasa announces softly without even sparing me a glance. He points to a rahle towering with goatskin scrolls. 'Any longer and you fail this assignment, resulting in punishment. The material from this week's texts was on the battles of the Camel Road. You must translate a prompt from old Adamic linguistics and then answer it through a discourse. Begin!'

Removing my sandals and sitting behind my desk – a rahle – it takes me two tries to unroll my parchment. The script is jumbled letters of ancient Adamic.

After using a flat stone to weigh down the parchment, I cut the nib of my reed pen and dip it into a pot of dissolved gum, honey and lamp soot, remoistening the ink, which wastes ample time. *A quarter of an hour.* He hopes to fail us.

Translating the glyphs into standard Sajamistani is a trying task, as I am no native in its language. 'Ten minutes,' the scholar says gruffly. Sweat beads down my neck. He begins tapping his fingers against his rahle, a music of damnation.

I finish decrypting the language. It reveals a simple prompt – to explain the clan alliances of the Camel Road. I glance up and the scholar stares at me, calm. This feels intentional.

But in history, I cannot fail.

'Time is up, rukhs!' Scholar Mufasa raps his staff against his desk. 'By the Easkaria code, examinations separate the studious warriors – the ones who aspire to be true intellectuals – from the indolent novices who assume being a warrior simply constitutes throwing a fist or wielding a blade. Each scroll shares a common theme – the art of reducing the enemy's will, a worthy lesson in our history.'

He paces before us. 'Pupils must learn the essence of warcraft. War is the art of reducing the opponent's will physically and mentally until an aim is achieved. It's countering an opponent's strengths and exploiting his weaknesses by out-positioning him in peacetime or warfare. And thus, we start after the Great Flood by understanding its themes in every major onset that fractured peace, beginning with Azadniabad and Sajamistan.'

He scans the first row. Initiates straighten their backs, fearful of becoming the target of his temper. I can sense it congesting the air, a living thing waiting to pounce.

'Rukh.' He points at an initiate. 'Present your answer.'

The boy crumples his parchment. 'Scholar Mufasa, I did not finish translating it.'

Mufasa stalks to the boy. 'Emirhan, tell me your answer.'

Emirhan pales to a waxy complexion. 'I said I didn't—'

Mufasa snatches the scroll, smoothing the creases. He emits a displeased sound before ripping the parchment to shreds. 'You did not read this week's material. Stand at the front. Do you not know better than to neglect your readings?'

'C-certainly, my scholar.'

'Your excuse is what?'

'I have none, my scholar.'

Scholar Mufasa gestures at his tunic. Complying, Emirhan unfastens the gold-buttoned latches, revealing a thin undergarment. With little preamble, the staff strikes his back. The room jumps.

Emirhan's mouth opens, to cry, curse – I cannot be sure except that his teeth sink into the meat of his tongue, red staining his teeth – but still, no sound escapes.

Scholar Mufasa flogs his back quickly, neatly. My hands tuck under my thighs, resisting the urge to clamp my ears against the din of slapping skin.

It's not the flogging unnerving me – such a punishment was frequent in the monasteries from my childhood. It's Emirhan's lack of protest. There is no whimper. His submission stirs my curiosity – like looking at a dead body in fascination even when you should not.

After fifteen lashes, Mufasa gestures to the entryway. Emirhan shuffles like something is wedged between his legs, drawing attention to the yellow on his pale trousers, the piss odour permeating the room.

I glance away in mortification as if I can erase the incident by not looking.

Mufasa sighs. 'Mark my words, that's the last you will see of him,' he says before he resumes checking parchments of the rukhs named Yima, Sharra Aina. Finally, Mufasa's sandals reach my kilim. 'You, Azadnian.'

I rise to my knees before inclining my head. 'Yes, my scholar.'

He glances down at my inked parchments. 'Explain the alliances of Tezmi'a.'

When I speak, my voice cracks but I smooth it out, knowing better than to parade my fear in front of scholars. *Be the clay*, I will myself. *Smooth and hardened beneath the sun.*

'The Camel Road—'

'Speak louder,' he snaps.

I clear my throat. 'The trade nodes of the Camel Road between the empires to the north and south and east are guarded by the Dawjad, Usur, Khor and Qan frontier tribes. In the Tezmi'a gorge, the Xasha and Qan clans allied beneath the banner of Usur-Khan through proposed marriage alliances,' I pause but he gestures at me to continue, 'until the raid of 508.'

'Stop.'

My lips clamp.

'Sit.'

My knees collapse like an obedient dog. The room suffocates with a warring tension.

Scholar Mufasa holds my gaze for a long moment. Years of paying attention to the emperor's every action clue me to his foul mood. His eyes, though calm and steady, do not trick me because his knuckles tighten on his staff. I have done something terribly wrong.

'You believe the words you've just uttered,' he says, pressing me.

'Yes, scholar.' Because hesitation would upset him more.

His grip tightens further on that staff of his. He punished one student today. I wait for a hit, a strike. Around me, students exchange glances. Still, he does not speak.

My lips almost part to beg punishment. I've learned fear stems not from pain itself but from the inability to foretell what form it will take, even as you sense it is forthcoming.

'You have read the manuscripts for this week?' he finally asks.

'Of course,' I answer.

'And this was your interpretation? Marriage alliances, instead of raids across the borderland to bring the clans to submission and force the allyship? What else prompted the final raid that annihilated them?'

'Famine,' I state carefully but my fingers dig into my ankles as my head begins pounding.

Mufasa snorts but simply steps past me, green scholarly robes swishing against my shoulder.

From my right, Katayoun shakes her head. 'Do not speak more.'

After listening to the rest of the rukhs' answers, flogging only two more pupils, he passes the class. He addresses the chamber. 'These prompts prepare you for the final Wadiq tests at the end of the winter, the most difficult examinations in the entire institute. Today, after my lesson, you will be expected to scribe my lecture again, to test your rate of retention. To prepare you for the Wadiq tests, in the last quarter of the hour, we will run through strategy simulations about a chosen battle. Who will go first?' he asks.

When pupils raise their hands, I grit my teeth. Yabghu had said the scholars' classes influence rankings in the city. So I raise my own, before Katayoun grabs my arm, yanking it down.

But Mufasa sees it. A malicious glint flits through his gaze. 'Oh, the Azadnian has more to say? Taking the curricula we'd assigned and warping it to your own conclusions?'

I drop my hand. 'Scholar, I don't follow.'

'You fool.' Katayoun briefly shuts her eyes.

The scholar points to my parchment. 'You answered the question, which saves you from punishment, but you interpreted it to fit a narrative typical of your kind.'

'What narrative?' For years, I'd had the tutelage of the Azadnian scholars, but being in Sajamistan, none of that education seems of any worth. 'I was born in Tezmi'a. I know my own history.'

'Bias and pride.'

'I have no pride.'

'Then tell me, *how* many raids had the Usur clan instigated for the Azadnian emperor?'

'None.'

'Are you certain?' Mufasa's chuckling tone grates on me like he is the emperor administering a poison test.

My willpower snaps. *'Yes, scholar.'*

He waves a hand dismissively. 'The same pattern of violence continued and continued until the Zahrs rose to power on the heels of invasions, taking the Camel Road to maintain their rule on its trades. At the cost of thousands.'

My ears feel hot. Uma was right, they hate us. They lie even about our sorrows.

'Every Azadnian dynasty, from the Stone Empires down to the Zahrs, used the Camel Road as their fodder to fund expansion and stoke more war against their sworn enemies. They never cared about the people on the land, not when the land of the Camel Road was more valuable than any human life, to feed their rule.'

And what of your empire, that threw me out of my birthlands in the first place? But the scholar speaks more, and it becomes harder to breathe. My senses clog, my surroundings blurring like I am underwater until I am floating out of the planes of my body. *He is wrong*, I repeat to myself five, and then ten, times.

I know how to defend against attacks. There exists a countermove for every offence, but how does one defend against an unseen manoeuvre? This battle is not one that can be blocked with fisted hands. The room begins to sway. I wish to crumple, but in a space full of enemies, I can do nothing except become still and obliging.

To distract myself, I start counting, skipping in twos, fives, tens, hundreds. Again and again. Behind the scholar, wedged in the corner of the chamber, No-Name is silent as the shadow she is. She is almost invisible, but when my eyes meet hers – I think the first time I've purposefully sought her attention – her body solidifies.

I imagine her small, scarred hands covering my ears; I imagine I am not in this room, and all of the liar's words are muffled. Though Mufasa speaks, I find a counterbalance. An argument is only effective when acknowledged. I must ignore it.

It helps. When the scholar finishes his tirade, I remove my gaze from No-Name.

The flush in my cheek subsides, veins no longer burning. I send thanks to my father for teaching me tears are a weakness. Glancing around, I imagine the emperor.

You are my left-hand vizier, his voice reminds me. *And tacticians in one moment of patience prevent a thousand regrets.*

'You have one last chance.' Mufasa lifts the parchment I received at the start of class. 'Re-answer this question for me, but without your molested version of history. Perhaps then I will reconsider your potential in my halqa.'

I know better than to throw this chance away. My mouth opens to respond before I realise… I do not recall the question. *What was it?*

A pressure builds between my eyes and I recognise this sensation, where I confuse words and time before failing to recall anything. I've time-blanked.

Mufasa's eyes narrow, holding my parchment. 'Answer the question, rukh.'

'I-I do not know, scholar. The question, can you tell—'

'*Answer it.*'

'I cannot!' I speak louder.

He slams his hands on the desk. 'Worthless.' He faces the class. 'This is not a past we are learning, but a conviction. You train to become the greatest Heavenly warriors to stave off another, greater evil. Or else…' He dips the corner of my parchment into a smokeless-fire lantern. Ash weeps down like grey tears. I pretend it weeps for me.

'… you become another forgotten aspect of history, a failure for the future to laugh over.'

But that is only the first day.

For the next two weeks, to make a point of his disdain, Scholar Mufasa ignores me. Though he poses questions that I know – martial conundrums that are simple – he refuses to pick on me.

'Explain the hierarchy of bone density in Eajīz warriors, dating back to Temirkhan.'

I answer before he selects a student. 'Seven, like the levels of Heaven. A warrior begins iron-bone training with a spiritual bone density of three. With each ranking, it becomes a multiplicative factor of seven. The highest Eajīz warriors of the seventh rank have a bone density over 700 times that of a regular mortal.'

The scholar carries on as if I had not spoken, picking on a student who regurgitates my answer.

Later, he asks, 'Tell me, in the Battle of Arsduq between the forces of Warrior Temirkhan and the Magician Junja Jazatāh, who was the hawk and who was the heron?'

For a moment, students take their time to scribe answers. I discard the parchment and stand on my cushion even as Katayoun yanks on my sleeve. Still, the scholar bypasses me.

My mouth opens anyway. 'When one blazes through obstacles to achieve their goals, with ideas calculated in absolutes, they are a hawk. When one pays attention to little details, understands the world as complex contradictory parts and shifts strategy to take advantage of changing circumstances, then they are a heron. An apt leader is a heron but at times is required to make bold, hawkish decisions. Temirkhan used the glaciers of the Black Mountains to eviscerate Arsduq's southern pass. He is the heron.'

The scholar pauses. 'You spoke without permission, and thus, I did not listen. Why listen to the words of a girl who taints our history?'

'My answer was correct.'

He whirls round, his outer robe flowing with the movement. 'You may claim to know the answer, but any structure is worthless when the foundation is weak. No rukh of mine succeeds without knowing fundamental Za'skar manuscripts.'

My teeth grind together. 'Then tell me which fundamentals. I will read them.'

'You will break before you can. However, if you thirst for a challenge, I cannot stop you.' He leans on his staff, as his apprentices watch me wide-eyed. 'If you wish not to be sent to the pazktab or banned from the final examinations, you must memorise all five annals from the Great Library on the Jazatāh Era. Give thanks to the Divine, an Azadnian is granted the benefit of a proper education.'

Another trap. 'All five annals? That's… thousands of parchments.' Would my broken mind even let me accomplish such a task?

Displeased, he crosses the room and, with frightening speed, jams his staff into my knuckles. 'That's for answering without waiting for my permission.' He lifts his staff again, slamming it down.

My eyes bulge as he leans toward me.

'We know victory well, stateless brat. We tasted despair at the end of a shamshir blade when the ground was bathed with our bodies under your heretic kind. Your attitude,' he says calmly, 'is unacceptable. You must submit to a greater will, be obedient to your superiors, consume knowledge without question instead of fighting your masters at every turn. So yes, all five annals. Or get lost.'

Rivulets of sweat plaster my hair against my neck, the result of humiliation more than the sticky air. Glaring into Mufasa's swollen face, I make a vow: *I refuse to lose to a reeking poisonous snake.*

He removes his staff from my hand. 'On you, I read defeat. *You are nothing*, you do not belong here.'

If he thirsts for abject surrender, oh, I will state it as if it's a proud name.

'I am nothing, I do not belong here. *I am nothing, I do not belong here.*' I say it clearly, no tremble to be heard.

The scholar studies me as if seeing me for the first time. 'Get on, rukh.'

I avoid Katayoun's stunned look, unwilling to be in the room for another second. I've been handed a warning and the scholars are not in the business of mercy to hand another. So, I get on, not bothering with a bow while Mufasa addresses the halqa behind me.

'She does not possess an honourable bone in her body, but what honour does her kind have? Rukhs like her rely on the brutality of martial arts. If any of you fail my class, I will ensure you never climb a single rank. You will stay as you are, a Zero-Slash, unable to participate with any squadron in the Marka.'

At those words, I still against the archway, my fingers biting into the latticed wood. Can the scholar do that?

I feel the other students staring at my back. Perhaps the Sepāhbad was correct in his read of me – feeble Khamilla, with no conviction, shuffling between halqas. She's bereft of a clan, unaccepted and unbelonged, from not only her empire, but now by the scholars of history.

15

It's dry-rutting hot in the Easkaria's corridors, the stench of sweat clinging like clammy cloth against an armpit. I am unsure where to go, like I am drifting through borderlands, despised by all. Using the collar of my ochre tunic, I fan my neck. The rage only smoulders. My hands ball, cheeks hot: hating with force, hating the scholars, hating everyone.

'Old fool,' I mutter.

Sajamistan did nothing to deserve these institutes, these mountains of old parchments. More power, schools, trade, bodies. It was a stroke of fate. Once, my brother told me Eajīz's affinities are tied to land, that is why Sajamistan has so many of them. A city of jinn magick and the resting place of Adam and the Heavenly Birds.

Scholar Mufasa is a damned Za'skar strategist and historian, the very type who constructs ideological weapons against my people, more powerful than even the sharpest sword. It is the winners of history who justify wars, who put ink to paper, scribing lies, who shift blame for strife from one empire to the next. I fear this man in a way I fear none other, not even the general of generals, for all revolutions are defined by their victors. And the victors are not kings and queens, but the historians – the living spoils of war who write their own stories.

My eyes screw shut. The daf sounds, indicating the next halqa. I straighten my tunic. A breeze from an open balcony, slanted by the mountainside, cools the flush in my cheeks.

'I had a feeling,' a sudden voice emerges with scathing frankness, 'Scholar Mufasa would oust you from his class. Took him long enough.'

Cemil's smooth tone only reinvokes my anger. When I turn, his gaze falls to my bruised knuckles.

'He didn't oust me,' I say.

'Oh?' He raises a brow and somehow, he makes it look elegant.

'I left on my own.'

His chin juts to ward the class chambers. 'On my first day, he punished me by rapping my knuckles twenty times. I paced this exact corridor as an initiate, cursing the old fool. But by the next moon, I crawled back like the masochist I am. He respected it and quickly he favoured me.'

I wonder about the purpose of his words. At my silence, his grey eyes harden.

'If a comrade gives advice, rukh, better to answer rather than posture there like a mule.'

'Am I your comrade?' I raise my brow back.

'No. But I'd rather best my rivals, than have them taken out before the battle begins.'

'How honourable. Katayoun exists too. What of her?'

He snorts. 'Know her long enough and you quickly learn she has no ambitious bone in her body. She doesn't care for rankings; she's in the battalion for the meals, shelter, the land benefits. At least she's honest in her goals; I can admire that too.'

'Well, I am fine in my goals.'

His smile is sharp. 'Fine by me. Isolation attracts the worst of jinn – a shai'tan. As the Qabl sages always warn: a lone wolf in a valley is more susceptible to the devil's mischief than a creature in a pack. But your kind knows that well, fractured by warlords who refuse to unite.'

My jaw clenches and I shoulder past him to my next halqa.

The rest of my classes are other versions of failures. Scholar Hawja in ethics disapproves when I flounder in my interpretation of Easkarian philosophy. I realise my upbringing only taught me the metaphysics of the 1000 Wings of Crane Monastic School, unlike Sajamistan's zeal for the Heavenly Raven.

In quadrivium, astronomy and metaphysics, my work is plausible but the scholars pay me no attention, leaving me to fade amongst the initiates. Lexicography is good, a small win. Cartography is a disaster when the scholar finds my drawing of the map's borders highly unusual.

'Yalon belongs to Sajamistan. And half of this territory in Tezmi'a is administrated by Sajamistani clans.'

It was as if all my life, I'd studied a different version of knowledge.

No, I want to cry as the rukhs receive the approval of superiors.

Failing, as usual, the emperor's voice slithers in my mind, and I sink low in my seat, my eyes burning. *These death-worshippers achieve the correct answers. They climb the ranks of this army. Is this how you will avenge me?*

Somehow, it's my ability to complete the tests on time that saves me from harsher punishment. The ones who do not are punished so severely, their chances of climbing the ranks of this city slim by the day; imperfection cast out.

16

My last hope lies in trifecta training. We iron-whisk our limbs in rapid tapping motions until red dots wink through our pores. As rukhs fracture their bones and split their fingers, our masters extend little care for the injuries. By night, my skin blotches purple from the iron. But to procure the iron-bone for which Za'skar martial artists are notorious, we continue.

Slowly but surely, my muscles tighten into dense sinews to maintain the nine stances. The transformation encourages me as I trade from a measly training knive to my sharper khanjar. We grow eager to mimic Za'skar high-ranks who seem to make the air clap and explode from the sheer force of their stances.

Our next lessons are conjoined with Overseer Negar. I recognise the warriors under her trifecta: the first is Dara, a lithe man of Second-Slash ranking, with deep-set eyes smudged in black sormeh; then Aina, a clever Zero-Slash from my classes and one of Katayoun's cousins; last is Aizere, with a delicate face, dark, pretty eyes and brown skin except where a thick pink scar bisects her cheek to collar.

'Pair up,' Overseer Negar orders with a crude smile. She points at a copse of date palms nestled between shrubs of mugwort behind the Easkaria school. The sun beats against our heads in a ferocious heat, the light rays bending the air.

'One of you will hold the trunk of the tree, while the other will punch it. Do this, and you pissing seedlings of Adam will become real warriors.'

Katayoun and I exchange cautious looks and just as I step toward her, Aina appears at her side, pulling her toward a tree. I blink at them, despite knowing that Katayoun has family, acquaintances – *comrades*

– outside of classes. A bond my fellow rukh and I most definitely do not have. As if strength is not her sole purpose, as it is for me.

Dara and Cemil stand together before a tree, both of equal ranking… leaving Aizere with me. She wears an expression of disinterest as we walk to a tall gnarled date palm, the trunk two handspans wide. Aizere positions herself behind it, and, by instinct, my eyes drop to her scar before quickly averting.

'Do not be a coward.' She seems to read my thoughts, sounding dour. 'Stare away. It's your people who paid me in kind.'

I'm given no chance for an appropriate reply because Overseer Yabghu barks, 'Hit the tree with one finger.'

Right. I've never been one good with words. My hand claws back and I let my hips guide me. In a whooshed breath, I obediently jab the tree with my finger.

Snap. My hand rebounds back at a sickening angle. I lift my mangled finger for the overseers, while Aizere watches on.

'D-did I do it right?'

Yabghu examines the fracture indifferently. 'Yes.'

Behind him, Overseer Negar laughs darkly at the other pairings nursing similar wounds, finding sick pleasure in our pain.

We switch positions. Aizere exhales and stabs the tree without breaking her gaze from me. Her hand snaps back but she too does not flinch. For a second, we glance at each other's twin injuries.

I turn around in time to see Cemil raise his finger and swoop into second stance. Through three breaths, his finger punctures a circle-shaped crater in the tree. To this, our overseer remarks, 'You've improved, Cemil,' making my jaw clench.

Then Yabghu pitches me a sidelong stare. 'And you, at least… understand the cost.' He raises a finger callously, and drills a precise hole. The sheer force causes a hole to erupt on the other side of not one, but *two* trees in a row, frightening a flock of perched humas, the birds' smoky shrieks carrying loudly across the entire metropolis.

'Rukhs must begin with finger taps,' Negar explains across the week, as we make our way through gruelling finger taps to punching in the form of iron-bone fists. 'Even the distance between each finger is a precise science. The goal is to create a hole in the trunk by sheer strength without breaking your fingers *or* utilising Heavenly bonds. It's a mathematical application of iron-bone multiplied by force. With this, you use the First-Stratum through your bonds, to cause holes in four trees simultaneously. The goal is to eventually master Ifrit's Strike of Death, where the martial artist uses their finger's vibrating internal Heavenly Energy to target an opponent's bond location like acupuncture.

'An Eajīz must strikes in multiples of three. The lower the multiple, the greater the force required to debilitate the opponent. The higher the multiple, the larger the risk, for going too far may break each of your fingers. If done wrong, your opponent could be paralysed. If done right, their bonds are disabled and they collapse. If taken too far, they die. Weaponise your opponent's energy against them until they cannot rely on their own bonds. Be merciless. Only when they lose hope is your battle won.'

A sudden thought reverberates through me. I recall how the Sepāhbad defeated me outside the Ghaznian citadel, disabling my bonds. 'The Sepāhbad is capable of this?'

'Every Qabl master is.'

With my uninjured hand, I grip the khanjar the Sepāhbad had bestowed on me, the hilt naked without a slash. I want that power.

As we progress, my overseer instructs Katayoun and me to spar with our affinities, first with only the manipulation of Heavenly Energy to reinforce our offence. Gradually, he permits me to use my nūr to face Katayoun's affinity: a virtue of fortitude, where her bonds create a Veil to intake and deflect the opponent's Heavenly Energy.

When I hold my own against her, Yabghu allows me to face Cemil. On the day of the sparring, with No-Name's arm clinging on my shoulder, I grit my teeth before stepping into the gardens. This is my chance.

Without a greeting, Yabghu lifts scrolls of parchment while chewing on an arak root. 'Many of the scholars report that you are failing your classes.'

I snatch away the scrolls. My heart twists in resentment and his voice enters my mind again.

Failing, as expected, the emperor whispers as No-Name stretches her arm around my throat. I swallow panic, pressing a hand against my chest as if it can lift the weight there, but it simply grows.

I want to change it; I want them to perceive me as better, until they bow at my feet. I long for approval, I *like* being right, riding that high the same way I craved passing the emperor's poison tests. To prove to them an Azadnian is equally matched; that my clansmen deserved to live. How will I return to the Zahr clan with intelligence if I wallow in the lowest ranks?

'Have you asked Katayoun or Cemil to help you?' Yabghu asks, leaving me unable to answer. 'You can moan about unfair treatment but I watch you during mealtime and training; you are alone. That's probably why the pazktab children taint your meals with sand and bugs. You turn students away; you provoke their ire too. Remember, rukh, your success here is determined by alliances. And shared pain, whether it is surviving war or training together, is the best form of solidarity.'

'Scholar Mufasa has already made an example of me,' I point out. 'Why would any rukh help me?'

He pats my shawl in a shrewd version of comfort. 'Prove yourself. The captain told me he sees potential in your affinity – your strength. If you fail like this, forget any hope of moving to First-Slash. He will never draft you for his Marka squadron.'

'That has yet to be decided,' Captain Fayez puts in, trudging toward our trifecta. As the most senior in the squadron, he rotates, observing the trifectas under his command. Today he will watch our sparring.

Cemil snorts from the marbled archway of Little Paradise gardens. His noise disturbs the sparrows splashing in the azure bowls.

'You seem confident,' I say but my bravado is empty. Cemil does not insult me further, and the truth of it is scathing. He finds me so pitiful, I am no longer a prospect of a rival.

In a clearing surrounded by poplar and citrus trees, Cemil dips his finger into a geometric glass fountain and closes the distance between us, pulling my arm into him. He's never touched me before.

'What are you—'

He reaches up, wet finger grazing my cheek feather-light. It takes me a second too long before I break away, an ever-present nausea curdling in my gut.

'Why did you touch me?' I snap at him.

He shrugs with a mocking smile. 'As the Qabl sages say, an ignorant opponent suffers the greatest loss.'

From the corner of my eye, No-Name huddles against a citrus tree. 'No good, no good,' she repeats, rocking back and forth.

Cemil returns to his side of the field and tightens the black muslin rounding his temple. He slides on a martial mask, bone-stone glinting under red sun, and I withhold a flinch. In a bow stance, his left hand twists a marbled khanjar with two ivory slashes scored across the hilt, blending into the light.

Discarding my robes, I roll up my tunic sleeves and exhale meditatively, loosening stiff limbs and evoking a warm surge of Heavenly Energy. I do not don my mask.

The captain walks between us, his muscles gliding smoothly. His black eyes hold steadfast like an iron will. Of course the man is the embodiment of iron-bone. And in his voice, I hear its hard conviction.

'I look only at a warrior's pride and strength. A simple calculus, if you wish to earn my favour. Now begin.'

I hardly manifest a glimmer of nūr before my cheek slams into the dirt, Cemil's blade digs under my neck, and his lips hiss against my ear, 'And you are dead.'

My heart is a pathetic flutter. He *perception*-blitzed my senses.

'How?' I demand face down in the dirt, sandy grits of it in my back teeth. His arm eases and my neck cranes to face him, still pinned. For a moment, a deep-seeded fear crawls under my skin, seeing him towering over me in a raven mask, an echo of a forgotten past.

'My affinity,' he answers simply before climbing off me.

I hadn't had an instant to use my Heavenly Energy – I did not *see* him.

'His affinity is a virtue of diligence,' Captain Fayez explains from across the gardens while his thick scarred fingers toy with a bone-pendant. 'It's a Messenger affinity; he marks a spot before battle and uses an activated Heavenly bond on his limb to arrive there first, at the speed of a jinn, by travelling through the Veil of the psychospiritual realm. He simply needs to write a glyph upon his target; he can use water, blood, ink – *anything*. And the mark remains there unless he swaps it for a new target.' He nods at Cemil, satisfied. 'Good work.'

'We are not finished.' I lift my blade. 'Again.'

That morning, I spar with Cemil many times, but it is of no use – as a Second-Slash, he disables my attacks, leaving me in the dregs of his affinity.

It isn't until our eleventh spar that I manage to snake my arm up, but he grapples me to the ground through an ankle lock. He lifts his khanjar and—

A burst of pain explodes down my arm. My vision goes black, for a breath. I squirm on the ground and hear a *squelch*.

'Eight Gates of Hells,' I gasp out.

Through my blurry gaze, Cemil is frozen in place.

I dare a look down, a bout of nausea in my throat.

His blade has crucified my forearm to the dirt, skewered like a slab of meat, tearing right through the gold-threading. Every movement shoots agony up my arm.

'No good, no good,' No-Name continues repeating from behind me.

'You are so helpful!' I snap at her, but Cemil seems to think I am addressing him.

His mouth opens and closes, smirk gone, eyes wide. He kneels, hand reaching out toward the khanjar.

'Do not touch me—' I lurch away, forgetting that I cannot move, making me choke on my words as the blade wiggles against my penetrated arm.

Another test. Another failure, the emperor tuts inside my head. My eyes shut and I curl up, counting up and down to calm my breath, but his voice only grows louder. I've failed the scholars' tests, and, now, the sparrings.

'Khamilla.' I feel Cemil's hands on my shoulders and my neck muscles spasm. 'Be still and breathe, or the wound will worsen.'

'Was injuring me intentional, so the captain does not select me for the Marka?' I breathe out.

His eyes, dark with remorse, search me before he nods toward the khanjar. 'Don't be difficult. Let me unpin the blade.'

'That's the last spar, the both of you!' Overseer Yabghu, who was sparring with Katayoun, begins to run over, ripping the arak root from his mouth and tossing it away.

'I've got this, Overseer,' Cemil throws out. He holds down my wrist. I bite on my other arm, refusing to cry out. He yanks out the khanjar and the pain nearly makes me pass out.

'We must take you to the Qabl medics.'

I cradle my arm. 'My overseer will take me,' I say coldly.

We both glance at Yabghu, who is searching for his arak root. He pauses and straightens. 'Of course.'

Yabghu reaches me and uses his martial wrappings to staunch the wound, before helping me away from the gardens, blood blotched through my tunic. I catch Cemil staring after the crimson trail on the grass, jaw clenched.

No-Name follows us while we head past sand dunes full of other trifectas training under the punishing sun. It is not until we climb the sandstone steps of the monastery, toward the healing quarters on its third tier, that my voice breaks the terse silence.

'He is more powerful. Surely, there must be a limit to the targets Cemil can use in battle.'

My overseer tilts his head. 'Cemil's limit is three in any given battle, unless he swaps it for another mark. As he grows stronger, that may increase. There could be other weaknesses. The Divine can bestow the same affinity to more than one mortal, and yet an affinity adapts itself differently to its wielder's soul – based on their Heavenly Contract, bonds, morals and, of course, creativity. Past warriors with the Messenger affinity marked their targets differently. But Cemil uses his contract with Heaven in this method – by writing upon his targets.'

'He uses it well,' I admit and my overseer does not soothe my fears. 'Captain Fayez will pick Cemil over me for the Marka.'

Yabghu reads my gaze. 'As you ask about his progress, he pesters me about you.'

'Why?' I face him, fighting the quaver in my tone. 'He has no need to worry. My path leads to a life of the lowest ranks. Scholar Mufasa swore to never let failed students participate in the Marka; to always make them remain a Zero-Slash.'

'That old bastard.' His lips twitch up. 'As for Cemil, a good warrior never underestimates their rivals, low as they are.'

'I could hear you, Overseer.' Cemil's voice rings out and we turn to see him panting slightly at the bottom, as if he had run across Za'skar. 'Telling her about the weakness in my affinity.'

Yabghu shrugs. 'You injured her. It's only fair. I ought to flog you.'

'Why did you follow us?' I break in.

Cemil steps upwards and his eyes drop to my cradled arm.

'I assume to check if your blade pierced me deep enough?' I press.

He continues walking forward.

'To ensure I cannot train and—'

He reaches our step and my voice falters.

'Overseer, you may leave,' Cemil says. 'I can accompany her the rest of the way.' Then he addresses me. 'I'm not desperate enough to intentionally injure you before the Marka. If I wanted to, then on your first day as an initiate, I would not have shattered the poisoned teacup.'

Yabghu observes us, deft eyes narrowed as if perceiving something.

Cemil presses a finger between my shoulders. 'Let's go, before you bleed all over the steps.'

'I am fine.' I shake off his arm and step through the monastery's wrought-copper doors. Above me, a vegetally patterned plaque greets followers with death and peace, in illuminated calligraphy. For me, it's only a bitter remembrance.

There are as many bonds to the Divine as there are breaths in man before death.

A junior healer spots my bloodied arm, pushing me toward the infirmary, but before the door shuts, I catch Yabghu thwacking Cemil's head and dragging him away for a flogging.

In the infirmary, I stare at my marred arm in disbelief. I believed I could succeed in this city, but now it felt like climbing up a mountain only to see you'd merely reached the path's end and had yet to graze the peak. Both Cemil and I have affinities effective in short-range battle but the chasm between our strengths is irrefutable.

Across from my floor-bed, No-Name balances on the beryl ledge of a medicinal shelf. Her skin is less pale and her features have altered, eyes wide and green.

My breath escapes my lungs. 'You... look almost like Uma. Why?'

She touches her face before dropping her hands. 'I suppose you wish me to be.'

I turn away, curling into the bedding. But my aches do not subside. I miss them. My clansmen. My brother Yun. My slain sister Azra. The easy nature of Zhasna. And Uma, most of all. I miss her gentle hands. I miss her salted chai with two sugar cubes under my tongue. I miss her wet, broken eyes that calmed when my fingers touched her cheek, weak though mine were.

I miss Uma. In her short life, I could do nothing to save her. And still in her death – I raise my bandaged arm – I have *this* to offer her.

My eyes shut, hearing Uma. *The Sajamistanis surround you like vultures as you flee across the Tezmi'a Mountains,* she says. *Their arrows sink into your back; they delight in your screams. Your whimpers become the music of a well-tuned lute as the Sepāhbad takes your hand lovingly in his own before pressing his khanjar against your thumb. You continue screaming. He slices it slowly. And then he slices the next finger, and the next—*

My eyes reopen and dart to my side. Suddenly, it's not *my* head conjuring terrifying reminders for myself – it's No-Name on the bedding beside me, wrapping her arms around my waist, voice slipping into the forlorn tune of Uma, saying the grotesque thoughts. Her face has shifted until she's undeniably my mother.

The horror makes me straighten. No-Name flinches. The answer hits me.

'Change to who I need.' I speak the command.

Uma disappears. No-Name's skin becomes a smooth olive tone, head thick with black curls, an elegant crane-feathered qaftan flowing to her calves, until she is the emperor in the flesh. Stricken for a moment, I cannot help the bubble of hysteria in my chest, wondering why I had not thought of this idea before. What else propelled me to master jinn-poisons in a feat of masochism, day after day?

All I need is the emperor to remind me – no, to *command* me – that it is okay to become a living, breathing Sajamistani to rise in this army. If I can deceive my brain, I will not time-blank. I can pass.

I walk to No-Name-Emperor and he takes my cheeks into his hands. His voice sweeps through the past, mangling into the present. 'What did I tell you about loss, daughter?'

'Loss is acceptable to a good strategist as long as it's never a concession in the greater war. To deceive the enemy, one must become them at all costs.'

From the vestiges of the past, he leans into the shell of my ear, uttering orders I've longed to hear. 'Yes, there *is* no victory without pain. The pain only ends when a winner is determined.'

'Now I understand,' I murmur. He taught me that no fear makes you arrogant. Too much fear makes you a slave, a puppet to the whispers of a master who longs to control you. But a good amount of fear will become your wisdom because fear means you hold a stake in a battle. Fear can save you. I fear this city more than anyone, and with that, I understand its stakes well.

Wrongly, I thought I needed no allies, that I could preserve the part of me that is Zahr-zad while living alongside Sajamistanis. From the way the scholars single me out, allies are all that will save me.

I face No-Name-Emperor, his features similar to Scholar Mufasa. They merge together, one my father, the other a scholar, but both my teacher. I could learn to love the scholar too – *I will be a good pupil* – for a mere semblance of his satisfaction.

In fact, I smile, *it's a labour of love*. Scholar Mufasa must only be harsh because he longs for me to succeed; his style of cruelty is his fashion of teaching as a patriarch.

I will claw my way to the top. It's exactly what was done with the poison: I felt the pain at first, but, achingly slowly, I built tolerance.

17

I have a plan: collect information on the captain. The next day, when the heavens above are the barest candlelight of dawn, I go to Little Paradise gardens, climbing up the citrus trees to train, while I mull over my objective.

Halfway into my stances, a tall girl shoves someone into the gardens.

'Leave me be!' A cry resounds through the air, almost awakening the slumbering karkadann bulls.

I glance below to see a familiar-looking pazktab girl, her fingers digging into the arm of a boy – the same boy I'd saved from an attack months ago. She has wide jade eyes, a necklace of buffalo bones tight around her collar, and dark hair braided with raven feathers into two spheres on her head. She looks fifteen or sixteen years at most.

'Did you bring it?' The girl kicks at the boy's satchel, loose barberries and apples strewing about.

'Yes! Leave me be, Arezu!'

Your success here is determined by alliances, rukh, Overseer Yabghu had advised me, and, seeing the boy, it shines a great deal of light on to my dilemma.

I leap down from the branch. The boy's eyes meet mine over the girl's – Arezu's – shoulder, lighting up in recognition. Before she can react, I clench her by the collar, turning her. My leather-sandalled foot connects with her torso, sending her flying into the bramble.

'Be gone,' I warn her.

'What the Hells.' She staggers to her knees and spits phlegm at my feet, but when I step closer, she runs off. Then I turn on the simpering boy.

'I've saved you twice now.'

I watch in bewilderment as he throws himself at my feet.

'You are most generous, even for an Azadnian,' he says. 'I promise to never spit on nor spoil your meals again.'

My mouth gapes open. 'It's been you? You've been putting beetles and scorpions and sand in my food—'

'*And my spit.* Forgive me. The other pazktab students do it too. It wasn't my idea!'

I work my jaw. 'Now you owe me another debt.'

'Debt? Me?' He glances around.

'How old are you?'

'Thirteen.'

'What is your name?' I ask impatiently.

'Sohrab.'

'You will do my bidding?'

'Anything if you train me.'

'*Train you?*' I repeat to Sohrab. 'You owe *me*.'

'The monks say pazktab children are too young to learn the advanced ways of Eajīz arts. But if I become your apprentice, the other younglings will think twice before hurting us. You can teach us Azadnian martial arts.'

'Who is *us*? There is only one of you.'

He turns and I spot two more pazktab students, younger than him, crouching behind the glass fountains. 'Yahya and Yasaman are siblings. The other students force us to steal from the kitchens.' At Sohrab's gesturing, they walk tentatively forward.

'That boy is hardly five years old,' I say, seeing the gap-toothed child named Yahya.

'Four years,' Yahya corrects, standing shly behind his sister.

'And I am thirteen,' Yasaman adds, as if it's a proud fact while she gnaws on a long strand of her ebony hair. *By the Divine.* I grimace at the sight of them. But I need discreet allies for this task, and children will do just fine. The more numbers, the better.

'I only have the Friday and Saturday free from trifecta training. If I agree to train you before dawn prayer, here in the gardens, will you fulfil my task?'

Sohrab speaks for them. 'Yes.'

'Then swear an oath on the Heavens that you will speak of this to no one. I assure you, my task is not treason.'

They exchange glances but swear the oath.

I reveal the task: 'When you serve food to the warriors during mealtime, go to Captain Fayez and his low-table. Anything the captain speaks of, you must convey to me. If you hear word about the Marka tournament – any strategy, who he intends to draft for his squadron – inform me immediately.'

'I have heard Captain Fayez mention your name, Usur-Khan, and something about the Marka,' Sohrab says slowly, and my pulse hitches at the possibility that he's considering me over Cemil. 'But if we're found telling you information, we'll be lashed. We deserve to know the reason.'

I sigh. 'Getting selected for a squadron and performing well in the Marka is an opportunity for low-ranks like myself to move up one rank. I need this information, as a last assurance. In exchange, I will train you… *as my ally*.' I can hardly force the words out.

'Is this as the martial tales go – the loner master adopts pathetic students who become worthy?' Yasaman blinks up at me.

Usually, masters are leathery things from old monastic schools. I hardly qualify to call myself anyone's master. But if they'd like to believe this… I squint at the three stupidly ambitious children who look like stalks of barley.

'Yes, stalk of barley.'

'Barley?' Yasaman echoes.

'Yes. To me, you are barley. Thin, small and pathetic. Line up.'

Sohrab grins. 'You will train us, Master?'

I wince at the honorific. 'Something like that. Now say your prayers and promise.' Sohrab merely smiles wider.

At my instruction, they begin orbital stretch kicks to loosen their muscles. Yahya watches us, clumsily following his sister, given the four-year-old he is.

'O Blessed, save us from this evil eye.' A voice comes through the citrus trees. I follow the sound, spotting Arezu sitting on a branch, tapping her cheeks as if to ward me away. So she never left.

'Evil eye?' I ask. 'Well, I did thrash you twice.'

Arezu laughs, the sound rough for her age. 'You are training Eajīz children? Azadnians are child killers.'

'I love children.' The claim burns in the back of my throat.

'You love children?'

'Yes. Look around you. These students can be exemplars of young martial artists—'

Yahya quits after his second attempt. 'This hurts.'

'Do not be so soft,' I scoff and nudge him. It is a mistake. He falls over. Then he bawls, the gasping, wet kind that sends disgust through me. His sister stoops low and lifts him in consolation but his weight makes her stagger.

'This is your training?' Arezu tuts her tongue. 'These *exemplary* martial artists?'

I ignore her comment. 'How do we stop that... sound?'

'You mean his weeping? He likes to be held,' Yasaman explains.

'Something else.'

'Food.'

'Which kind?'

Yahya pauses in his tears. 'Lamb-stuffed non.'

Inwardly, I curse. *Lamb-stuffed non? How could a child have such expensive tastes?* I grip him gingerly by the shoulders, my robes a barrier to his tear-induced snot. His fists wrench violently near my curls.

'Be careful,' I hiss at him and his eyes well again, before I add, 'I will bring you non.'

With a lingering look of disgust, Arezu recedes into the bramble of citrus trees surrounding the clearing. Above her, No-Name drifts on to a branch and watches the students, occasionally making faces and sticking out her tongue.

Yahya squirms, hitting my injured arm, so I prop him higher. 'Today you can watch, but this is the only exception. Next time, you must do ten orbitals.' I pray that if all goes well and I am chosen for my captain's squadron, there will not be a next time.

Sohrab pauses in his kicks, pointing forward. 'Who is that?'

A voice barks out, 'Who am I? *Who the Hells are you?*' Overseer Yabghu stalks up the slopes of Little Paradise's hills, his eyes thunderous on me. 'Rukh, you have a babe in your arms!'

Panic twinges in my chest. I drop Yahya on his bottom. 'No, I do not.'

We stare, in a standstill as the pazktab younglings, slick in sweat, gaze in dread between us, little more than chirping crickets scampering in the grass.

'You just dropped the babe.'

'I do not know this child. He was lost and crawled into my arms.'

Sohrab raises his hand. 'Mast—' He cannot call me *master* in front of Yabghu.

'Young students,' I interrupt. 'This scolding man is Overseer Yabghu. A high-rank.'

The flimsy distraction works. Sohrab's eyes latch on to the etched lines across Yabghu's khanjar. 'He is a Fourth-Slash!'

Yabghu only addresses me. 'I do not know what possessed you to speak with pazktab students.'

My expression does not shift. 'Overseer, I saved these students from an attack. They asked me how to defend themselves.' This, in truth, is not a lie.

He thinks otherwise. 'Ah. You lie, drawing a line between yourself and your only ally amongst the high-ranks.'

'What do you mean?'

He studies the children. 'Do not let her sweet appearance seduce you. I am her master; I know her well. You learn quickly – in Za'skar, sweetness is disguised behind a cloak.'

I glower at him with no sweetness as he drags me away from the gardens.

For the second part of my plan, I must win over the scholars. The next eve, after tongue-fasting, I resolve to find and use Cemil. He sits on the stairway to the Great Library, a bundle of scrolls surrounding him. His turban is untied, the muslin tossed round his neck, his dark hair gathered in a small topknot with raven feathers. His eyes are squinted in concentration, sormeh sharpening them. When he perceives my approach, a weariness slips into his gaze before he returns to his parchments.

I clear my throat.

He does not look up.

I clear my throat harder.

'What?' he snaps at last. Then his eyes drop to my bandaged arm and he hesitates.

I prey on his remorse and speak fast. 'Scholar Mufasa challenged me to memorise the five annals on the Jazatāh Era. Only then will he permit me back into class. Yabghu advised me to come to you for your... genius. I need—'

Help. The request lodges in my throat, unwilling to be admitted. Cemil waits. 'I need your help,' I choke out.

He leans back in a casual stance. 'Such respect. Where were these proverbs of my genius when I spoke to you in the school to *help* you?'

He will not let me live this down. 'Please,' I say in disgust. 'You won't refuse my grovelling. You enjoy it.'

Cemil is silent for a long moment. Then he gestures with his chin. 'Your arm? Has it healed?'

'It has hardly been one day. What do you think?' His eyes linger on my slitted sleeves. The hint of skin displays logos – like his own, except his are ravens – a hallmark of the Camel Road lands, divided by empires. I yank my sleeve down.

Then he smiles sharply and I recoil. 'I do enjoy your grovelling. I will help you on one condition.'

'Was the way you knifed me not enough?'

He ignores it. 'On the last Saturday of this moon cycle, the captain is taking his favoured soldiers from Squadron One to visit the Sixteen-Gated Grand Bazaar. It's the Festival of Lights, to celebrate the first harvest. You might join us. We go before he drafts his squadron for the Marka.'

'During the evenings, I study.'

His nose wrinkles at the thin excuse. 'It's my condition.'

Around us, torchlights of smokeless fire along the grand staircase cast shadows against the bedrock, playing against Cemil's face like an omen. A cool wind clatters through the waning evening. He waits, but my instincts prickle in warning.

'I do not know your intentions. I cannot agree.'

Unsurprised, he stands. 'For anyone, it would be an easy choice, but not for you. You may live in Sajamistan but the Azadnian in you is clear as day. No wonder the scholars despise you. Your paranoia, your isolation… you are forever the lone wolf prone to the devil in the empty valley.' He bends to my ear. 'I'd watch my back if I were you,' he says, before shouldering past me.

I stagger at the force, left to watch him walk up the stairway.

'Wait.'

He continues walking. I rush forward and block his path. He steps around me but I catch the front of his tunic. He pushes my hand away, lightly, avoiding my injured arm. But I yank him until we are nose to nose.

'I changed my mind. I will go.' I swallow my nausea.

He stares at my hand until I release him.

'You need the oldest Jazatāh annals,' he finally says. 'The Keeper of the Great Library guards these ancient scrolls. For him, we need something first.'

Cemil disappears across the road, into the monastic apothecary, reappearing with a foul-smelling pouch in his left hand. I follow him inside. The Great Library lives in tales scrawled across the continent; its ancient archives are the confluence of jinn-folk and human knowledge, a portal between the material and immaterial realm through sages and script.

Golden light hovers in a halo around the emerald domes above the imposing library, a grand stairway climbing to shimmering gold balconies and entryways disappearing into the dark mountain, as if it is a slumbering beast and we are ants crawling into its bowels, scared to awaken it.

Tamed phoenixes crouch atop the filigree-laced wood flanking a bone-stone entrance. Ababil birds streak circles across the dark sky as if compelled by some unknown force to guard the round roofs. The wings of parî form feathered shields across the ivory walls carved in vibrant epics.

Seeing us, the parî bow and smile. Their cheeks have a rosy pink tint, pointy ears twitching, skin shimmering as if the Divine ensconced their forms in starlight.

'It's easy for initiates to wander lost and never appear again.' Cemil yanks on my hemp waist cord, guiding us through a maze of corridors; hexagonal walls painted in miniatures about the Stone Empires dating to Adam's first descendants. Long palm shelves hold scrolls secreted from the Unseen world into the greed of human hands. The tiled walls carved from merciless bedrock depict various stelae of warriors slaying azhdahak by feeding the winged serpents poisoned cow.

Not even hate can rival fascination. I admire the architecture, the old creatures, the mounds of mineral-inked parchment, even the friezes of bone-stone, strange as they are. Above us, on patterned tiles, it reads:

    SPECIAL THIRD BUREAU OF MARID, JINN AND
    UNSEEN SCROLLS.

The complex widens into shelves that descend into eight layers below, filled with thousands of scrolls, ringing in spirals, eventually tunnelling into underground crypts.

I still against the archway. 'What is this?'

On the first level are hundreds of low-ranks sprawled across kilim rugs. From training, I recognise Aina and Gulnaz, Yima, Dara, Sharra, Adam and Aizere, the last looking especially disgruntled.

'Khamilla?' Katayoun spots us at the entrance, her russet braid aglow beneath the lanterns. She taps her chin. 'Cemil, are you feeling generous?'

I wait for a protest at my presence. None comes.

'Not generous,' Cemil corrects Katayoun as he enters, releasing my cord. 'We're here to find the Keeper.' He glances at me warily. 'This is where trifectas gather to study. We can return here after finding the annals.'

Small wonder the other students are succeeding. A little wide-eyed, I watch the rukhs parse out assigned manuscripts; trifectas debating, as united units, against others. I'm unwilling to admit how easy it would be to fall into their communal routine, as if deceiving myself into believing I can be one of them – that I can enjoy this curious studying as an Eajīz, where we fuel each other's answers.

'The Keeper?' Katayoun scowls. 'That old ass.'

'Who is the Keeper?' I remember to ask.

'He is the Sepāhbad-vizier for the jinn. The jinn-folk have their own tribes, wars and rivalries. The Keeper is a parî who handles their affairs in Za'skar City, for peace.'

But the Keeper does not live up to his grand status.

Deeper inside, at the centre of the alcoves, upon golden cushions, reclines an unimpressive parî. He chews areca nuts, his other claw smoking – I discreetly sniff – charas. The parî are mischievous creatures granted permission to leave the Unseen and guard ancient texts in the mortal realm. By doing so, they atone for their past sins so they can return to Paradise.

'I thought smoking was banned in the army,' I cough through curling smoke.

'Well, so is hashish. But the Keeper is not a mortal, so he's absolved from the rules,' Cemil answers, pointing at the parî.

'Surely *that* cannot be the Sepāhbad of the jinn-folk.'

'Am I a soldier?' The Keeper does not glance up as he starts tying knots with a black thread.

'Scholar Mufasa sent us,' Cemil says to him.

A scowl.

'The scholar will have my head if I do not memorise the annals,' I add.

The Keeper pouts. 'Can one piss without causing a smell?'

Cemil chokes on his breath. 'I-is this a jinn's riddle?'

I answer anyway. 'No, urine tends to have an awful odour.' The Keeper finally looks up and stares. After squirming, I add, 'Unless you drink plenty of water. Then the urine is clear.'

He sighs. 'I see. The fool always thinks he's not reeking up the place, sending pupils to bother me. Tell that to Scholar Mufasa.' He holds out his hand. 'As for my payment.' Cemil bows and digs into his pouch, pulling out a leaf of...

'Hashish?' My eyes bulge.

The Keeper accepts it and leads us through the archives, hopping over the kilim's embroidery, ensuring his heel does not graze any lines. I struggle to hide my annoyance.

He stops at a spiral of shelves. 'Jazatāh scrolls,' he says. I reach to graze the bleached-bone papyrus with unworthy hands: knowledge shared by benevolent jinn, channelled and scribed through Qabl sages. The Qabl Order: spiritual intellects of Za'skar who commune with the jinn-folk – by crossing their souls temporarily through the Veil that separates jinn and mankind – to gain knowledge.

'I would not touch those just yet,' the Keeper warns.

'Use this.' Cemil places a cold, wet bone into my hand, forcing my wrist toward the shelf. Before I can flinch away, the smokeless firelight flickers around us, dimming the library. Something sharp gnashes against my palm and the bone disappears. A manuscript tumbles out.

I jump back.

'Old guardians from the Unseen world. They help students find a text if you bribe them with food, meaning bones.' Cemil watches me in amusement.

'A warning would have been nice.' I extract my hand from his.

'Please continue,' the Keeper interjects. 'I'd love to see the aži serpents and zār demons sink their fangs into a novice brat like you.'

I shrink against the marble columns. 'Zār? But these are archives.'

'Archives now, but millennia ago, long before even Adam and Nuh, this was a jinn-kingdom's abode,' he corrects. 'Beasts have festered for millions of years, guarding ancient relics tucked into tombs, finding homes in obscure niches.' As if to prove his point, a hiss emits from below. 'Knowledge in our language holds thousands of meanings, not made for human comprehension, and forever lost in script. Nothing is translated without losing its original meaning. We are the Veiled; *our knowledge remains Veiled*. You read our texts with unfasted eyes, and we guard them. Bones are a simple price to pay.'

With that kind warning, the parî wanders off to hunt for the other manuscripts, Cemil trailing him. Beside me, No-Name leans the slit of her nose to the pages, giddily. She's changed her appearance into a younger version of Uma, as if preferring it.

'I've never seen so much parchment,' she says. A scroll catches our eyes, embossed with a triangular seal. I feed the shelf a bone and pull out the faded paper, the material woven through with silk threads. The parchments illustrate cuneiforms of the monoglot Jazatāh tribes, magicians who worshipped jinn and magick.

After flipping through the leathery pages, at the halfway mark, I find pictograms demonstrating monks in meditative states. It's a text for the monastery — Qabl sageism is how they meditate through the Veil to the world of jinn.

The Keeper returns to me, admonishing, 'Tongue-fasting begins soon, hurry and go.' He pauses when he spies the text I'm holding, and for the first time, his eyes flicker with unease. 'Those sageism scrolls are too advanced.'

'What are they?'

'A Za'skar monk travelled to the Mist Mountains and convened with ancient jinn. Those jinn had eavesdropped on Heavenly matters, copying forbidden knowledge. Later, when angels were sent down to teach magick as a test to mankind, the Jazatāh learnt and added more to these texts. You've no need for it.'

'I think I found the fifth annal,' Cemil interrupts and the Keeper turns away. I tuck the scroll into my satchel.

18

With the texts secured, I order No-Name to change at my whim to become the things I love and fear, so I do not time-blank.

In the beginning, she shifts into Uma, gazing out the window. Later, she changes into the emperor and manifests objects such as tending to a cage of courtly cranes. But for some reason, she is most effective when she manifests into my parents' corpses. The gore is a steady reminder of my purpose: to climb the enemy's ranks and destroy them. To earn my way home.

No-Name follows me as I study the manuscripts in Little Paradise, hanging upside down in the citrus trees, an old habit from the Azadnian capital.

'In the first Jinn Wars, the Dawjad clans united with which tribes against the Jazatāh?' No-Name tests me from the annals.

'T-the Arsduq tribes?' My memory fails me miserably.

'No. Which tribes?' No-Name repeats. Her face flickers between the emperor's features and her own unremarkable face before she shoves me off the branch. 'You failed his test.'

'I am aware.' I rub my shoulder. 'This cannot work unless you change into his corpse. I need to remember.'

She pauses. Her features pinch into the emperor's long face, those ebony eyes, that jaw as sharp as a shamshir. But blood trickles down her torso too, the wounds that caused him to die forming welts on her limbs, stealing my breath. She grips my jaw hard, prodding my memories, making my head spin, and suddenly, I'm on my hands and knees, dry-heaving.

I have willed myself to hide the details of how he died; to not dwell on the memory because I know if I had simply obeyed him – *if I had simply stayed* – he would be alive. Now his wounds taunt me; his depthless eyes stare with potent disappointment. I do not question this, for I find that I like the pain: its honesty, its simplicity, the way I can control it.

'What were the tribes?' No-Name demands again in his eerie voice as she walks to the fountains, peering out at the city with a black gaze.

'The southern Izuri lands belonged to Hunjin tribes under the banner of the Heavenly Crane,' I answer, my gaze focused on his corpse.

After that, the days stack like fired brick against brick; as No-Name reflects my parents' gruesome forms, I memorise manuscripts from the Easkaria school correctly.

No one else experiences periods of blankness, of confusion, of gaps in time. The reminder is blunt – these tests are difficult because of *my* mistakes, *my* unreliable memory. It is my fault, so it is *my* responsibility to prepare better. If my head forgets things, then, like people, it can be bent into submission. An old, familiar routine.

With it, I attend the Easkaria, applying myself vigorously despite languishing at the bottom. To the surprise of the scholars, I improve. Sajamistani history, philosophy, strategy, logic – everything is recited until I become a walking paragon of Sajamistan myself.

In cartography, we memorise and map the empire's terrain. In alchemy, we master rudimentary methods to create naphtha-throwers and distillate with sulphur and charcoal. In mathematics, the teacher is determined to make proficient artillerists out of promising wartime mathematicians. She teaches field problems concerning the flight of projectiles, the arithmetic of cannon devices, or the direction of moving objects and their velocity, but I find myself confused. In battle, would I have time to solve triangles?

Later, I learn these techniques save a squadron, for any good tactician worries themselves with logistics in advance, winning the war of systematisation.

Time smears: the week the autumn equinox arrives and the windy season of sandstorms infiltrates the scholarly city. Our tunics are replaced with thicker wool; in the eves, the chill forces us to round the shawls across our chests. The loving desert wraps us in her unwanted embraces; wind funnels and flings sand into every crevice of our hovels, fingers, scalps and breasts. I let her break me as I break my body.

No-Name tricks me with reassurances in my ear:

In the morning, you will see your clansmen.
Reading these pages is an order by the emperor.
You will be in Azadniabad if you succeed.

I listen to these promises when I am tired, when I am in pain, my mind falling for those seductions, one lie after another; again, again and again. I dare not resist the pain; I dare not go soft. It becomes a game. I find I love games. In a strange quirk of fate, studying in Za'skar does not vary from my years in Azadniabad; it's a routine of harsh monks and masters, a time of parchments and contemplation.

My superiors note a shift in my behaviour. Overseer Yabghu nods smugly when he runs across me – reluctantly – enlisting Cemil's help to memorise the Jazatāh annals in the Great Library. But my overseer was right; Cemil challenges my knowledge like no other initiate, probing for a hole, refuting with his own interpretations, and forcing me to build defence after defence in my logic, like a war decided by the planes of the mind.

Outside of classes, in the monastery, the Qabl monks begin physical training to complement our spiritual arts. They hand the novices a string of menial orders to complete on Friday and Saturday evenings. Parchments to ink, manuscripts to stringently illuminate, floors to sweep, cattle dung to shovel, garden pits to dig and date palms to trim.

Vaguely, I wonder if the monks are using the initiates to do chores, or if the labour holds any greater purpose. At other times, the monks command us to not eat for three straight days to understand the body's responses, to recognise primal, animalistic hunger, so we know true bodily poverty, an infinitesimal glimpse into death. They command us to meditate on bone-stone tombs before ordering us into the rose and citrus gardens, to balance our Heavenly bonds; else, warriors who only meditate on death go mad into suicide.

They proclaim: *The speaking body shall not be ignored. Awareness is the body's greatest weapon, for only then shall one acknowledge its faults.* I hate to admit that it is not a worship of death, it is a respect of it.

For weeks we haul muck, and the Qabl monks chuckle as if sensing our low morale. 'Wipe those snotty faces, pigs. The purpose will reveal itself. For now, you must build the foundation of enlightenment to reach the bond between life and death.'

The purpose is revealed after we finish digging the sixth pit outside the monastery. With a cramped back, I rest with the other Zero-Slashes, between Aina and Katayoun.

Suddenly, Sister Umairah looms above the grass, which is swollen with rancid nuts and overripe mulberries that squirt dark juices all over our ochre tunics.

'You require water?' asks the grandmaster. We nod eagerly. She folds her arms. 'Indulge me: did any of you think to use Heavenly bonds and escape the material world to relieve stress from the corporeal body? Did you even chant the Divine's names to contemplate death? Our faith loves death, for it's the highest honour to die in martyrdom. Then you are truly Qabl. If not, you become prone to jinn influence, even possession. Attacked by our enemies, will you crack?'

A shamed silence dwells upon us.

'Now let us begin real Qabl training.' She slaps the trunk of a fig tree. 'And I shall enjoy these figs.'

The monastics explain how the world is a thousand illusions and a thousand covers. To seek truth is to behold, then shatter these constructs. Even when I look within myself and examine my own considerations, those, too, are an illusion viewed through a veil of doubt, and to understand this is to shatter myself. *Enlightenment*, they emphasise. In Qabl meditation, one must be struck in a flash.

As I meditate, a sage slaps me across the face. On impact, I glimpse a white flash. 'Was that thus enlightenment?' I mumble, through a swelling cheek.

'No.' He pinches my ear until I yelp. 'I think it was your consciousness manifesting the pain of my slap. Not true enlightenment, but rather a self-defence mechanism.'

'Is enlightenment supposed to be painful?'

In a wide-toothed smile, the sage says, 'Very,' and slaps me again. I do not resist.

At other times, I time-blank, forcing him to berate me.

'Your memory is pathetic.' His breath reeks, the smell of a fasting monk. *By the Heavens*, I pray for his sake.

The sutras claim that Veils appear everywhere, not solely in the Unseen world, but in the cosmic equation riddling the material world. Other Veils exist – between the mind and the heart, the corporeal self and the soul.

Time is spent emptying ourselves, counting bone-shards and edging closer to the spiritual dominion to relinquish our bonds with the material world and accept death. We find truth, until all that is left is lies. Some days we are closer, some days we are further, but the monks temper our inconstant nature, whittling to their roots the impulses of youth.

The monks snap the assumptions from Azadniabad within me one by one. *The spiritual domain is an internal planetary system; the mind is the sun that knowledge revolves round and round.*

The monks throw questions at us, too.

Are you simply a unit of consumption, eating, shitting, breathing, talking, filling space?

At another practice, Sister Umairah asks, 'The soul is the window. To read it, you must polish its surface and gaze through. What do you see?' The answer dangles on a thread before me tauntingly, but still out of reach. 'What do you hear?' she urges.

My Zahr clan. Louder than myself.

These meditative enquiries provoke a thousand fears, forcing me to acknowledge things that I wish to forget. So, I burn the memories in myriad flames until they crumble to ashes.

Questions are wrong.

Sister Umairah frowns at me, levelling a stern gaze. 'Remain steadfast, pupil. The bountiful rain falls, flooding the valley, yet rather than sowing and reaping, all you do is watch.'

Every second is ideological warfare, but a warrior must love it, must become obsessed with it. Between martial classes, the school and the monastery, my trifecta trains relentlessly. We continue a peaceful routine, wedged into the violent crevices of our soul, until we are stitched into a tapestry of contradictions. We are good at that. Humans like to take peace and make it a symbol of war.

We recite every text. We protest nothing. We bow and grovel. We answer ridiculous questions and, most of all, we listen. When the scholars and monks insult us, we thank them; when they praise us, we remain silent; when they remain quiet, still we bow our heads in shame as if we committed a wrong. We willingly become everyone's pathetic pupils, hoping to become extraordinary masters.

After several weeks, close to the Marka tournament, Cemil tells me I am ready. It is time to try my hand again in Scholar Mufasa's class. Tentatively, I enter the martial halqa, the chambers pluming in frankincense.

'Do you have a death wish?' The scholar begins with no greeting. I catch Katayoun's eyes, seated between Aina, Sharra and Aizere. To my surprise, Katayoun nods to me, and that acknowledgement makes me step further in. Other students notice and murmurs of disquiet cause my heart to flutter like moths against torchlight.

I loosen a breath. 'Scholar, when I am wrong, you must correct me. Are you and I not alike, both students of knowledge?'

'A student is an easy name to claim. Whether you are one or not is a different question.' He snorts hard, flicking off my flattery. Even his wrinkles fold upon themselves like pruned grapes.

He snatches his copied parchments of the Jazatāh annals. He jams a finger into the middle of the codex and begins reading. '… The Jazatāh magicians did not believe in the natural cycle of death. Eajīz believe in bonds representing…'

I know this section, as well as my tongue knows the inside of my cheek. '– our resurrection. Eajīz must shred mind, body and soul before rebuilding it, the way the soul is made by the Divine, killed and resurrected. The first magicians neglected this relationship.'

Mufasa licks his thumb before unrolling a parchment closer to the beginning. 'Ancient Jazatāh civilisations travelled to the City of God's Gates, in ancient Za'skar. This city was the first metropolis after Adam had passed. A wicked empire, the birthplace of black magick—'

I remain quiet, in thought. This scholarship is about the Jinn Wars.

Around us, the low-ranks stare, some in open fascination and others in terror. Katayoun bends her head as if she senses I am one mistake away from bearing the violence of the scholar's staff.

A memory of Emirhan punished on my first day flashes through my head, trousers saturated in his own piss. *That will be you, Khamilla.* I fear not the pain, but the disappointment. I replace the scholar's face with my father. *They both are the same*, I chant inwardly. It recalls the memory.

'They,' I put out, 'held an asymmetry of power through black magick. Using the dark arts, the magicians invoked all types of jinn-folk who soothsaid in their favour. They committed infanticide by magicking wombs to produce stillborn babies, sacrificing souls to feed their power.'

The scholar's finger lifts, quieting me. The class looks on in equal surprise. No-Name treks down the kilim rugs before coming to a stop behind the scholar. Her shape appears like a younger version of the emperor, cross-legged at the low desk, touching parchment and reed pens as if writing letters. My eyes follow her movements.

'I am not done with my test,' the scholar grunts as he rifles through the manuscripts again. But I miss nothing, quoting by heart.

At the end of the hour, the scholar finally places the last codex down, speaking in a thick voice. 'You think memorising is intelligence. Anyone can learn modes of reasoning, but intelligence – true intelligence – is to seize the material, dissect each line, rearrange it and make it one's own. Indeed, you have demonstrated that you are a puppet, spitting the words required of you.'

I flinch and No-Name looks up from the desk, smiling at his words.

Then Scholar Mufasa waves at the other rukhs and I almost miss the gleam in his eyes. 'But I am a man of my word. You have studied the foundation, and you might even perform passingly in the yearly examinations. So go on.' His nostrils flare. 'Before I change my mind.'

19

In the chilly night, dozens of trifectas crowd around the gates of Za'skar to depart for the Festival of Lights in the Sixteen-Gated Grand Bazaar. Apparently, Captain Fayez intends to announce his squadron tonight.

'I find it a Divine miracle that you've left the libraries,' Yabghu tells me as he knots a raven-feathered shawl under his armpits. 'This is your first outing into Al-Haut?'

'Yes.' My tone is short. *Do not expect it again*, I want to tell him.

'Her expression says she would rather be studying,' Cemil remarks from my left. Tonight, he wears a dark muslin kerchief round his temple, making the grey in his eyes appear black.

'Because the examinations are in three weeks and the Easkaria scholars would like to fail me.'

Yabghu smirks. 'But you came, anyway.'

'Cemil made me swear an oath.'

My overseer glances between us. 'An oath? How did he manage that?'

Cemil has the decency to be truthful, but a sardonic smile plays at his lips. 'Bribery. I agreed to help her in her studies if she came.'

'Finally, you realised the use in bribery,' Katayoun mutters.

I give them a disgruntled look.

'It's good she came. The captain might be selecting the Marka squadron tonight...' Yabghu's voice trails off as the crowd of trifectas abruptly stops at the citadel.

'Bow,' Yabghu suddenly orders us.

From a distance, our captain's voice cuts through the air. 'May death be a peace upon you.' Other soldiers bow to a figure entering through Za'skar's gates.

'Bow,' Yabghu hisses again because I have not moved. Shock has frozen me. I rub my tired eyes. *No*, my sight is not mistaken.

The anger takes me by surprise. That it is still so whole and pure after a year — when I had kneeled before him in the frost, with the deaths of my parents as my hidden wound — is a relief.

A flock of advisers and two senior officers stand between us, surrounding him. Crouched against his neck is a courtly raven that fixes its beady eyes in my direction. The power of a clan's vengeance: it cannibalises itself without end, and I thank its resilience as I stare at the Sepāhbad, willing every ounce of my bloodied oath into the microcosm between us.

As if sensing its prickle, the Sepāhbad turns slowly. The wind exhales a bout of sand into a dusty swirl and I hold out a quivering hand to stave it away. The belly of the clouds rumble, bloated and grey, with an occasional blister of moon, yet no rain falls. Heaven's ominous warning is not lost upon me.

Just as the Sepāhbad faces me, I know better than to stare. I drop into a bow, only daring to look up when our shoulders brush as he guides his snorting white steed into Za'skar.

'May death be your peace.' He greets the trifectas softly.

My gaze lingers on his receding back. Cemil stares after him, too, but for reasons opposite, a hunger swimming in him.

He rubs at his jaw before casting a sidelong glance. 'You look shaken.'

'It feels like years since our encounter.'

'You've spoken to him?'

'It was he who recruited me into Za'skar.' Cemil and Katayoun still at the revelation while Yabghu looks unsurprised.

Cemil presses me further. 'Are the rumours true, then? Did you see into his eyes?'

'His eyes?' Katayoun asks.

'He can control the Heavenly bonds within his eyes,' Yabghu answers.

My thoughts slide back to his attack at the Ghaznia citadel, a part of me curious about his manipulation of Heavenly bonds. 'That is what he used on me.'

My words echo louder than I intend. Other soldiers turn, Dara and a Third-Slash named Dil-e-Jannah.

'Impossible,' she scoffs. 'You'd be dead.'

'It was a misunderstanding,' I speak quickly, omitting that he'd snapped my leg as well. 'I looked into his eye bonds, and I could not move before he used Ifrit's Strike, disabling my own Heavenly bonds.'

'Count your blessings that you live,' Yabghu says grimly. 'The Sepāhbad's affinity is a virtue of the original cosmic sphere. The scholars call it Spring of Heavens, for he can control the substances that make up the springs of life. Based on the conditions he set with the Heavens, he can pull water from the clay, air, rivers or the corporeal body. Wielding eye bonds is a rare ability, even for Seventh-Slash warriors. If you use it, opponents are forced to fight you almost blind, for if they look into your eyes, the Heavenly Energy paralyses them for a split moment. Eye bonds guarantee an affinity hitting its mark. This is the move Sepāhbad Jezakiel used to defeat *her* – the former Sepāhbad – in a Duxzam battle, to become our martial-vizier.'

My mind flashes to a distant memory of my girlhood, recalling the female general I saw then.

'Why did Sepāhbad Jezakiel overthrow her?' I ask.

'He took advantage of the fallout she faced for aiding Akashun's insurrection against the Zahrs,' Yabghu explains.

'I've hardly seen the Sepāhbad in Za'skar,' Katayoun comments.

'He returned today from the Camel Road,' Yabghu answers. 'With the strange disappearances in our borderlands, and the melees in Yalon province, led by Emperor Akashun—'

'Akashun,' I interrupt, the sound of the warlord's name another shock. More wind lashes my face until I am forced to raise my shawl over my head.

This is the bitter reality outside Za'skar's gates: my clan is fractured; Warlord Akashun still rules Azadniabad, and raids grow between our empires. Nothing has changed. Another reminder of my purpose.

'– and after the Marka tournament, I'll be departing for the late winter campaign at our northern outposts,' Yabghu continues as the guards of the bazaar wave us through the crumbling bone-stone walls.

Surrounding us, the bustle of the bazaar makes Za'skar seem like a separate realm. Though night draws a dark curtain as the moon teethes between the city's suspended glass bridges and palaces, weaving high amongst looming mountains, Al-Haut does not rest in its mercantile trade. The Grand Bazaar is located within the eastern quarters of the capital. Attached at points to the citadel walls, sixteen welded gates of mosaicked stained glass and indigo calligraphy in geometric designs stand large, undeniably crafted from jinn masonry.

I gaze at sword dancers who perform aesthetic martial arts, to the delight of gawking onlookers. Craftsmen dye swirling blue-threaded raven designs on the arms of children. Enormous smokeless-fire filigree lanterns shine along each sand-packed alleyway, as if breathing out a false dawn. Large triple-domed temples glitter, and priests, after evening remembrance, stand amongst open prayer niches in complexes made of glazed ceramic turquoise with raven epigraphs.

'The Heavens have abandoned humanity,' a priest bellows to a gathering of worshippers inside an open sehan. 'We have no prophets nor revelation. Cursed are we, like the tribes swept away by the Great Flood.'

The din of shouting shawl-makers pierces the market; they display glistening coins embroidered on tunics, printed from shuttles of wooden blocks. Carvers lift wares of worked bone: pendants, pottery and ivory seals. How so many of us fit in such narrow streets is beyond me. Dialects from Sajamistan's different provinces chorus the air, so unusual compared to the barks and orders of Za'skar.

Notables wear raven-feathered turbans while sat cross-legged playing saktab, sipping steaming cinnamon kahvah from palm-sized coppery cups. A wave of envy at the capital's diversity hits me. Are these bazaars common in Sajamistan? Do they always laugh and trade while on the other side of the city, children train for war?

'Is something the matter?' Cemil slows, letting Yabghu and Katayoun drift ahead with the other trifectas. I watch the warriors marvel at sizzling skewers of sumac and saffron lamb kebabs, and piles of pilaf garnished in slivered carrots, barberries and cashews. How can I be here, tempted, while my clan burned from these very same hands?

'Khamilla?'

I startle. 'What?'

He watches me for a long moment. 'You look pale.'

'It's the chill.' I glance away, anywhere but at him. 'I think it will storm tonight.' My hands wrap my shawl tighter.

As if on impulse, Cemil's hand reaches up, brushing a loose strand of hair into my shawl. His finger lingers on the thin black braids rounding my temple before he retracts his hand suddenly. 'Perhaps you are falling ill.'

'That would be your fault. You forced me here.' I step away before I let myself conclude that I do not despise the warmth of him.

To my left, Overseer Negar lingers with her rukhs Dara, Aizere and Aina; she catches my eye and leers. In her arms, she carries something obscured by a shawl.

'This way, rukh,' Yabghu calls out to me before I can look further, while Cemil splits off toward Negar.

Yabghu stands with Katayoun and other low-ranks from my halqa, Emirhan and Gulnaz. I spot a high-rank as well, Lukhman.

I hear Katayoun say, 'You are our master, this outing should be on your stipend,' her lips smirking.

Yabghu scowls but pays six coppers for each meal. The merchant offers up clay mugs of stew with torn semolina noodles, green lentils, reeking black garlic and dark beans. Yabghu tries to hand me one, and a kebab to Katayoun, his attar a comforting perfume of white clover. But I am rooted to the ground, watching the bazaar from afar.

He nudges it closer. 'Are you not starved?' Yabghu asks.

'No, I... I'm feeling ill.' I jump back quickly. 'And this is *rotting*.'

Yabghu frowns. Training is one thing, but accepting his outstretched food is a betrayal to my own kind. My head pounds and I back away down the alleyway, past merchants and smokeless lanterns. I did not know it was possible to be surrounded by throngs of people but feel helplessly alone.

At the end of the path, No-Name is there but distracted. Her long pale fingers flicker over a tea stall. Her form shrinks until she is a girl dressed in a crane-feathered qaftan. My feet slow.

No-Name changes, somehow becoming more than a single person. Now she's a wispy girl on the shoulders of her brother, who is dressed in monastic robes as he flaunts her across the bazaar, their laughs tumbling forward from the past.

'*Stop that.*' My breath catches as the memory slides into place like two lovers snug against each other. It reflects to me: my arm pulled by my half-siblings toward a bazaar beneath showers of stars, smelling the wealth of velvet in stalls, walking my fingers across rolls of silk before we all gather under platanus trees between evening poets.

My hand grasps out to the bright memory, yearning… *for who*, I cannot be sure, but, like nūr, the light is extinguished soon between my fingers.

I return to the present with wet cheeks, not from tears. Thunder quakes the skies; the clouds have broken. Huddling under my shawl, I watch the rain punish the late crowd, beating paths on the sand, forming long puddles.

I back away, right into Cemil.

'Usur-Khan.' His voice is tight, hand steadying my arm. It slides down, finding the old scar he inflicted on me.

'Has Yabghu summoned me?'

He hesitates. 'Yes, but it was a mistake to have you accompany us.'

Does he expect me to be offended? In fact, I am a little relieved. 'I agree,' I tell him. 'This was a waste of my time. But if I leave, Yabghu will—'

'No.' His grip is almost bruising. 'You have to go. *Now.*' He glances over his shoulder before shoving me forward. 'Go—'

'There she is.' Overseer Negar looms over Cemil, replacing his hand. 'It's good that she's here. Captain Fayez has decided to draft the squadron, *now*, in the bazaar.'

Cemil presses his lips together and speaks no more. My eyes narrow but I've no choice but to obey an overseer's orders.

As we walk toward the assembled squadron, merchants shutter their stalls and city folk flee toward the temple or find cover in grasping date trees, palms flipped outward in prayer. Preachers seize on the omen. At least this fear, both empires share: rain, a moment for prayer to remember the Great Flood.

Captain Fayez must not fear the rain, for he grins from the centre of the bazaar, calling out to us. 'What better, more sacred time than during rainfall to announce the underlings of my Marka squadron.'

Wiping my face, I slide on to a flat stone beside Katayoun beneath palm trees. No-Name comes forward.

'I think we should go,' she says quietly. 'I sense something. It makes me uneasy.'

Captain Fayez prowls round the centre, overseers flanking him. To the side stand two captains from other squadrons, here for the show: Madj and Osman.

Fayez begins drafting low-rank warriors. Many are inevitable: Lukhman, Dara, Gulnaz. Thirty rukhs out of over three hundred. In some trifectas, Fayez skimps, and in others, he selects two low-ranks.

Eventually, Fayez reaches our trifecta, the last one.

Rain is frightful for it reminds the people of how Nuh's nation was forsaken. My head tilts up, taking in Heaven's grief. Fayez too looks at the sky, and parts his mouth, rainwater trickling in. He swallows and licks his lips, accepting its curses as if he's beyond forsaken. Then his eyes come to rest on me.

'Usur-Khan.' His fingers fiercely grip the bone-pendant strung around his neck, until his nails bleed white. I stand, watching his hands. 'You would like to be in my squadron.'

It is not a question. My gaze flits up. 'Yes.'

'Will you obey my first order?'

'Order me.' I bow.

He unlatches his waterskin and pours it on to his sandals. 'It's simple. Lick this kahvah off my feet.'

I unfold from my bow. 'W-what?'

'Will you?'

I blink at his condition. A prideful sort. This is a simple decision. As I summon an answer, he suddenly faces the crowd of Za'skar warriors.

'In the face of an enemy, what does Squadron One do?' he demands of them.

'Snip the strings of fate, fan the flames and devour the ones who march against us.' The torrid wind carries their chant.

Fayez nods like the script hails from a holy book rather than the mouths of military dogs. 'Does *she* understand it so?'

It takes me a moment to realise what he has done. I gaze mistakenly, at the hundreds of eyes drilling into me and then Negar's slow smile, so I miss Fayez's quick movement. His iron-fist slams into my torso. I stumble back, legs collapsing to the dirt.

He hit me. The wind screeches, the wet air an invasion rather than a cleansing when it sweeps grit into my lungs.

'This is the enemy.' Fayez grounds his heel into the old injury in my leg. Pain blisters up my nerves. 'As if I would allow an Azadnian into my squadron.' Then I see it, the deep fury in his eyes – the hate. How was I blind to it? 'But you were an excellent rival to string along Cemil, bringing him to such potential.'

His foot slams down again, and the iron-bone makes my head flinch against a rock. Distantly, I hear Yabghu yelling. My eyes seek Cemil, but the deceiver is unable to meet my gaze, hands clenched into fists, veins corded up his neck.

'What potential?' Glaring at them, I smear away blood. 'I see no hawkish raven, but a soft yellow tit, or – dare I say – a snakebird. At least have the gall to look me in the eye, Cemil.'

Fayez grins at that and slams his foot a third time, sucking away my words.

'Captain!' Yabghu wrenches me upwards and shoves himself between us. 'She is still my student. And you will incur *his* wrath; you do not know that the Sepāhbad recruit—'

'Has my own lieutenant turned against me?' Fayez snarls. Yabghu's hand eclipsing my wrist tightens but he cannot disobey his superior before the entire squadron.

'Enough,' I say with an equally ironclad tone. My fingers ready, clammy, and my legs crouch. But I cannot throw a fist. My breath slows and I count upwards then downwards. 'Captain, you brought me outside of Za'skar so the senior officers will not see this offence. But you mistake me for someone with pride. Tell me, how do I show you that I deserve a place in your Marka squadron? You asked me to lick the kahvah. Shall I do that?'

The captain looks down his long nose, scrubs his rough, splotchy, henna-dyed beard. I meet his gaze. My legs bend until I am on my knees, moving toward Fayez's feet. I think about my scattered clan; about Hyat Uncle waiting for me to feed him information; about Older Brother Yun, surrounded in Arsduq, facing Sajamistani incursions at the borderland.

My overseer blinks in naked astonishment. 'Usur-Khan? Have you no self-preservation?'

'None at all.' I smile.

'Your ambitions will cost you your life,' Yabghu hisses. 'No one in this army will respect you.' Then he glares behind me. 'Grab her.' He grasps my left arm; a small hand takes my right. To my bewilderment, it's Katayoun attempting to drag me back, her right hand holding her kebab. I shove both of them away, lowering back down like an onager, face hot even in the wet. My pulse pounds militantly against my throat. *Pride does not matter in my battle.*

The captain grins through my humiliation. His sandal comes to rest atop my head, forcing it into the dirt. 'See, she loves it. And *I* love an Azadnian begging. It simply proves our theorem. You are Azadnian. Lesser.' His hand raises. 'Bring it.'

Overseer Negar thrusts forward the object shrouded by a shawl. Fayez whips the cover off. A surge of bile fills my mouth. It's a cage. Inside is a delicate white creature smeared in russet brown. A crane. Three long talons dig into its belly… a raven, pecking at its rotting flesh, which swarms with brown locusts, legs curled into its matted feathers.

'See that. This is natural. Just like this.' His foot hammers into my neck and I spasm out blood-tinted saliva. 'Like your natural inclination to bow at my feet. To never resist. To obey. A hierarchy of power; this is good for order. You are trying to break that order. Cemil is two ranks above you; a stronger martial artist.'

In the captain's shadow, Cemil wavers. He takes one step toward me but does not move closer. Once again, his gaze settles on my forearms, so like his own with its gold whorls, yet so different. His gaze hardens with an imperceptible anger. It is laughable: our fates on opposite ends. What separates us is an arbitrary border stroked in sooty ink that puts his tribe into Sajamistan and my maternal tribe into Azadniabad, both from the Camel Road. Yet, no one blinks an eye, accepting him as their own. Perhaps I should be grateful, saved from the fate of being him.

'The difference between you two is pride. Cemil would never beg as you do, below me,' Fayez says.

'No.' I splatter blood into my hand. 'Pride is chains to a warrior. I have no pride. I do not need it.'

'Pride keeps order.' Fayez glances round the bazaar, a reflection of his words: an orderly metropolitan that deceived even the jinn into labouring away to produce the riches of this city. 'If you proved yourself stronger, if Azadniabad conquered our lands, I would not hate you. I would accept the natural outcome,' he crouches, finger grazing the blood against my lips, 'and I would respect you. Not begging. Not petty tricks.' He recedes. 'For this, I will ensure no squadron will ever select you.'

'You are worse than Qabil.' I spit at his feet the curse of Adam's son. 'Violence is your natural order.'

'Tell me, do the bites of fleas affect the might of a flying serpent? No. Your anger, your attacks, do not affect me. I am an azhdahak. A flying serpent.'

I feel so small that I kneel lower, though I yearn to stand at his level. The illusion of equality is better than the truth of inferiority. My fists bury in the wet sand. Months of grovelling in this army and I haven't managed a single rank, while my brethren are cornered by this empire and vultures like Warlord Akashun.

I've tired of this helplessness. I will force my way into the Marka even if it requires a squadron of my own. My throat burns as I swallow hard and look between Fayez and Cemil, smearing the blood from my face on to my palm, presenting my vow: 'You force my hand. And you will regret this. My kind does not forget a blood oath.'

From behind them, Katayoun sighs, and lifts her skewer of sumac lamb, indifferent. 'This is the outcome when you have useless ambitions,' she says before her teeth tear into its meaty flesh.

20

In the gardens of Little Paradise, I perch on a soft hill and await the pazktab students. Below, the city of Za'skar awakens under the newborn sun. Dawn strikes through the dark in the sure command of the Divine, as He approves the celestial's rise after her prostration at His throne. Under its light, the gold vistas of the land carry warriors in trifectas in imitation of their revered raven who promises obedience at the feet of its master. I think of Captain Fayez and how the soldiers gazed on him with that same conviction. I will break it.

No-Name treks around the oases, shifting her form until her body flows in robes hemmed in crane feathers, dark hair shorn across her head. She crouches at the fountains, petting the soft blue pelts of ababil birds. My heart thunders at the spirit of my past.

'I despise when you take this form, when you appear as *him*,' I tell her, unable to utter my dead brother's name.

'You need this reminder, because what you intend to do is imprudent.' She voices my doubts.

'I have no choice,' I tell her. 'I've come too far to stop now.'

Soon Sohrab, Yasaman and Yahya arrive. I tamp down my nerves and declare with no preamble: 'I will continue training you. On the condition we become a squadron for the Marka of Za'skar.'

My captain has ensured no other superior will draft me, but there is a different gullible class to exploit. *In fact*, an eagerness swells, *children are the easiest to manipulate.* And that is the kind of squadron I need: one that is easily controlled.

The younglings look blank. 'Marka?'

'Yes. Marka, the tournament in four Fridays, on the winter solstice. A strategy battle of squadrons. Imagine the ancient art of mountain polo

– in this game, whoever collects a majority of enemy banners wins. We will register on the eve before, so it is too late to stop us.'

Sohrab laughs. 'Very funny. Why would you have children help you on your team?'

'I waste little time on jokes. And I would not waste yours, either. I need this – in the Marka, the well-performing warriors are rewarded. It's the only way for me to move up a rank.'

'The whole idea is a joke. You waste all of our time. We would perform awfully.'

'Have I not helped you? I will train you every day.'

A new voice chuckles behind them. 'So they owe you a debt because you trained them for a few weeks?' I glance over, recognising the bruising girl. Arezu. Her jade eyes glare into my own. 'You risk your reputation, leading a squadron of pazktab children. Is that even permitted by our masters?'

'Reputation? I've none. No captain recruited me for the Marka. And the captain said it himself: any inhabitant of Za'skar may create a squadron. As Eajīz – young and weak though you are – you are still inhabitants of Za'skar.'

Sohrab mulls it over. 'A battle… a *real* battle. It's—'

'Frightening,' Yasaman suggests.

'Rare,' Sohrab says, deciding, and I note, for all his impulsiveness, he might be clever. 'We have nothing to lose, but she,' he points to me, 'has everything to lose, and gain.'

The youngest, Yahya, shakes and then nods his head rather unhelpfully.

'I promise, we will not be humiliated in the Marka. Any effort is better than how we are seen now,' I say.

'How are we seen?' Arezu prods.

'Well, I am a loser in Za'skar. And you are pazktab students without a patron from the royal courts. You are losers as well.'

She studies me so scathingly gooseflesh erupts down my arms. 'No. We are different than you.'

'How?'

'You are a debt collector. I've met your kind. My family are plant-dyers from the lands of Khor. Our landholders give cheap promises by advancing ingots, to keep us borrowing cotton. You are like that. Cheap promises tricking us into crippling debt. Everything is a bargain with you, *master*.' With a perturbing look, Arezu walks away.

A cold feeling jolts into my stomach, that of an icy truth. 'My idea will not change. I want you in my Marka squadron.'

Something resonates amongst the other three students. Sohrab's lips twist mischievously. 'On one condition.'

'You are in no position to offer conditions to me.'

'You admit you need us for your plan. Listen to our condition.' I stiffen warily as he says, 'Beat us at our games and we shall play yours, *master*.'

With a chorus of laughs, Yasaman and Sohrab leave me dumbfounded in the gardens, taking Yahya with them. The mountains splotch pink from the sunrise. My cheeks heat with it.

'How dare they?' I say to No-Name.

'Patience, Khamilla.' She speaks in the familiar tone of the brother I once knew, still stroking the head of an ababil bird. 'They are merely children. Impatient, and young. Not all children are like you, living under the thumb of a ruler. Not all worship their pain.'

As I leave the hills for monastic training, my braids prickle and I rip off my silk tassels to find a cockroach prowling on them, two hairs clutched in its little legs. *It is so small*, I half muse. The urge to squash it consumes me.

No-Name looks bemused. 'A cockroach?'

'Those little asses,' I say, seething, recognising what they have done. This is Sohrab's condition. Just like the first day they spoilt my meal. These tricks and ploys with bugs… I know what I must do.

In the pavilion during mealtime, Yabghu intentionally sits between Cemil and me; we have not spoken since the night of Fayez's humiliation. Earlier, during trifecta studies in the Great Library, I spoke through Katayoun instead of directly addressing Cemil.

I turn away while Yabghu forces a wooden conversation between Katayoun and Cemil. Surrounding us are pazktab students crossing to and fro between tables. My eyes latch on to Sohrab and Yasaman, Arezu at the front. As they pass me, I lift my cup of kahvah, dumping it in their paths, causing Sohrab to slip on the bone-stone tiles.

'Usur-Khan?' Yabghu berates me. When the pazktab students pass me, I do it again; my actions confuse my trifecta but I do not explain them.

In return, during the dawn breaking of fast, the pazktab students retaliate with ants squirming in my barley porridge, where I mistake the bugs for specks of cinnamon.

After trifecta training, I spend hours collecting cockroaches in teacups before releasing them in the kitchens during the breaking of eve fast.

When I find bitter anise powder in my waterskin, I leave the pavilion early and lace the children's sandals in roughly ground chili collected from the Za'skar gardens to blister their feet. When I am at the women's quarters of the bathing river, I discover mounds of mushed figs and dates inside the tunic of my uniform, moulding my small chest into the opposite of modesty.

I will not be outdone by their ridiculous games. And in games, I always win.

And that is exactly what transpires. The next morning, my path to the monastery's terrace is intercepted when the students sprint toward me, dark blue and white tunics splattered in turmeric, armpits stained mortifyingly mustard as if with day-old sweat.

'We concede!' Yasaman breathes out heavily.

'Oh?'

She glowers. 'Fine, we agree to be your squadron. But it's madness!'

'A good kind of madness,' I promise.

Without wasting time, I pursue training the pazktab students that day. They ask me many questions, some as a product of curiosity and others of their ineptness.

'Meditation is a bore; when do we learn iron-bone?' Sohrab asks.

'Boredom is the failure to pay attention and meditation is the cure for boredom. Breathing is half the war. Controlling your breath determines who lasts longest in battle, and—'

'Master, enough with the parables,' he moans out.

Beside me, No-Name leans against a citrus tree and leaps up to grab a fruit that swings out of reach. She speaks with each jump, becoming increasingly impatient. 'Training these. Foolish students. Cannot work.'

If I knew of a faster way to create my own squadron, I wouldn't be helping them at all, I counter.

Her pale lips curve up bitterly. 'There are many ways if you open your mind. But you choose to block your mind, relying on children, rather than me—'

A growl rumbles from the citrus groves behind us. I still. 'What was that?'

The students rouse from their meditation, glancing around for the source of the sound.

'Help!' a voice cries. From the orchards, I spot a karkadann sniffing near the trunk of a tree.

'Get up,' I hiss at my students, and they oblige. 'Back away slowly to the pond and continue meditating.'

The beast's conical horn shines above a bullish blue torso, jaw hung with a sagging, scaly dewlap. It's both majestic and terrifying and my head pounds at seeing its red eyes. Even the birds from the Paradise fountains warble excitedly at the commotion.

'O, Divine!' the voice cries again as the karkadann grunts toward the tree. I follow its direction. It's Arezu.

She hangs from the top branch of the citrus tree, her fingertips clinging for purchase, blood streaming down her hand where she must have scraped it. Attracted by her voice, the karkadann charges the trunk, shaking the tree, and Arezu slips to a lower branch, her feet now only a handspan away from its head.

'Arezu?' Sohrab asks, but I cover his gaze.

'Do not stop meditating, no matter the distraction,' I snap, as an idea comes over me. Teaching pazktab students is a difficult challenge – unless I have a primed student to inspire them, to lead with ambition and to make them complete.

What are you doing? No-Name follows me as I face Arezu.

I have found it. I point. *My solution. I want it. I want the angry one.*

As if she's... a thing.

Yes. She is rude. I like her rebellion. It means she craves a fight.

But it will break your order. Worry sweeps through No-Name's gaze. *You need me. Not these foolish allies. Besides, the girl is almost sixteen, wiser and more stubborn than the rest.*

Then I will bring her into my order. All people can be subdued with time, all wills crushed.

'Her what?' Sohrab asks from behind me. 'What are you muttering?'

'Nothing.' I walk cautiously toward Arezu's tree, avoiding the karkadann.

Her eyes widen at me. 'Help!'

'I do not take kindly to rogue girls spying on my lessons. If that karkadann fells you, well, I think you deserve the mess you have put yourself in.'

Shut it, Azadnian heretic. Arezu struggles, her face reddening from maintaining her grip or, perhaps, embarrassment.

Swinging her legs, the momentum flies her back on to the branch. She attempts to shoo away the horned beast as it circles the tree languidly.

'I will help you on one condition,' I offer.

'You are a jinn,' she spits. 'I will not be in your Marka squadron—' A clamouring rustles the branches above her and, to our surprise, a furred arm smacks her face.

She cries out. 'Monkeys!'

The creatures swing through the trees, down and up. Arezu huddles low, shrieking, trying to dodge them. My pulse quickens but I affect a blank look, to not clue her into my inner panic. It is what I am good at, pretending my problems are small.

I dare closer to the karkadann. Arezu throws a lemon at a monkey but misses.

'If you recite remembrance about the Divine, the beasts might leave you,' I tell her.

She screams more.

I gaze around the clearing, thinking fast. Once, I had known the secret to fell a karkadann, but that part of me died a long time ago. All I've left is to recall Yabghu's words from my first day. He alluded that karkadann and monkeys dislike…

Incense. In my satchel, I unlatch my attar incense from the Qabl monks and throw the ash behind the beast. It does not work. Angered, the karkadann rams into the trunk, and the branches quiver.

To my horror, Arezu begins crouching, moving into first stance, as if she could fight the creatures.

'That stance is dangerous against them.' I raise my voice above the cackling creatures.

'*That stance is dangerous*,' she mimics, smirking. 'True grandmasters would stance train on treetops to learn balance. Yet, you train students on the ground.' But the smiles slides off when the karkadann gives a great thrust. Arezu's foot slips and she plummets backwards. I dive and catch her before she smacks into the hard ground. Retreating, I take us into the safety of the fountains.

I dump her on the ground. 'If you fool around with the karkadann in amateur stances, you will be attacked long before the bones of your body break.'

Her face tightens. 'You think you are better.'

'Yes.'

Her eyes darken. 'My formations are good.' Unsheathing an onyx training knife, she moves into second stance.

'Good,' I say flatly. 'Try to throw the blade by using the Heavenly bonds in your feet.' She pivots but remains flat-footed instead of rising on to the balls of her feet. 'You will twist your ankle.'

Her lips grimace. 'You want to rope me in with the rest of those gullible fools.' She gestures to Sohrab, Yasaman and Yahya, watching us from the far fountains. That is true.

She shifts her elbows into a line before throwing the onyx knife.

Carefully, as if approaching a ravening beast, I chop behind her knees before pressing a palm lightly between her shoulders at the sensitive point. She folds to the dirt.

'What the Hells!'

'Your centre of Heavenly Energy is pathetic. You look pretty but aesthetics are irrelevant. Instead, open the bonds beneath your feet. My overseer told me it's the First-Stratum of summoning. But you would know this if you joined us. Your potential is good.'

Her back straightens. Bewildered at the change, I wonder if I should compliment her more to win her over. 'But you are still awful,' I add quickly. 'Anyhow, we can make it work.' I examine her height and scrawniness.

'*We* are not making anything work.'

'You know, Sohrab needs a sparring partner. And you could benefit from a teacher.'

She barks out a laugh. 'What kind of master are you? Half the time, you hold Yahya in your arms because he sobs like a fat babe.'

'No, I don't!' Yahya cries.

Now it's my turn to be embarrassed. 'I hold him for a *quarter* of the time because he cannot handle the training as much as the others. *And he's four years old.*'

'Whatever. Watch now.' She readies her fists.

Yasaman, sensing what's to come, shoots to her feet. 'Arezu, do not—'

Arezu barrels toward me but I catch her fists. 'I will snap those fingers. Know that I've made good on worse threats before.' Another lie. Not a single threat I've made in this city has ever come true.

'But why do *I* need *you*? I am fine by myself.'

'It's a matter of heuristics. An Azadnian monk once said: one cannot learn to be a warrior by inaction. A tactician does not learn sufficient warfare through study only. There is no substitute for experience—'

Arezu rolls her eyes, saying, 'O, Master, thank you for that parable. Please quote more sagely scrolls,' before clambering up into a tree. 'I will do nothing with you.' Like a sparrow, she hops away branch to branch.

'She left,' Sohrab points out.

'She will be back.'

The next morning, she marches up the hill. Sohrab grins widely.

'I'm here to observe,' Arezu snaps. I catch her fingers curling into her blue tunic as if she awaits my scorn.

'I see. Would the new pupil like to introduce herself?'

'We are well acquainted. I enjoy thrashing Sohrab,' she mutters. The others wince. Arezu glances at my kerchief. *'O, master?'*

'Yes?'

She bows extra mockingly. 'There is a cockroach in your hair.'

I stare. Sohrab looks accusingly to Yasaman, who shrugs mildly. 'It's my affinity.'

If I show scorn, they will use it against me. But if I ignore it, I set an ill precedent. Children, I have learnt over the weeks, must be handled strategically.

'I am the fool for not noticing.' I fling the cockroach at Arezu, and she screams.

21

The final examinations of the lunar year – the Wadiq tests – arrive a week before the Marka tournament, a public affair for the low-ranks to demonstrate their potential. The first set are of martial affairs under the proctoring of Scholar Mufasa.

Yabghu sits our trifecta on the first tier of a limestone pavilion, where a sehan boasts clear oases and lush roses blooming under the cool day, the white and red flora like embroidery. Palm-wood rahle are arranged in neat rows, holding ink pots, soft moulded clay tablets and nipped bamboo reeds on date leaves. Unfamiliar faces mill about, hundreds of notables and bureaucrats from the royal courts greeting scholars and students, the ranks of their status dyed in black-threading on their palms.

Before we go, Yabghu passes around a sloshing mug of goat milk, steamed with turmeric and crushed almonds. 'It sharpens the mind,' he says. 'Like last year, I give the same advice. Many rukhs falsely assume your performance in the Easkaria holds no importance on rankings. But the scholars influence it as much as a Marka, or martial duels like a Duxzam. May the Divine bless you with the knowledge to succeed.' His eyes settle on Katayoun. 'Please, at least put in the effort to pass.'

As I trudge to my rahle, Cemil intercepts me. 'Khamilla,' he begins. I stiffen at the informal use of my name. It does not belong on his tongue.

'Usur-Khan,' I correct and sidestep around him. His decision to speak to me now, on the day of the examinations, is intentional – to throw off my attention.

He reaches for my shoulder. 'I was unaware of what Captain Fayez would do to you. I'd invited you to the bazaar because of camaraderie.'

'I prefer Katayoun. She is livelier to converse with.'

Katayoun glances at us from her low desk as we get to our seats. 'I do not prefer either of you. We do not converse ever, at all.'

'We will after this,' I promise her.

'Khamilla, I warned you on your first day, the captain despises Azadnians.' Cemil is blunt but sounds solemn. 'He would never let you compete in the Marka.'

'Then it is very well that I don't need him to do it.'

He cocks his head. 'No squadron would have you.'

'That is what you assume. Because you prefer when we are like this: you above me, chiding, while I am below, relying on your hand.' To make my point, I gesture at his hunched shoulders, his head bent so I can make out the dark flecks in his grey eyes. Then I nod to his empty rahle. 'You should have a seat before the scholars notice. As you remarked once before: I would rather best you myself, than have you taken out before the battle begins.'

'Master!' A voice rings out and Cemil turns to it. A throng of pazktab students, led by a scholar, straggle around the courtyard. Sohrab and Yasaman break from the group, running toward me. Arezu lingers behind them but does not come forward.

'That pazktab child addressed you,' Cemil accuses.

'No. Get on.' I shove him away. Reluctantly, Cemil takes his seat at the rahle but, in unabashed suspicion, watches Sohrab and Yasaman arrive at my station.

'Master, what are these tests?'

'An examination for low-ranks.' I bend toward my desk. Sohrab's eyes light up. Aware of Cemil watching, I give short replies.

'Will it be difficult?'

'No,' I say, deflecting.

'Have you studied?'

'With my trifecta.'

'Are you nervous?'

'No,' I lie, beginning to regret acknowledging Sohrab at all.

'Why do you do that?'

'Do what?'

'*That*. Not actually answering.'

I straighten my reed pen. 'I feel sorry for anyone who insists on speaking to me at all.'

'You are odd, master.'

'I promise to apologise after this conversation.' My eyes catch on the scholars lining up in the courtyard, including Scholar Mufasa. 'Which is now. My examinations are beginning. Sorry. And farewell.'

'Well, we pray for your success,' Yasaman adds meekly.

My hand stiffens around the reed pen. No one has ever wished for my success. I am accustomed to my clansmen anticipating my inevitable failure – even the emperor. My lips twitch but I pray I do not do something ridiculous, like almost smile.

The scholars pair students for the first round and Scholar Mufasa veers toward my low desk. I put down my reed pen and glance to No-Name, who curls up beside my rahle, tucking her face into my neck. *I need you to change*, I urge her.

Her changes are becoming quicker; in a breath, she resembles my father again, his black gaze pressing against my own. To the emperor, memories, feelings were useless. He raised me to be his vizier, to be his prodigy, to be cool and calm, deft in tactics. Strategy is *my* domain.

My mind clings to that conviction as in lightning-attack simulations, I winnow through the first few rounds with ease, beating Sharra, Aizere and other Zero-Slashes.

'What were the principles of the Al-Haut siege during the first wars between the Sajamistani and Azadnian clans?' Scholar Mufasa asks.

'Fire was concentrated on one point, and a breach was made, and the equilibrium imploded. And thus, a concentrated blow must be aimed at the enemy's strongest point in order to achieve a decisive result,' I answer first over Aina.

He asks in the next test, 'How should besieging Azadnian forces collapse the defences of Al-Haut?'

'The logical step is to dam the stream that leads into the confluence, depriving the city of water,' Yima, the First-Slash explains, continuing on about commando tactics.

The scholar cocks his head. 'That does not mean condemning as many as you can to death?'

A trick is woven deftly into his words, for of course death matters in a war – but he's speaking strictly in absolutes. It does not matter how many die; it matters *who* dies. It's the difference between cutting off an emperor's head or slaughtering mere subjects. The best generals strike a balance in every calculus of death when conquering.

'Poisoning the stream affects the same supply lines that feed our forces,' I rebut and cross my arms. 'I would order half of our mules poisoned instead. Then I'd melt half our weapons.'

'Of course *you* would speak of poison,' Yima smirks.

'In the past, siege engines flung poisoned cattle, causing rampant disease. Order fifty of your soldiers to launch cannons filled with the sick animals' entrails. It's biological warfare when the catapults fling disease at the enemy. That would be enough to weaken portions of their forces. Then, retreat with your flanks behind the moats of Al-Haut – as the enemy notes the movement, they will conclude you are repositioning because of the fear of disease. But this allots our forces time to dig, then blast, molten lead inside the fortress. When the metal has cooled, scale the walls and invade. You must obtain surrender by the enemy. Complete, utter surrender.'

Scholar Mufasa nods but his frown lines are like wizened cracks against dirt. For the first time, I wonder how much war he's seen and how many decisions he regrets.

I fight through a dozen more rounds. It's not until an examiner tallies them all up that I realise just three of us are left. We are brought to the centre of the courtyard, where hundreds of bureaucrats and warriors gaze on us. Scholar Hawja looks at my khanjar with bulging eyes, like I am a theorem to puzzle out. No one knows that I was learning martial tactics under the tutelage of Azadnian viziers.

'A Zero-Slash. The last time such a feat was achieved by a novice rukh was when the Sepāhbad was a recruit.' The scholar is not alone in her bewilderment.

My two opponents sit cross-legged on the kilim, around a rahle.

'Odd, indeed,' the Third-Slash echoes, Dil-e-Jannah.

Beside her, Cemil's face looks both sharp and pleasing, his body taut beneath his tunic. Our eyes meet and he raises both his brows twice at me.

I raise a brow back as if to say *what of it?* before I consider what I've done – cheeks burning – like we are allies.

He smiles but I catch a swell of embitterment. 'Nervous?'

'I've come this far with few nerves,' I respond flatly.

The scholar fiddles through her parchments and a hush falls upon the crowd. 'Study this map made after the fall of the Jazatāh Era.' She taps with her reed pen. 'At Azadniabad's encampment, located in eastern Arsduq, the khan, ahead of the Tezmi'a River, plans a campaign through the mountain pass that connects with our summer capital in Khor. In the north-east, Sajamistan's frontier troops have discovered the bulk of Azadnians allied with Zayguk. The frontier troops have scant time to stop the enemy forces from crossing through the Black Mountains, which would open a two-pronged invasion. The tribes along our Ghaznian border have fallen, leaving the Black Mountains undefended.' She spreads the parchment between us. 'You have four nights until they reach the pass.'

The three of us lean in, drinking in the map's contents. The encampment is detailed with steeds, sleeping tents and a winding qanat irrigation system fed by the river channels.

After a moment, Cemil shrugs at us. 'I suppose we are expected to ambush this encampment, burn their supplies.'

I nod until he suggests, 'But I would not expose our position. Instead of engaging the camp directly, from the elevated mountain trails, I would block the pass by burning the surrounding shrub and woodland, before redirecting the Tezmi'a River down the slope. This would induce a landslide, because the dirt cannot absorb the impact of water, mud and rocks colliding. Classic scorched-clay tactics. Envision the landslides used by Eskander against invading mobile armies when he retreated between the mountains of the Inner and Outer Camel Road to resist the Jazatāh. It's nearly suicide, but a guaranteed loss for the invading forces. With a deep-cut valley, it would block the pass, ruining the pasture, starving frontier tribes—'

My stomach clenches and my gaze darts to No-Name thrumming her fingers over the parchment. She is smaller – *so small* – and—

I am no longer in the present.

From her is a reflection of images: a girl standing in a deep-cut valley that tastes of ash. Around her, the Tezmi'a pastures are flooded, weakening the husbandry, starting a famine. And finally, a dead milk-brother's corpse carried away.

Was this not the outcome for my maternal tribe? Acting as scapegoats? My chin dips low as I watch Cemil speak casually about inflicting these conditions upon the Camel Road for the sake of Sajamistan. He must see something in my expression for his words hitch slightly. A cold awareness floods through me. Is this what is required for victory? Then war is not guided by the fingers of morality and war is not concerned with justice, it's cupped by the hands of greed. War only ends for the dead, and the ones who lose will always be accused of opposing peace.

'– this defeats any potential for a two-front war in Azadniabad's favour,' he says. 'As their peripheral tribes grapple with the obstructed pass – which will destroy irrigation systems and cause famine – this increases strife between their warlords, a benefit for us when they swing between loyalties. Just as what happened in Azadniabad, the infighting between warlords that led to the Zahrs' downfall.'

A begrudging part of me is awed that he would erode an entire region, especially when it includes north-east Sajamistan. In grand strategy, one seeks to preserve the possibility of coalitions, since allies increase one's relative power over other adversaries. Cemil is using scorched-clay tactics to block a mobile force. In long strategy, the tactic is deemed high risk for high reward, because altering the mountain pass will cause problems: damaged caravans for buffer tribes, rising warlords, disrupted trade flows for the enemy.

I mull this over, as Dil-e-Jannah presents her answer about a mincing strategy. I think back to my tribe. Why have the Black Mountains mattered in the Camel Road?

Finally, I address the scholar. 'I would have their supplies burned just to pester them.'

Cemil rubs the back of his neck. 'This is not the time for black humour.'

'In fact, I would allow the enemy to pass the mountains.' The adjudicating scholar has been deceptive; she offered the map to distract us with insignificant skirmishes, diverting us from the objective of the larger war.

'You are mad,' Cemil accuses.

'As mad as you,' I return. 'Grand strategy always runs counter to pure strategy. In this case, you forget the Black Mountains around Arsduq are the least favoured transit between the empires. Multiple buffers exist. I've seen them, even young.' I pause because my throat pinches, and I fear they will somehow hear the wound in my words.

'Nomadic tribes with shifting loyalties live between the borderlands, and control lucrative trade flows; they raid across the borders, salivating for whoever promises them greater coin. For this reason, in the Black Mountains, hordes of clans swear neutrality in any empire's affairs, letting armies pass through. But the neutrality only holds until a raid is committed against their clans.'

'So what would you do instead?' Dil-e-Jannah puts in.

'We should have tribes in our slice of the Camel Road – raiding tribes, excellent scapegoats – cross through the pass, ambushing and raiding the Black Mountain clans, breaking their alliances. In exchange, Sajamistan would give them control of the trade pass. The archers and horsemen, in retreat, would set fire to Azadniabad's camp. The Black Mountains clans would then raid, breaking neutrality.

'Sajamistan benefits in two ways. First, Azadniabad wouldn't be able to cross the pass. The Black Mountain clans would never ally with Azadniabad because they live to pillage Arsduq territory in raids – so unless Azadniabad wishes to compromise their alliance with Arsduq prefecture and its governess, no alliance with the Black Mountains will happen. Second, the pass becomes a war ground, and unlike Cemil's, my tactic does not destroy the valley, disrupting all caravan routes for the buffer tribes. No matter the outcome of the battle, a scorched valley leads to peripheral raids, dangerous for an empire bent on centralisation.'

'Even if what you claim is true, how would Sajamistan manage to thwart their army?' Dil-e-Jannah leans in.

'Azadniabad could never cross the Black Mountains without encountering the clans. If they do, Sajamistan clamps the enemy inside the pass. It's only in cramped terrain where numbers become a disadvantage, because troops are unable to facilitate wide manoeuvres. Trapped, Azadniabad's one escape route is to retreat to the west. And the Black Mountain tribes are in a natural position – an ideal screen – to stall Azadniabad as we converge the bulk of our forces from the south to intercept a potential invasion in the north-west through Yalon province. By then, we have the numbers to force any clans' surrender too.'

'You are a fool.' Cemil finally speaks, brushing aside the parchment. 'My tactics are the principle of calculated dispersion. By dividing, then inducing the enemy to disperse their forces through the landslide, you are in an ideal position to follow with a swift re-concentration of your own forces.'

'No,' I refute. 'You re-concentrate your allies to divert the opponent against a new enemy. It's isolation stratagems, *fool*. Eskander exploited neutral clans in the past, plundering them for resources, too, before pitting them against each other. Why should we not do the same?'

I cross my arms. Despite setting a dangerous precedent for this particular war, the hope is to destroy any neutrality in the first place, because why do principles matter when you have everything to lose? In war, the cornered enemies are the most dangerous, and for that, any gamble becomes practical.

Cemil's tone remains steady but something dark burns in his gaze. 'In your stratagem, you risk a new player. An ally who will readily turn against you.'

'War is a numbers game. No clan in the Black Mountains would risk turning against Azadniabad and Sajamistan simultaneously; it would be suicide. Scapegoat the garrison tribes.' I smile bitterly as I think of my uma's tribe. 'Then all of the frontier regions will be forced to pick a side, and from there, we levy trade to coerce alliances. This is an invasion; we must make our numbers equal to them, or larger. This is how you win a war, not a battle.'

Cemil's eyes narrow and I keep a neutral expression despite my doubts.

Scholar Hawja studies us. 'Brutal, decisive actions are required in reducing the scope of war, instead of indirect actions that increase the likelihood of drawn-out conflict.' She singles me out with a scowl. 'The long-term implication of your answer means those tribes will detest us, resist, even. That only protracts the war. A good general opts for swift, bold decisions but negotiates peace at a moment's notice. For that, Cemil wins the strategy examination.'

The courtyard fills again, surging with bureaucrats and soldiers. I remain seated. My fingers carefully crease my parchments to calm the simmer in my blood, but it tears beneath my nails.

'Usur-Khan,' greets Scholar Mufasa. 'I enjoyed the defeat despite your potential. You remind me of a former pupil.'

'I do?' And from a traitorous part of me, perhaps I have earned a semblance of his respect.

He continues. 'A leader must possess two qualities: a general's knowledge and their wisdom — for a leader requires objective information, but only wins the war with wisdom. You may have failed today, but wisdom is the far greater prize.'

I open my mouth but he is not finished, his eyes glaring. 'For many commanders, their victories bloat their heads, cost them empires. Because common sense is like air – the higher you climb, the thinner it becomes. Today, I heard your answers. You have talent, but like those commanders, you possess weaknesses: hunger, greed, *rage*. And I fear nothing will temper these faults. Even today's results. That is why you lost.'

'Will anything I do show you otherwise?' My words burn hotly.

'Have you not learned?' He turns his back on me. 'In Za'skar, there is no such thing as second chances.'

His warning is all but neglected when my thoughts boil over. I cannot help it. Anger billows, a nasty thing.

'Do you see?' No-Name hums from behind the rahle before she wraps her pale hands over my shoulder, tucking her face into my neck. 'They are brutal. With this loss, you cannot rely on anyone but me.'

I watch on as praising soldiers flock to Cemil; many scholars bow to him. Captain Fayez claps him on the shoulder with a sneer thrown my way.

At last, Cemil steps to me in acknowledgement. The anger I saw in him earlier has vanished.

'I was not sure who would win.' His words are dulled, instead of having their usual sharp edge. 'Perhaps next lunar year—'

I bristle. 'Pity is worse. You speak to me with kindness because you were drafted for the Marka, and now you have won this. When given what you desire, you compliment.'

I push away from the desk but his hand snakes out, before pausing above my arm. He does not dare touch me.

He gestures to my gold-threading: marks of circular cranes, then the shape of an ark between golden inverted whorls, a motif of the Tezmi'a Mountains. His voice drops. 'You spoke today as if you knew my stratagem well.'

'I don't.'

'Yabghu told me you hail from the steppes of Tezmi'a,' he presses.

'I see. You ask our overseer about me?'

He coughs. 'No.'

I glance at his arms, blue-threading obscuring the gold. I study the motifs of Sajamistan – three-headed ravens, seventy-seven bonds in swirling lines and even a three-tiered ziggurat.

The words leave my mouth before I stop my curiosity. 'And where is your tribe in the Camel Road?'

His expression darkens. 'We were not nomads. My people settled long ago in Khor's township.'

He abandons me in the centre of the courtyard, crossing toward Captain Fayez, who takes him to a group of senior officers. I go still at seeing who is amongst them.

The Sepāhbad. He'd observed the Wadiq tests? My brows furrow further when a scholar leads a gathering of pazktab students eagerly toward him. I lean forward and watch the Sepāhbad speak to Arezu. What could he have to do with her?

I turn away. After stuffing my parchments into my satchel, a shadow falls across me and I look up.

'Usur-Khan,' his voice greets me.

My fingers tremble in anger, and it takes everything to keep my tone flat. 'My Sepāhbad.' I muster a palm up to my chin.

His hazel eyes study me, a courtly raven perched, as ever, on his shoulder. A tight silence ensconces us. As he glances at the space between us, the bonds carved into my soul thrum like that of horsehair strings on a fretted lute. I frown, wondering what he perceives — that I am the same girl who knelt in the frost at his mercy, or now a soldier who is subsisting against all odds in his violent army?

His next words take me aback. 'You still have it.' He nods at the khanjar strapped around my upper arm. The very blade he accorded me.

Keep my blade as a reminder. If your oath is broken, your last duty ends with this blade and your blood running through your fingertips.

'Of course. It was my oath.'

His mouth twists wryly, a little bitter. *'Was.'* He steps past me. 'Indeed. You did well today, but a shame about the outcome.'

22

My pazktab students seek me out in the early dawn near the Great Library. Alone, I linger beneath a pair of wide gold gates obscured by the wings of parî guarding its entrance. It's silent, save for the occasional shriek of fiery huma birds curled upon the crumbling stone steps. The Sepāhbad's khanjar twists between my fingers as I stare at its naked marbled hilt. Last eve, Cemil earned another slash for winning the Wadiq tests; he is now Third-Slash.

'Master.' Arezu treads up the stairway reluctantly. 'I did not expect you to have the mind for passing the examinations. You were in third placing.'

'Third means nothing.'

Yahya pulls at my waist cord. 'Victor to me,' he says.

'I do not wish to be *your* victor. I wish to be *the* victor. And don't touch me.' I stand with a frown, dusting off my trousers. 'All the more reason to train in this last week, for we have a Marka tournament to ruin.'

During the predawn before trifecta training, to the students' delight, I introduce martial stances to complement their Qabl meditations.

We begin with horse-stance, the mother of all stances and the foundation of martial arts. I demonstrate the basics before they practise it for hours alongside orbital training, the art of circling your limbs through different planes. For the true challenge, the next day, after rummaging through the vegetation, I produce four sticks.

The children stay silent as I attach the stiff branchlets to straighten their spines and balance their shoulders.

'Walk,' I order. To their pain but my pleasure, they hobble, the sticks creasing into the smalls of their backs.

'We look ridiculous,' Arezu says after several minutes.

'Become used to it, because the stick will be your new companion. Go now and fetch your rationed waterskins, teacups and incense sticks.'

They arrive back reluctantly with the requested items.

In the deeper horse-stance, they crouch painfully low with knees out, feet parallel and palms clasped in front of their chests. I tie the stick once more with flax rope.

'Master.' Sohrab shifts from toe to toe. 'We do not train like this in the pazktab.'

'Quiet,' I say after I double-knot it. 'That is the purpose of the stick. Your spine cannot collapse.'

It takes another moment to distribute their rationed water into twenty-four cups. One by one, I place bowls on their shoulders, upon their wobbling thighs and lastly, their parallel elbows. With my cold nūr, I light the longest incense stick on the wooden coaster, placing it on the ground.

'What is this?' Arezu whispers but panic edges into her question. The truth hits them at once and I grin. *They cannot move.*

'Training,' I reply. 'The rules are simple. I have lit an incense stick. You are to remain in horse-stance until the incense burns to ash. The branch attached to your spine will maintain your form. You will feel pain, embrace it. Your bones will crack, ignore them. If you disobey my instructions, naturally there is a cost. The cups containing your rationed water will topple from your limbs. The dirt will lap up the scarce moisture and there will be no way to earn it back, leaving you without rations. At each instance that a cup falls, I will refill it with more of your water. Now pray to the Divine for a miracle.'

'You tricked us!' Arezu accuses me, but from the force of speaking, her arms jitter and the teacup upon her left elbow crashes to the ground.

'Enough mewling,' I intone. 'One cup of water is gone. I would save my energy.'

'This is impossible!' Yasaman joins her.

'An Eajīz's power can only grow through pain. A linear relationship. In the pazktab, the scholars read beloved martial tales, warriors accomplishing impossible feats at high adrenaline but desperate moments. Saving your water serves as an incentive.'

'But the incense will take an hour to finish! This is not—'

'Just?' I offer Sohrab, stripping my voice of any emotion. 'Where is the morality in this army? If you wish to be a Za'skar warrior, it demands a high cost.'

The memory of the Sepāhbad flashes in my head, his quick-witted movements making me helpless; my captain, the stern scholars, their cruelty.

'I am giving you a taste of what the future holds. I am preparing you for the vices of Za'skar City.'

For the next hour, No-Name and I observe the students maintaining horse-stance. I chew on neem and clove-scented root to do away with my boredom. At the half-hour mark, the children's cries rebound through the clearing in an uncomfortable din, Yahya's the loudest.

'Breathe in the direction the remembrance shapes your teeth and tongue,' I add unhelpfully.

Yahya pleads the loudest. 'Master!'

Shame braids through me but I fling it away. His posture drops like a sodden blanket and his features pinch together, eyes rounding into a glassy sheen. Silent sobs wrench through him and my spine shudders as if they are carving through me too. For a wavering moment, No-Name reaches out to the pained child but at a second blink, she's vanished.

I blame that sound for my foot moving forward on pure instinct, stopping only at the last moment. The teacup rolls off Yahya's right shoulder. I let it fall.

'I am to teach my students, not rock you in my arms like a wailing babe.'

Only Arezu does not complain. She merely blinks open an eye. 'You do not care.'

'Not at all, no.'

More teacups topple, but I muster past the students' whines until the hour flounders by and the incense is reduced to a blackened stub.

'Good work.' I untie the staffs. Immediately, the students curl up, groaning and rolling in the tall grass. It's eerily silent. Clouds have crept in, brushing the tail of the rising sun. All four passed the exercise with at least one bowl of water intact.

I crawl into a copse of citrus trees, where I hid my supply of water. To the group's surprise, in exchange for succeeding in my test, I portion my rations to recuperate their losses.

'What would happen if we failed?' Sohrab asks between gulps.

Arezu meets my eyes. I don't answer. Instead, I order, 'Tomorrow, you do it again.'

After three days of repeating horse-stance, the students graduate to affinity summoning. I've not the time to wait for children to learn slowly. Instead, I need a squadron to squeeze its merit's worth. And as young things, I discover their motivation.

Sohrab carries a jostling bundle of nuts and fruits. My eyes drop to slits. 'What is that?'

'Food swiped from the kitchens for… Yahya… and me.'

'I see,' I say, snatching it before he can blink. I shell a pistachio and toss the green nugget into my mouth. 'Are you upset? Would you like to spar with me?'

Sohrab shifts his feet at the unlikely outcome. 'No,' he croaks.

'Then begin stance training.'

Sohrab stretches into a high mountain-stance. A half-hearted effort. Unimpressed, I scoop up pebbles and whip them at his limbs.

'Ow!'

'Your stance is so weak, pebbles are unbalancing you. Pathetic.'

'I'm hungry!'

'Your stance should be sturdy enough to withstand seventy times your body weight. Success equates to food.'

Arezu is the sharpest in her stances, Yasaman is the fastest, and Sohrab is efficient in his kicks.

'Better to be a master at one technique than mediocre in all.' I have Sohrab focus on one kick, repeating it over and over again against the trees.

After the completion of different breath cycles, I toss figs and skinned almonds into their mouths. If they are on the cusp of quitting, I dangle a fig close to their lips before snatching it away. Soon, I force them to meditate with the water bowls while perched atop tree branches.

'Master, I want to spar,' Sohrab protests.

'Sure, imprudent boy.' I pass his bowl of water to him before pointing up. 'I will hear no complaints.'

'I read about this in a martial tale,' Yasaman says.

I glance at her in amusement. 'You like many martial tales.'

'And folktellers,' she answers and I pale. 'One day, I will be a scribe for Za'skar, under the Sepāhbad.'

My amusement disappears.

'The Sepāhbad,' Sohrab laughs. 'You would have to be the best of the scholars.'

'Fools, we need to survive first. If we fall, we could die,' Arezu points out too sensibly.

'And?' I raise a brow.

Arezu smirks. 'Her kind is cruel to children.'

'Was this not what you wished, Arezu? To stance train upon the highest tree? You fall, you break your bones. How pitiful. Now begin.'

Arezu spits her date pit into the sand. Then, obediently, they climb up, except Yahya.

'Why are you still down here?' I ask.

He holds out his short arms. I sigh and grab him, hoisting him on to my back before climbing up the tree.

Perched upon trees, we meditate through dawn. At times, they scratch or pick their noses, and I swat them. Below us, No-Name crouches in the dirt; today, the shape she takes on is akin to my uma. Her long hair curls down to her velvet waist-sash, wrapped around a pale qaftan. She does not acknowledge me as she yanks out thin weeds.

Later, we practise summoning. Through her Plague affinity, Yasaman can summon a swarm of the cursed creatures from the scriptures: locusts, scorpions, white beetles, fire ants and rattlesnakes that invaded sinning tribes in the past.

Slowly, Sohrab, with his Clay affinity, is able to manipulate ores from the ground. But there are limitations in his Heavenly Contract; he cannot yet extract large metals from it. He requires a pocket of metal on him to work with. Even with this, he cannot expand it greater than the size of his own body.

When Arezu demonstrates her affinity of Brother-Nature with the virtue of temperance, she manipulates plants and three black dahlias, bending their spindly stems.

At an attempt to produce more flora, her concentration breaks. 'I told you, my affinity is useless compared to the others.'

I shake my head. 'Every affinity of the Heavenly Birds holds importance.' I rub the dahlia between my fingers.

'That is easy to say when you have nūr.'

Behind us, No-Name continues to yank at weeds. At seeing this, a sudden memory from my girlhood bleeds through my thoughts: Uma bent over the royal gardens in Azadniabad, trimming weeds and flora with the monks.

I blink hard. 'The best power is subtle. Flowers grow beyond anyone's estimation. Think of the Great Flood, the raven, the crane. In Azadniabad, we believe Brother-Nature's wrath is immense. I've seen it.'

'Flowers are not made for battle.'

'Great warriors have died by mere flora. How did Eskander the conqueror die?'

'He was poisoned…'

'By a blue-dotted dahlia from the Unseen world. A jinn-poison.'

Her eyes redden. 'Well, I cannot control the Unseen. It's enough for me to train in iron-bone.'

'Well, flowers can be poisonous.' I incline my head and my lips curve up bitterly. 'If it's poison we must study, I can help you with that.'

She begins pacing in circles around the glass fountains, the francolins inside slanting to follow her movements. 'Fine. But I only know the flowers I tended back home.'

A curiosity piques my interest and I remember what she told me. 'You are from Khor?'

Arezu glances away. 'Yes.' Like Cemil.

Khor is an established trading node in the central Camel Road, south of the Tezmi'a pass. I turn away Arezu's word, not wishing to know more. She is nothing but sand flying on the breeze, pricking skin but easily dismissed.

'So this is where you disappear to before the fast?' Yabghu's voice cuts through the air, as he crests over the hill.

'O-overseer,' I stammer.

'What is this, rukh?' he snaps. 'I've caught you again with pazktab children.'

Arezu's gaze swings between us. 'We are her students.'

'What she means is, these students are targets at the pazktab school. They have no clanhouse nor patron to protect them. So I thought to teach them… as a good deed,' I hastily explain.

Yabghu's eyes twitch. 'In our months of training, not once have you expressed piety. Pray that I never see you again with them.'

Something strange happens. Arezu throws herself at Yabghu's feet with flushed cheeks.

'Please!' she cries out. 'By the Divine, she teaches us. Do not doubt her good deeds!' Yabghu tries to leap back but Arezu clings to his leathery clogs. 'She is our only hope to withstand the pazktab schools!'

Yabghu grits his teeth as Arezu's tears wet his pale trousers. 'Enough, child,' he relents. 'I believe you. Perhaps my rukh can be well intentioned.'

I struggle to maintain a neutral expression as I help Arezu up, bending to her ears and breathing, 'Thank you.'

'Master, do not expect me to do that again,' she only whispers back.

An idea strikes me. I brush Yabghu's sleeve. 'Overseer, perhaps you can help me train them for the hour?'

His eyes drop to my hand on his arm. 'By the Heavens, I will not—'

Arezu's eyes dampen again, and he falters. 'Only this once.'

After I convince Yabghu to guide the students through the First-Stratum of summoning, other pazktab students begin to take notice of our morning work. By midday, fifteen pazktab students have joined us.

My recruiting is not finished. After trifecta class on the monastery's terrace, I intercept Katayoun. I tell her about my intention to enter the Marka.

'You have fallen under the same mad spell of ambition as Cemil.' She does not sneer nor raise her voice, as if that too is an effort that she does not intend on wasting.

'Ambition is not a sin,' I retort back. 'In my first month as an initiate, I watched you. You completed the monks' tasks well, but never more than what they asked of us. You are unremarkable. Everything about you is economical.' Evidently so – she hardly blinks; she cannot muster the energy of being offended. 'I need you in my Marka. I cannot compete with only children.'

'Drafting me is as terrible as having a squadron of children,' she says before continuing down the stairs.

'My stipend,' I say to her back.

Katayoun stills.

'If you join my squadron, for the rest of the year, half of my earnings go to you.'

She leans against the bronze balustrades of the stairway, considering. 'If I join you, it's inviting the hatred of our masters and Captain Fayez. I am the way I am, to survive. When you were recruited into our trifecta, you replaced a rukh who died. I do not share her death wish.'

'If we perform horridly—'

'You will,' she reminds me.

'– you remain comfortable at Zero-Slash. If we do well, you become First-Slash. You lose nothing, while gaining my stipend.'

Katayoun marches back up the stairs. 'I am only one person.'

'Of course.' I lean in and place several ingots in her palm. 'You will get more if you convince another low-rank to join.'

'Cemil will murder us.'

'My stipend,' I repeat, curling her fingers around the copper.

As nimble as a fox, she pockets it. 'There are only two fools who trust me. Sharra and Aina.'

'That's good enough.' I hide my triumph.

During mealtimes, my students continued to report information gathered from the other captains' Marka squadrons while they served food. From this, with Katayoun, I begin contriving my plan.

The next day, I announce the last piece needed to complete our entry:

'I went to the Za'skar bureau of duels to register our squadron. Your task is to convince the other thirteen pazktab students to join us, making us over twenty, the minimum number required to compete.'

Yasaman raises her hand. 'It will not be not easy, master.'

'They are young. Promise gold and glory.'

'You expect *untrained* students to battle in the Marka?' Arezu arches a brow.

'I expect them to distract. We are following Eskander's strategies, outmatched in power but unmatched in speed and diversion. No one will have predicted it.'

Arezu smirks. 'Even if we convince them, they do not trust you as an Azadnian.'

That is a good point. 'I will make them trust me,' I insist.

'But you rarely speak kindly,' Sohrab remarks and my mouth gapes open.

'You are inept at social interactions,' Arezu adds.

'Master holds me,' Yahya protests and I feel a little reassured.

'In truth, you are terrible at making friends. You berated and beat Arezu when she thieved from me,' Sohrab dares to say.

'Because she *hurt* you.'

'Which proves my argument; then, you tried to teach her how to steal from me better.'

'Okay, enough.' I pretend to straighten my tunic. 'May the Divine reward your honesty, you pigs.'

'You prove our point again. To draft pazktab students, you must charm them.'

'Charm?' I recoil.

'Yes, charm.' Arezu sidles up to me. 'With pretty words and your pretty looks. Make them believe you are their next Eskander. Pazktab students are suck-ups to the older soldiers.'

And because I cannot argue with sound logic, a better plan strikes me.

'You are bribing them?' Arezu screeches the next morning, pointing to the hastily gathered thirteen pazktab children. They line up across the fountain gardens.

Yahya, who insisted on being held, laughs at her and I switch his weight to my other arm.

'Katayoun inspired this idea. I tried to speak of glory but found it hard to convince children who cannot wipe their own asses properly. Why persuade them on the merits of bravery when we are all cheap and swayed by primal greed? You claimed I should be Eskander – he would approve,' I explain.

I jangle my satchel, containing my year's saved stipend. 'One copper ingot for each child, a low bargain. It hardly matters to me.' I shrug. In actuality, it does. Due to my Azadnian descent, I receive little benefits from enlisting in Za'skar except for this measly stipend. The senior officials have frozen land benefits from the royal court. This reduced me to borrowing a healthy weight of ingots from Yabghu – whose stipend as an overseer is much grander than my own. I claimed that I wished to buy more prayer garb and I would pay off the debt soon – which I have no intention of doing.

'Which of you would like an ingot?' I ask the awaiting students, whose mouths part like gaping fish.

'They are young,' Arezu argues.

'Greed does not discriminate. Besides, you are sixteen, now.' I place Yahya back down but he reaches for me again.

'You must stop this horrible habit. You mistake our relationship. I was compliant before but now, I will be firm. I cannot hold you, especially during a battle. It's disgusting.'

'Please,' Yahya insists.

'You pig, put your arms down.' I carefully step a hair-width of distance around him. 'Must I remind you all, we have a Marka to scheme for and enemies to destroy.' They are not listening.

The corner of Arezu's left eyelid twitches. 'When do I receive an ingot?'

'You are older and wiser. Tell me this.' I prod her chest. 'Do the scholars teach greed or have you learnt this on your own? Do you not heed the priests' sermons on Mondays?'

'I do.' A student named Firat perks up.

'– ten, eleven, twelve…' I raise the coppers.

'Wait,' Arezu says.

'… *thirteen*. Arezu, I train you without expecting payment,' I say. 'You get no ingot.'

23

On the morning of the Marka, angels gaze down from the Heavens at the white salt-blown desert, its clay cracked open to reveal hideous scars. The whole of Za'skar arises in a bustle for the ancient tournament, bureaucrats scramble into the gated city to place bets, wizened warriors wonder which soldiers would rise to take up their mantle next, and clanhouses scout promising Za'skar strategists to patronise in their armies.

As my squadron pads across the sand dunes, a shock spreads like wildfire through the ranks of the city. Soldiers halt in their trajectories, gazing at the bevy of pazktab students at my back.

'This is madness! A mockery of Za'skar customs!' Scholar Hawja squawks out as we trek along the paths of the Easkaria school. 'Summon the Sepāhbad at once!'

'He would never dare interfere in the customs of the Marka,' Scholar Mufasa says from an open balcony, staring down at us. 'Not when he led a Marka not much older than a pazktab student himself.'

Katayoun shifts beside me, ducking her head until her russet braid falls forward, bone-pendants clinking. 'I told you this *is* madness.'

'I bribed you,' I remind her.

'You didn't pay me to keep my mouth shut.' Her lips crack into a grin. The humour soothes the nerves fluttering in my chest.

From the bottom of the Easkaria, Squadron Three stands in formation around Captain Madj. At seeing us, the captain nods subtly in my direction.

'What was that?' Katayoun asks, bewildered.

'Captain Madj is Fayez's rival. A clever strategist sows discord in their opponents before the battle begins,' I tell her.

She glances at the pazktab students flanking us. 'Look at the discord of your flock first. One of them will wet themselves.'

'For spiritual calm, I ordered them to perform ablution in the way of Adam, and to slather incense and black seed oil over their limbs,' I explain.

She grips the layers of leather gird around her hips. 'You must do more. You must speak to them.'

'I explained the stratagems—'

'No. You must inspire their loyalty.'

'You speak as if you care,' I say curiously.

'I have my own earnings on the line.' She speaks in a low tone. 'And I am thinking of Yabghu. He always gives a talking-to, until my ears bleed. But he does not quit, even when I quit him. Embody our overseer.' She looks away with blushing cheeks.

I dwell on her words as we arrive at the Marka battlefield, where desert creatures crawl across the six territories that are cleaved onto a separate plane within the salt desert, between the immaterial and material world. Katayoun explained that the parî blow a psychospiritual Veil upon the Marka. In its dimension, the sun beams hotter and the air becomes vibrant, sizzling with otherworldly energy. Cypress and vegetation dot the pale terrain in a green shock of flora along thin gurgling streams.

The seventeen pazktab soldiers align in three uneven rows in Territory Six, adorned in the martial tradition of white and red wolfish raven masks. In the nick of time, Aina and Sharra sprint toward us and I sigh in relief.

'Go on.' Katayoun nudges me.

I take a deep breath. 'Warriors,' I face them, 'we are the smallest squadron in a battle to capture enemy banners. The squadron to capture a majority of *four* banners is the victor. The challenge is the trade-off between stealing another squadron's banner or protecting our own. There are six squadrons. Enemy squadrons, when they discover our presence, will target us to get an easy banner. Only abide by the strategy we discussed: do not engage directly.'

'Like pesky rodents,' Arezu speaks out.

I shrug. 'Rodents are thieves. They play dirty, never fair. But they survive.'

Firat, the same age as Arezu, shifts uneasily. He is short, hardly a quantifiable person, merely a bundle of thick skin and bones. 'I cannot do this,' he says doubtfully.

'Well, I already paid you,' I repeat.

Katayoun tugs at my waist cord, leaning forward. 'I told you to inspire them,' she hisses.

'I am.'

'He might piss himself,' Sohrab mocks the student.

'I will,' Firat admits. I decide I do not like him.

According to Katayoun, I suppose I am to speak comforting words. Shall I compliment him? Or coddle him? Disgust surges through me. I am not Yabghu.

'That could be a problem,' I admit. 'But your pathetic weakness can have worth. Hold it in until the enemy is in range, then piss on them.'

'I will be scrub to the enemies,' he gasps. I search myself for sympathy, even a smidgen, but discover none. For months, my training has amounted to this: my only chance to climb up the army's ranks.

Across the blue salt desert, squadrons scurry to their respective territories, but incredulous eyes find us: Overseer Negar with Yabghu and Captain Fayez, Captain Osman of Squadron Four. It's not until all of Squadron One spots us that the daunting task of the Marka needles me painfully. It's obvious: our chances of success are as thin as a horsehair.

Yabghu jogs over, ripping off his martial mask. For the first time, I glimpse his true anger. 'You were training these students beneath my nose for *this?*'

'I vowed to participate in the Marka.'

'Listen to yourself. You are picking a battle with high-ranks with the scraps of *the pazktab?*'

'These are the finest warriors the pazktab has to offer.'

'Finest warriors?' Yabghu seethes, moving around me. 'At least I should reason with these children. Why would you agree to her mad idea?'

'She paid them,' Sohrab offers.

Yabghu's neck strains against his collar, veins stark against his brown neck. '*This* is why you borrowed from my stipend? I am not a patron to fund your madness!'

My heart hammers. 'I-I will pay that back.'

'Khamilla,' he nearly growls, and I step back. He has never broken formality like this. 'We both know you won't. Besides, do you understand what this will do, my own trifecta defying me in such a mortifying manner?' He turns on Katayoun, his glare lashing her until she flinches. '*And you.* The girl who could not even pass the Easkaria suddenly finds herself in a Marka?' He prods her forehead. 'Has the Azadnian spun black magick on you?'

'Enough.' I yank Katayoun behind me, shielding her from his glare. 'Today, there are no trifectas. Only the order of a squadron. You will not speak to my underling like so.'

With a curse, he backs away, but my heart twists in something close to remorse. No matter what I think of Sajamistan, my overseer has always been a kind, forthcoming teacher. The only kindness afforded in this city.

As I turn my back, a hand wrenches me forward.

It is not Yabghu's fingers gripping my tunic. Cemil's thunderous gaze pins me in place. 'Khamilla,' he hisses.

'Peace unto you, Fayez's dog,' I greet him.

He tightens his fingers and I cough from the fabric creasing around my neck. 'Are you one for insults before a battle?'

'Not an insult when I only speak to what I perceive before me.'

'Ah, so polite,' he grins sharply. He studies the trembling children and laughs. 'I told you allies are good, but this is hardly what I meant.'

'And?'

'*And?* You have not an ounce of dignity nor honour: you are unfit to be a Za'skar warrior. You've children waddling after you like roosters at an uma's back.'

That snaps me. I grip his chin and lean close, until he is forced to acknowledge the long-dormant rage simmering in my gaze. 'If they are roosters,' I whisper fiercely to him, 'they are *my* roosters. And only I am allowed to insult them, not you.' I press my palm to his chest until he steps back.

'If you thought he despised you when he ordered you to crawl, then you will face his true hate now. He will murder you.'

'I assume that includes you? You love when I crawl.'

'No mercy,' Cemil promises, before reproaching Katayoun. 'And how much did she bribe you?'

'Glad you can see through Khamilla's methods so clearly.' Katayoun's smile is as sharp as his.

'More like you're so transparent,' he tuts at her. 'Fools, my comrades.' He spits at our sandals and goes to rejoin his squadron.

'I have had worse,' I call out to his receding back. 'You can piss on us.'

'No thank you. At least I preserve my honour. We are still a trifecta,' he replies without turning back.

'Ass,' Katayoun mutters. 'This is why I prefer Aizere. She is angry but not a fool like the both of you.'

'You are here,' I remind her.

'I guess I am a fool too.'

'Did he mean that?' Yasaman cries from behind me. 'They will murder us?'

'It's intimidation. Standard in any battle,' I attempt to comfort her. *But it's working.*

The group of students cling together, eyes wet, uniforms hanging loosely over thin frames. Perhaps I am in over my head, a mad girl indeed. But what choice did this Hells leave me? To scrape at my superior's feet? To wait years and never climb one rank?

Arezu steps across the flanks of young warriors. '*I warned you.* Her own captain stomped on her in the bazaar. He made her kiss his feet.'

I pause. The rumours have reached even the pazktab schools.

'Imagine what he will do to us. I've seen battles before,' Arezu continues, blank-faced.

'What will he do?' Firat asks.

'In a raid, I saw enemies take a babe as small as Yahya, all jiggly with rolls. And they stretched him apart until he burst. Children are the easiest prey.'

I hurry forward. 'Arezu.' I take her by the arm. 'You are scaring them.'

I begin to drag her to the side as she struggles in my grip. 'I am only preparing them.'

She is one of the oldest amongst them but, I'd forgotten, still a child. And though I do not understand children – hardly recall being one myself – I understand this, the need to speak your fear out of existence, pretending it does not matter. To share the burden of those scars. I know how to deal with the beginnings of a monster.

'I see why you warn them,' I reassure her.

Her fingers tuck into the necklace of bones around her throat, but I catch the tremors. 'I have seen battles before; I have seen good warriors die. And we are not even good.'

'The Marka does not allow for murder.'

She rolls her eyes. 'I mean wounds! Those other warriors hate us. Their violence will prove it.'

Before I can think further, my fingers slip out the melted Zahr khanjar, flipping the handle to show Arezu. 'See this? My dada gifted me this blade after I passed a test.' A part of me despairs in mentioning him, sharing such a private memory, but she is staring at me so intently, I swallow the cowardice. 'Before he'd gifted it, I'd failed many tests. I choked. The blade felt unworthy.'

'You failed?'

'Between us… many times. But that is our secret. Every warrior has a weakness that manifests in our lowest moments. But the true test is if it manifests in your battles. For me, my weakness is memories. At times, I stop thinking. I am caught in the past. For you, your fear from what you've seen in your childhood will burden you.'

She frowns but does not dispute it. 'Then I am weak.'

I shake my head. 'Weak? No, Arezu. This anger you carry, it's a strength. It's why I sought you for this squadron. While you are here pretending not to be miserable, I understand. I understand why you trained in solitude before you allowed me to be your master.'

Her green eyes flit up, wary. Curiosity stretches between us, the sparks of friction snuffing for once.

'You desire power. You crave the rush like me, and you are angry. I do not know why, and in truth, I do not care.' I hope Arezu cannot hear my own fleeting resolve. These are the words my father would tell me, a conviction for me to cling to. 'You may only master your power if your conviction bears the weight of its burden. So, tell me, the moment you improved your affinity, was it not the best feeling? The thrill of knowing no one could hurt you, no one could stop you just for a moment?'

Her lips twitch, as she regains her bearings. 'It felt good.'

'Remember it.' I gesture at her hand. 'You have your strength.' I lift my blade. 'And I have mine, always,' I promise.

I return to my squadron. If only these students were not wallowing in their own hysteria. But they would not have survived for so long in

Za'skar if they had not faced terrors inside the city's gates. I need only to remind them of this.

'Squadron Six,' I bark, dragging Yahya alongside me. 'Lines.'

The seventeen students stand in stern order, with Katayoun at my side, Aina and Sharra behind us.

'Our opponents laugh because they smell our terror,' I begin. 'But they are ignorant of one fact: that you have faced greater enemies. If you can accomplish the pain of stance training, if you can handle *me*, or the abuses of ruthless pazktab masters, nothing is worse. Today you are warriors.' My tongue burns from the magnitude of the lie while Katayoun fights to keep a neutral expression. The students straighten. 'Answer your captain: how will you fight during an enemy's ambush?'

'Stab the khanjar in the enemy's toes,' the young squadron shouts in unison.

'How deep?'

'You bury the blade to the hilt to pin them,' they drone louder.

'Excellent,' I murmur. 'At the parî's signal, the Marka begins. Focus on your tasks.'

I do not know my soldiers well, but I try for an encouraging look. From the horror in their gazes, my attempt is more awkward than comforting.

A sudden light illuminates the desert planes before a great parî soars above the salt flats. It's the Keeper of the Great Library.

He lifts a clawed hand, huffs of silver power rippling into a Veil. My ears pop and my mouth dries. Through the murky haze of the Veil, I can make out the shadowed forms of thousands of soldiers, scholars, officers and bureaucrats observing from atop the mountainous cliffs enclosing the desert. The back of my neck crawls. I trained for this my entire life: to defeat opponents who outmatch me, for is that not Azadniabad under Sajamistan? If I fail this, I do not deserve to be martial-vizier of my clan.

The Keeper bows his head. 'May the pain of this battle bestow upon you the bond of the Heavens. Begin!'

We sprint in different directions, each Zero-Slash leading a division of the pazktab students. Yasaman and Yahya flank me on the left of the saline oases. At the first tree, I snag a branch from the ground. We fasten the stick at the centre of our territory, supported by a boulder.

The banner of our territory is a calf-skin flag located along ridges of red and white sediment.

After grabbing the real banner, we circle to the south, dirt kicking up in a whirlwind at our feet.

'Breathe to ground your Heavenly bonds into the incense,' I encourage Yasaman, as all three of us crouch behind a cluster of cypress trees.

Sweat trickles down her temple. 'I think I did it.'

Ahead of us, Squadrons Two and Four, led by Aygul and Osman, charge into our open territory, only to come face to face with each other. The battle is quick, decisive, as I predicted.

Squadron Two engages in a clear, bow-shaped line, dividing their numbers into two flanks. The flexibility of the formation is like that of a pulled bow. The captain orders her soldiers right, deceiving Squadron Four, whose captain assumes that they will be overwhelmed on that flank. But Squadron Two counterstrikes the left-hand position. Squadron Four sacrifices the entire left flank when Osman tries a full-weighted frontal charge despite the gaps in his wings.

In short time, Squadron Four is forced into a concession. The parî flash into the arena, carrying injured soldiers outside the Veil. With that, Aygul of Squadron Two emerges victorious.

I exhale in relief. 'Are the fire ants in position?'

'Yes,' Yasaman answers.

Fire ants commanded by her affinity crawl below the soldiers' feet. No one notices the cursed critters, let alone the infinitesimal shard of steel from a welded blade that each ant carries in its pinchers, courtesy of Sohrab's Clay affinity, which manipulates the alloy into sliver-sized amounts.

My wrist lifts; I inhale the dabbed scent of my attar. Through a flicker of my finger bonds, a thin string of nūr threads from my hand to a metal shard, flashing light. Soldiers in the vicinity will mistake it for mere sunlight.

Ten beats later, Sohrab, from the opposite end of the territory, enlarges the metal shards gripped by the ants into thin, sharp needles.

A cry sounds, but Squadron Two is too late. The metal skewers into their heels, up through their feet. All but twelve from Squadron Two howl from the grave injuries.

'Breathe and rest your bonds, subdue the Heavenly Energy. Then summon the third creature, the white beetles, to the stick in the centre of the territory, for the next stage.' I turn Yahya on my lap, so his face is positioned below mine. 'This will be difficult, but I trust you. You must go collect more bramble. After the Marka, I will use my stipend to buy you lamb-stuffed non.'

His forehead leans in. 'Yes, master.' Then he scurries into the cypress trees. Again, we wait. Captain Majd of Squadron Three darts into our clearing, her thirty soldiers capitalising on a situation ripe for victory. She pierces through the remaining forces of Squadron Two as I predicted. I had sent a missive that offered a low-stakes alliance, inviting her to invade our territory before Captain Fayez, in exchange for roving through any surviving squadron.

Captain Madj snatches Squadron Two's banner and spots our decoy flag, posting guards in front of it, assuming it's real. Squadron Four must have left their flag in their territory and split their forces to defend it.

Even from our positioning, Madj's voice carries a grin. 'Bait-and-trap tactics by an inexperienced squadron of children. What else should we expect? The Marka is a simulation of conquering, not defence.'

Not baits and traps. We're a moving barrage.

Stationary defenders committed to their territory are cattle to any roving troops who strike in quick successive blows. But my troops will cause trouble by nibbling stubbornly at the enemy – like ghûls gnawing on a corpse – before constantly retreating. We will not practise defence until the last possible moment.

Our current position offers us natural obstacles that we can use: while they are defending themselves from our bites, we are manipulating them into geographical traps. By forcing them to swallow our bait, we divide them and survive the course of the Marka.

The problem is that Captain Fayez has not yet arrived. I expected him to engage our territory straight away, eager to make fools of us, especially when he saw Madj was there.

'My gamble for Fayez failed,' I note. And when Madj realises she holds a decoy banner, our alliance will alter in his favour.

'Master, what should we do?' Yasaman asks, his tone uneven.

We manipulated the first squadrons to eliminate the others for us. Now I hope to manipulate a third team into stealing our fake banner. It's crafted from Yasaman's white-walking beetles, a species the Divine used to plague Stone City, a destroyed apostate civilisation. The wings of the beetles mimic any pale colour of their surroundings. Its success hinges on Yasaman's ability to command the beetles to take on the appearance of the banner while the real one is with me.

To conform to Marka rules, no territory banner is allowed to be covered, so our real one is tied to my back like a glaring signal against the vegetation. We have minutes until Madj realises her flag is a ruse and spots the real one.

'Follow me,' I order. My subordinates and I circle the oases toward Sohrab and Arezu, who wait near Territory Five. At the boundary of the plains, Arezu stoops below a date palm, splattered head to toe in sand.

'Was it done?' I ask her.

From her fretful look, anxiety squeezes my chest. Sohrab brushes stray dirt from her hair as she answers. 'Squadron Five's territory has the largest oases, so I summoned the poisonous cacti with my affinity until it caged their warriors. But Captain Fayez's squadron arrived and defeated their squadron. They are charging in a southward direction toward our territory. I was forced to abandon the other pazktab students…' Her voice trails off.

'What happened?' I demand.

'Look.' She points to the boulders. I climb up alongside her before pausing at what I see.

Below, three students who were tasked to hide beneath the cacti to snatch Squadron Five's flag are exposed. Overseer Negar and two warriors surround them, dumbfounded at the sight of children. One of them, Dil-e-Jannah, has a khanjar sticking out of her left foot, which almost makes me smile. But from her annoyed look, it might as well be a pinch than an injury. Overseer Negar sighs and gathers her hands; the ground below cleaves into a crater, plunging the pazktab students safely into it.

'Should we save them?'

'No,' I say, deciding after a moment, disappointed. 'They were scrub for the opponent anyway.'

The Marka has hardly begun, and I am down three precious bodies.

'Master, if Fayez has an idea of our plan, we have failed.' Arezu voices my exact doubts. 'If we could just engage Madj head-on, to take her out before Fayez arrives—'

'You are going about strategy all wrong. Nine out of ten times, frontal charge is contingent on numerical superiority. We are small,' I correct her. 'In a melee, we focus on mobility, to enforce our own natural positioning.'

'That does not sound like the purpose of the Marka,' she says reluctantly.

'It is only a game.' I return to where I left Yahya. Fayez must have a distinct idea of my strategy using Madj, or else he would not have targeted Squadron Five first. Had he predicted this? Perhaps he isn't underestimating me at all.

I shut my eyes. It is easier to envision the Marka as a saktab gameboard. My surroundings fade. I imagine six territories, placing us on the outskirts of the sixth. We are outnumbered two to one against the other squadrons. If Arezu controls the plants again, and can tighten a noose of poisonous flora, trapping Fayez's troops, it will be a bloodbath. Fayez's squadron will be driven against Madj's forces with my soldiers on the outskirts, exploiting their openings. A tactic modelled after a fish caught in a stone-weighted net.

From the barrier of cacti, we will cut off their communication lines; they will have no way to inform their other flanks.

After explaining the amended idea, Sohrab, serving as my messenger, darts to tell the students holding our position in the east, and to Katayoun with Yasaman, ordering them nearby in Territory Five with all of our flags, where no one would think to look for them, since Squadron Five is defeated already.

To Arezu, I say, 'Continue circling vegetation around the perimeter of our territory in dense rows but use a three-breath meditation technique, like what we did on the treetops, to maintain Heavenly Energy. Divide them.'

She nods, scurrying off to her position.

From my satchel, I apply three drops from the attar bottle the monks bestowed, one on my collarbone and two on each wrist. In seven breaths, my soul escapes the confines of the corporeal, travelling to the psycho-spiritual world. My bonds reach Heaven and I demand the firmament acknowledge my wish. A rush of power greets my soul, filling the seventy-seven bonds with the scent of the attar.

Not a moment too soon. Fayez's squadron emerges below in supple flanks, intercepting Madj in our territory. Each squadron possesses a flag at the centre of their formations. Before they converge, the ground, moistened by the oases, cracks as roots entangle the warriors' feet. I smile.

And then it breaks.

'Destroy all of this,' Fayez's voice thunders through the plains. 'I've had enough of these petty tricks. Expose their positioning.'

Negar lifts her right foot. I blink and the entire territory shudders. Clay arises in a wave of dirt, crushing Arezu's fragile plants, burying them beneath a smooth wall of pale, saline sediment, forcing me to scramble back. I pray my soldiers were not buried in the landslide.

'There she is.' Fayez turns, spotting me far in the distance on the rocky sediment, with no trees to obscure me. 'Humble your dog,' he roughly orders his lieutenant. I flinch as Yabghu breaks away from his flank. He clasps his palms and the air plunges into a scorching warmth. A Smokeless-Fire affinity, the same energy used before mankind's existence to create jinn.

His shoulders round back before a stifling heat wilts Arezu's flora.

It's clever. Captain Fayez prepared Yabghu as a direct rival against my defences; he predicted I'd use Arezu to fortify the perimeter.

'I am not finished,' I mutter before raising one finger, using the Second-Stratum of summoning, which condenses Heavenly Energy and combines multiple bonds. Nūr teases from my hands and feet, splitting into three dense ropes of cold cosmic light until it solidifies. It slithers down the blue slopes of the salt ridges.

As it reaches Yabghu, the nūr erupts, lighting the territory into a flash of white light, temporarily blinding him.

'Again,' I bark loudly at Arezu. She weaves her flora into four tall brackets. Before Yabghu could stop her, Madj's soldiers spill into the clearing, and I sigh with relief.

'Their sight!' I order loudly. Arezu's cacti whistles thorns into Fayez's isolated flanks.

'My eyes!'

With the soldiers blinded, pazktab children from the eastern flank choose to charge like proud cowards. They bellow toward the first square in the net formation. It contains seven soldiers against ten of mine, and in its centre, I spot the enemy squadron banner, guarded by two opponents.

I rush down the slope on to the battlefield, switching to First-Stratum summoning.

The fundamental key of the Marka is the rule of no deaths: a necessary provision that ensures any attacks by affinities must be conservative; it's less about a display of power and more a test of how one can control and wield it.

My foot sweeps low, impelling gales of sand into the eyes of Adam, the first warrior I spot.

A second one thrusts her khanjars out. Gulnaz. The sharp glints a promise of pain. I spin, heel kicking back, bonds blasting a shield of concentrated nūr.

Gulnaz throws up her arm from the light, but Za'skar martial artists can manoeuvre deftly even blinded. Arching back, her wrists twist, blades shooting forward so fast they almost cleave my stomach, like a butcher to a lamb. It must be an affinity, somehow manipulating the air currents around her.

I twist left, the blade nicking my ear. *Too close. If I could just—*

I stoop down, dodging another blade that would have slashed my neck. *She wants to inflict grave injury.* I leap, closing the distance between our attack zones, my fingers pinching the tip of her khanjar before it thrusts forward. Blood beads down my knuckles.

Her head reels back to slam against mine, but my right foot hooks around her ankle as I sidestep with the other, my arms driving through the momentum into third stance.

Our khanjars intercept. My blade twists up against her, whining from her weight. Teeth gritted, she presses harder into my side, the pressure building. I strain, heels sliding back against the dirt.

Our eyes meet briefly. Snarling, I abruptly leap back, following the air current, our locked stances suddenly off balance. Nūr ignites the tip of my khanjar before the blade rolls into my pinkie. I spin inwards, knifed palm slashing into her with a brutal spleen strike. Gulnaz's stance crumples.

Seizing the opening, her other comrade, Dara, dives into my path, but I am ready. Nūr shoots from my finger bonds into two spikes, lashing out like snakes at his ankles.

Dara's knees buckle but he only grins, mouth opening – *he uses his tongue bonds*, I realise. Above, the Veil ripples like a grey duvet and the sky crackles and booms. I've read about this affinity from the seventy-seven, a Heavenly Contract that asks the angels of the Divine to manipulate a storm flood on the Eajīz's behalf.

'No,' I cry. The hair stands erect on the back of my neck before purple light ignites the square plane.

I'm knocked off my feet. My body smacks against a cluster of cacti, puncturing my arms in a shocked sting. Warm blood dribbles down my sleeves.

Dread carves down my back as the next lightning bolt destroys nearby flora. The plants scatter, exposing my squadron's position to the other flanks. Cursing, I roll as Dara's khanjar punctures downwards.

My two shoulder bonds expand, dense nūr slithering toward Dara's back, then erupting before he can finish me. With a cry, more from surprise than pain, Dara stumbles forward, and I crawl, snatching the banner and retreating before he can lunge toward me.

Just then, three soldiers under Captain Madj enter the square plane, and I sprint away, spotting Sohrab on the opposite end, behind our last thin defences of cacti, clutching a bloodied arm against his chest, Yahya strapped to his back.

'We are going to die, master,' Sohrab moans when I reach them. 'Take him, I cannot hold him any longer, my arm is not working.'

'Retreat with the second banner,' I order after taking Yahya. 'Fayez and Madj are occupied in battling each other. For now, find Arezu—'

I cannot finish my thought because in the distance, I spot Arezu cornered on the salt crystals at the edge of the territory's cliffs, Cemil above her.

Sohrab notices, too, eyes widening.

'Retreat!' I shout, but my voice does not carry far enough. 'Do not engage—'

Arezu's head snaps to the side as Cemil shoves her. My heart stutters. Cursing, I thrust the flag into Sohrab's arms.

'Retreat!'

Arezu is fodder, all of these students are supposed fodder – the thought is like glass cracking beneath pressure. If Arezu is injured, any hope of winning the Marka is snuffed. *And Cemil* – my fingers dig into the meat of my palms – *I warned him not to insult my students.*

'Take Yahya,' I tell Sohrab, but he shakes his head and bolts away.

'Where are we going, master?' Yahya asks as I heave him up against my side.

'To save your foolish comrade. Hold on to my tunic and do not let go.'

'Cemil will kill us?' he asks with growing dread, a boy only now coming to realise his dangerous circumstances.

'Shut up,' I hiss. 'My students are not allowed to die.' Murder may be outlawed in the Marka, but anger has a way of yielding ever so gruesome accidents.

By the time I round on Cemil, his back to me on the craggy salt cliffs, he is gripping Arezu by the wrist. I have only seconds. Angling nūr through my left arm, I attempt a horizontal barrier.

'You are like a buzzard, Khamilla. I need only a worm as easy bait,' Cemil tuts before spinning, yanking Arezu forward with the force, his palms out. He disappears from my vision.

Yabghu told me he can only mark three targets at a time.

An arm wraps around my waist, the other twisting my right elbow to my lower back. I grit my teeth to fight a gasp as he pulls me flush to his chest.

'And I always have you marked,' Cemil hisses into my ear, his blade digging into my spine. Yahya babbles out a cry and Cemil stiffens against me, only now noticing the child on my left hip.

His hand loosens for a split moment. But the distraction is enough for my shoulder bonds to shoot a dart of nūr into his neck as I lunge to shield Arezu. I cannot wield my full nūr without injuring the students.

Cemil's hesitation at the sight of Yahya – whose watery eyes and quivering lips would make even a shai'tan reconsider working for the devil – is all I need. Cemil may be inclined to attack Arezu, a sixteen-year-old, but the true test lies in this: would he attack me as I hold a four-year-old?

I think not.

Cemil tugs roughly at his kerchief. 'This is unjust even by your low standards, Khamilla,' he says, seething. His fingers ready at his khanjar hilt but he does not instantly use his Messenger affinity.

My mind scrambles through the possibilities. *There must be a distance- and time-delay restriction between each use of Cemil's affinity, depending on what he transports through the Veil,* I note. *Transporting himself must be the highest threshold for his Heavenly bonds.*

'However, a Marka is a Marka. With a child on your arm, you make this too easy,' he says, stalling more.

I adjust Yahya and yank Arezu behind me until we are back to back. With my right hand, I flick my khanjar into a reverse grip and crouch into first stance. 'Fool, do not underestimate a woman with both a child at her hip and a blade in her hand,' I say before he darts forward. As a Third-Slash, he is the superior fighter, but I am no wheedling novice.

'Arezu,' I order under my breath just as she stamps her foot bonds. I spring leftward, using Yahya's added weight to rotate. Below us, the boulders splinter from a lumpy root of some entombed tree shoving through the salt rock.

Cemil rears back as the ledge shakes, but somehow, with pure strength, his knife muscles through the opposite momentum toward my ribs. My left knee juts up into a split kick, knocking away the khanjar, my heel slamming into the tender underpart of his jaw.

'You don't listen, you've just done it,' I spit as that same foot's bonds gush out nūr.

But he is faster, his Messenger affinity sucking the Heavenly light into a Veil. I do not wait to fight this battle. Arezu hops on my back and I dive sideways off the edge of the small cliff with my students clinging on to me.

I misjudge the force of the fall. We roll in a shower of loose sand. Our limbs jerk and tangle, raw dirt scraping our skin until white flakes crust like thin paper. My shoulder slams into the ground but I manage to absorb the impact to save them from injury. Just as I guessed, Cemil does not transport to me – there is a geographical restriction to his affinity.

Cemil curses from above and Yahya bursts into tears. I waste no time in sprinting to safety behind the layers of Arezu's cacti. Still, the foolish girl huffs as if I have done her a great offence.

'I didn't need you,' she says as I set her and Yahya down against the trees.

I grimace. 'You did and it was impudence to provoke a high-rank. I had to save your life.'

'But you said I'm good at anger and I should use it!'

Exhaustion and fury spear into my veins. 'Yes, but too much of anything will be your downfall. Use the anger productively!'

'No yelling,' Yahya says weakly.

'Squadrons are not democratic; they have a command structure, and soldiers are to follow it *obediently*. Unless you wish to be abandoned in the throes of battle.'

Arezu's teeth flash. 'I would rather be defiant than be what you are: completely, stupidly empty and hell-bent on insane Marka plans.' She shoulders me roughly before scooping up Yahya.

At times, Arezu irks me. Her face makes my blood boil, her words make my ears ring. No-Name was correct: this girl is everything I despise.

Though older than the others, she is still a child; I hate children. She is impulsive; I hate impulsiveness. She is loud; I hate loudness. If only I could force her wilfulness into submission, shred it to pieces before rebuilding it. *But she is a human, not a weapon*, my mind reminds me.

'Arezu, I have faith in you, by the Divine, but you cannot battle Cemil; he's a Third-Slash with the strength of a Fifth.' I force myself to check both of them, relieved they have no grave injuries.

Sharra rejoins us with ten pazktab students and Sohrab, still clutching the second banner in his grasp.

'He did it,' Sohrab announces.

'Who did what?'

'Firat, he pissed and shit on Overseer Negar and her soldiers. Yellow everywhere, I saw!'

I decide I actually like Firat for that. 'He stalled her advance. Sohrab, this gives you time to hand the banners to Katayoun. Order Yasaman to summon scorpions. And tell Katayoun that three students are within Territory Five, trapped in Negar's sinkhole. She must free them.'

'We have another problem,' Sharra cuts in as my makeshift page. 'Madj's and Fayez's soldiers are no longer clashing. They engaged with whatever remained of the other squadrons, to finish them. Fayez had three banners total but we snatched one; Madj still possesses two, one of which is our decoy. This also means—'

'Madj has allied with Fayez. Against us,' I finish stiffly, wondering if I should be flattered or if I'm to begin digging my grave now. 'At least they assume we have only one banner.'

Arezu crosses her arms. 'How do we fight two entire squadrons?'

My mind slows and I imagine a saktab board again. I find it easier to breathe by simplifying it.

'Master?' Arezu says nervously, as the rest of the squadron exchanges uneasy looks. *Inspire their loyalty*, Katayoun's voice penetrates my thoughts.

She was right. I cannot do this alone.

'Heed me carefully,' I say. 'In Za'skar, our true school is not of texts and parchments, stooped over our desks in a life of philosophy. The application of these lessons, the simulations of history, and the living personalities of conquerors and the fallen: that is Za'skar.' I am starting to realise as I speak it. 'How a warrior leads, and how the weak fall. The Marka may appear as a gameboard – and I might have called it as such – but it is not a game. This is an abstraction of war. Za'skar… is the study of man and how to conquer them.'

I level a grim look at my underlings and then out to the enemies. 'We are baby tits surrounded by herons, foxes, snakes and vultures. Your monks will not save you. The powerful here win. And to have power,' I point at each of them, forcing them to hold my gaze, 'you must steal it. Three squadrons have fallen, yet we remain. But we are not going to fight anyone. We would lose. For now, we steal banners and run as if hordes of magicians are at our backs, leaving destruction in our wake. *We can win.*'

As Arezu forms more cacti, with Sharra's counsel, I formulate our plan. At my orders, she leads the pazktab students to the north while Sohrab sets the last of his metal around the perimeter. He extends the metal into tall spears, sweat streaming into his eyes. I reflect nūr into the metal spears until light criss-crosses across the territory in beams, blinding the two and a half squadrons within its vicinity.

I re-enter the square plane containing Madj's banner. To taint our opponents' expansion of Heavenly bonds, at my command, Arezu summons sand-shrooms, a stout flower I studied in Azadniabad that emits toxic fumes. The poison will weaken our opponents' sensory abilities, but not disable them.

I light the sand-shrooms with nūr. The line catches like a blaze ignited on dry twigs.

Madj's troops split at the sudden light. 'Retreat to the west flank!' Madj barks, diverging from Fayez's lines.

Meanwhile, Yasaman's scorpions scamper to the banner, fortified against rocks and dirt and guarded by a soldier. Quickly, their claws tear it away during Squadron Three's hasty retreat. Sohrab moves between them and replaces it with another ruse of a banner, takes the real flag and flees to Territory Five, where Sharra and Yasaman await.

'Arezu, using the left flank as cover, bring a small handful of students to me. When Fayez charges, they will close the gap,' I command them.

As Aina leads Firat and the remaining pazktab students around as my reinforcements, Fayez and his soldiers enter the chaotic battlefield, a sheer force of numbers.

The captain shoves through his squadron lines, clutching his left eye, shot red from sand-shroom fumes.

I study his formations. I might as well be nipping at his squadron's skin instead of inflicting bodily harm. Like any adept general, he's adapted to form three flanks – two wings and one at the tail to pull from. I didn't see it before because Fayez used Madj's troops as a buffer, rather than using his own soldiers to weaken my numbers.

Fayez raises two fingers in command code. An enraged Negar – tunic damp with piss yellow – flattens her hands against the sediment, a tremor shooting through. With little preamble, the ground beneath me gapes open, obliterating Arezu's flora and any way for my underlings to hide.

'Fall back,' I bellow to Sohrab, yanking Yahya against me as the entire south-east is uprooted.

Fayez begins calmly but the strength of his voice carries. 'You are cornered by two squadrons. Surrender now to prove that even an Azadnian is capable of an ounce of dignity.'

I rub dirt from my cheek. 'I've thought about it. No thank you.'

His jaw clenches before his fingers raise again. A line of twelve warriors charges, aiming for us.

Leaving a gap wide open in the back, the banner exposed. Fayez's tail soldiers rush forward, slightly delayed.

With Aina leading, our subordinates close on the rear while the captain fixates on my presence. I flicker nūr to bait him toward me. My eyes blur as Fayez's affinity ripples through him. It's the Three-Feathered affinity, allowing him to take on forms of one of the three aži sky creatures. His skin morphs into luminous amber scales, pupils forking white: he has the strength and muscles of an azhdahak serpent.

In a blink, I shove Yahya away just as Fayez smacks me against the dirt. My left leg twists beneath me and I hiss from the old injury. From beside me, Sohrab foolishly charges the captain.

'*Get back,*' I yell, but there is no need because Yabghu is suddenly there, twisting Sohrab's injured arm, dragging him away.

Straddling my hips, Fayez uses the spikes along the azhdahak to crush my torso; my organs clench, even as I thrust my arm out to lessen the pressure. He cocks his head, almost curious at the sight of my helplessness. But the curiosity must be a tangle of darkness because he lets me struggle, enjoying it. His taloned iron-fist rears back.

Instinctively, my head turns as it slams into my jaw, nails raking three bloodied lines. White spots dance across my vision.

'You hardly resist me; how can *you* be a Za'skar warrior?' Fayez asks quietly before slamming my head once, then twice, against the clay, causing me to see stars.

'Using children is cowardice.' Overseer Negar looms above me, watching Fayez slam my head again.

'Enough!' Cemil runs to the captain, yanking him off me. 'She could die.'

'N-no. Please continue,' I wheeze out, drawing to my knees.

Around me, the remaining pazktab students are attacking both squadrons. With no defences to conceal our positioning, we are cattle. Still, through sheer bravery, the children flirt with the remainder of Madj's and Fayez's troops, who toss them around easily until the last of the students are subdued, a laughable melee. A cry rebounds through the fields and I watch Negar retaliate against Firat, clenching the student with an arm around his neck.

I cough out blood. Fayez straightens and turns, hunting for our banner as Katayoun – ahead of him – runs in the opposite direction.

'Even your subordinates abandon you in the face of their opponent,' Fayez says, leering before nodding to Cemil, who summons his affinity to eat the distance to Katayoun, marked from trifecta training. Before he reaches her, she stumbles and drops the flag, then flees. Cemil turns to snatch the banner she left behind, but any triumph slides off his face when it disintegrates beneath his fingers into white beetles.

'What the Hells?'

'The fool is you, Captain Fayez. I was your bait.' I wipe blood from my lips and grin.

The realisation dawns upon them. Fayez assumed the flag would be protected at his rear, but instead of making the pazktab children my bait as he predicted, I chose to sacrifice myself along with them. A hard lesson learnt but realised at the right moment.

As Yahya had collected the branches at my order, to plant this final deceitful banner, Yasaman, from the southern flank, supported the deception by summoning beetles to cover the branches, making them appear as ours. Relying on our pazktab forces to charge Fayez, Aina and Arezu used the opportunity to retrieve Fayez's banner.

None of Fayez's soldiers had noticed, for they had no choice but to hold back my other roving students as one would swat stubborn flies. They may be flies but, in a swarm, they are an acknowledged presence.

Horror plays across Fayez's features before, in a mad dash of desperation, his azhdahak body swoops across the territory.

'Now!' cries a young voice as three pazktab students tackle Fayez – the very pazktab students from the sinkhole that no one had bothered to account for, who Katayoun had freed at my order.

Cemil lunges forward but he cannot manifest his affinity so soon, with the time and geographic limitation.

'Run!' Katayoun's voice rends the dusty air, as Aina passes the banner to Arezu, who scrambles up the salty ridges of Territory Five, to join Yasaman and Sharra at the top.

I limp to Katayoun, vision bleary. We watch Arezu climb with her bloodied hands, holding the fourth banner as if it's an emanation of hope. Yasaman pulls her to the top, clutching three other banners. Scrawny and underestimated by their enemies, the two children slam the banners into the cliffside before Za'skar City.

The warriors gawk in horror at the four banners in my squadron's grasp.

The Keeper dissolves the Veil and declares Squadron Six the victor.

I stagger into Katayoun and collapse.

24

The Heavens seem pleased despite the day's violence. A pale mid morning through a shock of white sun, a blink of pleasant warmth above the burnished sand, stretching her limbs beneath the sky's belly; the bickering shouts of warriors a comforting tune. My sticky curls cling to my neck, my thin kerchief plastered through with blood. I sniff sharply: the potent taste of triumph bitter to my senses. My tactics were unconventional, and for that, is there pride in my win?

I cannot dwell on it. The emperor would remind me that true success has not been earned until I have a rank to partake in military assignments and collect intelligence on our enemies.

Katayoun and I brace each other's weight, limping forward. 'Where is Cemil?'

'There.' She nods her head. Cemil is on his knees, staring at his hands. 'He fell for our ruse.' She meets my eyes, a warning brimming in them. 'He is confused, and confused men with wounded pride go to great lengths to avenge themselves.' Before I can mull over her words, a cheer emanates from our squadron.

'Do you hear that?' Katayoun actually smiles.

'Those are children, drunk on victory,' I say as the pazktab students shriek at Yasaman and Arezu carrying Yahya across the sand dunes. I gaze at them in fascination. Za'skar displays its sharp contradictions. On one hand, a lot of these warriors are violent and merciless. But between its sheaves are the displays of camaraderie, the tempered kind, thrumming low and slowly.

'A part of me is still in disbelief,' Katayoun admits. 'I doubted you.'

'At the very least, Yabghu will be relieved of lecturing you. Will you try to earn more ranks?'

'No.' Her cheeks redden, and she gestures at the injured warriors surrounding us. 'Never again. And I believe you owe me your stipend.'

I fight the urge to smile. Soon, Aina bounds across the fields and Katayoun leaves me to greet her cousin. The sensation disappears as I look up at the craggy mountains, where officers and bureaucrats are amongst the dense crowd of onlookers; most frowning from bets lost. Amidst them, one grabs my attention. Even at a great distance, I know his gaze meets my own, before he turns and descends the cliffs back to central Za'skar.

Perhaps the Sepāhbad permits the Marka because of what it yields. Perhaps horrid violence unites people when pain is shared and victory is the consequence. Perhaps the point of conflict is surviving it together.

'You realise,' No-Name begins from over my shoulder, and I turn. A breeze relieves the heat of my wounds, but her monastic robes stay vast and still. 'Your vengeance will end the lives of those students.'

My body tenses. 'What do you mean?'

'You ache to reclaim your clan's throne and to be their left-hand vizier. You slave away in Za'skar to gain any information; to bring victory and unite the warlords. You wish to destroy Sajamistan. There is inevitability to this fate; will it not cause the death of every warrior here? The Eajīz children who will grow up and enlist?' No-Name clasps a hand against my cheek.

I gaze into her bleak eyes. 'I cannot think about a future that has yet to exist.'

'You are blind to the true enemy.'

'Enemy,' I repeat quietly. 'The enemy is the man they worship. The man who is the general of generals. These children may be naïve now, but in a few years, they will be trained beasts licking the Sepāhbad's hand, murdering another's clan.'

No-Name grins with sharp teeth. 'Who from your clan? Your uma wasted her life.'

'*Shut it,*' I breathe, shoving my face in to hers. 'Sajamistan did this; they left many like her to be abused in raids. They bred her fears. They killed her.'

Revenge. I'm determined to sustain the thought, but dread shadows it. Was revenge not my purpose – my vow? What honour remains for me if I cannot keep the promises I made even to myself? No one, not even children, will stop me.

'Be gone,' I order No-Name. She does not heed my command. Her features are fuller and familiar, as if I gaze into a reflection of myself. Hers aren't simple whispers; her words are blades that open old wounds. And I cannot blot them; they only bleed more.

'Master!' Arezu choruses with the others, but I cannot look at them anymore. Za'skar and its copper gates and its bone-stone walls absorbing the crimson dawn is a city only satiated by blood. If its students did not bleed, the beast that was the city would not rest. A disturbing image. But I cannot say such a thing to the students, for it would ruin their dreams.

And of course, children are children through their dreams. Children only become monsters when all the dreams fade away.

The crowd of officers and warriors surges across the desert plains, patrons of disgruntled clanhouses cursing their warriors for their losses. I pass Fayez, rage blazing in his dark eyes as he snaps to Yabghu, 'You failed to mention she's a strategist.'

My overseer turns and says thoughtfully, 'I had no idea either.'

I step around them, heart thundering.

'If those loathsome tactics even count as a strategy,' a new voice snarls. An arm lashes out; a hand wraps around my throat. A strangled sound escapes me. It's Negar, her tunic stained and wrinkled, bone-pendants strewn across her mussed hair.

'You reek of piss,' I tell her placidly. Her other arm lifts, fist of iron-bone slamming against my cheek.

'Negar!' Yabghu peels her away. I sputter a cough before shoving her. 'Usur-Khan!'

I glare at my overseer. 'She committed violence against an underling, unprovoked. It's an offence.'

At that, Negar spits at me. I do not flinch even as the dark goo slides down my jaw.

'I do not mind,' I encourage flatly. 'After all, I warned you of my blood oath. The captain stomping upon me in the bazaar was paid in kind today.'

By now, the warriors and officers tread around us in a loose formation. Negar straightens, wrenching her anger back, an understanding settling in this mental battle. She failed to provoke me, but I provoked her, and she does not wish for me to do it again.

Captain Fayez shoves his way toward me.

'What did you think of my natural order?' I look about. 'You respect power and its natural outcome. This is mine.'

'Bringing children to a battlefield,' Fayez scoffs. 'Are you not a warrior with honour?'

What an absurd notion. Quite the opposite. 'Yes,' I lie.

'You disgracefully used waste as weaponry,' Negar juts in.

'It qualifies as biological sapping,' I reply coolly.

'A young student pissed over my warriors.'

'The best tacticians have foresight. A shame that you were unable to predict the creative novelties of my warriors.'

Yabghu steps between us. 'Usur-Khan, you are delirious and bleeding, go to the healers.'

'The Easkaria teaches that victory is achieved not solely through knowing yourself, but through understanding the enemy.' I turn to Fayez. 'Today I learnt you are shit. As was your strategy – shit. As was your leadership, also shit. All that makes you reeks, my captain.' I tack on the honorific, unsure if it is an offence to forgo it now. 'Bested by damned children despite being a Fifth-Slash. You walk so haughtily, you are blind to the strength lurking below.'

Yabghu's gaze flits helplessly between us. We do not dare move.

Fayez curls his fingers but does not touch me. 'You sacrificed pawns in battles, flinging them like rocks at jinn. If this had been a real battle, you might have won, but you would be the last one standing.'

I stare back. On the battlefield, he thinks I would resort to petty baits, that I would have my warriors devoured by a beast. Even so, what of it? Soldiers are meant to be pawns. We are all pawns.

'The best commanders do the things nobody else dares do, the things the world would hate them for, but the things that are necessary. Swallow your pain or let it fester, it makes little difference,' I say.

'And if this were a real martial duel, coded by honour?'

'I would win again,' I state carefully.

'A Duxzam duel, the truest test of strength. Gamble away, imprudent warrior.'

Murmurs of disquiet ripple through the crowd.

'Duxzam?' I taste the word, recognising it. The martial custom for high-ranks. Yabghu said the Sepāhbad used it to become martial-vizier.

My overseer's eyes grow large. 'Fayez. She is yet to be a ranked soldier; she isn't First-Slash!'

'With the Marka's outcome, she will be First-Slash, and permitted to duel,' he says ominously.

'This is foolish. She will be obliterated by you, in seconds,' Negar scoffs.

'Speak openly,' I demand.

'The Duxzam existed before the creation of humanity, before Prophet Adam, when the tribes of jinn-folk settled disputes for land and honour through holy battle. This is now a custom in the martial clans of Sajamistan. By declaring a Heavenly Oath, two warriors agree to gamble a stake on mutually agreed terms. The winner of the duel takes the stake. If they break the vow, their souls are condemned, losing Heavenly Energy. Battling in Duxzam is how high-ranks have grown stronger; how matters and disputes are settled in Za'skar and beyond; how even the rank of Sepāhbad is decided. But a warrior cannot always battle at the Duxzam, for each Heavenly Oath comes with a severe cost. High-ranks partake in a duel each lunar year.' Fayez grins roguishly. 'No man nor jinn-folk can interfere in the holy battle unless by Heaven's will.'

I nearly fall at this. 'What do warriors gamble in a Duxzam?' I ask breathlessly.

'Wealth, land, honour, Heavenly bonds, military assignments, postings – anything.'

'Captain, you promised *me* the duel.' Cemil is suddenly there, forcing himself between us. Negar acts quickly, wrenching an arm around his neck before throwing him to the ground. Fayez does not blink; does not even acknowledge him.

'No one interferes, rukh.' Negar digs her foot into Cemil's back. He meets my eyes, his blazing in contempt.

I force myself to focus on the captain. 'So you wish to duel me,' I say, fighting a swell of hope.

'Khamilla.' Overseer Yabghu's voice rises in warning. 'This is the high of your victory speaking. Fayez has nearly mastered the martial system of iron-bone; he is a Fifth-Slash—'

Fayez's eyes cut to him. 'One more word and I will gut you.' He returns his glare to me. 'Name your stake.'

'You are a Fifth-Slash,' I speak slowly. 'If I win our duel, I will take your highest-ranked military assignment scheduled this coming year.'

Fayez's lips tilt up menacingly. 'A high price,' he warns. 'My assignment is not as an auxiliary. To pay me equally in kind is through the next most valuable currency.' His expression tightens. 'Time. If you lose the duel, for three years you will not participate in a Marka, examination nor battle. You will rot and remain in First-Slash as my dog.'

'What?' I share Yabghu's horrified expression, and the warriors surrounding us appear equally surprised, angry… and some hungry for my demise. 'How is this a fair currency?'

'One successful assignment with the high-ranks and you will never have to beg for another in your feeble life. That is, if you win the duel.'

'One year,' I plead instead. 'The same benefits but a less ridiculous amount of time.'

'Two and a half,' he counters. He has trapped me. To refuse is to admit that I have nothing of value to a high-rank besides my own time. And it is true. 'Is it not the philosophy of the Duxzam, to gamble away what one cherishes most?'

I clutch my chest, a cluster of wounds. Somehow, if I do win, I would be assigned with the high-ranks, accessing the best military intelligence on Sajamistan. Perhaps, I'll gain enough from the assignment to defect from the army and return to my exiled clan.

Grimly, I nod. 'When is the duel?'

'After the month of reflection before the spring. Duxzam is forbidden in the fasting days marking Prophet Nuh's departure from the ark. Perhaps you can plead to the Divine to save you.' His grin widens like the expression of a soon-to-be rich man. His eyes remind me of the leopards I once spied roaming the Ghaznian mountains in the silvery nights, snapping the necks of white hares slinking along the trails.

Staggering back, the blood loss finally creeps in. I fall to my knees, unsure if my dizziness is from injury or the frenzy of a hare backed into a corner.

'We must bandage your leg,' a Qabl medic tells me.

I support my arm on the window. The infirmary is attached to the monastery, with embossed schemes of greens and bronze, mosaics of paintings showing horned creatures treated by sages. My eyes dart upwards at the stars, living, flickering things against the black.

I imagine the cosmic light is my strength and if I so choose, I can light the dark world at the snap of my fingers; I can follow that light's path to home. The fantasy is gone too soon at the reminder of the Duxzam: the key that returns me to my clan or the one that locks my chains in this city.

After the healer ties the bandage, she places at my floor-bed a tray of figs, mulberries and a bowl of yakhni floating with a film of milk fat and lamb bones before leaving. No-Name crawls to it and dips a finger tentatively into the bowl, then brings it to her mouth.

'It tastes odd,' she murmurs. She turns to the mulberries, and after licking one, her black eyes grow huge. 'This is good!' She dives into the bowl, but the mulberries fall past her tongue, unable to be swallowed by her immaterial form.

'Stop that,' I snap before rolling over in my wool quilt.

'I'm hungry,' No-Name cries, as I wonder how my students are faring in the other rooms.

As if thought brings them into existence, a flurry of footsteps rouses me. 'Master,' a voice hisses. 'Are you awake?'

I sit up. 'I don't have a choice it seems...' My voice trails off at seeing Arezu and the other students shepherded in by Katayoun.

She sighs. 'They ruined my sleep and forced me to bring them to you.' With a raised hand, Katayoun leaves quickly.

Arezu's cheeks are bruised, a sleepy Yahya on her back. Sohrab's arm is in a splint, and beside him, Yasaman looks well except for bandages around her fingers.

'You should be resting.'

They exchange glances. I wonder how they do that, speaking silently in their own understanding.

'We are,' Arezu eventually answers before they slip on to my bedding.

Yahya throws himself across me, and the breath knocks out of my chest.

'A-at ease,' I sputter.

'Order them to leave,' No-Name says as she tries to snag a mulberry. Over the bowl, our eyes meet. *It is only one night.* Her expression furrows. 'Hungry,' she murmurs again.

Yahya snores into my chest and, gradually, after shoves and snatched blankets, the other students quiet into light dozes. Except Arezu – she clutches her stomach, curling in beside me.

'Were you injured during the Marka?' I glance down at her.

'I was only wounded on my arms. So why is my,' her voice drops, almost mortified, *'stomach sore?'*

After a moment, I ask, 'Have you ever bled?'

She shakes her head. 'I've heard the other pazktab girls speak of it, but I've never had it.'

I study her, dumbfounded. At sixteen, Arezu has not had her bleeding-cycle? And is it not the duty of a parent to tell her about these matters? A curiosity ensnares me, but I bat it away.

I cannot fathom being a parent; children are fat whining pigs. Who would willingly choose to have them?

More aggressively than perhaps I should, I grit out, 'When it happens, come to me, then.'

She pauses, not expecting my offer. 'Something has changed within you. I-I am still waiting… for a scolding, for disobeying you in the Marka.'

'You are not a babe nor that young. I am only a few years older.' But I feel much older.

'Yahya was almost hurt.'

'He shouldn't have been there in the first place,' I admit with a swirling mass of guilt in my gut.

'Arezu deserves a scolding,' Sohrab mumbles, eyes opening sleepily. 'When my uma lived, she would scold us.'

'Scold,' I repeat. 'I am not your uma.'

They go quiet, and again, a peculiar feeling resonates through me. I regret my words, unable to parse why, except that I would never blame my failures on someone else, least of all them. If I cannot give them the scolding they want, is that their fault or mine?

'Uma?' Yahya brings his head up from my chest. 'Master, my uma.'

They all still at that. The light voice, the light words that seem so small – do they not understand the weight? The responsibility?

'I am your master,' I whisper. 'Not uma. *Not uma.*' Yahya's lips tug down and, to my horror, his eyes water. 'Wait—' I panic and Yasaman goes to grab him but I halt her. My hand comes atop his dark curls, soothing the frayed strands until his eyes droop again.

A curiosity takes hold of me and this time I do not fight it. 'Where are your clans?'

'Here, in a small village of Al-Haut.' Yasaman stifles a yawn. 'Uma was a bone carver; she was martyred giving birth to Yahya.'

'And your dada?'

'He was a bone merchant who travelled north and disappeared.' She frowns. 'Fortunately, I was chosen as an apprentice to a court librarian; he even sponsored Yahya in the pazktab. My old master taught me my letters to be a scribe.'

I blink. 'You truly wish to be a scribe? Not a warrior?'

'Like the scholars, Yahya and I will specialise in the Easkaria, to be scribes for the vizier.'

'Tell me the point of writing pages of suffering? It's worthless,' I mutter.

She flinches. 'War is more worthless,' she snaps, loud enough to startle Yahya. I glare above his head. 'You cannot study a war without the scribes.'

'Master,' Arezu scolds. 'You love your proverbs; here is one for you: the ones who claim books are beneath them fear the knowledge they possess. You are being a coward.'

'I am trying to save her,' I snap back but I am no longer there in the room. I am drifting far, far away. My voice lashes in a way it never has before. 'I've seen it. I've lived it. I made her mistake. Accepting the *stories* of a people is a burden she will never be able to fulfil. It's the worst curse to pen the history of the past. One day she will *break*.'

'Master?'

I tuck Yahya into the quilt and hobble on my good leg. Something is wrong with me; I have lost my cool over something so small.

Arezu lurches forward, catching my arm at the entrance. 'I see you now.' But I fear what she reads inside of me.

She follows me out into the corridor and we slide down the cold marbled wall. As if to mollify the taut silence, Arezu offers a question. 'Master, why throw yourself into another battle after the Marka? Why take such risks when the odds are against you?'

'You would not understand.'

She pins me with her gaze. 'Then make me understand. I hate when you are like this: here before us, but also not.'

I lift my forearm of gold-threading and dare close to the truth. 'Like you, long before this, I had a home. My tribe was determined to ignore the outside world, but the world was determined to take every bloody bit of its offerings from us. I was accepted into a new home, and I do not want it pillaged again. Now I train in Za'skar because I want to save it.'

My words are still honest, for she does not know what home I refer to. To her, home is here: Sajamistan.

Arezu says, 'In Khor, we faced all kinds of raids in my village; many Sajamistanis did.'

She calls herself Sajamistani when she is of a Khorinite tribe. I swallow my protest. I call myself Azadnian, despite being born in Tezmi'a. It is easier to cede to the empire.

Arezu continues, 'You think we are not alike, but my own brother died from a raid when he was only two.'

I now understand how she grew to be so fond of Yahya. 'I didn't know.'

She looks down at her bandaged arms. 'There are many things you don't know.' She smiles; how fondly her jade eyes glisten. 'A warrior saved me the same time my affinity came into being. So, do not tell me I do not understand. I may be younger than you, but I intend to enlist the next lunar year. To fight like the Sepāhbad.'

A hero to one and a monster to another. But I think about the Azadnian villagers who came to help me on the night of the raid – they were my heroes too. Tonight is a night of contradictions.

'You should have that warrior train you,' I say lightly.

She bends her head. 'I embarrassed myself before them. In Khor, each time that I'd see the warrior, I'd follow them, clinging to their cloak, until they would sit me down with kahvah to silence me. They warned me of Za'skar and its schools. But because of my stubbornness, the warrior agreed to bring me here, despite my family's protests. I do not see the warrior often, but sometimes, when they return, they greet me with kahvah and rose faloodeh.'

I almost crack a smile. 'Faloodeh?'

She flushes. 'Who doesn't like faloodeh? But that's not my point. All of us are here, fighting to be warriors. You are no different.'

My right knee tucks into my chest. How can I explain to her this wrangling conflict between the desires caught in the past and the desires of the present?

'While in training, you assumed I felt nothing,' I say. 'But in truth, all I feel is anger. Not loud anger, but the gentle, simmering kind, like tea above a slow-burning fire. The kind that does not leave, even in prayer. I fear that is all I will feel until my last breath is anger.'

'Well, is it *your* anger?'

I cannot meet her eyes. 'Go rest.'

I only wish the anger were mine.

Throughout the night, I watch the children slumber. Yahya rolls here and there, pressing his cheek against my chest. Something rises through the curve of my throat; I am unused to this kind of contact. I cannot recall ever doing this with Uma. But pressing against my discomfort is a fierce urge to take hold of him and promise to protect him, wielding my blade. Are not all warriors maternal in how they defend?

As the changing hues of dawn shimmer through a stained-glass window like strokes of paint against the canvas of the students' skin, my hand reaches out, wishing I had the courage to brush their hair as an uma might do. Is this how it feels to have a child? To hope for their best, even against the cruelty of empires and warring men? Was this my uma's world? I never understood her, not even her death, but right now, I think I understand more than I ever did before.

'I am hungry,' No-Name whimpers again, taking my hand into her mouth trying to eat it. Her eyes are no longer upon the bowl of mulberries. They are on the children.

A growl rustles me awake. I must have fallen asleep.

'Take her into the exorcism ward!' The distant shout of a Qabl monk. I struggle to my feet and peer out of the room. Across the hall, above the bone-stone archway, it reads:

SPECIAL SECOND BUREAU OF EAJĪZ JINN
POSSESSION AND EXORCISMS.

I recognise Sister Umairah and two junior monks dragging a young woman between their arms.

'She arrived today?' Umairah asks, her robed form obscuring my view of another figure.

'She broke her contract with Heaven. The pressure of the siege made her crack.' I hold my breath at hearing the Sepāhbad's low voice. 'The fool attempted the Gates technique and her bonds corrupted, attracting the jinn. I suppose you know the feeling of jinn possession well.'

She sighs. 'Given her past as a prisoner in Azadniabad, she's more vulnerable than most. It's always the youngest who become a Corruption.' Umairah clutches her prayer beads. 'Beware, my Sepāhbad, jinn possession increases in your ranks.'

The possessed woman rends her nails against her own neck until her scaly flesh peels into ribbons. She growls, spittle foaming at her lips. Her black eyes dart up, down, and then – *to me*.

My head pounds, a flurry of memories squirming out of the bloodied sinews of my mind. I stagger forward. That cannot be. This is—

The possessed woman from my childhood.

I cower against the vaulted wall, suddenly in the past, seeing a young woman surrounded by cawing birds in the meadow, throwing me down, teeth bloodied, before Older Brother struck her unconscious with an exorcism.

My head shakes. *No.* I must be mistaken. It was years ago; I cannot remember her features well. I assumed that woman had died. How is she in Sajamistan years later?

Something tugs within my chest.

Impossibly, the space between the woman and me shimmers. A gold silky line – a Heavenly bond – connects the warrior's spasming body to mine, but it vanishes just as quickly.

'Take her.' The junior monks drag the girl into the exorcism ward, carrying the scent of blessed olive and black seed oils. The Sepāhbad rakes a hand through his hair and pauses at seeing me against the wall. I flee back into the room.

25

A week passes until my leg is healed enough to return to classes and trifecta training.

On the steps of the Easkaria, Katayoun halts me. 'Avoid Cemil. He has not nursed his wounds well.'

'I will.'

She works her jaw, as if it hurts her to say this. 'Perhaps your ambitions were not misplaced. You've wounded their pride. For that, win your foolish Duxzam. If any warrior can demand even the Heavens for an impossible victory, it is you.'

My tongue fumbles at this. 'I... I will. And I was being honest, in the Wadiq tests. I prefer your silence over Cemil's company.'

'Wouldn't anyone?' She holds out her hand expectantly. I hand over a pouch clinking with my monthly stipend.

We step through the corridors, as straggling low-ranks eye us. Upon entering the martial history halqa, a long line indents Scholar Mufasa's forehead, from dismay or approval, I cannot guess. Dozens of Zero-Slashes stare coldly at Katayoun and me.

The scholar stands from his rahle. 'I declare your Marka victory an embarrassment.'

My head bows, hands curling in.

'However, pride does not win battles. You used the resources around you – unbecoming as they were – cleverly. And for that,' his voices loses its edge, 'we bestow you this.'

He unsheathes from velvet my khanjar and Katayoun's khanjar, each with one ivory slash scouring the marbled hilts. 'You are hereby acknowledged as warriors of First-Slash ranking.'

*

The days bend into a new routine. In one week, Yabghu is to depart for a military rotation up north; we will merge with another trifecta until his return. He increases the vigour of our trifecta training on the monastery, particularly challenging Katayoun after the Marka. A stone-faced Cemil and I avoid speaking to each other.

Outside of trifecta training, to prepare for my duel, I apply myself to martial arts. I posit various questions to Sister Umairah, until she tires of me.

'If Captain Fayez is a master at iron-bone, I cannot beat him,' I tell her, thinking of the Sepāhbad and his iron-hard fingers, precise and dense.

The grandmaster considers my words. 'Fayez understands the conditions of reaching enlightenment in battle. I only see veils inside you.'

I startle back. The veils the monks speak of exist most persistently between me and the memories of my past; between myself and my emperor's demands.

'I was like you, I desired strength – until it nearly cost my bonds to the Heavens.' The grandmaster crouches on the cushion before me. 'Answer me, what does it mean to become the best warrior?'

'Victory.'

She squints. 'What do you desire?'

'To be knowledgeable in all.'

She smiles and I feel gifted with something precious. 'Any being of desire must suffer adversity. That is Qabl. One must be pulverised into dust particles, one must become nothing until they are asked their name and reply *nothing*. Ironically, slave of the Heavens, you are a liar when claiming to seek truth, for when you think you long for honesty, you instead ache for the cover of lies, aware that any shred of honesty requires sacrifice. With sacrifice does knowledge choose to reveal itself. Do you know who you are?' She nudges and I scowl.

'You do not heed her; you ignore the truth.' Fear ripples in No-Name's gaze.

The questions seep feverishly into my bloodstream, like a slow poison. *Who am I?* My identities wrap like silk binds. I am a daughter of the Zahr emperor; I am a nomad of Usur-Khan from the Azadnian borderlands; I am an Eajīz of Za'skar in the Sajamistan Empire.

And I am Khamilla.

But that truth seems so far away, so irrelevant. Because names are undeniably vast and powerful but so utterly meaningless.

Instead of seeking further help, I back away from Umairah's knowing smile.

After the Marka, the dynamics in my classes change. Word of my duel spreads, leading to other First-Slashes seeking me out in the evenings by Katayoun's urging, to spar, instead of ignoring me as I expected. To prepare, I train in the wild woodlands behind the barracks, and practise my stretch kicks and stances, so by the time they join me, I am nimble and ready to go. Combat manoeuvres are reduced to the same mathematical formula: strategy plus brute force and power will equal victory.

At the end of the first week, after finishing a spar against Gulnaz and then Aizere, I remain seated on the sandy fields, struggling to massage blessed black seed oil into my weak leg.

A shadow bends across the packed sand.

'Khamilla,' Cemil says in greeting – the first words we've spoken all week.

I study him. 'Why acknowledge me now?'

He crouches on the field, crossing his legs. 'To understand my mistakes.' His hand stretches to the clay pot of oil. 'May I?'

My fingers slow on my shin.

'What,' I begin before he snatches the pot, 'are you doing?'

Cemil waits, leaning over my exposed leg. A silence creeps between us. Though this is unbecoming, after a long moment, I release my leg and nod, if only to find out his intentions.

His fingers catch my ankle on to his lap. My eyes avert, unwilling to acknowledge his touch.

'Tell me, why you are duelling the captain?' he says as his hands dig into my calf. Uncertainty floods me, for I do not find this pleasant nor unpleasant.

'It is the law of power in Za'skar.'

'Power.' His smile slips and the pressure of his hands presses into my muscle. I hold myself steady.

'You could duel other high-ranks.'

His head shakes. 'There are thousands of soldiers, but only so many Fifth-Slashes, who duel once or twice a lunar year. Why would a different captain duel me, when Fayez was there, telling me that I could challenge him if I help us win? I was close – so close – to contesting Fayez's power, *if* we'd won the Marka. No other high-rank has any reason to challenge me. I didn't help us win the Marka even though I warned Fayez.'

'Warned him of what?'

'As soon as I learnt about your squadron, it became as glaring as the dawn that your strategy would be a roving pincer.' His hand treks down to my ankle, clamping it hard, like iron. 'The fool did not acknowledge me, even though my strength rivals his.'

'If he was a fool, then you, too, were the fool to follow him.'

The force of his grip increases and my surprise hampers my next words.

'Never will I make that mistake again.' Our eyes meet and he suddenly yanks my leg forward over his own until we are face to face. His fingers tread away from my foot, but my hand clenches his, arresting it. He flips our hands together and studies them, interlaced. I pull mine back. *Seize it*, I order myself. When I look up, he is staring as if it is the first and last time that he will do so.

'You are not yourself,' I say, slowly realising.

'I am grateful to you.' His voice tightens, and my instincts whir.

'That is difficult to believe.'

'You've reminded me of what is at stake in Za'skar. Perhaps you were correct, honour cannot matter.'

'Release me.' My voice drops. 'An overseer will see.'

He searches me like I hold an answer for him – of what, I cannot fathom. In his face, what I took as struggling detachment shifts to veiled contempt. A cold feeling spears me.

He pushes back into a crouch and offers his hand. I do not take it, and he frowns when I draw myself to my feet, leaving him to cross his arms, muscles flexing in a way that whorls the gold-threading like a warning. The dusk darkens his eyes beneath the muslin wrapped around his temple. A yak-tail bone through his earlobe swings with the lilting breeze.

The warmth of him lingers, making me confused – that I even let him touch me so is a betrayal. I wait for the sick to rise up my throat but it does not. As if my body is betraying me.

'You will duel Fayez through Duxzam, for it is a law of power.' He speaks quietly without the honorific. 'But you do not duel me.'

'We can spar in trifecta training.' I go around him but he yanks my arm, pulling me back into his chest.

'You accepted a captain's Duxzam. Certainly, you can spar a Third-Slash. A simple knife battle.' I register Cemil did not ask, he quietly demanded.

Cemil is more powerful than that; he might be equated to a Fifth-Slash.

'Only a spar?' I grasp at reassurance, but the decision is not shared as No-Name digs her bony fingers into my shoulder.

Cemil's teeth flash. 'Of course.'

Every master warns their students to never spar alone. The thought crosses my mind as I glance about.

'Khamilla, this will not end well. Leave.' No-Name's voice edges to panic.

Quiet the mind. Think of the Qabl monks; a bone-shard to meditate upon.

Other warriors take note of us. Katayoun is at the steps of the Great Library with Aina and Dil-e-Jannah. She spots me with Cemil and frowns, hurrying toward us. Others follow – more and more crawling from the outskirts.

On the sparring circle, Cemil and I bow, clawed palms parallel to our chins. I bid away the material world. Our surroundings dim, everything fades, and bonds buckle beneath my soul, tightening as Heavenly Energy circulates inside me. My khanjar blade twists around my finger and I crouch, curled into first stance.

Cemil follows, yet his first stance is a coil of lithe muscles, and his eyes hold a warrior's measured surety. For a second, I meditate into the spiritual realm, gazing at his bond expansion before regretting it.

The width of his Heavenly bonds imposes on the psychospiritual world, not thin strings, but a golden substance malleable to Cemil's every whim like melted glass masonry.

I return to my mortal body, my grip on my khanjar tightening.

One blink and Cemil is in front of me; the next my ears are ringing, the air a whoosh of sand like a flourishing storm, pealing grit from his sheer speed. He launches straight and high, his shadow swallowing my form, then he slashes low – *without* his affinity.

In the nick of time, my wrists cross, my nūr-engulfed blade clanging against his knife in a splay of sparks. I barrel forward in a low feint before my arm arcs upwards to his head in a crooked slash.

'Pathetic,' Cemil sneers, his head sweeping the ground, planting both feet against my chest. Like a leaf tumbling in the wind, I fly to the other side of the circle, smacking on to the hard clay, my lip bursting with blood.

'This is your strength? This is the one who stole from me,' he says in disbelief. With no chance to rest, I roll right, his khanjar stabbing by my ear, shaving skin, and I gasp at the anger behind it. What have I done?

'Stole what?' I snap.

'My Duxzam,' he grits out. *'It was mine.'* I'd sensed the hunger from him on my first day – his ambitions in classes, our trifecta, the Marka.

Warriors collect on the sand dunes around us like swarming bees. Cemil's eyes dance in mirth as he lunges.

My mind fleets to Yabghu, reminding me of positions, slashes and combinations. In a split moment, I drink in his stance positioning. *I will not be backed into a corner.*

Spitting blood into his eyes, I curve my elbow around his ribs and jam into his back, collapsing his spine, my legs twining around him in a mount until I am above. His back arches, his ankles locking around my calves to squeeze my lower body. My injured shin strains.

I have this. I must only—

His hand darts out, snatching my jaw in a clamp. With a curse, I try to move, but the iron-bone behind it presses harder until I fear my jaw will shatter.

'A lovely face to carve into my personal relief. See how your arrogance costs you,' he hisses before his hand twists, using his grip of my neck to flip us with a resounding *smack*. My vision streaks white and my neck muscles tear.

He could kill me. He almost snapped my neck. This is not a spar.

I assumed we had an alliance of sorts, our animosity trickling away. But this hate is matched to the rage boiling inside of me. Had it been there the entire time?

Swiftly my foot's bonds tighten into the sand, and I scramble up. Barely in time for my knife to parry and slash his.

'You've gone mad,' I spit out, ducking from a strike. 'You almost killed me!'

'How rich. But that is Azadnians, they invade and steal our lands, heretics of no honour. I warned our overseer that he brought a poison to this city,' he says roughly, swiping forward. My arm raises. It's no use, less than a deadlock when every block of mine is a second too late.

My back hits a fortress of flesh from the circle of bloodthirsty warriors, my khanjar grinding against his blade's edge. I hear the First-Slashes yelling at Cemil to halt this, but the others' roars drown out their cries. Of course he fights. Cemil is only content when I fall below, but the moment I am on top, he cannot bear it.

'Concede,' Cemil barks.

I push forward. 'I would rather fight than fall as a coward.'

Smoothly, his wrists twist down before spinning and driving to my right. The changes in direction are unpredictable, no longer linear. His elbow crunches into my nose.

'What else would I expect from an Azadnian?' His knife cuts across my cheeks.

At every offence, he rebuffs my blade. He is strong in every respect – size, speed, even range. But the most maddening thing of all is that his sheer will, without his affinity, outmatches my own as if this is a vendetta, not a mere battle. And this is a *fraction* of his strength. He could toss his weapon and fight with fists against my blades and still win. He could move slower, yet still outstrip me in strength. His movements are a tricky calculus; he never wastes a breath so he can outlast me.

He *is* better. In every possible way. I cannot win, not against his conviction.

We circle each other like crazed beasts and when he advances again, he proves his masterful approach in the art of knife fighting. I receive a blow to the side, a kick to my bad leg, another slash at my neck. His blade kisses flesh like a sickeningly obsessed lover.

'I understand now,' I sputter with a bitter laugh, twisting away from a slash. 'You want me so injured that I can no longer duel our captain. You want me to forfeit the Duxzam.'

He does not deny it. No matter my attempts to endure his pace – my high arches, my low swoops – nothing works. *Nothing.* At last, he throws me to the ground.

'You are sickening, Qabil's spawn,' I hiss, cursing him.

'As sick as you.' He digs his foot into my abdomen, and I cry out. '*Concede.*'

'Is this the point you wish to make? Never against your kind.' I am seething through bloodied teeth. This is a different kind of cruelty, where emotions are as painful as fists. 'You stomp upon my limbs, spit in my face. Tell me,' I try to breathe, 'are we both not monsters?'

'*Monster?*' He stoops down. 'I break my body every day to destroy your kind. I will never forget what your people did.' He yanks on my arm, the gold-threading an omen between us. 'I cannot understand how our superiors let you into this city. Your empire burned *our* homes in the borderlands. My clan, wishing to return, still holds the bone-shards from the bricks of our hovels. Azadnians pillage *us*. Let the warriors witnessing this duel remember that her kind does not care; they peel babes' skin, hanging them on walls in triumph.'

'And what of you!' I burst out. 'What of *my tribe?*' My surroundings dim, black splotching. I taste blood, I smell smoke, I see a spear piercing the khan's head.

'If you ache for a monster, I will show you a monster,' Cemil promises. He wraps his hand around my throat, ripping me away from the past, and I dig my heels into the sand. But he does not squeeze. He stares at me struggling beneath him and I wonder, is this it? Is this the ceiling to his anger? Or will he snap and do it?

'Master!' a familiar voice shrieks.

Cemil looks back and, to my horror, Arezu flings herself at his back. But the Third-Slash simply catches her by the wrist. She flails, trying to punch him, but in little more than a twist, he tosses her aside like a bug.

'Do not touch her!' I struggle to rise against him. '*Do not dare touch her!*'

But I am *weak*. I am *nothing*. *He is stronger than you*, I can imagine No-Name telling me. She watches, stricken in fear while the crowd leans in to my demise. My senses slosh languidly and I feel myself gazing at the world from afar.

Justice does not exist; justice will never exist.

I am skin and bones. Weak and pathetic. A girl who drifts between borders like a swirl of dirt in the breeze. A girl with a piece of everything but nothing whole to belong to. One who will never amount to anything but repeated failure.

'Do you yield?' Cemil demands again, fingers slackening at my throat. He is trembling.

'*No,*' I wheeze, thinking about my massacred tribe, and then my Zahr clansmen. A Sajamistani will not see me break, will not see me scream. Never again. I need this Duxzam.

He speaks calmly, but a slow horror quivers beneath. '*You are not normal.*'

I attempt to imagine what normal means. I did not cry as an infant. Uma said the devil did not prick me. I know that is not normal as well. Normal means having a name, a clan; being kind; not time-blanking. I only know how to be the blade of a fallen emperor.

Normal. I am unsure of its meaning, but I know I do not ache for it, either. If I am not normal, I will be ugly. So in pure animalistic panic, I drive forward, smashing my head against his. I know it will not win me the fight, but I am angry, I want him to hurt, I want his pain so raw, he yells. I want to feel his skin rip beneath me, blood pouring like water for a thirsty monk in a sun-ravaged desert.

And yell he does before he slams my arm against the ground. 'You are not fit for this city. You are unbelonged.'

Humiliation sears like a hot wick. But these are my uma's warnings coming to fruition. Hers were not spun fables of lore, nor an attempt to scare me into submission. Her sensationalism was grounded in truth. One of us acts out of line and we all pay. One of us utters something despicable, we are all blamed. I am not the city's scapegoat; I am an empire's scapegoat.

And you are doing the same, No-Name reminds me.

Suddenly, Cemil is wrenched off me.

'Disgusting,' Overseer Yabghu sneers at him, Katayoun and Aina at his back. They must have alerted him. 'Thrashing your own trifecta is beneath a warrior's dignity, Cemil. Sparring in a high with Heavenly Energy alone without a convenor will result in this, a high of bloodlust.' Then Yabghu pulls me up. 'And *you* should have conceded, foolish girl.' He surveys my injuries. 'Who cursed me into having this trifecta?'

A wave of guilt crashes into me. The rage in Cemil's gaze dims as he glances around us, realising what he has done. Yabghu helps me limp away but as we pass Cemil, I pause.

'You should have done it, coward,' my words tremble quietly, 'for my anger is greater. You will regret that you did not end me.'

In the Qabl infirmary, Yabghu does not speak to me. His foot shoves me into a chamber before he departs without a word, leaving me to fester in a pool of my blood.

Later, as a Qabl medic tends to me, my anger muffles the pain.

They will regret this. Cemil, Fayez, Sajamistan – all of them. My hands fist, the rage another bandage binding my wounds tightly.

No-Name crawls from the corner to my side, laughing. 'I warned you. I warned you not to battle him. Clay-beings always seek an excuse for violence. He claims victim, you claim victim, and then you fight, drawing blood until it ends with no victor.'

My skin fissures from the blood caking it. I curl into myself. 'You cannot erase human brutality. Not when it exists inside of us, as innate to the body as air.'

26

My eyes open to Arezu's looming face.

'You are awake!' she cries, jolting Sohrab.

'What are you doing here?' My voice scratches out.

'Your battle was mortifying, master. You could have done better,' Sohrab says as my jaw clenches. 'Well?'

I keep my voice level. 'Your words are frustratingly logical. I have nothing to say.'

'Good.' Arezu smiles. 'If it is any relief, during mealtime the low-ranks said Cemil's been brutally flogged; it's all they're talking about. And apparently he's been disciplined for the rest of winter.'

I notice purple splotches on her arm. Shame flushes through me. 'Thank you for intervening in my fight. But *never* do it again. He was in a high because of Heavenly Energy and could've killed you.' I point to the door. 'Get lost, please.'

The students sigh, exchange looks, bow and get lost.

Alone in the room, Sohrab's words smart. I dreamt of being the vizier of my clan, swiftly cutting Sajamistan by collecting intelligence against them.

Pointless. The word rises sinisterly, and I see the emperor walk to the corner of the room, raking his hand through his hair, looking out at Za'skar's grandeur.

'I am sorry,' I say, and my fingers grip the woollen quilt. 'You named me but I could never bear its burden.' Grasping hope is like cupping water, only for it to stream through your fingers. The harder you try, the deeper your failures.

As a child, I knew this. I was so weak. But my father reclaimed us. It was a folktale: a great emperor whisking a lone mother and wide-eyed daughter to his rich courts. He became my master. He made me. I vowed to be worthy of him, broken though I was. Even a shattered porcelain plate can be pieced back together, shards and all.

If I lose the duel, for years I will be trapped in my ranking. Discovering my identity, the Sepāhbad will torture me before this city, and worse. I imagine his tranquil features, his amusement while I scream.

My eyes burn, but, like always, no tears flow forth. To become stronger in a matter of two months, I must destroy my assumptions and my body – limbs torn, muscles shredded, mind wiped – before rebuilding, restitched piece by piece with blood and bone.

Glancing at No-Name, I know what I must do.

I hike to the woodland behind the barracks, the dregs of the stream dribbling against the riverbank. I prepare myself for what I must do, peering at its surface. The panoply of stars streams into the Simorgh's constellation, the sister of my power, alike in its omen.

There lies my answer. 'No-Name.'

She appears behind me, standing amongst a copse of pistachio trees. She has changed, taking to the moonlight as stardust; her white hair curls long, her pale skin shimmers, and her eyes dampen like spilled black ink, swallowing the hint of white. A discomfort itches through me. Her face structure has softened. Her features are mine.

A good believer would feel there is something unnatural in my intention; it defies the iron-rod conviction of belief to the Divine who rules over the Heavens and clay. But my eyes betray my faith by drifting to No-Name, fraying my will like worn yarn.

'Change,' I whisper.

No-Name morphs into Cemil, eyes blazing in hate. It awes me. It terrifies me. I bestow a rare smile. No-Name returns it. The Divine's bountiful gift to me is my mind, and my mind is a cave of degradation. I can compress months of training into mere days, for No-Name can be anyone and anything, and she can hurt me in ways no one else can.

At my command, Cemil-No-Name moves with a jinn's force, blades skinning my torso, spinning me to the dirt before I can even blink.

'Azadnians are the enemy,' Cemil-No-Name says, leering. 'Heretics, the killers of the Heavenly Birds.' Pinning me, he digs his blade beneath my wrist until the skin splits opens, red gushing down. His hand muffles my scream as the skin peels like pink ribbons until he reaches bone. His voice becomes soothing like Uma's, explaining how Sajamistanis hate me, how they will kill me. My hips buck him off, and he vanishes with the immaterial movement of jinn-folk.

Then… my wounds disappear. Only shallow cuts remain. I do not know what to make of this. My stomach flips and I bend over, hurling the contents of my stomach all over the wild weeds. After I smear the sick from my lips, the smell curdling, I simply hiss, 'Again.'

In the beginning, as the weeks crest and fall, No-Name wins every spar. She embodies not only the warriors of Za'skar, but even my clansmen. Some days she morphs into my siblings, Zhasna or Yun, wearing their faces to remind me of my mistakes.

The worst is when she drapes herself in indigo monastic robes, turning into *that* monk. I look away, refusing to believe it.

'Don't you recognise your Older Brother?'

'I had no monk as a brother. I only recall a traitor,' I reply, remembering what my father ordered of me.

Then she guts me, intestines spilling out like long worms; she jabs my eyes until the pupils burst into liquid. I feel the pain – every blazing second of it – when she tears my body apart and my heart stops beating. But at the end of each fight, my wounds disappear, and only a small amount of pain remains.

It is awful, *so awful*, the urge to curl up is dizzying. At my lowest moments, the temptation to concede overwhelms me.

The gore of it puts me in a fervour. I no longer sleep; I hardly eat; my eyes ring in shadows; my bleeding-cycle does not appear again. Every morning and night, I wrap my broken flesh with cloth to conceal it from prying eyes. I hurt myself to become stronger and I begin to like it. When the urge to rest for even one day, when the traitorous parts of me whisper that one evening would not make a difference, No-Name careens into the emperor.

My presence becomes rare in my trifecta study sessions. As the First-Slashes engage in discourses in the Great Library, a pang resonates in my chest; I was there because Cemil showed me it, but it was he who thrust forward my weakness. And so, No-Name clamps my ears, ensuring I'm never tempted to respond to other First-Slashes. I make no more allies and I do not care. I do not want friends if their companionship is a ruse shielding their violence – like Cemil's hatred. I want power.

Katayoun notices the change. It's the end of the month. The days of fasting have arrived, and with them, spiritual acts. Monks lecturing about Nuh's lessons. The exorcism wards emptying. Shops closing and reopening only after sunset. With no water or food to supplement my energy, my endurance increases and my Qabl meditation soars.

After convening for trifecta training, I hand over Katayoun's portion of my monthly stipend.

She fingers through the pouch and takes one ingot. 'Keep the rest.'

'But you are not generous.'

She yawns. 'Listen. You can bribe me any which way, but you look so pathetic, you might need this more.'

I flinch. Evoking pity from the girl married to greed feels somehow lower than the thrashing from Cemil.

'You've regressed back to your initiate days. You hardly speak, even in classes. When Yabghu returns, even he will notice.'

If my methods are so wrong, why are they working? After a string of losses, I begin to hold my own in the spars against No-Name. And with this obsessiveness, something within me changes like the weather – one day sun, and another day storm. At night, darkness grins at me. I see creatures as if the Veils of the Unseen are peeling back. The shadows accompany me wherever I go, a warning of my forsaken path. Instead, I turn the Sepāhbad's khanjar in my hands and repeat my vow: he shall regret gifting this to me.

No-Name changes, too, into more woman than girl. But I fling these disturbing observations away. Fear is weakness. Pain is strength. And the thrill of training through pain is the bleak reward at the end – an addictive high – and I crave it, hoping to get it again and again.

In the last weeks before the Duxzam, the pazktab students seek me deep in the woodlands, finding me hanging upside down from a tree.

'We have a proposition,' Arezu announces.

Sohrab shoves her away. 'Please!' he begs, falling to his knees. 'The Marka is over but we need you! Be our master again!'

I sit upright and squint, pretending to think about it. 'No. You expect me to continue holding your hands?'

'Yes, please. Hold me.' Yahya tugs at my tunic.

To my startlement, Sohrab's features harden in the first streak of genuine anger I've ever seen on him. And I am stunned at how much I despise myself for causing it. 'You need us.'

My shoulders lift. 'Not anymore.'

'We are your only friends. The other warriors resent you for the Marka victory.'

'I have friends,' I defend. 'Like Yabghu.'

'Yabghu hates you. He is forced to be your overseer, and you defy him at every chance.'

My teeth clench. 'It is the allure of our blossoming friendship – built on hate, but all a pretence. Besides, I have Katayoun.'

'You pay her into your loyalty,' Sohrab argues.

'Such honeyed lies, master.' Arezu smiles coyly. 'The victory has bloated her head. Goodbye and may death never be a peace on to you.'

At Sohrab's elbow, Yasaman drops to her knees with a scowl and Yahya clumsily follows.

Arezu sneers at their backs. 'You fools concede so easily.' Her jade eyes flick to me, cold. 'My proposition is simple. We help you, and in return, you train us, for a reduced time.'

I glance at No-Name, who shares my scepticism. But the students' watchful gazes make my guilt well like blood on a shallow cut. So I announce: 'Half of the hour.'

'And if we want more, will you refuse to train us?' demands Arezu.

If I admit that, it will make me awful. 'Yes.'

Sohrab speaks in Arezu's ear and she suggests, 'Fifty minutes.'

'Thirty minutes.'

More whispering. 'Forty-five.'

My mouth curves. 'Thirty.'

'Thirty-five.'

'A generous thirty-five it is, you pigs,' I hiss. But I do need them. And yes, I admit I miss them, the feeling so foreign.

'You must awake long, long before dawn. Drink your water at night to dampen your sleep. With your bladder on the cusp of exploding, you will shoot to the latrines, wide awake.' I shrug. 'The warrior monks do this.'

But our training is short-lived. In the week before the Duxzam, they change their minds. As I await them, I watch Yahya cling to Arezu's back while she scrambles up the hill. The breeze teases me shyly, the early morning encased in a light smoke leaking from the central capital.

Yahya's laugh carries through the air, forcing its way into the mess of my heart. If I could steal a laugh, it'd be his; I yearn to hear it every day, the happy abandon of a child even in a place of cruelty.

When the students reach me, he pauses mid grin. He climbs off Arezu before wrapping his fingers around my middle finger. 'Master is unwell.'

My arm recoils. 'What?'

'Yahya is right,' Sohrab cuts in. 'You look awful.'

'I will pray for your offended sight later.'

Suddenly Yahya raises both his hands. 'No training.'

The students exchange looks, lowering their blades.

I glance between them. 'Have jinn possessed my students?'

With her khanjar, Arezu slices her forearm until red weeps down her light brown skin. 'I'm injured. I must head to the medic.'

I drop to my knees. 'Do not hurt yourself! Why would you do that?'

'If self-infliction helps…' She shrugs. 'You hypocrite. I've seen you use this tactic.'

'What?' I stare in horror. *Arezu used pain to prove a point. I am supposed to do that. Not her.*

Yahya gazes at the wound, almost curiously. The heat escapes my body. I want them to be nothing like me, left with blood and disappointment. But as my eyes linger on the crimson claiming its mark on her, I'm afraid it's too late.

Squaring my shoulders, I yank the blade from her grasp. 'I didn't teach you to abuse blades in such a manner.'

'You would not understand.' She looks away. 'We will see you after we break our fasts. And you *will* eat. Or I will report this to your overseer.'

Arezu yanks Yahya away, the others following, but the breeze carries his words. 'Master look sad.'

Arezu must have spoken to my overseer, because when Yabghu returns from his military assignment on the Camel Road, he finds me before trifecta training, curious, using his khanjar to pick at his teeth. His scent of white clover attar is almost comforting.

'You are foolish,' he states. He takes the khanjar out of his mouth. 'The way you train into pain and exhaustion is the opposite of the Qabl methodologies. We meditate on death, but we balance it with the life we receive through prayer, fasting and incense. This balance should not be ignored. You are too far into death.' He snatches my arm forward, tugging my sleeve up to expose fresh bruises. 'What punishment are you inflicting upon yourself?' I scramble for my blade but Yabghu stops me. *'Enough.'*

'Did Arezu or Katayoun snitch on me?' I scowl.

'They didn't have to. Your masters are not blind. I was beside myself to have my own trifecta. Then immediately I lose one rukh and now have you three under my tutelage. Truly, the Heavens are testing me.'

'When you were a low-rank, who was in your trifecta?'

'Negar and Fayez.'

'Of course,' I mutter.

'Know that I speak from understanding my comrades well: I've watched the bloodlust in Fayez. My only regret is that Cemil fell under his influence.'

'Do not speak of Cemil.' I glance away.

'I will.' Yabghu massages his jaw, studying me. 'Fayez is a Fifth-Slash. And a Third-Slash thrashed you black and blue. Wait, instead. You can become a brilliant Za'skar strategist and duel warriors in your own rank.'

My gaze roves through the woodland, with its chirps of red-tailed myna and the caw of a raven. 'You do not understand me, then.'

He follows my gaze to the raven. 'You are angry. I know you did not lift your blade against Cemil first; his jealousy compelled him. Cemil is like the son of Adam turning against his own, I suppose. See, Cemil has a weakness. He cannot distinguish if he should like or resent you because he sees himself in you.'

'What?' I wrest back my attention in surprise.

'Hate and affection are on the same path, quick to turn on the other. He is confused and does not know if he should hurt or ally with you.'

I blink. 'That does not sound like a man but a child.'

My overseer snorts. 'That is obvious. But you, rukh, in some ways, are no better than him in your singular goals.'

He has his dagger again, carving it down the blue-threading on his arm as if it's a reminder. He does this often, I note. Then he spins it up, and my blade crosses his.

'You remind me of a woman from my past.'

'Who?' Our blades spark.

'My mother. She knew only two truths: that man in its arrogance convinced itself not to bow, even if it meant walking to its death, and two, that to fight was to give meaning to our short lives.'

'You did not share her feelings.' I parry his slash.

'She died practising her philosophy and I lived to see it undone. We hail from Bavnah province; she resented our governor for joining

Sajamistan, and believed our tribes should govern.' He smiles, and light as air, curves the blade against my ribs, bringing a sting of pain before I could even register his shift in direction. 'She was a severe woman who died for her principles, even at the cost of her loved ones. That was her freedom. An unsatisfied woman, my mother – even my sister.' He meets my eyes and any amusement leaches from his gaze. 'You are an unsatisfied woman marching to your grave.'

'You should be proud. I've truly become of Sajamistan.'

He taps my shoulder with his Fourth-Slash khanjar. 'We like martyrdom to serve its purpose. Not foolishness.'

If I embodied his beliefs, my life would be simple. If my tribe of the Camel Road did not resist, Sajamistan would rule this continent.

'You say this at your convenience,' I say. 'Your uma's name does not exist, not even in history, because you betrayed your kin's beliefs.'

'But many of us live,' he cedes with a sigh. 'My sister. My cousins. Myself. We live and she is dead.'

Deciduous pistachio leaves swirl in intricate patterns through the wind, as intricate as his tale as he whirls inward. My knife twists down. His ankle comes between my feet, our bodies at a standstill like our principles. We both step back at once just as our words find an equilibrium.

He frowns as if unimpressed with nature's gall.

'I recall when Fayez stomped around me,' I finally answer. 'You could do nothing as his lieutenant. Because you love the rules and being a bee in a hive. You are not like your uma. You like orders fed to you without thinking twice. But that will never happen for me. You are content where you are. I am not.'

His eyes grow as sharp as the nib of a reed pen. 'Even so, what of it? Not all of us aspire to become a general. Some of us know our place in the world and are wise enough to accept it. I have my stipend, a place to sleep, a noble career as a warrior.' I nearly grimace at *noble*. 'The ones to die gruesomely are the leaders, while the rest of us quietly disappear, and run with a new pack. I have nothing else to prove except defending my empire. Ever been in a battle, Khamilla?' The rare time he utters my name. 'Your entire outlook will change when you fight in your first.'

I have.

'If you even survive,' he adds, with a rough laugh through his teeth. It slithers into my ears long after he departs.

27

On the Duxzam evening, the amphitheatre is crammed; it is an event more eagerly anticipated than a Flood Festival. Thick wagers fly amongst the onlookers. The bone-stone complex can hold over 20,000 people, and tonight it's full to the brim. The wind is too calm for the promise of violence.

'Those are not only Za'skar warriors.' I slow outside the tunnel entrance, gazing up in awe. From soldiers to scholars, bureaucrats and the great noble clanhouses of the capital, they mill about the eight tiers of the amphitheatre in elegant emerald and gold and crimson brocaded tunics stitched with raven seals. Their hands glisten with whorled black-threading, an indication of their status. Some have donned oxidised headdresses and bone-pendant jewelled gauds. Seated in the topmost row, shadowed against the constellations, chins resting on their palms, I discern advisers and strategists from the royal palaces. 'Why would noble clanhouses watch a First-Slash duel a high-rank?'

'This duel is about what you represent as an Azadnian. When man's pride is wounded, the only path to salvation is vengeance. Why not too the violence of a duel?' Yabghu answers me.

'And gambling,' Katayoun interjects, from the sandstone tunnel. She kicks away from the wall and crosses to me. 'Our overseer's honour didn't allow him to tell you—'

'Katayoun,' he says, glowering.

'— the noble clans make a sizeable fortune from gambling on Duxzams, despite it being outlawed in our faith. They even gamble on the time it takes for a warrior to win.'

My stomach turns at the stale stink of my own fear. 'I imagine the stakes are low. I cannot imagine anyone gambling on my victory.'

'To my knowledge, three have.' She slugs an arm around my shoulders. 'Make me a wealthy woman tonight, comrade.'

Yabghu glares at her. 'You use gambling as an excuse. You do care.'

'You go too far, Overseer.' She pushes back with reddened cheeks, and I find myself almost smiling at them before I stop myself.

Yabghu straightens his turban and glances up at the sky with a thoughtful look. 'Though you march into defeat, if I was a sinner, I would gamble on you as well.'

I look to him in surprise. 'That is your honour speaking.'

A softness enters his gaze. It cools my heart. Still, I resist any hope. Hope is but a bit of gilding, obscuring the horrors of a ghastly world. It changes nothing. I remind myself of that before he suddenly pulls me into an embrace. White clover and jasmine pervade my senses. In a panic, my eyes dart to Katayoun, who looks on awkwardly. What is this odd touch? I stave away confusion and try not to shove him. A part of me wonders: what do I do with my arms?

'At ease,' Yabghu whispers into my braids.

My shoulders drop and I stay so very still. With shut eyes, for a wavering breath, I am no longer in Sajamistan but in Azadniabad, with my half-siblings, the scent of firelotus and blue poppy engulfing me.

Yabghu breaks away just as a voice calls out, 'Fool, you would side with her over Fayez?'

'She's still my student.' Yabghu faces Overseer Negar who leads her trifecta, Aina, Aizere and Dara, near our tunnel.

Overseer Negar shakes her head, henna-stained braids swinging with the momentum. 'She is an outsider. Whoever dared to let her into our city was a fool—'

'Then I am the fool,' a voice adds pleasantly, and I feel someone warm step up beside me. Everyone bows, save for Negar who looks on in surprise before hastily following their lead. But she is not wrong in her distrust.

The Sepāhbad, flanked by an old man, glances at them. His head turns over his shoulder and our gazes meet. He still speaks pleasantly, but his eyes are cold, 'Shepherd girl.'

Confusion floods me, and with it, a familiar rage. 'Sepāhbad,' I force out.

'Let us pray this is a promising duel.' The older man hardly spares me a glance.

'By the Divine, Adviser Arash,' the Sepāhbad answers as they stride past us, climbing the steps of the amphitheatre.

'We should go,' Yabghu says gruffly, but his expression has dimmed.

We walk through the clay-rammed tunnels of the amphitheatre side by side. My overseer bestows a final lesson. 'Fayez has nearly mastered the iron-bone. If he reaches the zone of enlightenment,' his lips press together, 'the duel will be as good as over for you. But your strength is your durability. And your creative use of the environment. Remember that.'

With that dour advice, he climbs to his seat on the bone-stone rows beside other high-ranks.

'Master!'

My pazktab students run into the tunnel behind me as I near the stairs leading down to the sand pit. Wearing unnerved expressions, they mutter prayers. Their weak faith in me makes it hard to swallow.

'Take this,' Arezu says after I remove my sandals, feet cool against packed sand. She unclasps her necklace, animal bones jangling and ugly.

'This I don't need.' I back away uneasily.

She scowls and rounds me before forcibly knotting it behind my neck. 'Yasaman carved it for me. But I give it to you, master. When they say you don't belong in Za'skar, they will see, you have a part of this empire upon you now.'

My quivering fingers hook around the bones, tempted to rip it off… but I cannot. It's her gift.

Slowly, I descend the stairs into the womb of the amphitheatre and the crowd hushes. My gaze roams through them as I peek out from the bottom, catching on a bruised Cemil seated beside Squadron One. In the middle are scholars and monks, Mufasa and Sister Umairah on the bottom row with a group of pazktab students.

The amphitheatre's pit is expansive, peppered with bedrock and date palms. I remove my robes, to reveal a white bare-sleeved tunic with an amber waist cord and dark trousers. I wrap my joints in močpič cloth before flicking my left earring, the only reminder I have of my parents. I count the throwing knives and khanjars on my belt. Dabbing the rose attar seven times on my arm, the incense waffles the air, warding away lurking jinn from my bonds but also solidifying my Heavenly Contract. The rose pervades my soul as if it originates inside me rather than from the external world.

Rage rinses away the fear. Months of pain, sacrifice, disorder, all leading to ten minutes that will determine my fate. The blade is my sacred art, and now, it must be my extension.

Fayez and I walk to our respective sides. My gold-threading glows beneath the lanterns blazing with smokeless firelight, and his blue-threading shimmers and ripples, as if our duel is between empires, not people. Above, the Keeper blows a shimmering Veil upon the arena, ensconcing a plane of the Unseen in the material world.

'The stakes of this holy battle are scribed and seen by Heaven's witnesses,' the parî announces from above. 'There bears many costs to breaking your Duxzam gamble: an alms-tax of a quarter of your wealth, fasting thirty days and paying the toll of an orphan's upbringing. If you are unable to fulfil these terms, the clergy's courts shall dictate what means of charitable labour you will undertake. And of course, you will become a Corruption, falling to jinn possession and curses. The Divine knows your intentions; no man can break a Heavenly Oath.'

I nod, queasy at the firm warning.

'My warriors, come to attention and greet peace.'

'My foot.' Fayez spits on the ground.

'Fine. Here is my peace.' I raise my palm and slit it with the khanjar, letting crimson patter to the sand.

'What is this?'

'A blood oath,' I say, but not of my own. The blood of my clansmen wronged by his empire.

Fayez smooths into a stance, right hand poised before his neck, eyes narrowed, legs wide. He unsheathes his blade, the vibration a song of steel and fury before it drops out of sight for a conceal and slash tactic. He speaks serenely. 'Let us see if holy light makes a holy warrior.'

I enjoy his words as I splay one leg back, my foregrip angling the khanjar perpendicular to my neck. 'With pleasure.'

'And those pazktab students will be next.'

My muscles tense. 'You lay a finger upon any of them, I will rip your tongue out and skewer it so far up your backside, you will find it right back in your filthy mouth.' Then I drop into first stance, shoving the hilt of a second khanjar into my mouth, sliding a third into my free hand. I recall my clan's oath:

Forged by blood, bound by duty, I offer my soul by the white blade. The enemy who wrongs one will face the Zahrs' wrath.

My wrists remain loose, ideal for direction change; my grip is reversed, to slash as my primary attack and thrust as secondary. My awareness of the psychospiritual realm increases. The seventy-seven bonds interweave in a pulsing gold, each thread throbbing in mirror to our heartbeats, reminding me that I can only summon twelve bonds while he can access three times more.

Tension stretches thin like thread to be spun. One instant we stare, and the next, the daf echoes, and the thread snaps, breaking our stillness.

We pounce, clashing together in snarls and flickers of light.

Fayez's blade slashes forward, then cuts low, but I sidestep, breaking the linear direction and spinning around him, feet planting against his back. Like stairs, I shoot high in the air.

Arching, both hands slam my nūr-drenched khanjar down.

At the last second, he whirls inwards, his right arm swooping up in a feint before his left hand snakes into a lancing palm strike, knifed fingers paring my torso.

With a grunt, I sail back, landing on my left foot.

Everything was fast – too fast to process.

'Is that all you have, rukh?' grins Fayez.

Behind the Veil, the crowd is no longer unappreciative; instead, they are stunned that I am holding my own. No longer a one-sided wager, but a full-fledged duel.

I meditate seven breaths, the material world fading until our souls exist in a sea of darkness, buckling with uncontained Heavenly Energy. They dance like birds, bonds contracting and expanding, testing each other. Next, I crack my toes, more bonds expanding.

I charge, nūr engulfing my wrists and blade. Each step light, each breath a calculation.

A pace from his attack zone, I feint left before cutting low, the khanjar in my mouth slashing at his ribs, spraying blood. He pivots, a right-armed hook glancing off my cheek. One direct blow from him is like playing with death, so I jump right and then drive low. The movements dance, too rapid for the naked eye as we whirl faster and faster, each clash of our blades a deadly song, each drop of blood nourishment for the clay.

But he offers no chance to breathe. When I scramble for space into the date palms, he closes the distance; when I parry and counter into his attack zone with a slice of nūr, he shuffles back. His Three-Feathered affinity hardens his skin into the leathery cast of an azhdahak serpent to snuff out my meagre Second-Stratum nūr against his all-encompassing Third-Stratum.

My chest burns from an open wound. The crowd senses my pain, jeering. Fayez headbutts me, crushing my nose before flipping me to the ground, his grappling techniques unparalleled.

Doubts creep into whispers, dwindling my strength. And Fayez loves it. He pounds his foot on my left leg.

'Is this it?' he snarls. 'I expected a decent fight.'

Colours burst in my vision and with them, a collection of memories. The taunting as Fayez had me crawl to his feet. I trained, more than him, more than anyone. *You made a vow, Khamilla. You win by rage.*

My arm lashes out, fingers gripping Fayez's neck. 'Fool.' Spitting out the khanjar, my tongue opens, bonds erupting with nūr as my head crashes upon his.

'Another feint! She uses a tongue bond!' The crowd baulks as he stumbles away.

My arms lift. One leg. Another leg. Now I am standing. My left leg threatens to collapse but I rewire the bonds, the muscles left no choice but to obey. My hand wipes away blood on my cheek. I cannot use a tongue bond again without sacrificing immense Heavenly Energy.

Everything slows as the metaphysical reality blossoms, rearranging Fayez's bonds into neat lines, *predictable lines*. Delving into my rose-scented bonds, I will them to tighten into Second-Stratum, summoning which combines Heavenly Energy through multiple bonds. My body is limited and my muscles shred.

I float back to the human realm, time galloping forward. Before me, I do not see Fayez: I see enemies, I see the Sepāhbad, I see Akashun. I even see the emperor. I see people I fear. I see my mistakes. I see a test I shall pass.

Fayez recovers from my hit, transforming his balled hands into sharp talons. Flashing a lethal look, he says, 'Now the duel begins.' He lunges and I roll on to the ground before my face gets battered. A barrier of nūr rises around me, forcing him into a wide berth.

With the barrier, my left leg rotates, bonds expanding as Second-Stratum compresses the nūr into a dense formation of golden chained tails lashing around Fayez's ankles. It singes his skin, but his legs thicken into the coiled scales of an azhdahak, deflecting the worst penetration.

To this, I stomp with bone-breaking force, splintering the nūr into miniscule needles to sink into his scales. It slows his movement, leaving him no choice but to counter with long-range manoeuvres. He rolls six throwing knives between his fingers before his scales explode around his wrists.

In a burst of steel, the blades whine toward me.

Crouching into a narrow but weightless third stance, I whip out a second blade, twirling my khanjars around my fingers. Inhaling deeply, my vision narrows, nūr engulfing my blades. The speed of the projectiles slows from the meditation, and in a flurry of movements, I deflect the knives in clanking slashes.

It works in his favour. I turn at the last blade, exposing my side, forcing me to rotate my shoulder bonds. I throw up a vertical shield of two planes of nūr, but his scaled body erupts with a fiery burst, shattering through it with a hidden blade. Pain hisses across my chest and I blindly dive, left arm swinging under, clocking him on the jaw with knuckles covered in nūr.

He reels back and I gather my bearings. *He could have punctured my heart*, I realise, if not for my wild punch.

Unrelenting, he throws hook after hook, pursuing me to the edge of the arena. My forearms rotate through each blow, muscles trembling. I suddenly slash up, but his scales shift, azhdahak affinity bursting with fire, liquidating his skin. My knife skids up into the air, flying high. His eyes brighten and he pounces.

My feet slide back as I counter: flick palm, flick palm, wrist cross, turn, thrust, *there!* I sidestep outward, and stoop, palms slapping into the dirt. '*Die*,' I hiss. My toe bonds expand, bathing my legs in nūr, slamming into his chest. He soars back, but before my relief manifests, he curls mid-air and rolls, landing smoothly.

I stoop into ninth stance, thumbs at the pommels of my blades. As I channel a rapid seven-breath meditation, my skin ignites with nūr from my soul like white fire. I urge the bonds to pulse faster, the compression so dense, the clay cracks beneath me.

We are at another deadlock, the momentum of battle teetering on an edge.

I wipe sweat from my brow, jaw clenching. When I feel the Heavenly Energy peak inside my soul, I shoot forward, faster than he can see. The force propels me to his side, and I stick out my knife to slash, tearing his ribcage, across his neck, jaw and leg.

At the final thrust, he uses my hunched form and cracks his elbow into my back.

'*Ququoos,*' I hear him chant as I roll forward, only looking up in time to see his affinity transform him, *again*. This time the second feathered creature: a winged ququoos. Red fiery wings blaze the metaphysical arena in tremoring waves, and I throw up my arms at this mesh of human-phoenix form.

My mind scrambles at the unexpected positioning. A clever move by him, for his large body gives me no space to manoeuvre.

To his surprise, I throw myself on to his large scaled back.

He rolls his wings right to crush me, but I twist to cement my feet, mustering Second-Stratum, ninth stance, which steadies my body in the wide staggered position. I twist and flip along the scales even when he lifts his wings. *Second stance, fourth stance* and *fifth stance*, before I run to the top and leap, twisting, my feet hammering on to his fiery head.

My skin burns and we go rolling in a tangle of talons and limbs. His knee snaps my jaw and blood leaks into my eyes. But my arms blindly catch his talons. Through strained, bloodied teeth, I pull backwards. His ququoos form shrinks and he slips from my grasp.

Cursing, I pivot with my right heel, crunching my hands into dense balls of Heavenly light. Compressing them, I launch the spheres in quick succession. A blast hits him in the chest. At the next projection, his fiery wings bracket his body, fire absorbing the nūr in a crackle and ejecting it.

The explosion knocks me on to my stomach into a bundle of date palms. Blearily, I pick myself back up, glancing at the trees. Yabghu's advice returns: use my environment. What if I create my own?

I crunch my hands again; instead of aiming for Fayez, I gamble on the Heavenly Energy reserves I have left and sprout dense walls of nūr around the amphitheatre, using the structure's pillars to form them. My form trembles when I manifest eight different walls of nūr like a forest of cosmic light. I leap over them, on to the topmost ledge of the amphitheatre, the sandstone fissuring from the force of my Heavenly Energy–imbued body.

On either side of me, officers lurch back a bit, though the Veil separates us. I stalk around the ledge, stepping over them, my bare feet leaving bloody footprints on the sandstone. Shoving the hilt of another khanjar between my teeth, I pass Adviser Arash and the Sepāhbad, who leans back with crossed arms, watching me form barrier after barrier above their seats.

Fayez turns in a slow circle. My breath labours from maintaining so many walls, but I start to leap from one to the other, my movements growing too fast for his perception, behind him – *beside him* – over him. He turns at each brush of wind created by my passing, whipping his blades, but he is half a breath delayed, unable to pinpoint my location. Instead, his knives shatter the maze of barricades. I forcibly erect a new wall each time.

I squat over the barricade behind him, my hands curling on the top. He whirls around, sensing me. But that one second is enough to target him. I clasp my hands and fall back from the barrier.

'*Dragon scales,*' I order through the khanjar. My finger bonds burst wiry tendrils of nūr into the wall, merging them together with my leg and back bonds to form a net formation of amber whipping upwards, right into his face. The density skewers his jaw.

I hit the ground and do not wait. I pounce, as he howls from my needles of nūr. *This is it.*

When I am a breath away from his hunched form, time slows. Something is wrong. His lips move as if he is channelling breaths. His fingers curl inwards. My heart stutters and the air crackles around us.

The tip of the khanjar in my mouth kisses his neck. Fayez's eyes rise slowly – patiently – as time slows.

'*Maximum iron-fist.*' The words are uttered calmly.

I do not see what happens next.

One second I am there and the next, I see a flash of glowing eyes, a white spark, and then I am in the air, sailing back across trees – no, *through trees*. My back smacks against the bedrock, but I splinter through it, landing in a crater of dirt, sand and debris.

The sky shakes above me like Judgement Day, and I realise it's my tilting vision. Blood seeps through my clothes. I cannot sense my right hand, two fingers crushed. My left leg is unrecognisable.

I cannot feel anything – cannot hear anything. My mind disappears from the material realm, and horrifyingly... my seventy-seven bonds connected to Heaven flash and stutter. To my disbelief, four bonds snap and wilt to the ground of the psychospiritual world. Those were my feet bonds.

A laugh pulls me back to the present.

Fayez stumbles forward, clutching his bloodied face, laughing and laughing. Dread spears through me.

'Enlightenment,' the crowd murmurs in a sardonic swell. The scholars exchange long, impressed glances. Older clanhouse generals look on with cocked heads from the top of the amphitheatre, and some nod, content that one of their own has reached the maxim of the spiritual arts. Only Yabghu is on his feet pushing against the Veil, fear naked on his face, with the look of a teacher about to watch his student die again.

My overseer warned me. *Enlightenment*: the martial phenomenon where the Heavenly bonds are heightened; where one's senses are all-seeing; where eyes flash white as their spiritual energy encompasses everything. One blow can *sever* a Heavenly bond.

I've caused a man to evolve into a monster.

Even Fayez did not expect this. He shudders. 'I have never been able to master a maximum iron-fist,' he says, as if the awakening of Heavenly Energy has him baffled.

But this warrior is powerful. This warrior is Za'skar. From the lessons of Sister Umairah, the maximum iron-fist is the densest punch of iron-bone that martial masters can use; it snaps the connection of several Heavenly bonds. In my case, my foot bonds. It will take me weeks to recover, after a spiritual cleanse, from such a brutal attack.

My nails dig into the sand, scooping pebbles and dirt. My eyes search the uneasy crowd, moving up to the advisers. I cannot give them the satisfaction of watching me concede.

With a prayer, I use a tree to pull myself out of the debris, leaning on my right leg.

Fayez's smile ceases. 'How are you still moving? You should be done for; your crucial Heavenly bonds have snapped.'

My legs tremble, but I grit my teeth, imagining a string pulling me up forcibly.

Fayez rolls his shoulders, then lunges so quickly in his state of enlightenment that I cannot see or predict his movements; they no longer form a pattern. *Use your environment.*

I hardly blink before pain explodes in my torso, then jaw, then throat with bone-crushing force. One after the other, his scaled half-quqnoos fists pummel me in an iron-fist barrage, obliterating more bonds.

'At least fight back,' he laughs, enjoying this. He spins, and the heel of his maximum iron-bone foot smacks into my chest so hard I find myself against the other side of the amphitheatre, crumbling the entire wall in a human-shaped crater. He gives me no time to recover, whooshing high in the air at an inconceivable speed, both hands clasped to hammer on to my face.

'Run!' I hear Yabghu screaming at me from the other side of the Veil.

I will myself to push away, knowing Fayez's move will crush my entire skull.

Use your environment, I remember, feeling the sand still clutched in my fist.

When he is a split second away, I throw the pebbles and dirt into his eyes and roll. It slows him for a breath that saves my life. My arms go up and suddenly he's behind me, scoring his khanjar across my shoulder blades. He tears it deeper and deeper, cutting through sinews, and I finally scream.

He laughs, and with all my strength, and sheer instinct, I swing around on my right heel. His eyes flash like ivory flames again and his ankles wedge in, flipping me on to my torn back. He slams his longer charay blade down, but with another rock flicked into his eye, I manage to shove my knifed hands into an *X* to parry his thrust.

My weaker wrist snaps. With a cry, I gather my bonds under my hand and brace the khanjar against his blade even as my muscles splinter from his mount.

'Your affinity fails at critical moments,' he says, not with a sneer, but a solemn look. His eyes grow almost completely white. My knife wanes while he leans harder.

My head turns sideways, lungs contracting. The crowd bends forward, sensing my end. Yahya buries his face in Arezu's chest.

The humiliation crests with the despair. Searching inside, the anger is there, holding out her arms, and I cling to her with the fervour of an abandoned soul tracing light to the mouth of a cave. *If only I had mastered the Third-Stratum. If only this battle would tide in my favour—*

Fayez's knife tickles the thin linen of my battered tunic, death breathing down the nape of my neck. This is inevitable, is it not: the hare clenched at last in the jaws of the leopard. But the thought breaks off, refusing to accept its finality.

Hovering behind him, No-Name reaches out a hand. Our eyes lock. *'Heavens, please acknowledge me!'* I scream.

The metaphysical world claims me.

In the tales of old warriors, even the strongest found themselves backed into corners. But Eajīz, the first monk and apprentice of the Heavenly Birds, had simply prayed.

I am cross-legged, breathing through the attar in a space of the psychospiritual world. My lips beg in prayer.

'O, Divine, I ask you, throughout the Heavens, to grant me the power I was born with to defeat my enemies. For I am a daughter born from an alchemy of blood. I am the vengeance of every wronged clan, and I am the reddest storm sweating the warriors facing its wrath. Bestow this mercy.'

I know not victory, but I do know pain. I am war. And its anger will shrivel the sharpest fighters at my feet.

In the present, my hand reaches from the immaterial into the material world, the answer from the Heavens appearing in my head.

As Fayez's blade punctures my neck, my left fist buries through the dirt, feeling the Heavenly Energy pulsing through Brother-Nature throughout – a lesson from my girlhood where I meditated on the harmony of the Heavenly Crane.

Every bond in both of my legs are disabled, so my left-hand bonds absorb the energy from the natural world, evoking a ribbon of nūr to slither beneath my sweat-slicked body. Like a gold wire, it wraps around a chunk of boulder from the crumbling amphitheatre wall.

Use the environment. My fingers, grasping the dirt, clench into a fist. The ribbon of nūr answers the call, smashing the engulfed boulder into the back of Fayez's head. His eyes flicker from white to black, his scaled body slackening for a valuable second.

I imagine the Qabl monastery. If I believe my body is light, not weighed down by my injuries, this can work. I breathe: *I am the bone of a light Heaven-bound corpse.* My left hand pushes off the dirt, the force sending me soaring above Fayez before he overwhelms me again.

I twist in mid-air, condensing my last conserved power. I send all of my Heavenly Energy from my body into my hands, pouring like water off a cliff. The spiral in the core of my soul alights.

The Third-Stratum of summoning rushes into me at once, unlocked. Upturned in the air, I cry, *'Seventy-seven Binding Art,'* to the back of Fayez's head. My fingers pinch into a snap.

The cosmic light protrudes into seventy-seven glowing arms.

Fayez whirls around. 'What is this?'

'Gambling.'

I release the snap and the immaterial arms surge forward. I land, wobbling on my right knee, watching the sheer force of the nūr's compressed arms wrap him like bandages, sealing him in silver agony. The impact sends him tumbling to the ground, an inhuman cry ripping from his throat.

Blood reverberates in the air and I breathe it in.

I do not wait. I sway upwards, and heave into his trembling body, with No-Name at my back, her palm pressing between my shoulder blades. 'Finish this,' she whispers softly into my ear.

My left hand curls. With no Heavenly Energy inside me, I have to rely on pure martial arts to end this with the risky Ifrit's Strike.

My hand lashes around Fayez's blood-slick throat, pinning him to the Veiled wall. Above me, officers and warriors – who bet on Fayez – rush down to us, but the Veil does not break.

With my broken right hand, I claw three fingers before stabbing one finger after the other in successive strikes into his abdomen. Yabghu said to use three-fold strikes, a way of dispersing energy to attack the opponent from the inside of their soul against pathways of bonds, rather than inflicting physical damage outside first.

Fayez's bleary gaze widens, a fellow martial artist understanding the danger of this predicament. My internal energy paralyses his movements.

He is a tree, I chant. *And I, the martial pupil, must drill a hole.*

At the third multiple, his knees scramble to jam upwards. With convulsing fingers, I begin another multiple, daring myself to reach twenty-one. Faster and faster I jab, recalling how the Sepāhbad used this on me. My hand cracks at the twentieth count and when his left foot sneaks to shift balance, I spin, curling my broken fingers.

Now or never. I stab below his heart, reaching the twenty-first multiple and disabling his strongest bond.

My finger snaps from the pressure, a wave of pain rushing in. Fayez collapses, squirming like a spider. My eyes catch on the bone-pendant at his throat that he's always toyed with. It's small, as if belonging to a child. I yank it forward.

A loud mewl spills from his mouth.

I take the string and snap it. Then I crush the bone, to snap his will too.

Backing away, I hack blood. My head leans down.

'This is the natural order that you speak of. I am the Azadnian standing atop you. I have made you bleed. And I savoured every second of it.' My tongue tastes copper. Whose blood, I do not know. I smile, realising I am only capable of grinning in the thoroughfare of destruction.

My foot rolls him over and I pretend he crawls like a dog; I pretend I am his master. For once, I maintain a semblance of control, and though it is control over one man, the power crashes in intoxicating waves. Even the blood slithering about him is fascinating.

'Warrior,' the parî hisses. 'The Duxzam is finished.'

'But he did not concede,' I say, a little disappointed that he is alive.

The Veil falls. My hands drop. The amphitheatre is silent.

I did not know I was capable of this, not the battle, not the power.

Nobles of clanhouses descend on to the sand pit, staring after Fayez as healers lift his body in disgrace. From the astonished faces of advisers and warriors, including Yabghu, nobody predicted this. Even my pazktab pupils are stunned. But I have won against a high-rank. It pleases me in a sick way to bask in their begrudging validation.

'Rise,' a voice rings out. Sister Umairah steps down from her row and raises the flat end of her khanjar to her forehead.

Slowly, with a scowl, Scholar Mufasa lifts his blade. Then Yabghu, and Katayoun. Great warriors around the amphitheatre, thousands upon thousands, raise their khanjars and bow. Only Cemil does not. He stands with an unreadable expression, and I realise this enmity has not ended; it has simply grown, for his potential as a martial warrior far exceeds Fayez's.

But the other warriors' gazes do not hold the anger I presumed. Instead, I sense an unexpected acknowledgement, bonds built on spilt blood.

I study the deep callouses on my palms. These warriors understand the hold of power. When it is thrown into your lap, you refuse to let go. The line between virtue and evil has always been fine. How often have I crossed it?

Staring at their lifted khanjars, empires and clans fall away, until what remains is a warrior acknowledging another warrior. I take the khanjar that the vizier bestowed to me and raise my blade back, slamming it to my forehead.

'The bond to Heaven is forged in war,' Sister Umairah declares.

'The bond to Heaven is forged in war,' I repeat back.

My only hope: that I haven't yet crossed beyond the possibility of mercy. Someday, evil might devour me. If it does, it would be a fool's dream to long for return, because I would be no different from the ones I call my enemies.

Uma once said humans are made from the dirt of our graves, thus all clay-beings have sown in them a part of death. I think of what the emperor taught me, a part of me sown in violence. And I, the child, always to return to the true womb: death.

'Go on, warrior.' Sister Umairah nods to the tunnels, and I realise I must walk on my own. I must leave the duel on both feet.

My gaze moves to the pazktab students. Only Arezu's lips break into a smile, and a warmth shoots through me, bringing me down from the high of victory.

The pain hits me. How many bones have been shattered, I cannot tell. But the pain is engraved in my soul. My vision tilts, my legs quake. *Go*, I urge myself, lungs rattling as I limp, dragging my left leg. I know I won't make it. Yabghu rushes down the amphitheatre, Katayoun beside him.

As darkness blotches my vision, delirium takes over. I see a young man in monastic robes, and a girl beside him.

'Eliyas...' I blubber. My hand grasps, trailing his jaw; and then I see Yun instead of my traitorous brother. To his left a girl, no longer Katayoun, but instead my sister. 'Zhasna.' My voice catches. 'You are alive.'

Their hands surround me, pushing me onward. 'You must walk alone. To fall is to show them weakness.' The voice wavers between the present and my past.

'Yes, Older Brother,' I speak through bloodied teeth. The vision fades as I walk past notables and scholars. I no longer have my siblings. That was simply Yabghu and Katayoun. *No, our enemies*, I remind myself.

Staggering through the tunnels and sand fields, the monastery looms ahead, and just as I reach the staircase, I collapse. With a cry, I see the skin on my forearms tug and pull. Something crawls beneath.

'Come now,' a warm arm lifts me up, 'you are almost there, Usur-Khan.'

'I do not understand.' I try to speak but my tongue spasms.

'Bring forth the olive oil, and incense.' The cold voice floats above before he glances down at me. 'The shaking you feel are shai'tain attempting to possess you, to break your Heavenly Contract. In the duel, you overused your soul. Your vulnerability allowed the jinn to attack you.' His calm gaze meets mine. 'Meditate through it.'

The monks swarm me with oils and blown words of script. A growl emits from my mouth, not belonging to me, but to something worse.

As a child, I vowed never to become this. My hand scrubs the flaking blood upon my cheek. Before me, No-Name grows taller, her smile as raw as an open wound. *But of course this is our only path now.*

PART THREE

The Gates of Heaven

The burial of Adam's son was guided by the raven who scratched the dirt. The healing after the flood carried by the crane. The wisdom of humanity preserved by the simorgh. Our tribe stands between the Heavenly Birds but that is our downfall.

As Qabil said, Woe to me, for a raven showed me how to bury my brother; this creature is wiser than the haste of man.

Verily the ones with knowledge have a gift and a curse, for they can foresee the patterns of the future, but no one shall believe them.

—ORAL TALES OF CHIEF FOLKTELLER
BABSHAH KHATUN, USUR CLAN, YEAR 498,
ERA OF THE HEAVENLY BIRDS

28

A red and ivory domed sandstone ziggurat rises from the arid dirt, ivory columns reaching upwards over the west quarters of the city. Yabghu waves at it, as I limp alongside him.

'White-Pillar is the administrative structure of Za'skar's military affairs and postings,' he explains. 'Beware. It's guarded by the ganj from curfew until sunrise, in imitation of the serpents guarding the royal treasuries. Only assigned warriors are permitted to be inside.'

As if to make this point, we shiver past a leathery serpent coiled around the copper gates.

One week has passed since the Duxzam. Fayez was demoted to Fourth-Slash, no longer captain. Yabghu's khanjar glistens with five marks – now a Fifth-Slash. As we cross into White-Pillar, different warriors greet Yabghu, including Adam, Lukhman and Dil-e-Jannah. Strangely, instead of skipping past me, they nod, clawed hand up, with sayings of death and peace. I halt.

'What's the matter?' Yabghu turns.

'Nothing,' I mutter, but the shock of their greetings sweeps through me; it should not please me.

Yabghu drops me at a wide gold hall with a bone-stone vaulted plaque that reads:

BUREAU OF SPECIAL ASSIGNMENTS.

Inside the administrative chamber, my body throbs from the toll of the spiritual cleanse I had that morning at the hands of Qabl monks. The officer nods to me and I sit on my knees before her floor-desk. My eyes stray to the corner. The fabric of space ripples. A shadow writhes and eyes glow—

'Usur-Khan.'

'Yes?'

'I was saying, you are going to bleed upon my parchments.'

'Forgive me,' I murmur, and lean back, touching the bandage around my temple.

The officer returns with a scroll. 'Are you sure this assignment was your stake?'

'Yes, my officer. I asked for Fayez's highest-ranked military assignment.' My ribs constrict. Had Fayez retracted his stake? Impossible, given the Heavenly Oath.

'Your Duxzam was rather pointless. According to the scroll, you were chosen for this assignment months ago.'

'What?'

She smooths the yellow parchment on the cedar table. There, in stark calligraphy, is the faded soot ink of my name, and a wax seal by a senior officer named Adel in a cuneiform of three ravens.

'No,' I say louder. 'Why would they approve me for a high-ranked assignment? I am only a First-Slash.'

She shakes her head. 'Missions are divided into several constituents. The superiors assigned Fayez for this, but that does not mean low-ranks cannot play a part. Every mission needs translators, pages, cryptographers – these smaller auxiliary roles are given to promising low-ranks as a test of their potential. A scholar must have written a favourable rank report and recommended you after the Marka. You were to be briefed end of this month, a standard practice. But regardless, you are here now.' Still smiling, she drips wax, confirming my placement.

I am an Azadnian. They would never approve me so soon. With trembling hands, I grip the parchment. If I had known, I would not have—

Destroyed myself. I grow light-headed, nearly falling over. I am unable to stop staring at the parchment.

The officer bolts forward. 'Usur-Khan?'

Then new footsteps. And a familiar voice repeats the question, stirring my anger. 'First-Slash, are you well?'

How can this be?

'First-Slash, your martial-vizier is asking, are you well?'

My gaze flickers up in slow realisation.

Above, the Sepāhbad cocks his head as if he is concerned, his hand outstretched like a false promise. But there is something gathered in that expression. What, I am not sure. The bone-pendant at his throat winks between us, catching the filtered light from the balcony.

'Are you well,' I repeat in a daze. His hand moves closer, and I force myself to take it, his skin calloused and warm. I bow my head. 'I am well, my Sepāhbad.'

It must have been him. He gazes at the scroll between my fingers, lips turning up almost knowingly. 'You look unwell.'

I can only stare, reducing my face to something cold. Anyone may mistake the Sepāhbad's expression for one of genuine regard, but I do not. My liver roils at a new fear: the Sepāhbad did this. But why?

He drops my hand and I tap the parchment. 'I earned an assignment. For that, I am pleased.'

He nods slowly and returns to the officer.

At his back, I bid farewell: 'Blessings of death upon you,' my words as clear and true as the promise of Paradise's rivers to martyrs. For once I mean the salutation. My blessings are only disguised curses.

Ten soldiers in auxiliary roles are granted access to White-Pillar briefing chambers, across from the Sepāhbad's intelligence complex. In the eve, senior officers direct our gazes to the goatskin map pasted against the walls.

Officer Samira says to us, 'Your posting will be north of Ghaznia province in the mining borderlands.'

I reel back at the circle of fate – to return to the place that brought me here.

She points to the map. 'Ghaznia province is located south of Arsduq prefecture in Azadniabad. The Black Mountains are a natural border, leading to the alpine pastures of the Camel Road. All of you will pose as labourers in these borderlands under the ortoq-caravan Dhab-e, to trace the disappearances of our villagers from the five settlements here, and the three there,' she says, guiding on the map. 'The bulk of vanished workers were either semi-pastoralists or miners under Dhab-e.'

The ortoq trade once consisted of aristocrats selling goods to peripheral governorships along caravan routes between Sajamistan and Azadniabad.

'In the past six months, villagers have disappeared from schools and monasteries in Ghaznia province and the western Camel Road, along with many labourers in the onyx mines. At first, there were excuses about collapsed mines or illnesses, but the pattern correlates with raids along the settlements, near Arsduq, connecting up to the north-east Izur prefecture in Azadniabad. Our troops' presence grows. If this continues, an invasion is the only option. We've sent spies to two mines on our north-western border. For this assignment, we are sending ten informants to infiltrate Dhab-e's recruitment of miners from northern Sajamistan *into* Azadniabad. Each of you will be assigned to a high-rank—'

Arsduq is the prefecture where Yun, my half-sister Bavsag and other Zahr clansmen reside. If the disappearances continue, Sajamistan would invade through Arsduq, into Izur. In fact, an invasion is the likely outcome.

My thoughts flatten. I have no choice. I must learn every name of Za'skar's informants in the mines to pass to my clansmen; even the positioning of their border troops.

The officer continues to tap at the map. On it, three bases are outlined with embossed circles, and troop routes are indicated in red streaks. The officer distributes scrolls containing the command signals, the defensive plans in the event of a raid and our covers as infiltrates.

I lean my back against the wall, legs trembling. If I do not warn the Zahrs about this infiltration, then an invasion into our eastern and northern prefectures would finish any stronghold we have left. I must warn them – the only leverage for my clan.

But I'd have no choice except to defect from Za'skar as soon as I am on this assignment. *To home.* But resisting that comfort is a cruel truth. My mind darts to my trifecta, and then to the pazktab students, wondering what they will think when they learn of my true nature – that I used and discarded them.

My chest clenches before cold hands grip my shoulder, No-Name frowning. 'You cannot have doubts now, not after your sacrifices.'

I clutch my conviction closely. *You owe this city nothing.*

The officer finishes by holding up a thumb-sized pouch. 'Powdered azhdahak poison. One lick and you die in the event of capture.' I cannot mention that I am immune to it.

As the assigned warriors depart, I catch sight of Scholar Mufasa outside the chambers, holding a stack of scrolls near a leathery map decorating the sandstone corridor.

It's of the Camel Road, heavily marked with cuneiforms of traded goods. Silver and glasswork, pistachio and sesame, silk, and steppe-camels, in pictorial drawings along the inked thoroughfare.

My thumb rubs against the dark lines of Sajamistan's borders, stark, unyielding. If any calligrapher attempted to blot it from existence, they would find the task impossible.

Scholar Mufasa scrunches his forehead. 'Usur-Khan.'

'Peace of death,' I greet.

The scholar follows my gaze to the map. 'You embark on your first military assignment, so study this map well. It reveals Azadniabad's constant weakness: its peripheries. Holding on to the Camel Road is the adhesive binding their economy together.'

I stare at Yalon, but on the leather, it's a province of Sajamistan. Once, it was the Zahr winter capital. 'It could also be lies. Maps seem to be very different interpretations of a story.'

He chuckles. 'Maps show that an empire-state's true borders represent an end to expansion. Azadniabad dares call itself sovereign, with no provinces and hardly any unified governors. But a true state has no need to war within itself. Isn't that how Akashun came to power, from infighting warlords?'

Conflicts that Sajamistan stoked, I almost hiss. But a small begrudging part of me acknowledges the sense. Sajamistan inks arbitrary lines upon a map, allocates their sovereignty and names it for themselves. Borders are spaces, they are barriers on maps. People do not know they live in cages, yet each day, by pen and paper, they choose them willingly. The entire notion confuses me, but if it's so wrong, why is Sajamistan superior in every way to Azadniabad? Perhaps Azadniabad should do this too.

'What is the point of this, scholar?'

His gaze turns melancholy. 'To open your eyes. You have one foot in Azadniabad, and another in Sajamistan. Both empires war over the borderlands of the Camel Road but Sajamistan has Za'skar, this is our epicentre. For Azadniabad, it's their tributaries in the Camel Road. You know this; you are from Tezmi'a. The vassals and warlords are a tower of hastily stacked mud bricks; snatch one from the bottom and the entire structure crumbles. Worse though for Azadniabad, the borderlands are ungovernable and the nomadic tribes are warmongers,' he chides, as if the notion of self-rule for the steppe-lands is a foolish idea. I flinch.

My hand strokes the leather like it's an intricate puzzle. I only wish I could reach from the Heavens above and switch the pieces of the map. As if I could play Divine.

I am assigned to prepare with Adel – a Seventh-Slash warrior in the Alif, an elite odd-numbered circle under the Sepāhbad – for the military assignment. It feels like an intentional decision from the seniors.

My first interaction with Alif Adel is not what I expect. When he steps into the briefing chamber filled with the assigned soldiers, I bow low.

To my bewilderment, he grabs my hands. 'After your performance in the Marka, I announced to the clanhouses that one day I would marry you.'

I baulk, 'W-what?' before remembering he is a senior, and keep my head inclined. Adel appears the same age as Yabghu, in his late twenties. His features could be mistaken as familiar, for he has a face that could be shared by any apprentice in a bazaar – with eager brown eyes, a smarting of black stubble around his jaw, and embroidered muslin strewn around his tall, lithe form.

'Of course, I have a wife. And a very young child. But—'

I glance helplessly behind him at Officer Samira and she rolls her eyes.

'– a shame, really. Your fish-in-the-net tactic; the mobile barrage; the use of young students to make your opponents' wills falter – tell me, whose brilliant idea was it to use that child's piss? After all, the best tactics are the cowardly ones.'

'My idea,' I say in a small voice. 'At least one warrior thinks my Marka win was not mortifying.'

'Mortifying? Who spoke like so?' He glances about, and no one answers.

I clear my throat and we begin. For the next few evenings after classes, I attend a phonetic halqa, practising the Ghaznian dialect again. The language is rough in its grammatical structure, with four noun cases. Outside, in the White-Pillar, Alif Adel and I practise our false identities. I morph from Khamilla Usur-Khan to Leila Mahsahzad, an orphan raised in a Ghaznian monastery to mine in the northern borderlands. We review signals, flicking our fingers or blinking in numbered sets; we create written codes for short reports to be relayed to another informant, who will convey the message back to the Ghaznian outpost.

Afterwards, when Alif Adel bids me farewell, he goes to the intelligence chambers to meet the Sepāhbad and his advisers. The Sepāhbad's triple-pointed bone-pendant flashes in his hands. I realise it's not a pendant at all but the same seal belonging to the vizier, used to enter his intelligence chambers.

An idea forms in my head. If I am to defect soon, this might be my only chance.

'You are taking on a great risk,' No-Name says, scowling. 'Why risk infiltrating the Sepāhbad's intelligence chambers?'

It's bath day as I follow Katayoun to the hammam.

I will be defecting to Arsduq, to warn my clansmen. If I don't seize my only opportunity to gather more information, it could cost my clan and the warlords our only stronghold in eastern Azadniabad. This information can regain the warlords' favour because we have leverage against our common enemy infringing on our territories.

'But you already have information,' No-Name presses.

My lips tug down. *I need more.* The fate of my existence as the fallen emperor's sword begs for me to do it.

In the women's side of the bathhouse, hot steam curls around my face. The baked brick cupola is divided into vaulted rooms, wooden partitions for segregation. Spring waters, from the oases' qanat system, circulates through geometric-tiled basins and hot stones, heated in part by the smokeless firelight at the top of the bathhouse. Attendants glide around the partitioned chambers, from cuppers to cleanse spiritually polluted blood, to bathkeepers and shavers: the only luxury in Za'skar, sponsored by a notable in the sultana's courts buying favour with the military.

Soldiers recline on marbled benches, propping their feet above the steaming stones. Others teeter in high wooden clogs – a precaution to avoid the molestation of the smallest, most perverted of bathhouse jinn-folk. Ceramic walls are painted with pictorial art of warriors on the backs of huma birds.

'Even if your idea is sensible, how would you take from the Sepāhbad?' No-Name pauses. 'After all, he is the most feared warrior in the empire. You cannot just steal it.'

I gaze pointedly at the partition between the bathhouse. *I will not steal the seal. I will borrow it.*

Instead of bathing, I tie my robe and walk along the latticed partition, stepping away from the women's quarters. Around the corner of the slab, in the public side of the bath, I see young men, scholars, even pazktab boys, relaxing shirtless in their loincloths, conversing.

The Sepāhbad is where I expect him, next to Za'skar advisers and Alif warriors. Even Adel is present. I can hardly see the vizier's profile, except that his back is flush against the centre of the filigree partition, the wink of the bone-seal secure against his throat. I try to calculate his exact position in my mind.

'You perverted girl,' Katayoun tells me when I return.

I jump. 'No – I... *that* is not what I was doing. I was... lost,' I mutter.

In the women's section, I test my theory. Katayoun hands me a loincloth and we disrobe quickly. I wade through the oily rose waters to the centre of the wall, back against the wooden partition. My hand presses at it. This slab of palm wood separates us by a nail's length but the Sepāhbad does not know it, not how close I am to him, nor what I am to do. If I was to stand and reach over the narrow gap between the partition and ceiling, he would be right below, hair merely a finger's brush away. Our proximity means the bathwaters between us are connected.

Sinking my hand deep into the water, I increase my finger bonds to one-third of their expansion. The bathwater clashes with the cosmic cold nūr – so dense from the Second-Stratum, it forces the water's temperature to drop. The smokeless fire above us flickers and sizzles, reheating the room to compensate. After twenty minutes, across from me, Katayoun flinches and – to my amazement – removes her bone necklace, placing it on the carved niche beside her. I continue this and watch other warriors remove some of their bone-pendants due to the hot air heating them, until immense steam rises and wavers like a white sheet hung by a thread, obscuring my sight.

After another moment, my left silver earring sears against my ear, the metal hot from the clash of temperature below and the heat above. It confirms my theory.

Short on time, the next week, on bath day, I execute my plan. If I am to temporarily borrow the Sepāhbad's bone-seal, I will need a bar of red clay soap.

I unclip my left earring and place it in the dressing chambers along with my makeshift soap-mould. In my loincloth, I settle in the springs with Yasaman and Arezu, who I'd told to join me in the hammam that evening. As they bicker beside me, I discreetly alter the bathwaters with my nūr. My back slides against the laces of the partition, gooseflesh tickling my neck despite the heat, for on the other side of this screen, a handspan away, the Sepāhbad should be with his advisers, sitting with his back against the slab separating us. Based on my observations, that is the same location where he and other senior officers tend to rest. My gamble is steep because I cannot rely on seeing him to make this work.

After cooling the waters with the densest nūr I can discreetly summon beneath the surface, I lift from the tub, tie on my robe and excuse myself from the students.

I round the women's section, pretending to walk to the dressing chambers. In the public corridor, I glance at the pale ceramic walls, containing a slight reflection of the public side of the bathhouse, revealing a view of the Sepāhbad. His seal is on his neck, still.

The smokeless firelight flickers and the skin around his neck seems to redden from the hot air. Adel reaches out, brows furrowed, and lifts the Sepāhbad's bone-seal, snapping something at him. At the moment, it is no longer around his neck but on the edge beside the niche of the basin, near Adel's hand. From the hot temperature, steam curls and thickens until the seal is hardly visible.

I return to the bath, which Arezu has left to try blood-cupping.

'Yasaman,' I say after a moment. 'I need help.'

She floats to my side. In a hushed voice, I say, 'Remember my earring? I think I dropped it below this partition.' I point behind me. 'It slipped through the cracks but I am too embarrassed to go to the men in my immodest state. Perhaps if you summoned the white beetle we used in the Marka – *discreetly*, as to not surprise anyone – you might command it to retrieve the earring. It's on the edge. I would be in your debt.'

Yasaman huffs, 'No debt needed, master.'

The guilt swirls in my blood. I remind myself futilely I did not train her for moral reasons but for my own utility. Still, a part of me worries that I will implicate her in my crimes. But the Sepāhbad would not hurt children, would he?

As Yasaman concentrates, I will more nūr beneath the connecting waters until our side of the bathhouse is a swarm of steam so thick,

I can no longer see. For the next minute, the Sepāhbad should not notice that his seal has vanished.

A short moment later, the bone-seal emerges through the cracks of the partition, the white beetle blending into the tile.

'That is not an earring.' Yasaman's eyebrows draw together.

I don't like where this is going.

'I wove it on to a string.' I snatch it before she notices my lie. 'Anyhow, I've things to do, student.'

With a wave, I rush out of the baths back into the dressing chamber. Inside, two Second-Slash women are changing, and I count beneath my breath. When they depart, I shove the seal beneath my uniform into the clay soap-mould, each excruciating second dwindling by. A moment later, I tuck the seal into my thin linen robe, leaving the soap under the rest of my uniform to set.

Yanking on the robe, I return through the public corridor, the steam a thick veil. *It has been only a minute, if I slip the seal through the partition—*

I collide blindly with a warm body; hands grasp my waist, fingers brush my ribs. I mistakenly grab the neck to steady myself against the slippery tiles.

'Forgive me,' I breathe, tightening my linen where the seal rests inside, against my heart.

The steam clears between us with a snap of a finger. Only one Za'skar Eajīz can do so, with their Spring of Heavens affinity.

'Underling.' The Sepāhbad looks faintly amused, eyes so close that I can see my expression in them, fighting despair from showing.

Tension suffuses the air like piled firewood begging for a spark. His wet cheeks are flushed from the steam, his black curls tousled from the humidity. In modesty, my gaze lowers. I suddenly realise it appears as if I am staring at his bare chest. Now, I lower my gaze to the floor.

'My vizier,' I force out. Does one bow their head even in a bathhouse half dressed?

He doesn't let me consider the question for long, releasing my waist and leaving without a backwards glance, his cloth brushing against me. I swallow the lump in my throat. He must think the seal is still with Adel.

He will not, I remind myself, *assume foul play.*

In the bathing chambers, Arezu and Yasaman are gone. I shove the seal through the gap in the partition, steam still thick. When the

Sepāhbad returns, he will assume the pendant had been beside Adel the entire time.

The celebration of midwinter arrives, my last day at Za'skar before my assignment in Ghaznia. In my pocket, the Sepāhbad's replicated seal threatens to burn a hole. I'd used the clay soap-mould to commission a replica in the bazaar with whatever savings I had from my measly stipend. Paranoid about the Sepāhbad's informants tagging me through the city if I went alone, I asked Yabghu to accompany me, pretending to repair my earring.

With tonight's celebration, there are no classes, for the winter night calls for prayer and charitable acts. In Sajamistan – unlike Azadniabad – this festivity symbolises the day where companions reflect on the darkness of night eating away the setting sunlight – like a twin of death – by speaking cautionary tales over the hearth to dispel jinn-folk lurking in the eve.

'Tonight there will be prolific shooting stars,' Yabghu tells our trifecta. 'Pray for a peaceful coming spring. The Heavens cause cosmic light to steal through the dusk, the death of darkness.' But like any celebration, the traditions supersede its intended purpose.

In the lemon and fig gardens behind the Great Library, warriors amass on red kilim rugs with ceramic bowls of ajil laid round with figs, dates and pomegranate paired with roasted nuts, and incense. Piping hot rose kahvah is poured into teacups and distributed.

It's the brink of sunset, and light scorches the courtyard like red scars. Warriors and scholars and pazktab students form trinities of groups; some read folkteller scrolls, others battle in poetic odes about the night, and many play saktab – the wind eating away the clamour of their voices. Adel spots me and waves with other Seven-Slash warriors.

But no one is able to resist the view of the evening, faces tilting heavenward where stardust streams like silver fire against the constellation of the Simorgh.

This eve is my only opportunity to infiltrate the intelligence chambers, while the officers are distracted by festivities.

In the meantime, I follow Katayoun and Aina as they grab saucers of kahvah while I pick up a board game from the Great Library. They intend to find a spot in the courtyard with Yabghu, Captain Madj and her trifectas. Cemil and I still do not speak, and shortly after throwing me a conflicted expression across the courtyard, he moves toward Dara and other Third-Slashes.

Before I could join the trifectas, I spot the Keeper of the Great Library at the bone-stone archway.

'I wonder if I will speak with you again after tonight,' he says while balancing manuscripts in one arm and holding a hookah pipe in the other, his ivory wings spreading across his back.

I bristle. 'I live in Za'skar. Of course you will speak with me again.'

He sniffs deeply. 'Lies. The smell is so potent from you.' The parî nearly bumps into a shelf jutting out, wheezing through another puff of hashish. 'Shall I reveal a secret?' he says, humming.

'I think the high of hashish is speaking, not you.'

His voice pitches low. 'Something awful cusps the horizon – a great new era. I have seen it.'

'This is definitely the hashish.' I frown. 'And are jinn not barred from soothsaying the future – from eavesdropping on Heavenly matters?'

'Live long enough and the cosmos becomes a series of repetitive patterns.' He yawns. Then he sobers, pinning me with a dark glare. 'I tell you this, *Azadnian*, because many jinn are attracted to your scent from the Unseen world, curious at your feelings in this city. Tread carefully: you veil yourself well, but even an impenetrable veil can be lifted.' He pauses before casting a wide smile. 'Consider my words a warning from the Unseen. My price is hashish.'

His chuckles scrape after me like a blade against stone. My hands turn over the board game, but at the sight of the gathered trifectas, my stomach twists.

I recede to the corner of the fig garden, the crowd of warriors thickening as they clink teacups. I'd forgotten these simple moments shared with kinsmen. Envy shudders through me as my chin rests on my knees. No-Name climbs up the mulberry trees and hangs upside down, smiling at something she finds humorous while sticking out her tongue. The last time I celebrated a festival was with my half-siblings before Warlord Akashun's invasion. I shouldn't be here.

'Is a game of saktab not better with a partner?'

At that voice, a pathetic lick of fear grips me – but I compact it like texts stacked on a shelf. When I fold on my heels, the Sepāhbad holds up a hand, the courtly raven on his shoulder as still as a bone-stone relief.

'At ease.'

'Peace of death be unto you,' I recite coolly.

'And you,' he replies.

The way he speaks is both sharp and soft. In our first encounter, I assumed the hint of warmth was a deceptive tactic, but here his voice reminds me of the monastery, of exchanging words in a gentle thrum between meditations. No wonder I thought him a monk; he speaks under a mask of peace. Seeing him here – unbeckoned – rattles the calm of midwinter.

'Well?' the Sepāhbad prods.

'I think so.'

His lips twitch. 'You think so.'

'My partner has not arrived.'

'And if I were to ask to be your partner?'

My thoughts slow. Our encounter at the bathhouse was unintentional. This, *here*, is not. Yet now he chooses to acknowledge me after all my time in his city? Not with a blade against my neck or in the amphitheatre, but in the open air as if we're companions? This catches me off guard.

'You are my Sepāhbad, you may ask of me anything.'

His hazel eyes, as beautiful as the gold sky, narrow. 'That may be, but we mortals like permission. It lets us feel like we engage as equals. Even if the outcome is the same, the decision is sweeter cloaked as a choice, yes?'

There is something to his words. I keep my expression clear, like wiping a salt tablet clean of engravings. 'Yes. Permission is an attractive concept.'

'Assuming honesty, then, underling, would you like to play me in saktab?' He smiles in such sudden charm that I frown, waiting for a condition. 'I assure you, there is no consequence if you refuse.'

Any game of strategy allows one to deconstruct an opponent's mind and discern their tactics. But it works the other way, too – both participants expose their stratagems.

'Say no,' No-Name hisses, but I cannot refuse.

To the Sepāhbad, I lie. 'I am not experienced in saktab.'

'I harbour no expectations.'

I wave at the lines of grain beneath the sandblasted board as wind rustles between us, my dark curls blowing across my face. 'Then I accept.'

He sits cross-legged, fingering the kilim.

'Marble or brass?' I ask. He spins a brass stone between his fingers. 'An agreeable choice, my vizier.'

The objective of saktab is to apprehend an opponent's strategy and anticipate their moves. For every push, there are a thousand paths; for every steal, a thousand captures. Saktab is a map of options, not only a path to triumph. And in our world of emperors, invaders and subjugators, it becomes a game of freedom and conquest.

'Do not stare long at the board,' No-Name snaps from my shoulder before she leans her head forward, parallel to me, studying the Sepāhbad coldly. 'He will read your intention.'

Strategies beat through my head like a chant.

'You may go first.' The Sepāhbad splays his hand toward the pieces.

I roll a marble between my fingers before placing it. Without hesitation, he drives his own. At every turn, we increase speed. We pause only twice, attempting to interpret strategies. The furore begins when I surround his first three pieces. In saktab, one must capture territory around the patterned grains of sand. He does not react when I place the marble on the outside of his net formation.

The Sepāhbad plays inside, instilling two separate interiors. The domain stops me from capturing his territory.

No-Name paces impatiently around us. The Sepāhbad bends low, studies my fingers grazing pieces before I set a screen. A bead of sweat trickles down my neck when the Sepāhbad places his brass away from liberty. Why, when he could have threatened to capture five of my squares?

On the left, he captures more, but I've the tact to stall on the right. I check his territory, finishing a conquer. I look up to see his gaze studying my face, perhaps to find a crack in the smooth surface, anything to give me away. I hope he enjoys trying.

His fingers drum the kilim like a warning. The board becomes muddier and the air shifts, the end nearing. All I must do is fake my final move.

A sudden light flashes the courtyard and warriors gasp, pointing up. My surroundings surrender to a glow of silver as if enclosed in smoke from a pipe, obscuring all but the spectacle above.

The sky blazes in the Simorgh's constellation. Celestials scorch through golden hour, the Sepāhbad's eyes reflecting the thousands of shooting stars streaking their wills like convictions yearning to be seen. For a moment, it's as if the sky is water to him – a thirsted man deprived of light and only able to drink his fill under the cosmic phenomenon. For that unnerving second, he reminds me of the shadows whirring in the corners of my vision.

His raven caws to Heaven, but the Sepāhbad no longer bothers to look to the sky, as if something in the board game intrigues him more. 'How ironic. The Simorgh and its nūr, in a shower of stars.'

I return to the board. 'Indeed.'

'In the scriptures, angels cause the running stars by dipping celestial rock in fire before throwing it across the cosmos against eavesdropping jinn.'

Now I look up coldly.

'Still, it's Heaven's beautiful light thwarting darkness.' And though he speaks of the skies, he stares at me.

'Then take the omen before you. The Simorgh and her nūr promise a new era.' I recite this like an ode but with none of the voice that should inspire it.

Then my fingers push a marble piece, cementing my loss in the game.

The Sepāhbad's thumb traces his brass before he switches tactics, shifting to the right. In my peripheral vision, his lips tease up.

'My vizier, you could have taken my territory.'

'And you, my lesser, could have connected around my last row of brass. It seems we both made incongruous errors.'

But a master tactician would never make an offhanded mistake like that.

Testing him, I leave an opening for capture, but he does not take it. I watch his expression as he leans forward, sliding another brass, before again, our gazes lock closer. This whole game, my strategy was to *seem* like I wanted to win, because naturally, it's what any opponent in a board game would expect. I stalled long enough, curious about his strategy in saktab. But this is the Sepāhbad that I face; trying to win would expose my tactics. All along, I have been staging my own loss.

If he realises it – well, the game would be concluded. Winning in saktab is not how you best the Sepāhbad; victory lies in throwing him off his own predictions. My brother once used this stratagem to prove a point to me, before his betrayal, saying he'd rather bite a loss to win the greater battle. It was working, but something has changed. There are three territories on the board, I realise.

I decide to speak plainly to provoke him. 'You wish to read something from our game.'

He does not so much as blink.

'You came here, regarded my gameboard and did not take my opening. I then left three as a test for you to have the win, and you rejected it.' As if to prove this, I take. Then his brass takes. I take. Three more moves and it becomes clear what has happened.

I inhale sharply. 'This is a loop.'

He does not look alarmed nor apologetic, which is worse. His answer echoes from afar. 'Pieces are sacrificed to set larger strategies in motion, because some concessions must be made to obtain the bigger victory. Victory for some is unpredictability. You sought to lose.' He smiles. 'As always, your masochism is breathtaking to witness.'

I blink twice. Somehow the Sepāhbad read my intent and contrived a stalemate by devising an infinite loop with no established winner.

We both straighten from the board. 'A stalemate, how good.'

Bemused, he stands. 'Flattery. It seems unlike you.'

I crunch the dirt, which stings beneath my nail beds. 'Sepāhbad, what did you require from me? I submit to my masters.'

The Sepāhbad only tosses his brass to the board, the stars dimming in his eyes. 'Shepherd girl, did we not establish an understanding? Having choice makes the difference. And, I think I have learnt what I wished to know.' He bows and retreats toward the inner courtyard.

Did he defeat me after all?

The question remains with me until the pazktab students arrive with the scholars. My eyes rake over their new garments, donated from some noblewomen. Red and emerald robes to their ankles, belted by amber hemp cords, the hems clinking with bone-shells, and hair woven with headdresses of animal bones. Sohrab wears a well-stitched robe over a dark tunic.

Yahya trips over his long crimson robe. I straighten it. 'You all look…' But there is no word to describe them because I have never used such words to describe anyone – the closest emotion that stirs is how I feel seeing fledgling birds. I think I would offend them if I called them baby buzzards.

After I arrange another saktab and explain the rules, Sohrab and I dive into a game.

'Master, I cannot play when you are so cruel! You are cheating.'

'There is no cheating, only clever travellers seeking the shortest paths.'

'Which parable did you find that from?' Arezu deadpans.

I look up. 'A text you clearly refused to study.'

'Dramatic woman,' she mutters and my lips twitch but I raise my hand to hide it.

'Snivelling pig,' I counter and Arezu clamps Yahya's ears.

'Khamilla.'

With a sigh, I move from the board while Sohrab shakes his head. 'It's tradition to join the other warriors and listen to their folktales.'

'And poetry,' Yasaman adds, holding up a stack of papyrus scrolls.

'You are free to join them,' I say. 'But I do not desire the other warriors' company.'

'Master can tell us a story.' Arezu's eyes alight in challenge.

'I have no stories for midwinter.'

'You liar,' she says. 'Don't forget what you told me after the Marka. You come from a tribe of them.' Then her eyes pinch bitterly. 'I suppose with your assignment tomorrow, your mind is on other things. In truth, it's hardly fair.'

'What's not fair?'

'We fought alongside you in that Marka, yet you were promoted.'

I almost laugh. 'Because you are a pazktab girl. You are not ranked.'

'So?' she demands. 'I'm only a few years younger than you. Your lessons always preached to *never let youth withhold our ambitions.*'

They did do that. I am realising much of my advice to these students follows a cosmic loop, coming back to bite me. 'You, child, are far from Za'skar's ordeals.' She flinches and I straighten, aware that my words carry weight.

Her bitterness stretches into a smile. 'I suppose to you we are never worthy, most of all me?' Her fingers dig into the kilim, nails pale. That confusion stirs again – *no* – a strangling inside my chest. It takes a moment to understand: Arezu is not upset; she is frustrated at something beyond her control. Because of me.

'Of course, I think you're worthy,' I say thickly. 'Just not of this.'

'And now you admit it.'

'What would you have me say?'

'You are leaving tomorrow,' she repeats, with the same expectation held in Sohrab's gaze, but where he looked hopeful, her eyes are red. My heart begins burning; the stab, like pricking needles, fractures through the denial I've built, giving way to the urge to tell her she is worth more. 'You are leaving,' she repeats again.

'I am leaving…'

You. It hits me. *What is this strange ache?*

Not a pain I have chosen or walked into, but unwanted pain. Invisible pain. The numb blanket that has cocooned my entire life, the reliable comfort I chose to slip under, was nothing but a cage at the border of agony.

This child, who I called my student for my own selfish purposes, is in pain and so are the rest of them and I continue to be blind to it. And I am not sure why, but tonight I *feel* it as keenly as she does. With it, an emotion I think everyone is familiar with, but to me so foreign – a deep worry, hoping to always guard them from harm. Like how one feels when they sight a wounded bird. But the emotions are stifling; how does one bear this many?

I could do something, then. I could do one thing right. I cannot discourage her hunger, it wouldn't work. Instead, I could mould it into something better. A pang squeezes my chest. Masters do not comfort their pupils like this.

Then who does?

'Your dream is to become a Za'skar warrior to help your village in Khor. But it requires true patience to rise in this city,' I finally answer. 'Clearly, that's a quality I lack, but you – I trust you to have that patience.'

'Trust.' Arezu is sceptical. 'You trust me?'

'Of course.'

A silence settles. Arezu opens her mouth several times but stops, as if afraid to break the odd peace we share, as if we both are obliged in our roles to constantly push and pull at each other. *Speak*, I will her.

'It feels strange not being in Khor tonight; our storytellers rivalled those on the Camel Road,' she finally says.

'No, they did not. Ours were—' I blurt and stop myself.

'You are doing that again.' She presses as if this is what she had hoped for. She shoves my arm. 'Don't you miss your tribe?'

I glance down, admitting, 'I hardly remember them.'

'One does not need to remember to miss someone. I hardly remember my own.'

Something clicks within me, as if the odd emotions untangle into fine threads. I do not recall much of Uma's tribe, but Arezu is right; at the mention of Tezmi'a, there is an ache there, deep inside, echoing a call.

I surprise myself by reaching out, tapping Arezu's chin up. 'When I miss home, I look to the sky.'

She blinks. 'That's odd. The sky is the sky.'

'Perhaps, but someone told me – someone who I no longer recall, but whose folktales have stayed with me, even as I fight against them; I think, in this moment, I am grateful I have them – she said there is comfort that the sky in its magical symmetry is shared by all, even home. The sky gilds the same sunrise, sunset and moon. The same constellations peeking slantwise against the black.'

'And you say you do not have stories,' Arezu answers in a sad sort of understanding. To my surprise, she leans her head against my shoulder. 'It's okay, master. Sometimes remembering those stories can be painful.'

My throat clogs. How does she know – how does this girl, years younger – know the pain in my heart before I speak? Why cannot I understand hers? Why am I so selfish?

She gives me one of those smiles, too small for a girl with so much life burning inside her. 'Tell a story,' she urges.

I am more than a master to them, even if unwilling. They give me titles I don't deserve, in foolish hope.

'Perhaps I know one tale,' I announce. 'My overseer said that stories carry us through the night's death to light.'

'I did say that,' Overseer Yabghu interrupts from behind me.

'She's going to tell a story,' Arezu tells him before I can stop her. My pazktab students run to gather other students, some who had been part of our squadron.

I prepare myself to do this. If I do not have my own kindnesses to share, I have the kindness of the dead who entrusted me with it.

Then my overseer is beckoning other warriors to hear the folktale: Katayoun, Aina, Dil-e-Jannah, Adam, Aizere and so many more until they are a sea of flesh. I see even Cemil, who does not sit but leans against the bramble, arms crossed, watching me silently. At the sight of him, fear rises up my throat, but I raise my hand and point at the circle.

In our duel, he spoke of what happened to his people, but he had never heard what happened to mine. This might be the first time any of these warriors have heard a tale coloured by Azadniabad.

From the corner of my eye, No-Name wears long monastic robes and gawks in reproach. 'You should not do this. Do not comfort the students or warriors. You do not need friends,' she warns. 'I am here, yet you do not rely on me – the one who has accompanied you in your loneliest moments, your entire life.'

But the homesickness rifling my chest tells me that my students give me peace. At this, No-Name covers her mouth as if that idea will make her vomit. 'Stop, please,' she begs and her form ripples, toppling off the tree. 'I-I cannot control who I can be…' Her voice disappears, body changing.

In her stead stands a young woman with watery grey eyes like weak milk-tea, a stern mouth and furred robes. I cannot place her name but her mouth opens, smirking. 'My apprentice,' she says.

I watch her as the crowd forms. My fingers stretch toward the constellation, ablaze in pink dew.

'Magicians are attracted to children; they hope to deceive them through their loneliness. But the tale I tell you tonight is one of companionship, one of comfort, to save you in this long night. Gather round and let me speak to you of the khan of nūr, the mighty Simorgh, who never flew below her abode, for she scoffed at mankind's greed to conquer. In this vast and strange world, let us pretend that all is well, war does not exist, our tribes huddle around a fire, and we are warm, and safe. Let us hold hope between us, and let me, master, and today, chief folkteller, speak of the healing firebird that saves us all.'

They lean forward in anticipation. My head pounds, my lips move, but they do not belong to me. I simply watch the woman of my past, shaped by No-Name, stealing her words:

'The Simorgh was a Bird King whose abode was the Heavenly Sea, in a tree which contained the seeds of all sustenance. Whenever the Simorgh flew to the tips of the Tree of Knowledge, one thousand branches snapped, and the seeds pattered into the water, nourishing our valley with plants, here and there, before it was destroyed by raids. The mystical bird raised the worthiest Eajīz warriors in secret, within her Mist Mountains, using her nūr – she was a Heavenly blessing at times of revolution. Her strength belongs to the ones who move from land to land; who walk with the wind and speak to the animals. She has watched the world burn thrice over. When the Tree of Knowledge she rested upon caught alight from the Divine's punishment, burning the universe and herself, she was reborn to tell the tale, living with an indestructible wisdom. As she witnessed Prophet Nuh's Great Flood, she let herself sink in its waters, reborn again to warn of its lessons.'

As I spin the tale, I look at the pazktab students, praying my words provide the companionship that my body cannot. I wonder, did my elders ever feel this sweetness? Was this why my tribe spoke stories by night? But why had Uma refused to tell a story? Had the stories lost their magick in a world that bent it for its own purposes? Had she forsaken the words because they held no more meaning after bitter life had had its way with her?

Or had she lacked the bravery to speak the words, to invoke their power? Words are a profound burden, and for the storyteller, words burn and reshape old truths into new truths. Words change reality. She could not ignore hers.

This knowledge carries me onward and the crowd listens keenly, watching the shifting cosmos etching lines against the black. My heart expands and contracts to their rhythm, finding relief in the bleak thought that humans are like the stars: a circulation of light, seemingly infinite but nothing more than a brief cosmic flash, leaving behind nothing but darkness.

When I finish the tale, there's a taut silence. By the time the crowd disperses, Yahya is asleep. I carry him in my shawl, the others stumbling sleepily to the pazktab communes. With the guard's approval, I follow them inside.

Bidding farewell, the hurt yawns into my heart, tired of existing. *These children are my firsts.* Of what... I cannot name just yet. The stubborn resistance to affection refuses to admit it. But know they are my firsts.

'Farewell, my nūr,' I whisper to them. 'I may be your master, but in truth I was your student, learning lessons that none but you could have taught me. Now I must return home.'

We are brought together by our shared ambitions but separated by them too. What I cannot confront is that I no longer know what home means – if it's a place or if it's this – this emotion evoked by them.

Arezu clutches my sleeve, a wide panic in her eyes but also an offering. 'Remember, we are your home.'

And you are mine, I wish to say, but I back away because I am used to every home I've had being destroyed; why not this, too?

29

When the last hour strikes before curfew, with most of the officers in the courtyards, I use my clearance to enter White-Pillar's briefing rooms, across from the Sepāhbad's intelligence chambers. In my satchel, I have only the bone-seal, some parchment, pen and ink.

Three soldiers cross the hall. When they turn their backs, it grants me three seconds. With two steps, I jab the imitated bone-seal into the circular space set in the door. It presses and clicks. I dart inside.

My back rests against the entrance door, waiting.

Silence.

Inside, palm-wood shelves are stacked with parchments; the balcony overlooks gardens and fountains, filigree balustrades obscuring the view. The room is wide, with other locked doors, and niches for texts. An intricate gold divan and a tea table with a copper teapot and fist-sized teacups are beside a warmly lit smokeless hearth. Beside the window hang tasselled tapestries. At the centre is a long floor-desk. Behind it, smooth ivory walls glow with embossed warrior paintings of Jinn Wars and scriptures. One catches my eye, of a raven with a claw against the clay, showing Adam's son how to bury the first corpse of mankind.

Smokeless firelight burns low from corner lanterns, shadows leering and lurching as I pass.

My lessons return: first, I note the dust; as long as the layer of motes on the desk remains the same as before I entered, the Sepāhbad will not suspect an infiltrator. Two, I must take care in sweeping the textured rugs, so they display the same directions of footprints as before. As long as I step with my heel to the left, no new footprint will appear. Three, I must not lose track of time; I have perhaps an hour.

I inspect the largest shelves near the balcony. My priority is developments in Ghaznia province and Izur and Arsduq along the Camel Road, because this intelligence is my empire's salvation. Parsing out thousands of parchments in a room holding revered intelligence is near impossible.

For the next half hour, I withdraw and scan scrolls, only the archived ones with broken seals. The papyruses are scribed in a mismatched code; it takes furious minutes to deduce the codes I am familiar with, but still I am unsure if I understand it. Several have a number script at the top, numbers I can rearrange. After a painstaking moment, I find scrolls allocated to Ghaznia province.

The first reveals troop developments along the valley, which I note; in another, my eyes catch on a transcribed exchange with a spy reporting on the disappearance of another informant in Dhab-e after receiving a spiritual cleanse from a local Azadnian monastery. My eyebrows furrow. From the third scroll, I learn Sajamistan's military is in correspondence with the eastern Zayguk region to obtain passage from the north-east front, into Izur, above Lake Xasha, in Tezmi'a. I nearly drop this scroll, cursing. Would Sajamistan intend to invade from both Ghaznia and the north-east, into Izur prefecture?

In the last scroll, my breath stutters. I find correspondence with a Qabl monk on jinn-poisons. The letter is short, vague and difficult to decode, but I make out a glyph of a huma feather and poison and the word for Ghaznia… *and Arsduq*. My brows knit as I lean closer.

'Soul contract,' I read aloud. Is this a jinn ritual? The symbols remind me of old sutras in the Qabl Order. But what would Arsduq prefecture have to do with a jinn ritual?

The main information I've obtained is on the north-east invasion and alliances — *this* is important for the Zahr clan's allies. After re-scribing the scrolls on my parchment, to memorise before burning them, I return the seals to their original order, blowing dust motes so it seems like nothing was disturbed.

When I am halfway across the room, the door clicks with a resounding echo. Time stretches in two drawn-out, impossible seconds.

As the entrance slides open, I lunge into the deep niche between the hearth and balcony, tucking into a ball behind the tapestry.

The Sepāhbad is here before curfew? Every fibre of me shakes with fear. *He will sense the water within my body with his affinity, he will wrench me from the wall before snapping my arms like branches.* By the Divine's blessing, the hearth is here; its smokeless energy might mask my own.

From my narrow view, I see the Sepāhbad enter, a courtly raven crouched on his shoulder, two scribes and Alif Adel at his heels. A gold cord trims the leader's black wool robe, flashing beneath the dim lanterns, his hair windblown. He silently hands the scribes a bundle of parchment before dismissing them. After sitting cross-legged behind a low-table, he dips his reed pen and methodologically inks a parchment before rolling it up and melting an Alif seal. He pushes back his unruly curls, flashing the pictogram on his left palm.

Alif Adel lifts the crook of the hearth, poking it into the low fire. 'Where is Yabghu's last report on the girl? If I'm to be on this assignment with her, I should read it.'

I frown at this. The Sepāhbad does not answer, simply flicks open a parchment and holds it out. A part of me has pondered why Yabghu, from the first day, was neutral – even at times kind – with me. It now seems obvious: he'd been tasked to report on me, the Azadnian. And I must not be the only Azadnian that the Sepāhbad gathers reports on.

Adel begins to read the parchment. 'I should warn you; I admire the girl's mind—'

'You have a family,' the Sepāhbad interjects drily.

'– but I have a feeling that you do not speak the full truth of her. You would take such a gamble of trust on this military assignment?'

The Sepāhbad's mouth curves wryly. 'When do I not? If what I assume is true, you would say my idea is one of a mad man.'

'Even you cannot predict one's actions like that.'

'My clan maintained a belief,' he says before switching in dialect. 'The path of the mule across the plateaus is not a path shaped by the primal instincts of hunger, but instead a great hand swirling the sea of creation, without a care for the consequence.'

My fear morphs into gutting shock. I know those words, that dialect and that verse from a proverb. My memory sails into the past. He said *his* clan but that would mean—

The Sepāhbad is from a nomadic Azadnian clan?

With renewed focus, I try to make sense of him. That proverb... it belongs to the nomadic tribes in the juncture between the Dawjad Khaganate in Izur and Tezmi'a; the very north of the Camel Road. The proverb, passed down for centuries, conveys that no choice is coincidental — every action is a piece within the great cosmic equation crafted by the Divine: the only designer.

Staring, I know in the deepest marrow of my bones that I am missing something. Something threading right before my eyes but too far to grasp. His words — it feels as if he was not speaking about the Divine at all.

With it, asperity rises, that he who is of Azadnian descent refuses Azadniabad. But how is he in Sajamistan? Does he descend from a clan in both?

After resealing the parchment, Adel bows and takes his leave.

A new fear reverberates through me. At any moment, in the quiet, the Sepāhbad will sense me.

'Having fun?' No-Name's voice is calm, but I startle, elbow glancing the wall.

The Sepāhbad's head snaps in my direction and his raven rises. My hands grasp wildly at No-Name. The shadows grow around us. *If only I could disappear like her.*

His eyes seem to pin me. He stares and stares. I open my mouth to say something, *anything*, to fill the horrific silence but—

No-Name clamps my lips. The shadows, *the darkness*, surge until I've melted into their black. I do not know how I command them — if I commanded them at all — or if it was No-Name's doing.

The darkness hides me. From the corner, the hearth folds into itself, a gentle core of red.

'I cannot maintain this for long. He cannot see or hear you either,' No-Name explains, arms around my neck. From his lack of reaction, she speaks the truth. A triumph thrills through my veins.

His eyes narrow and stray to the space between us. I follow them, unable to see what he can. Then his gaze flits upwards — to the corners of the room — and he mouths something before blowing against his fingertips in the direction of the hearth. It must be remembrance to thwart jinn.

The Sepāhbad stands and comes forward; I, too, creep toward him, until we are face to face. But he takes another step, then another, and another, and instinctually I back away as each foot of his scuffs my own, until I hit the half-opened balcony doors. His hand reaches out to my face, astonishingly close, but in the reflection of his eyes, I do not see myself. His hand curls, simply passing through me, yanking shut the balcony doors. My soul chills like the frost of black winter as his finger briefly touches my face.

After stepping back, his head cocks down to the raven curled against his collar. 'O, Rasha, speak of what you see.'

It can speak? The raven stares forward – through me – with the bereft stillness of death. 'Darkness, master,' it rasps.

At that, the warrior smiles with no humour and sighs out, tired. 'Like always, creature of the grave.' His finger grazes its feathered ebony head in one firm stroke. 'It might never leave.' The raven and Sepāhbad exchange a silent look. Then: 'I must forgo you, old friend,' he says, low, to the bird. 'Forgive me. We will meet again, soon, in the forsaken lands. Where you mourn.'

The Sepāhbad draws straight and his eyes narrow upon me once more, but he merely shakes his head. He blows out the lanterns, snuffs the hearth with a swift snap and departs.

'How have you made me disappear?' I ask No-Name.

'Everything I do is your will. We are one.' She vanishes with a secretive smile and a terrible feeling comes over me.

30

Ghaznia–Arsduq Borderlands, Sajamistan Empire

The terrible feeling follows me over the next six weeks, in the time it takes for the assigned informants, including Adel and me, to travel to the Ghaznian borderlands as labour miners in the Dhab-e encampment. Throughout this time – following river bends at the mountain bluffs, crawling into hollow pockets where streams level out, depositing jade and gold dust – we exchange coded interactions, even when nothing notable transpires. That is, until the third week, when three of the workers are transferred north without a word.

But Adel is unconcerned as we walk through shrubs. 'We are close. Be on the lookout; we will be next.'

'How do you know?'

He frowns. 'Dhab-e would transfer miners with no clan affiliations, no family. Why not us?'

I pause at that. If he is correct, we would be transferred across the borderland. I should be eager; I will be close enough to defect. But there is no relief in this outcome, only the cold truth that I am ascending upward in hope that my clan triumphs.

'Is something the matter?' Adel must read my hesitancy.

I glance at him, and the bitterness swells because he is one of the Sepāhbad's right-hands. The vizier they serve is also Azadnian, as Azadnian as me.

Or is he neither Sajamistani nor Azadnian, but wholly an identity of a borderland, one carved into this continent, rejecting the loyalties forced upon him? It had never occurred to me that such freedom could exist. He is everything that I can never hope to be. He has escaped the bonds of his identity, has he not?

'Nothing is the matter,' I answer.

After all, everything is as it should be.

Adel's prediction comes to fruition when, the next evening, my mining overseer informs me I will be transferred north with a small group of workers, past the border. My hands slicken in anticipation – I would be in Azadniabad, able to defect to Arsduq.

But that evening, our caravan rests for the night at a local monastery, near the mining village bordering the valley between Arsduq and Ghaznia.

'No one is permitted inside before blood-cupping,' an apprentice announces to the caravan. This is common in the mountains, to cleanse non-locals of the evil eye and lingering jinn. During evening prayers, an apprentice of the monastery sniffs around the labourers. At many, she shakes her head. Eventually, she reaches me.

'Come now, sister,' she orders. 'It's your group's turn for blessings.'

A question forms on my tongue, but curiosity wins instead. I've little choice but to have her take me through the clay-rammed tunnels, under the monastery, with two other labourers. As we billow through the deep labyrinth, my ears ring. Not from sounds… but from the lack thereof. My feet slow. My chest tightens as if my soul is convulsing behind my ribs.

'Sister?' the apprentice reproaches. Behind her, my eyes skim over veneers carved into the clay walls. Inverted three-pronged pictograms that I can hardly make out in the dimness, other carvings of figures around a distorted crane.

At the end of the tunnel, the apprentice presses her hand against a carved triangular red seal that somehow appears familiar. To my surprise, it shifts, the bedrock trembling, revealing more tunnels leading to partitioned cavities beneath the monastery.

The other two labourers are each left in a chamber before I am taken to my own room, which is barren except for the ceramic domes used for blood-cupping, a small cot and torchlights. Inside, there is another woman who introduces herself as Farzaneh. Strangely, both women wear teal scholarly robes with a mustard cord around their waists – a dark pictogram inked on their hands indicates their stature. Not what I expect of monastic clothes.

At my hesitation, Farzaneh places a hand on my shoulder. 'Behave.'

The way she speaks is wrong, and she wears a mask of indifference as she inspects me, her gaze sweeping over me like I am an animal, a thing. 'Now strip.' She nods coolly toward the corner. 'Clothes go there. Then we will begin.'

When I am bare, she circles me while scribing on her salt tablet. She prods my naked skin with a leathery finger. I begin counting in my head, up by fives, then down by twos.

She lifts my tongue. She pokes at my breasts, the rings of my hair, my spine. She pauses at the threading on my arms.

Then she lowers to my genitals, and I yelp. 'What kind of blood-cupping is this?'

Her eyes flash. 'Dhab-e is your coin, and you serve them. They work under the Great Father. Obey. We could make this difficult or easy. You choose.'

I want to hurt her. The thought is so sudden and violent, my breath hisses through clenched teeth. She moves to my feet and lifts a needle and spool of thread with the ceramic cup.

I feel a prick from the needle and thread in her hand. My eyes flit down. My foot is red from the cupping. Below my ankle is a strange triangular pictogram from the threading. I flinch back, wondering what I've got myself into. I only needed to reach the borderlands to defect—

My vision blurs, pain reverberating up my feet.

Her words are softly uttered but fill me with the kind of fear before an arrow thuds into its target: 'By the Great Father, young one, I am only following orders.'

I awake to rope around my wrists. The panic wells. From my position on a cot, I spot a low-table below me, holding a copper cup swishing with crimson liquid. On me is a thin, rough wool tunic. My head cranes, taking in the new chamber. We must be further underground, for the cavern is laden with wet dirt, the protruding bedrock etched with hieroglyphs across its jagged face. One emblem is stark: an inverted triangle seal glowing red, like the one on my foot, with the glyphs of a corporeal heart, eyes and body.

The soul.

There are many carvings; others show figures prostrating to horned creatures. One cuneiform shape is difficult to read, for it's inscribed backwards – completely inverted in its lines. Shadows bend at the corners of the chamber, and an odd wind fills the air – almost like an edifice of the Unseen, where the Veil has peeled away from the physical world.

I look down at coasters of incense aligned in triangular patterns along the cavern floor, but its perfume is choking, none of the comfort of monasteries. My soul tingles, the bonds etched within me thinned.

'She's awake.' A voice breaks through my fear. I jerk up to see two robed women standing at the entrance.

My lungs contract. This feels – *unholy*. I've only seen these triangles in the annals about the Jazatāh tribes.

'What are you doing to me?' My voice wheezes, arms shaking to budge the rope.

'Hush.' Now it is Farzaneh from behind me. She leans in and cups my jaw, as if meaning to soothe me. She's spoken in a southern Azadnian dialect. In what cruel blessing must it come from her lips? I tug again at the bonds.

She carries on with a thread and needle, poking above my chest. 'As the Jazatāh said, some of us exist for sacrifice by the universe. And today,' her brown eyes twinkle, 'our potential will blossom once more because of sacrifices like you. I give my thanks, barbarian.'

'Sacrifice?' I still, even with the frantic pull within me.

She says some kind of incantation before lifting a vessel of dark liquid. It smells… *familiar*. It writhes like it's alive. A needle gleams in her other hand, wicked in the torchlight.

My eyes shut and I release my meditations. Weakened as they are by the unholiness around me, still they work. My forearm bonds contract against the rope.

At once, compressed nūr cuts the bindings like a blade of divinity. My toes crack, a wire of nūr shooting outward. The force cracks one's neck. The second is delayed in unsheathing her blade as, in rivulets, the dense light drips on to her, bursting her flesh into oozing pink-yellow pustules. When she swings, I leap from the cot, arms locking around her neck until the vessels in her eyes bulge red and burst.

Horror shudders through me at the grim knowledge that I have *killed* someone after so long. I have killed two people so quickly.

Pain rips across my shoulder, Farzaneh's knife slashing down. My elbow rears into her fragile jugular and she loses her balance, screaming. I stomp on her left wrist, snapping it perpendicular until white bone juts out. Wrenching her collar, I stuff her robes into her mouth as another cry erupts.

'Now,' I begin, wiping my blood-stricken cheeks, hoping she does not notice my quivering hands, 'You will answer my questions.'

She continues mewling. With no choice, I take the nearest coaster and smash it like a stone on each of her knees, crushing the bones. She shrieks and shrieks into the cloth, face boiling red.

'You have one chance to respond. What is this place?'

I expect fear, panic, anything but the slow hope that bleeds into Farzaneh's eyes – the realisation that she has information I want. I loosen the cloth from her tongue.

'Y-you must speak to i-it,' she wheezes out.

'Who?' But her mouth spasms. So my fingers grip her chin until white blotches appear. 'You assume your life matters to your Great Father after letting me escape my bindings? You think your masters do not already look down their noses at you, like you are anything but a pawn? Why else are you here, probing at naked flesh and smelling filth?' I lean nose to nose. 'Wearing rich robes, yet living in poverty of the acknowledgement you seek. The only reason I don't have a knife to your neck is because you are replaceable. They will always treat subordinates like us as dirt.'

Her mouth opens, a fish gasping in air. Garbled words come out that I cannot understand. The skin around her face stretches, the muscles twitching as if…

I rip the knife from my shoulder and press it against her throat. '*What are you? You are possessed!*'

Her nose lifts and her eyes flicker black as she rasps, 'I smell it in your blood.' But her intonation has changed – younger with curiosity. 'How do our poisons run through your soul?' Her gaze darts to the copper vessel.

And the familiarity clicks. The blade falters. 'Jinn-poisons… this vessel has a jinn-poison. And you are a jinn speaking to me.'

Farzaneh's chest thrums with a contained laugh, her gaze running up and down my body. This must be a young one possessing Farzaneh's body. No-Name glances at me. 'The jinn is perhaps only a century old. A child. Curious and eager. We can pull information from her.'

I face Farzaneh again. 'Only the Zahr clan used jinn-poisons.'

She starts to struggle again, huge-eyed, jinn and human competing for control inside her. 'N-not anymore. For so long we have been servants, kissing the continent's feet. Mitra will change the paradigm through its magick. Can you blame us for making something powerful in a world that spits at us?'

The word *Mitra* tickles my mind… where have I heard this before?

She steadies, the jinn seemingly in control. 'How strange… you have his scent,' she murmurs. 'Akashun's scent.'

My head spins. 'You said magick. Black magick is forbidden.'

Quick as thunder, her face contorts as she growls, 'You Eajīz are narrow-minded, stranded by your arrogance. You believe in Heavenly powers when the jinn-folk's magick is untapped potential waiting to be exploited. Sajamistan will no longer have the forces of the Unseen. We have formed Mitra.'

'I don't understand—'

'To permanently transit jinn souls from the Unseen to the mortal world requires a bond of magick. That is Mitra.'

Disgust beats against me. The Jazatāh tribes, who once conquered this continent, harvested black magick and committed infanticide for ancient jinn masters.

'Black magick cannot be done without steep costs – sacrifices.'

She laughs. 'Of course, but that's power. To gain the knowledge of Mitra from an ancient jinn master, the wielder must sacrifice the heart of a soul.'

'Soul?'

'A nameless soul. They must sacrifice the heart of the soul of their *heir*. Then the wielder will gain the knowledge to form Mitra bonds. After that, it requires more sacrifices of other human souls to many jinn-folk. Making Mitra bonds requires years of contracts with the Unseen: the blood of humans is resistant to jinn-poisons; and it requires possession of human hosts to allow the jinn and soul to begin merging.' Even buried in the depths of her fanaticism, she acknowledges the high price.

My head pounds. 'The Zahr clan ruled for centuries with the support of the monks. How could they possibly accept and wield Mitra? It's against the creed of our empire!'

Her broken hand twitches and spasms, as she cackles, spittle forming at the corners of her mouth. 'Foolish girl. The Zahr emperor *began* developing Mitra with his clansmen. In exchange, the jinn master demanded the blood of the original sacrificed soul. But the emperor fell before the exchange could be completed. Akashun ingested the blood of the original soul, to form a bond with it. Then he completed the exchange, to become the true wielder of Mitra, before the fallen emperor had the chance to. A small circle of the emperor's monks colluded with Akashun, to wield its magick—'

My knees buckle as my mind returns to the past.

No-Name watches on, curious. 'Do you remember now, how your Older Brother was a spy? He was used and manipulated to inform Akashun about your father's jinn-poisons, about your building blood resistance to it – even collecting your blood for Akashun, creating the weapon. And what of the possessed woman fleeing the monastery? Your father used many powerful souls like hers to develop blood resistant to the jinn-poisons, and then fed it to the jinn master of Mitra.'

'—the Jazatāh tribes sacrificed many such nameless infants. When their souls were sold to the Unseen, the bodies became soulless,' Farzaneh finishes.

'Which soul did the Zahr emperor originally sacrifice?' I demand of both of them.

No-Name settles against the wall, her feet resting on the corpses. I catch the sick gleam in her eyes. 'Oh, you know the answer.'

'And why must the soul of the sacrifice be resistant to jinn-poisons…' My frail voice trails.

No-Name's leer is a blade's edge. 'Think about your childhood. Jinn-poisons make up the elements of different jinn-folk. You trained to become resistant to many creatures in the Unseen – serpents, ghûls, bulls, winged jinn – nearly all of them. Through this exchange, your resistant blood was given to the jinn master, who used it to send jinn-folk across the Veil into the human world. Akashun, being the sole Mitra wielder, is then able to bond and control the jinn to more human hosts.'

She does not describe a power in the hierarchy of seventy-seven affinities, but instead pure magick – lawless, unbound. We are taught that if an Eajīz draws colossal power while breaking their Heavenly Contract, they will face the repercussions. And when mere mortals use black magick, even their appearances wilt.

Akashun should have gone mad for using black magick. But he is alive, for the souls that were sacrificed are facing its repercussions – not him.

I gesture at the inscriptions around the cavern, seething. 'Why are you using the peoples of the borderlands?'

Still, Farzaneh's mask of calm is impenetrable. I want to dig my nails into her flesh, force her to lash back if only to prove that she is still partly human, capable of human responses.

Farzaneh chuckles, a mix of the jinn speaking. 'You mortals are so simple-minded. These sacrifices are being used for a noble purpose. Our Great Father Akashun is the first since the Jazatāh to have such a bond with the Unseen.'

She leans into my knife, mocking. 'It's a new era. The jinn of the oldest pre-Adam civilisations moved at the speed of cosmic light. Jinn can lift a thousand men, leap to the mountains, hear from thousands of paces away. But our weakness is our intellect; we cannot read nor write, though our elders' knowledge is vast from travels to the Heavens. For humans, this is a true blessing, for the jinn-folk would rule the cosmos and enslave man like infants. There are many: ifrit, dîv, ghûls – and shai'tain, the cruellest jinn – eager to cross the Veil. Because unlike humans, jinn have no permanent material body. With Mitra, the human becomes a shell for jinn to possess, their wills controlled by Akashun. This is a type of permanent jinn-catching. And it bestows upon the host *the strength of a jinn.*'

'The strength of a jinn,' I repeat numbly.

'Sajamistan may have the power of Za'skar, but against all of the Unseen, it is *nothing.*'

My ears begin buzzing. 'And their people?'

Farzaneh shrugs. She is proud. 'These are not people.'

I blink twice, her statement a strange echo. *Who speaks like this?* Like they harbour no identity, each person a mere limb of a greater political body. But I recognise this Azadniabad, where lives are meaningless as long as they serve the emperor. Where tribes are insignificant, and only the esteemed ruling clan is Divine.

A hand caresses my hair. 'You fool.' No-Name tuts her tongue right into my ear. 'You poor, hypocritical fool.'

At the same time, Farzaneh says, 'Other tribal confederations exist across the continent. Borders are being created; trade is flourishing. The Camel Road will always be prized, and others will salivate at the chance to sink their teeth into it.'

'Mitra is not a solution,' I hiss.

She covers the horror with cold logic as if that makes the reality better. 'Why should Azadniabad not line its own pockets using the vast realm within its reach? If we do not, we are doomed. A plunged economy is a womb for revolution.'

I think about Zahr rule: the slow raids from Sajamistan that poisoned our borderlands until our winter capital fell into their hands.

How else did Sajamistan grow after the Jazatāh tribes were overthrown as conquerors? The ruling clan used the domain of the Heavenly Birds: Za'skar. They attracted merchants, scholarship, kick-starting a shift from cold, barren feudalism toward civilisation, motivating people to move the wagon wheels of an economy.

As if reading my thoughts, Farzaneh adds, 'But you see, Mitra does more than produce an army, it's a *trade*. Eventually, we'll be able to trade and cipher a weaker version of both the knowledge of Mitra and its bonds to the other kingdoms, using the weakest jinn, durable and good enough. Even Sajamistan will have to forgo their limitations on the Unseen world. They will adapt; like the jinn, they will realise Eajīz are no longer all-powerful. With time the corporeal body will adjust where human souls coexist with jinn-folk. Power works that way – you give rulers a lick, they're satiated for a bit. When they start to agitate, crank a little more, until temptation overrides their restraint.'

I am too horrified to form a response. She is right. Any kingdom would salivate to seize a weapon of mass destruction, would they not?

'Business is where war begins, and business is where it ends.' Farzaneh grins. 'That's hard work. For Azadniabad to grow, Mitra will secure our stakes in the Camel Road, beginning with coercing the steppe-tribes to concede to Azadniabad, or they risk their youngest becoming Mitra hosts.'

'But…' My voice drains, pale like my thoughts.

For any source of labour with costs as high as Mitra, the empire must create depravity – must make the conditions of the borderlands so impoverished that the tribes have no choice but to accept Akashun's rule.

I imagine what it is like for a tribe like Uma's in the Camel Road – they raid us, they kill us, they burn the steppes and pastures, they destroy our subsistence and demolish our tribes and rape our lands. They create our poverty. And then they swoop in, declaring they will save us.

Mitra would simply magnify this. It vexes me. If Azadniabad controls the supply of Mitra, Warlord Akashun has a monopoly. It forces kingdoms to trade, because any two entities in a mutually beneficial relationship are bound to engage in concessions with each other. Things become symmetrical again, and against the rest of the cold, barren world, Azadniabad has *something*. The same way Sajamistan secured control over Eajīz.

But a thought pushes back. *Akashun used innocents.*

The natural order of creation is this – neither creature can become the other: human cannot be jinn and jinn cannot be human. Warlord Akashun is fracturing that reality. We would become no better than the Jazatāh.

Suddenly, Farzaneh spreads her good hand and takes my fingers gripping the knife, pressing it against her chest. She begins smashing her fist against it. Again and again, the crunch of bones unmistakable.

'*What are you doing?*' I say, yanking the blade out of her reach.

She smiles coldly, the abandoned coils of a woman cemented in her beliefs. Her eyes grow black, the jinn seizing control. 'What will you do? Put this woman out of her misery? She was going to die by your hands anyway. This mortal body is now unfit for me.'

Her teeth tremble in her gums, and one by one, begin clattering out. Like marble ingots. In her eyes, the pupils disappear. The knobs roll out of her skull.

Thud, thud, thud, wet rolling balls. I reel back, hitting the cavern wall. My gaze catches on a scar bisecting the skin below her collar.

Eyeless with two bloodied sockets, she cackles, 'Kill her.' Then her voice raises, straining. 'Kill me. *I want you to kill me.*'

I plunge my knife into her, so deep that my fingers slip into the bloodied hole.

The pain strikes me as if I'm stabbing myself – the oath to my clan once my conviction but now like my bird cage: *Forged by blood, bound by duty, I offer my soul by the white blade.*

'Such loyalty,' No-Name murmurs. 'Such beautiful loyalty.'

31

Outside of the chamber, I step into a corridor of bedrock below this strange edifice that they abuse as a monastery. Cavities stretch on either side of the cavern, long and uneven, descending into a rocky spiral, the bottom impossible to grasp in endless darkness. A stench wafts in the air. Rotted and bitter. I taste blood, as potent as if sticking out my tongue would coat it crimson.

The tunnels branch into chambers that appear to be praying rooms, with shuttered partitions and the slightest flickers of incense. There must be apprentices from the monastery inside. My bonds tingle, as if this place is carved from the bindings of time. From the blasphemous magick, I can hardly summon my affinity.

Quietly, I decide to investigate further, where the copper lanterns above provide the barest light. Where there is no torchlight must mean there are no apprentices. At the first row of chambers, I pause.

'Go in,' No-Name prompts me.

But the partition does not budge. I see an inverted triangular seal on the bedrock and press my hand against it. A sharp prick against my finger. I realise the seal stabbed it to draw blood. Aglow, the bedrock shudders and opens like a mouth.

Inside the chamber are more coasters in the triangular pattern, friezes etched against bedrock and… naked sleeping bodies. Three women, with sooty scars roving their necks. I step closer. Between their breasts, flaps of skin reveal dark cavities, empty of hearts. Inside each ribbed carcass, strings of black-threading form inverted cuneiforms with the symbols for the heart, ruh and corporeal body. I fight a gag.

A thread hews through the torsos, tying them together. I follow the string to the centre of the incense, seeing a trifecta of heart organs crinkled in a dark liquid. This must be a type of jinn-catching to begin the Mitra bond.

The next chamber reveals what can only be more Mitra rituals – men and women with strings seaming together empty chests with their hearts in a platter; in another I find mouths stitched up, with tongues snipped out and submerged in blood and jinn-poison. I recall monks teaching us how the ruh is manifested in the heart, eyes and tongue, but I'd never imagined it like this.

In the fifth chamber, I choke at the size of the bodies. Smaller. These boys could not have been more than ten years old. I imagine Farzaneh chuckling, saying the youngest souls are the purest – the easiest to tame for a jinn.

My hand lifts. Black gaping holes for eyes, and inside the sockets, thread stitches the cavities in a stringy mangle. The incongruity makes me stumble back. My hands drop and I lean over my knees, dry-heaving.

I go further down the maze, seeing men, women – *and children* – as still as corpses, but somehow in-between life and death, like black magick has withered their skin; there seem to be thousands.

The sheer number of bodies informs me that these are not merely labourers. How many tribes were raided in Sajamistan?

If war lacks a clear enemy, then what war am I fighting?

I begin rushing into more rooms. I see skin stripped off chests; some still with hearts, the raw, pink muscle thudding from an ebbing heartbeat. The deeper I descend in the bowels of the mountain, the more mutated I find the bodies. I see one with a tail; another with a stem at its spine as if to sprout wings – the soul between jinn-folk and man entwined.

The worst I find is a small crate, with a woman laid beside it, hands folded upon her womb. No-Name peers into it.

Two babes with horns curling out of their heads. How many women were forced into impregnation through Mitra?

I find that I am unable to look away; there is something mesmerising about the grotesqueness. One would not think any of them alive, but the smell of human blood and piss indicates otherwise. Or perhaps the quiet pain from those bodies is the most undeniably human thing left.

Who is foe and friend? Sajamistan? Azadniabad?

If I think too hard about why this exists, the meaning of what Azadniabad is doing, I will combust. Making myself see is the only way to keep my insides quiet, keep my thoughts to a whisper instead of a scream.

I ask myself questions, too. My hands trail a long black string.

How old was this body? Fifteen? Perhaps.

Which jinn creature is this? I do not know.

How much do you think they screamed? How long do you think it took for them to degrade as a jinn slowly possessed—

I can take it no longer. Trembling, I climb upwards, toward my original chamber.

Until I hear a clamour of voices coming from the brightest glow of torchlights. I lean around the partition, making out the glint of iron gates at the far end. There's a distinct smell of smoke.

I see scholars emerge through the open slit.

'– no, seven souls cannot contain a falak…'

I still. A falak? The great serpent of the Unseen?

My mind whirls. Perhaps to its scholars, this is the paragon of invention. My hands clamp over my ears.

'Your emperor was quite a clever man,' No-Name comments, oddly pleasant. 'You never once wondered why he had you test jinn-poisons?'

The part of me that is horrified clashes with the part that longs for assurance. My nails scratch into my right palm until the pain erases the rebellion in my mind, the one that will incite the emperor's anger, the one that will make him demonstrate to me that pain equals obedience.

He has hurt you; he has always hurt you.

'Face it,' No-Name says. 'You are a Farzaneh. You would be accepting orders without a care under your clan. In the hands of a tyrant, many become monsters.'

My knees lock. And then I retch. As I heave yellow liquid, her words prod more.

Studying the bodies is like gazing at my own mistakes. *How could humans be capable of this?* But a scarier revelation strikes me. *If I'd never left Azadniabad, would I accept this, too?*

Memories flash behind my eyes, ones that never gained purchase on my consciousness until now.

The night of the raids, morality did not matter, age did not matter. What mattered was victory, which the enemy would achieve by any means. Tribesmen were tortured and discarded. Rape was an act to bestow shame, as deftly as a dagger strike. Sajamistani tribes left us half alive or snatched, not out of mercy but as punishment. Our scars were a haunting reminder so we would die inside as we continued to live.

My eyes burn. 'The emperor could not have…'

No-Name shakes my shoulders. 'He sacrificed you. He called you wanderers – *barbarians*. He ordered you to forget your maternal tribe. *Think*. Which soul are they speaking of… which soul was sacrificed for Mitra.'

The air rushes from my lungs.

'Your uma was insignificant to the emperor, so you were left as a nameless heir. That was the exchange your father made to commune with the ancient jinn master, to obtain the knowledge of Mitra. And even in Azadniabad, when he learnt that you are an Eajīz, he threw you into jinn-poisons to progress Mitra. It's your resistant blood your father needed to access different jinn creatures. The same blood that Eliyas collected in your training and gave to Warlord Akashun, to ingest. When the emperor died, Akashun completed the exchange with the jinn master, to send creatures across the Veil for his Mitra bonds.'

'The Zahr emperor sacrificed me…' My voice breaks as I glance down at myself. But my soul is here, is it not?

I flee back into the room where Farzaneh's corpse lies, huddling next to bloodied teeth and eyes. It's better than seeing the broken bodies down there.

I face No-Name. 'What you speak of cannot be true. It makes my work for *nothing*. Who will give me orders? I always follow the clan!'

'The emperor is dead.'

'*No.*' I shove her to the wall until we are nose to nose. The anger, it flashes as keenly as the night of my parents' deaths. 'He's not dead. He's in me. *He has always been in me!*'

'Pathetic slave,' she sneers, 'the fear you feel is your own. He cannot punish you. *He is dead*. He was no noble emperor. Your Older Brother warned you.'

Is that why Eliyas turned against us, leaving the shelter of the clan's lies? I think about the girl I became. She was willing to kill for her emperor because she'd been taught to look at her opponents and glimpse only empty monsters. She had followed orders. She'd had purpose. She unabashedly liked her purpose. She was one amongst an empire of many. She was me. I'm terrified that I liked it.

No-Name continues. 'Powerful rulers can topple. And the emperor has.'

'Because he was *murdered*.'

No-Name frowns. 'Khamilla, you have a habit of creating things that are not there and removing things that are. You made yourself forget Babshah Khatun, the khan, your milk-siblings – even Eliyas, after your brother became a traitor to you. Haven't you ever wondered what other horrors you've forgotten?'

'Do not say their names,' I beg of her, but she carries on ruthlessly.

'If you had the chance to see the emperor in the flesh, *the true emperor*, would you?' No-Name asks.

My head throbs, the skeins where the soul meets the heart of the mind aching. I take laborious breaths as if Qabl monks guide me. Darkness swirls at the edge of my vision and, like parchment, I tear it from its corner.

My eyes open. No-Name merges into the countenance of the emperor: his sharp, handsome, but cold face. My father leans close, thumb caressing my chin. 'Little bird,' he greets me.

A whimper escapes me. Suddenly, I am a child again before her dada. A dada she misses. A dada she loves dearly.

'Dada,' I echo but the honorific tastes wrong. 'You are alive. You are here.'

He looks powerful. Exactly as I remember him. But then his thumb presses harder and harder. Sharp pain reverberates beneath my jaw.

'You are hurting me,' I whisper.

'Should I not return what you dealt me?' He bows his head. 'Tell me, who killed me?'

A mental test. 'Sajamistan,' I answer.

His image wavers in the chamber. 'You are wrong. But when are you not? You forget things, even when your hands are coated in blood. You time-blank to protect your coward self.'

My feet stumble back.

He nudges closer. 'Try again.'

My skin burns. 'Do not say anything,' I plead. *'Please.'*

'I speak as I will. I accepted your uma into my empire. I raised you from nomadic barbaric stature to nobility. I fed you with my hands. I trained you. And you repaid me with blood.' My eyes flicker shut. The emperor yanks my collar to meet his dark expression, wielding a vendetta that death cannot cheat. 'My *daughter* killed me. Say, *I killed the emperor*. I did not teach you to kill in shame, I taught you to kill with pride.'

And the words burst from me.

'I killed you.'

The admission settles like dust. I killed my own father.

My knees drop to the ground beside Farzaneh's corpse. And the memory jumbles out like a ghoulish lesion, skin torn, inviting infection.

It has always been the emperor lurking in the depths of my thoughts, judging my actions. Hissing at me to obey. The night of Eliyas's execution and then Warlord Akashun's invasion with Sajamistani forces, I remember now.

Uma had been surrounded by the Sepāhbad's soldiers while the capital descended into chaos. On the hill, I shoved the emperor away to reach Uma. And I did it again. I was angry. I felt it in the way my hands shook, the way my blood boiled, my head pounded. But I was not in control. I released slivers of nūr, piercing his flesh against the tree, and turned away. I had wounded him. I hardly realised that I killed him.

My anger bested the control of my affinity; anger at a man who let a daughter's mother die for his ambitions. At a man who executed her brother in a breath. At a man who used me night and day.

'It was a mistake!' I cry to him. 'I was angry. *So angry.* But you made me like this. You never permitted me to feel anything. You despised my emotions!'

The emperor crouches. 'You hated me. And now I hate you. Tell me what you did.'

'I killed you like Sajamistan. I did not avenge you.'

The emperor grips my throat and tightens his fingers. I could stop this – after all, it's by my command that No-Name is the emperor. But if I can choose anything, it's my own punishment. This is what I most deserve.

'You never hated it. You wanted me to order you. You had no home and wished for my clan,' he continues against my ear.

I wish to say no but that is another lie. He owns me. I like that he does because the not knowing of who would own me instead seems infinitely worse. If I escape him, who will swoop in and chain me next? The emperor is the poison that I choose, rather than handing my fate to another. The time-blanks are my checks and balances. The notion is morbidly laughable; the schisms in my mind are my own creation. I deflect memories. I erase them from existence. And why not? It's better to divide the brutality of my memories – the happiness, the urge to cry, the sadness – rather than feel everything at once. It's better to dam the memories than endanger myself with a flood of emotions.

My mind is my own gameboard, the planes a conquered domain. Here no one commands me. Not even my father. Only I can.

No-Name returns to herself.

'The emperor never hurt me.' The words lodge in my throat. 'When did he hurt me? Prove it.'

No-Name snatches my arm. 'He created Mitra from you. He hurt you when you failed your poison tests. But you loved it because it meant your father held a stake in you and some acknowledgement was better than none.' She throws my arm back down.

'Who cares if he hurt me!' The confession tears from my throat. 'Pain, everyone feels it, it's normal. The ones who complain of it, *they are weak*. It was discipline.'

'No. The emperor made you nameless. Until he discovered, that out of all his children, you were the only Eajīz, and to his embarrassment, bred from nomads.'

Nomads. Suddenly, I am no longer with No-Name. Memories bombard my mind.

I am in a green gorge with the ones I'd made myself forget.

In this makeshift memory, I walk into a yurt. My lips shape their names as I kneel before the hearth. Beside me, Usur Khan snips a gold thread dipped in amber dye and mare milk. Then *she* enters like a gall of wind – Babshah Khatun – yanking on my freshly threaded, bloodied arm. She guides me outside before the tribesmen. *The girl who felled a karkadann with her tongue and an arrow at the age of seven, it is she who will carry with her the tales of your greatest joys and fears until the end of her days. She is your entrustment.*

But I've forgone that oath.

Then I am in a different plane of existence.

'Eliyas,' I say. In this memory, he carries me on his back, whirling through the bazaar.

'Look at the Heavens,' he says in awe. We stop at a pit of performers, and he swings me on to my feet, and wraps his arms around me. 'Let me tell you a secret,' he whispers when I am not listening, eyes twinkling. 'I told the emperor to name you Khamilla Nūr-e-Sûltana, little bird of light.'

'I am not a light.' I curl into his chest, my voice shaking. '*I killed you too*. That is all I do. I ruin beautiful things.'

He tucks a small braid behind my ear. 'You were a girl, yet you blame yourself? I do not hate you. My regret is that I did not give you the home you desired.'

'I failed you.' My words tremor like a prayer. 'And more, the people we trusted failed us both. Your trust in Warlord Akashun was nothing as you imagined – he made worse the emperor's machinations – and my trust in the emperor was a lie. I am sorry.'

He smiles, forlorn. 'I wished for a hero. My other mistake was I dreamt more for our people.'

'You were my hero. You deserved to rule. Maybe then our enemies in Sajamistan would not have been able to take and take from us. But I had you killed. I could not save my tribe, my clan, my brother or my uma. But I swear,' my voice pierces my soul, 'to atone for my mistakes.'

I reach into the bonds of my past, fingers trembling. *I am sorry I'd forgotten you*, I tell Babshah and Eliyas.

My mind goes to other instances. The times when I would catch Uma with her arms around her stomach, tears dripping down her delicate cheeks. But the emperor hated tears. Perhaps it was an excuse. I cared, but my fear of the emperor was greater than my care.

The muscles around my throat spasm but nothing regurgitates.

How sick am I that I ache for my father? The warring world is worse than any pain from his love. Because he did love me. And I believe that.

'The Sepāhbad was right,' I breathe out. 'I have no conviction; I am worse than greed, for I only follow. If someone commands kill, *I kill*. And now, the emperor has let me down – but all my heroes do.'

No-Name shakes her head. 'You must cleanse yourself of the emperor; you must let him go. He is your poison.'

Desperately, I take her hand. 'Tell me. What is the antidote?'

Her rows of sharp teeth gleam in the torchlights. 'You must kill him.'

Then she is my father again. 'Khamilla,' he breathes.

My eyes well with tears. I imagine him hugging me.

Then he kneels. He *is* hugging me. He has never embraced me like this. He is solid. Real. Warm. My arms lift, the temptation great. A part of me understands, logically, what embracing him is doing.

He smiles so affectionately; a keen wrongness tugs in my liver. 'You've done it,' he says. 'You infiltrated our enemies. A worthy weapon for the clan.' But a frown disrupts that satisfaction as he sees us on the ground. 'Why are we on the floor?'

'Because I am in pain,' I whisper.

He is jarred at this. And why not? I have never told him my true feelings, about anything – least of all my pain.

'Rise.'

'Did you hear me? I said I am in pain.'

'Rise before your clan; it was what you were bred to do.'

'Your clan – *your children* – deserved better. Eliyas, Yun, Zhasna, Azra, they were pure.' My hands feel wet, and I think I am bleeding – from everywhere. But the emperor does not care. For he was the cause of it – even now, still *is* the cause. Does he not see outside his own perception of me or is he wilfully ignorant, liking that I straddle the line between daughter and dog, smiling at the master that chokes the chains around its neck. For really, what is priceless to an emperor who sees the world as a series of finite values waiting to be conquered?

As if sensing my change, his arms tighten so I am a daughter tucked in the crook of her father's arms. But love is for fools who will recklessly chain themselves to its corpse even when it rots. Love is not made for the ones who have nothing to spare.

I lean into him and wipe my tears. 'I already killed you.'

His face crumples. 'Foolish girl, we could have reigned if only you had stopped resisting.' His grip tightens. 'You need me. You can never go a night without my name upon your lips. It makes you feel useful.'

I back away. 'This is wrong.'

'Many things in the world are wrong.'

'No, *you* are wrong.' My voice is a plea, praying, hoping, *clawing* my way to the words so I may believe them.

'Would you believe me if I said, all this time, you were my strength, too?'

I despise the acknowledgement. At him, I smile. 'No.'

'You had one task,' he snaps. 'I forgave you for your failures, for your roots. I made you. You only had to avenge me.'

'You lied to me!' I burst. 'You lied about the poisons, about empires – everything!'

'The world is full of liars! What we know of it is determined by the victors. I became your father for *victory*.'

'I never asked to be your daughter!' My breaths rise rapidly. 'I never wished for your ambitions that destroyed us all. The clan – does it not matter? I am relieved the Divine made this your fate, to die from your own creation, for it released me from you. All the time I was obedient, but why – *why did my brother die?* Why did I have to abandon my tribe; why did I become a weapon that condemned the souls around us? Why did I lose my uma? *All I wanted was my uma to be safe.*'

'I did it for our home.'

'Not our home. *Your throne.*'

I do not know of a home. Is it possible for a heart to ache for both – for Azadniabad, across its prefectures, which deserves better than my father, and for Tezmi'a, in its rolling pastures? The emperor never let me love both, I was always forced to choose one. The land was my home, not the name. I was only to allow myself to be an Azadnian instead of an Usur of Tezmi'a, or a Zahr. If each home I've called such has been destroyed, what kind of home have I ever had?

But the emperor is not looking at me. For I've always been the barbaric daughter of a barbaric wife he never asked for. They like to call us barbaric in fear of our strength to conquer. Tonight, I can conquer him. I grab the khanjar from Farzaneh's corpse. I grasp the one emotion I've truly ever understood. The one that birthed and spat me out.

Anger. I was once a girl who demanded a fate from the Heavens. Despite my affinity, I have not changed. I refuse him. And I refuse the girl I was before.

'Even the grand khans of the world will fear a peasant who holds a knife to his throat. I was the peasant and you the great khan,' I whisper. 'Now die by my blade.'

Nūr lights up my knife and I thrust the light into the emperor. The nūr slams his skull on to the ground. Pink tendrils split from the middle.

My fists smash into his nose.

I deserved the pain he inflicted. That was not hurt, that was consequence. But the bodies out there, that is unfathomable evil. And it is my fault.

My father is not the first nor the last monster. Warlord Akashun today. Another will arise tomorrow. These men perceive themselves as deciders of fate, but who declared them gods?

Nūr punctures through him until his skull is caved in and planks of bone jut out. His body droops in prostration as if our roles have reversed, and I am his master. Sorrow carves through me.

It is not real. It is real. Neither and both. And for that reason, both must die. I sear this memory with fear, so at no time will I forget that he's irrevocably dead.

Then No-Name is before me again, staring in shock. I wait for my mind to clear, to feel unburdened and light. My body throbs all over; my teeth clank together.

No-Name is calm because I am not. 'Tell me, what will you do?'

'Do?'

I made this Mitra. A magick... created by my jinn-poisons. A weapon used to massacre Sajamistan and subjugate the tribes of the Camel Road.

'I-I – my brother...'

Yun... he is up north. He is close. But is he involved with Mitra? It would be so easy to take the knowledge from Za'skar, including plans for an invasion into Arsduq, and give the intelligence to my clan as an advantage against Sajamistan. To earn my rightful place as their vizier. But I think of my role in this. And my vow to Eliyas.

An understanding breaks like bitter foam cresting the sea. My eyes shut in disbelief. 'I cannot defect without ensuring Sajamistan knows about Mitra being used in these villages. Helping them feels wrong. But Mitra exists *because* of me. *I need to kill him* – Akashun.'

If I defect right away to Azadniabad, I fall into my clan's hands. Did Hyat Uncle know of Mitra – and for that matter, which clansmen are supporting it? I cannot be sure. If I inform them of Sajamistan's invasion into Arsduq prefecture, I will be powerless to stop those loyal to Akashun from escaping with Mitra. And it's the borderlands – and their bodies – that are raided for Mitra, inflicting damage on the larger empire of Sajamistan.

I cannot be sure who is right or wrong, and I don't think there will ever be a clear answer in the annals of history. The Veil has been lifted and the world is rearranging into meaningless lines of borders, dividing and conquering. But I do know what Akashun intends will always be at the expense of the Camel Road.

'What of Warlord Akashun?' No-Name asks.

'I still intend to defect from Za'skar – not yet, but soon,' I say, making the decision. 'Farzaneh explained that Warlord Akashun is the sole wielder of Mitra. If I am to destroy it, I must kill him. Perhaps then we will have an end to it.'

Fleeting hope crosses No-Name's eyes. 'How would you kill him?'

My mind drums with possibilities. I think of the Great Flood, a symbol of Divine decree controlling us, even now.

'Destroying Mitra means you might never return to Azadniabad,' she adds. 'The great clans would order you dead. Mitra is their hope against the rest of the continent.'

I do not know which clans have sided with Warlord Akashun. My heart tugs at this. If my clan has chosen Mitra, I must cut the thread between myself and my kin.

A low sound whistles through the air and the partition of my chamber curves inward before bursting in a spray of rock and dirt.

Alif Adel stands there, fingers bending to funnel — what I see to be — his affinity, Afflicter, to manipulate the currents of the planet through the angels.

'I found you,' he says and I baulk at the blood drenching his tunic. Unintentionally, my soul stirs, sensing the rippling bonds of a Seventh-Slash, still strong despite the unholiness of these caverns.

In two long strides, Adel reaches me. He leans in, forehead pressing against mine, so I have no choice but to peer into his trembling brown eyes.

'They will die,' he says in a low voice. 'Every single one of them who partook in this filth will die. *The Divine have mercy, I will make them scream.*'

32

'We have seconds before the scholars see this damage,' I say.

'We cannot escape without collapsing this outpost; it seems to be beneath the monastery. They have more across Azadniabad, but at least in destroying this one, it is one less evil.' Adel paces about.

At my frown, he stops and takes my sleeve, turning me so I look at him.

'They whored out villagers, they mutilated them. Azadniabad is begging for another war. These people need us.'

It would be so easy to poke at Adel, to incite his anger, which is as fluid as his warmth. His words are ironic: he accuses them of the very actions his empire repays in kind.

He continues, 'Za'skar has collected intelligence on the disappearances for over a lunar year. Our informants had shared mentions of soul contracts, but we'd never seen the end result, nor imagined it to be like this. If we don't destroy this monastery, the apprentices will note our escape and send caravans of this Mitra to northern Azadniabad. These bodies, they are jinn-folk in human shells. Their souls have merged but the humanity of them is gone.'

Then he reveals two blades in his sleeve, snatched from dead scholars. He hands one to me like a half-measured concession. If he notes my slight reluctance, he does not comment on it.

I take the blade. Our eyes flare as one.

At the gated entrance, I dry out the wells of my weakened ruh until immolating light permeates the material world. Nūr blasts from my leg bonds. Adel fans it with his superior Afflicter affinity, the currents of the world compressing my light into blasts.

The front of the bedrock crumbles as we run, weaving through corridors toward iron gates, Adel's affinity slamming two apprentices out of our path. Our attacks only manage to damage a quarter of the sprawling underground outpost. We do not stop running as we pour into the rugged courtyard outside the monastery, even as guards hound after us on our trail. We trample through shrubs until the path ends abruptly at the brink of a ravine. With little hesitation, Adel wraps his arm around me and dives over the edge.

I've no time to scream as we plunge to our deaths, but at the last moment, Adel summons a soft gall, tumbling us safely to the ground. The guards skid to a halt above us and we make our escape beyond the mountain pass.

Adel's perception of the currents steers us away from the borderland. We cross south and pass a village, where we steal a horse, which carries us to the nearest outpost.

There, our dealings are scribed into reports, then delivered through the parî courier system reserved for viziers, where ababil birds deliver letters at high speeds.

We are told to wait for the Sepāhbad's arrival from the central Ghaznian outpost. Hearing this, a cold sweat breaks out on my neck. Every moment I remain in Sajamistan is a risk of him discovering my identity.

'Is something the matter?' I hear Adel ask.

But my mind drifts to the raids of my childhood; to Sajamistan encroaching on our prefectures; to my uma cornered by the then Sepāhbad and Alifs before she ended her life. It makes choosing to help this empire a painful conflict. The equivalent of a knife slicing half of my body, leaving the other intact. For I have dreamt of the Sepāhbad's death a thousand times to soothe myself.

Before I can summon an answer, Officer Samira enters the room. 'The Sepāhbad has reviewed the reports with Adviser Arash.'

Alif Adel sits up, his eyes thin slits. 'Old man Arash is here?'

Her expression pinches. 'Please, do not pick a fight, my Alif.'

In the intelligence ward, the words go unheeded when Adel glares daggers at a familiar wrinkly man in a left-hand vizier's robes, decorated in amber birds, who stands beside the Sepāhbad. His greying hair pokes out from a feathered onyx-coloured turban, his eyes and mouth worn from a life spent more in battle than away from it; a dagger pictogram is dyed on his forehead through black-threading. On Arash's shoulder is perched a large, weathered raven. Flanking him are the outpost captains and their aides. Adviser Arash is not an Eajīz, though he is the oldest left-hand vizier to the Royal Council of Sajam.

The Sepāhbad looks on from a palm-wood table as we fold our knees on the kilim. He meets my gaze briefly. I feel hollow. The officers convene and discuss a potential invasion of the Mitra outpost. The Sepāhbad spreads a calfskin map of the terrain, the design of it adjusted by Adel's memory.

'Old man, have you come to your senses?' Adel speaks as the captains bow over the long stone table.

Arash cocks his head. 'And what would that be?'

'The uselessness of optimism and negotiations. We should strike first. I warned your little council of bureaucratic rats of the growing raids on the border and look where it has led us.'

'The local Arsduq tribes will accuse us of invading the buffer; they will deem it a breach of their alliances in the Camel Road and retaliate with Azadniabad, leading to a crackdown on the steppes.'

Adel huffs a laugh. 'Have you read the reports? They've been bribing tribes for months. The crackdown has begun.'

Arash's expression wavers like leaves pattering on to the surface of an oasis, but he stills himself. 'The bodies Azadniabad used were villagers on the frontier. We could be hasty in assuming these were from Ghaznia province at all.'

My jaw gapes open. Does he see *value* in Mitra?

I catch how Adel's eyes flick to the Sepāhbad as he delays his response, almost as if silently seeking permission. I realise Adel's jabs at Arash are an intentional provocation. Rather than arguing with Arash himself, the Sepāhbad allows Adel to steer the offensive. From this, the Sepāhbad plays the middle ground between the two ends of the spectrum, appearing appropriately neutral as necessary to his aides. The weapon of subtlety is more terrifying than blunt force; the politics of the martial-viziers makes my head spin.

'Old man, the war has arrived. Any cooperation in the past between our empires was a necessity born of a shared enemy. We have no shared enemy now.' Adel rakes his hands through his henna-stained curls, voice seething. 'You dare excuse torture; you excuse our own provinces' deaths. The only purpose for Mitra's existence is for waging war, fool.'

Adviser Arash stews on this. 'Based on Usur-Khan's report, they intend to offer a Mitra trade to create mutual assurances – their intention includes developing variations to preserve the human soul. We would be fools to dismiss the idea without considering it. Think of it as a weapons trade. Inventions come at the price of lives, which Azadniabad has already paid, and from which we could benefit. How is it different from the cost of inventing a weapon? Weapons are not magick but they are powerful. We cannot change that Mitra now exists. Azadniabad controls it; this opens a chance for beneficial relations because sooner or later, they'll salivate to try Mitra on Eajīz. They might need Za'skar for its ancient jinn-knowledge. If we refuse it, that is Akashun's opening to finally conquer our borderlands. Akashun will trade Mitra to our vassals on the condition that we receive no support in the event of war.'

I sit on my heels, leaning against the wall, my hands fisting. Adviser Arash would forsake his alliances with peripheral tribes, and our integrity?

'You would sacrifice our people for trade?' Adel seethes.

Adviser Arash chuckles darkly. 'Accuse me of greed, but humans like me only survive long enough to learn that pacifism, when possible, is the best option. In this case, it requires trading Mitra, a terrible choice, but sacrifices have to be made to save larger numbers of people.'

The Sepāhbad waits for quiet. 'Well,' he begins. 'Azadniabad wishes to unify its warlords and tribes into an empire. And empires are like newborn babes; they spend their early lives looking for an identity. Any state must develop an adhesive, an identity that unites every new clan and broken tribe, to be distinct from their past but also distinct from other kingdoms. Sometimes identities come at the expense of their own tribes. These are the prefectures and provinces.'

Adviser Arash raises a brow. 'Sajamistan is that, no?'

'Yes, while Azadniabad's identity has an adhesive in the form of a common enemy – Sajamistan. Mitra exists to counter our hold on Za'skar. And when they back us into a corner with Mitra – we would be forced to agree to their terms. This is hung on conceding our territories in the Camel Road. Tell me, in negotiations, when a knife is held to your throat, would the agreement be fair and amiable, or is it twisted coercion? If one party holds unparalleled leverage, it's no agreement at all, it's servitude. Akashun holds leverage, for *he* possesses Mitra. The possibility of a trade… or an alliance is a myth.'

Silence.

'I await your answer, Adviser Arash.'

'I stand by my words, Sepāhbad Jezakiel.'

'Then let them remain words. Now we begin,' he answers coolly. The room bows.

The Sepāhbad intends a double envelopment at the peak of the valley for elevated advantage. Four squadrons will station themselves in eastern and western flanks – replacing each fallen soldier by pulling from the elite centre cavalry concentrated with the most Eajīz – until the enemy is hemmed in.

An auxiliary will be hidden on the northern cliffs, arrows readied. At the Sepāhbad's signal, the flanks will form an outward line, and when we engage Azadniabad, they will fall back into a bow formation. The flanks will create a box, and from above, the auxiliary will pick the enemy apart. Capturing will not be a priority until the outcome of the invasion is determined. Given this is the frontier, we would only be battling garrison troops, not those of central Arsduq, ruled by Governess Bavsag. However, a drawn-out battle risks her reinforcements arriving.

'If we do this, then prepare for war,' Arash says severely.

'Mitra's existence means the war has begun. We are making the first blow.'

As the officers begin to parse out the logistics, I regard Adviser Arash with interest. Old men like him have achieved so much in their long careers through this kind of grey pragmatism, cutting furtive deals across enemy lines in shadowed corners. I've always thought of myself as coldly practical, but I see now that there is a spectrum of pragmatism, and his I don't know if I align with. I wonder if he would reserve his judgement if he'd glimpsed what I did in the cavern – the decayed bodies.

Decayed bodies. A slow realisation runs through me. Would we battle Mitra creatures?

And only from guilt do I force myself to speak. 'My viziers, if this underling may offer an urgent perspective.'

Adviser Arash turns his head, noticing me, for the first time, with a wrinkled stare. Though he is not the most powerful one in the room, somehow, he exudes authority. But it's the Sepāhbad who nods at me to continue.

'There might be more than Arsduq troops,' I speak quickly. 'In the depths of the caverns, I heard... I heard apprentices murmuring. They spoke of a falak serpent and souls used to bond it—'

Officer Samira baulks at this. 'Impossible. Even the Qabl sages have never communed with the ancient falak.'

'– and given the depth and dampness of the caverns, at least part of it must be located below a river grotto. Though we tried to destroy the caverns, there are likely more tunnels branching out beneath the valley. If this is true, Azadnian forces would re-route a bulk of their troops with the falak, from the south of our position, and engage in a two-pronged offence behind the mountains.' Still holding their gazes, I say, 'That is, unless we anticipate the serpent.'

The Sepāhbad contemplates my words. 'If this is true, we would have to risk changing the auxiliary's positioning on the cliffs.' He faces the room again. 'To verify the tunnel entrances, we send one scout. We'll feign a retreat to have them assume we know nothing of the tunnels. The bulk of our soldiers will be ready above the cliff side to pick them off like cattle. Or I drown them with the river.' He makes a whirling motion with his finger.

Another hour passes before the soldiers are dismissed, but the Sepāhbad nods at me to remain.

He points at my left hand. 'I have a theory I'd like to test. Can you summon a sphere of nūr?'

My bonds expand. 'May I ask what this is for?'

'Steam.'

Horror stills my bonds before I hold my expression to something neutral.

'You extinguished your nūr,' he points out.

'I was startled. How can this work when my nūr is not hot, but cold?'

'It's cosmic light. Through Second-Stratum summoning, when it becomes dense enough, it compacts infinitely without assuming space, which can potentially obliterate the state of water upon interaction. Or must I teach this to you?'

'No. I would never have thought of creating steam,' I lie.

Faint amusement lines his lips. 'You are flattering me again.' His Spring of Heavens affinity pulls water from the air before his hand hovers above my own. Quickly, I decrease my bonds, making the water stream uselessly through my fingers. He frowns.

'It did not work. We cannot create steam.'

'Then increase your bonds,' he suggests too patiently.

'To what extent?'

He crosses his arms and cocks his head. 'Are you a pazktab student unable to do basic bond expansion?'

I lift my hand before producing a swathe of nūr, his features wavering beyond the bright curtain. 'Will this do?'

He peers at it and nods before extracting more water from the air. 'This will be your first battle, yes?' he asks absent-mindedly.

I think of Tezmi'a, and then the capital Navia. 'No. But it's the first I am willingly partaking in.'

'Then see it as a history lesson.'

My eyes narrow. 'People will die; that is not a history lesson.'

He almost smiles. 'Not for the first time. This continent is founded on war. The pathetic thing about our history is that we coexist because no one was strong enough to conquer the other, not because we agreed to coexist.'

'I think the Easkaria is enough to teach me, though Scholar Mufasa is my least favoured tutor.' I sound bitter.

He smiles now. 'Mine too.'

I glance at the small smile, and then away before looking again. It hits me that we are in Ghaznia again, like this. He notices. 'What makes you stare like that?'

'I am only thinking.'

'Of?'

'A monk.'

He slows in pulling water. 'Do I continue prying answers, or will you answer less obtusely?'

I regret my honesty and decide a half-truth would appease him instead. 'I am thinking of how I thought you were a monk and how absurd that is now.'

He remembers and appraises me carefully. 'You assumed it. Though I wonder, you seem more provoked by this rather than the fact that I had your leg snapped in half.'

'A broken leg I can take.'

'And more,' he says, holding my gaze.

Remembering that for him I am a mere low-rank, I step back. 'Forgive this underling, my Sepāhbad.'

Ending the matter, he lifts his hand. I stare at my trembling fingers below his. The water clashes and hisses into thin clouds, obscuring the room.

'Steam,' he muses.

'Who would have thought?' My insides knot, reminded of his bone-seal.

'We'll be outnumbered three to one. As they dissect the troops with the bow formation, we'll create steam before the archers engage. For the enemy, a blind retreat.'

'Yes, Sepāhbad.'

He studies me through the steam, still amused. 'Who would have thought,' he repeats back.

Before I leave, his gaze flits to the space between us as if he sees an abstract thing that is out of my reach. He has done this often. Not for the first time, I wonder what he actually sees that I cannot. I hope I am not blind to this truth too.

33

Arsduq Valley, Azadniabad Empire

At dawn, we ride to the pass between Ghaznia province and Arsduq prefecture. At each rest, our masters sternly order the soldiers into the Eight Revitalisation Stances, a practice dating from the ancient armies who preserved Heavenly Energy to prepare for battle. We ride in stealth along the conifer trails crawling with bandits. In the high elevation, the mountains slash upwards through the fattened clouds that threaten to pour. We avoid the central roads, criss-crossing between nodes of buffer townships ruled by chieftains, who might sight our numbers and ride ahead to deliver the intelligence to Azadniabad.

The Sepāhbad orders the captains to divide the squadrons for concealment. At the slightest disturbance, we are quick to scurry like ants, dismantling our fire pits, uprooting our small yurts and ushering our horses into the conifer thickets along the higher snow-capped trails.

I had never considered these details, in even a small melee like this – the logistics of concealment. Of weaponising uncertainty against the opponent hours before the battle begins, or even baiting enemy scouts with geographical lures by creating falsified trails, so the now-anxious enemy assumes their opponent is dispersed around the terrain rather than concentrated in one location – the psychological aspect of battle beginning long before the violence.

We arrive at the frontward side of the valley, a considerable distance from the Mitra outpost. The jagged terrain cleaves the mountains into a wide alpine gorge. Below, an icy river gushes through bedrock. As the squadrons bend into their stances, I rub on attar, the rosy scent puckering the damp air.

'Are you ready?' No-Name rises from my shadow, but she looks pale.

No. I am honest. These are my people I will be fighting. And I am scared… what if I see a Zahr clansman? Am I making the right choice?

She looks at me, hopeful. 'Be steady. When you defect to kill Akashun, you might see your siblings again.' Then she vanishes.

The flanks gather at the apex of the valley, and soldiers acknowledge their comrades with the sober looks of people who accept they may not live to see another dawn. We roughly fasten our ivory masks. Battle applications are rehashed, flank numbers re-examined, and then final nods of approval. According to Officer Samira, as an Eajiz I am not to be on horseback, but I will remain alongside the elite horse cavalry, beside Alif Adel. Our aim is to feign the frontal charge before swinging at the enemy's weaker rear to sever lines of retreat. Then, I am to continue down that path to the Sepāhbad at the southern valley and create the steam.

Adel comes up beside me. His hand grips a papyrus, methodically folding it before launching it in the air and restarting the process.

'Is that papyrus?'

'Paper kites,' he corrects, flicking it upwards through his Afflicter affinity, the currents causing twelve more to encircle his body like a white halo.

I snort. 'Paper cannot kill.'

In response, one slices across my arm.

'What the Hells!'

'This is a celestial alloy sharper than any blade, from the Great Library, harvested by the first jinn who flew across the cosmos.' My awe trickles out like the contents of a smashed teacup, for he is still a Seventh-Slash, the peak of Qabl mastery. He turns fully and looks at the khanjars on my belt. 'Your first battle?' I nod. 'Stay close to my side.'

'How did you fare in your first battle?'

He smiles weakly. 'When I was a First-Slash, I almost wet myself.'

'That is comforting.'

We gaze at the worn valley, a mummification of ambition in the history of conquerors that have battled to win its lands. The mountain rivers reflect the midday sky, a false light of hope.

As scouts report Azadnian forces amassing, the warriors rush to their flanks. From my vantage point, I have a view of the blurring shapes of soldiers, their leather armour and crane-feathered cloaks flapping like wings. It begins with a swarm of hundreds of Azadnians in their indigo velvet garb riding across the outpost, dividing to engage each flank.

The blue figures begin staining with the red of blood. Screams pierce through the roaring mountain wind. Powers flare, bodies fly, and the grasslands upturn from the Eajīz scorching crater holes into Brother-Nature.

Panic mingles through me, that I am helping the empire that has abused me for so long, followed by an odd rush. A spar, a duel, it's different from battle. No matter how clever the general, no one can predict the outcome of a melee with thousands of possibilities.

The terror of it hits me, but I merely shove the hilt of a khanjar into my mouth before looping more into each hand. For battle, I must be blank. I cling on to a familiar anger. *These are enemies*, I lie to myself.

'Let us go,' Adel commands. Half of the centre charges, the other four lines splitting neatly to supply the eastern and western flanks as our mounted archers ride on steeds.

We pour down the trail and I remain at Adel's right, afraid of being caught in the oncoming herd. At the centre, the Azadnians forge through with cries for their empire, forking left and right, unaware of our mounted archers traversing above the mountain's many ridges, falling for the first misdirection tactic.

'Hold the line!' Adel orders.

Through the deafening roar, the first enemy clashes against us. My fear and panic fall, red bleeding across my vision.

From beside me, Adel arranges his paper kites into a diamond formation. 'Light the tips in nūr,' he orders, and I send wisps toward the paper weapons. With a huff, his tongue bond blows, scattering the kites to the enemy's lines. They zip across arms, slicing through sinewy muscles before the dense nūr bursts and soldiers scream.

We continue like this; when my guard is low, Adel shields me with a paper kite while I channel blasts of nūr. Through deft commands, he folds the kite into paper needles, flinging them inside mouths or penetrating eyeballs.

At every small victory, the next line of Azadnian soldiers follows, bursting from behind the valley. Too many. As soon as I can I engage, and the hair on the back of my neck lifts.

A crack splits from beneath me, and Adel flings a hand to form a thick current as a shield. The grasslands explode, blasting me off my feet. My shoulder smashes against a rock and I roll into a ball.

'Khamilla!' Adel yanks me up.

'I am fine,' I manage, seeing that though the Azadnian forces are overwhelmingly solely mortals, there are a few who are Eajīz. 'What was that affinity?'

He grimaces. 'A Heavenly Contract of Fortification where the wielder has unparalleled strength. They must have stomped upon the terrain to shake it.' He continues, 'Though our formation holds, their numbers are the problem. We must expand our blast's reach.'

I place my khanjar back into my mouth and combine my leg and arm bonds into Second-Stratum to form a horizontal barrier, so any attack is less likely to immediately overwhelm us despite their numbers. And though the odds are terrible, we spin back to back to face the enemy.

Adel rotates his shoulders, forming a vortex current that whirls puffs of dirt into a funnel. It's a grey angry monstrosity, rippling like smoke and uprooting the shrubs. As the grasslands shake and splinter below the net of grey, Adel flexes his hands, widening the vortex before us. Just in time, it absorbs the next wave of the Fortification affinity before spitting it back toward the Azadnians.

'At my next current, run and blast.'

Understanding his intention, I take two leaping steps, landing in ninth stance, ideal for dense bond expansion, compressing nūr within the heels of my palms. At his signal, my hand bonds fling gold ropes, bursting right into the funnel. Adel flattens the storm before erupting it mid range before the enemy.

I cannot see in the chaos of light and air, but the tremor carries into my feet before the thuds of bodies reach us in sickening squelches as warriors are shredded apart.

Twice more, we blast in the same manner. Eventually, we break their lines, allowing the rest of the central soldiers to split toward the flanks.

I follow Adel to the left wing in time for our squadron to engage the Azadnians from the rear.

Officer Samira turns at our approach but before she even speaks, her body stills and red gushes from her chest, a knife protruding in mid-air. To my bewilderment, the ground mutes into a dark chroma as if a great shadow has befallen this section of the battlefield. And then the knife rips from the captain's chest, cutting her fingers in sprays of red before careening into her throat and lopping her head off.

I lunge with a strike of nūr but the shadow skitters back across the battlefield. 'What was that?' I reach out, hardly processing her corpse.

'Reinforcements.' Adel breathes calmly despite the obscene death. He gestures ahead at the next line of Azadnians. 'This is a shadow art, from a jinn through a Mitra bond. I'm not certain how the human soul coexists in that warrior, but it seems Azadniabad has sent their best, a stupid sacrifice for a melee.'

As if summoned, a roar of fury rips through the air. Leading the charge is a lithe woman, black Veils rising from the ground at her command and shielding her comrades. She lunges from shadow to shadow – *no* – pounding on all fours like a leopard flying.

'Her strength is drawn from shadows on the ground,' Adel observes, his brown eyes alight, almost welcoming the challenge. The Seventh-Slash flattens his hand on the clay, sending rolls of currents to swerve them, but the shadows hold. 'A change of tactics, my underling. Cast your affinity to pierce her legs.'

Grounding my soul, sweat trickling down my back, I force the Heavenly connection through three bonds. The nūr becomes malleable from the Third-Stratum, pouring from my toes into a long wire before crossing the beams into textured threads. Flinging my arms, I raise them like a puppeteer commandeering a bonded creature to my whim. I mentally recite the prayer of the style: Seventy-seven Binding Art, a manifestation of what I had invented in my Duxzam.

'Hold.' Adel braces as he stacks a wall of currents around it. Then he surges it upwards, elongating the creation until the nūr resembles the long white spine of an aži.

'Now!' he cries, and I release the scaly bonds through seven exhales.

It crashes at the enemies' feet in sweltering waves of agony. Adel widens his hands to carve the nūr outwards into compressed blades. It impales Azadnians across their ankles so neatly; it is a startlingly grotesque art. Red crests through the valley.

I do it again, the mirage of pale yellow slithering into my opponents' mouths this time. My heart thuds faster and faster, an exhilaration filling me. They are no longer my people, but silhouettes of numbers. Things to destroy. Blackness curls in my vision, the shadows growing as Heavenly Energy surges into the spiral of my soul. My lips twitch.

One, two, three – more. The light blankets me, thick and heavy. *Why care for life when the Divine has bestowed on you the gift of death?* Nūr is a destruction, not a creation.

My fingers unclench again. For the next two enemies, tongues of light lap at their feet, crawling upwards, the dense mass pawing their faces until they slough off in liquidised flesh.

Adel suddenly holds a hand to his mask, and I blink out of the fervour. 'Was that the last of their flank? I must go to the Sepāhbad,' I pant, staring down at my arms.

'Wait.'

Then a cry erupts from their flanks. I pause in sheer horror. *How?*

Within the strewn bodies, a shadow writhes out, slamming through corpses. The wraith digs like a thumb in the meat of an apricot, expelling the dozens of soldiers it had cocooned. The remaining Azadnians rush to surround us. The same shadow-wielder leads them, baring her teeth at me while blocking my path to the cliffs.

'She won't let me pass—' I begin.

'They are stalling. As a Seventh-Slash, I can easily take on a dozen mortals at once, so let me handle the rest. We cannot let them break our lines,' the Alif orders.

There is no time to reply as the shadow woman lunges at me. Adel faces the others. A black wall at her command sprawls out like dark water but before it can surge into me, my palm pushes outward, bracing the metaphysical energy. She flings a dense Veil and I dive and roll, my nūr swirling around, absorbing the Veil through cuts of light.

But the Azadnian flicks her finger, gathering the shadows into a cesspool at my legs, and a part of me wonders how her spiritual wells are so full, how she has so much energy this far into battle.

I pivot, unbalanced, and she punches another black Veil that opens at my spine. My left leg kicks backwards, the balls of my feet intercepting her shots in a split barrage, sending wave after wave of nūr, so she cannot project it back.

But it's not enough. Exploiting my fragile balance, her ropes of shadow delve into the clay, erupting it beneath me. My foot bonds expand, and her shadows widen into a thin, dense net, forcing me to leap into different stances. Left, right, left and left, then right again, twisting frantically to avoid the tendrils. The warrior senses my delay, and she switches to close range, her shadow-engulfed shamshir swinging at my knee, her lips peeling back to grin.

My khanjar drops low, skip-catching to redirect her momentum before I rotate my torso outward and then duck, the blade between my lips driving through the enemy's shin, jerking up her calf, severing tendons. With a hiss, nūr explodes from my tongue bonds, hacking the limb off.

Her mouth opens, grey eyes huge. She cries out at the bloodied stump. I lunge and my palms open to finish her, but the black wraps her like silk before the attack lands.

With another yell, a string of black shoots from her mouth right into my neck. My breath catches, and my throat bond manages a hasty barrier, but the warrior seizes on my distraction, her next shadow stomping on my knees; I crumble with a cry.

The shadows curl around my throat, squeezing. My dense neck bone hasn't snapped, solely from iron-bone training. Her lips widen into something horrifying, though her eyes are wet.

'Barbarian,' she hisses, staggering on her good leg, the Veil propping her up.

My feet scramble for purchase, digging into muck. But she tightens the noose of black, my throat crushing beneath the pressure, my connection to Heaven winking out from my dimming senses, my mask plastered against my skin.

The pain is not real, it is not real, my breath wheezes.

The Qabl monks say to embrace pain in hours of meditation. *Accept the bond of death*, I remember, for a warrior's blade is not the extension of the arm but of the very soul between existences. It is the ache for Heaven running from the Hells.

Rise, I command my bonds. In this plane of frozen time, my opponent's soul pulses prominently at the centre of her ribs between a mesh of black-threading absent of a heart.

Biting back my nausea, I aim toward the pulsing. The nūr erupts from my chest bond to hers like a waterfall, snapping the shadows. She screams.

Not a human but an enemy, I remind myself. I know the world is not so simply divided, but my energy intensifies when there are no subtleties.

As the butt of my right palm rises, it jams into her nose, rearing her head back. My bonds tighten, left hand clenching into iron-bone fist. I stoop in the third stance that Yabghu had drilled into my head, knuckles connecting below my opponent's jaw. Her head snaps off in a clean nūr-engulfed blow.

Staggering up, I have my first look at her ravaged face. A maw of grief unfurls within me, and I teeter on the brink of falling. She looks so young—

Another Azadnian replaces her, yelling in fury at their dead comrade. A sword slashes across my side. My teeth sink into my lip, cutting my cry. I wedge my blade into the ground before flying around, my legs ploughing into a liver strike, collapsing his form before my khanjar plunges into the soft muscles of his neck.

One falls, the next rises, in a never-ending flow. Battles are not about martial forms, I learn. They hinge on endurance, who can last the longest, because battles never *damning* end. I had in some ways viewed Za'skar as a game – the examinations, the duels; it was a contest of minds and blades – but I had fooled myself about its purpose: we were honed to become war monsters.

I hack my way forward, covered in gore, while spitting out blood – whose, I cannot tell. I crunch limbs underfoot. I do it again. And then again. It's bleak. It's cruel. But I do my duty under the name of an empire I detest to absolve myself of another. That thought steers me onward.

As I engage my blade with another enemy on the cliffs, I sight a small flank of warriors on the opposite side of the valley, at the mouth of the pass, observing the battle from above while retreating slowly.

My soul stirs and my knees clank together. From afar, I make out a throng of crane masks, a young man at the front standing on the stirrups of his mare, an ivory khanjar strapped to his velvet waist-sash, features indiscernible. The world quiets, except inside of me, where invisible hands pluck my heartstrings to a tune I cannot hear. My lips move instinctually.

'Yun,' I say, somehow knowing it's him. And then I am yelling in abandon, '*Older Brother!*'

Mid turn, the horseman stiffens, as if the Divine has granted a small mercy and carried my cry through the wind to the other side of the river valley. He looks over his shoulder, but I cannot see his gaze, his expression.

His arm jerks up, commanding his men to follow him into the mountains. I back away. I cannot reach him; he is in enemy terrain. My clansmen were my home, but this is only the pattern of fate: that I should play a part in bringing about their demise.

I bury my face into my hands. Every instinct of mine yearns to run to my brother. Instead, I back away from the cliff. I don't want to be here. Perhaps because war makes one feel small. Perhaps because in battle one's worst fears are paraded before one's eyes, but there is no fleeing, only watching comrades perish.

In war, you are nothing but a piece to push upon a map, discarded when you have fulfilled your purpose – assuming you are not dead. After, you are simply nothing.

A yell rips me from the grief, and I whirl. An Azadnian lunges and my hand raises, but she abruptly stiffens, a shard of ice piercing through her throat. It bursts. She collapses.

The Sepāhbad stands behind her, a double-ended khanjar's hilt between his teeth, while his other hand crushes into a fist, a line of ice formed from his fingers to the Azadnian. He follows my gaze to the lip of the valley and it hits me as we begin moving.

'The scout. You sent a missive to central Arsduq,' I say, piecing it together.

We trek down a cliff-side trail until we overlook the confluence of rivers converging below.

The Sepāhbad wipes blood dripping down his mask. 'Yes. The governess of Arsduq is one of two prefects in fray with Emperor Akashun. Even at odds with me – her enemy – she is prudent enough to gauge that weakening Akashun works in her interest. The missive was a mad gamble. But victory will come by pinning the Zahr strongholds against Akashun.'

And it worked.

The Sepāhbad glances forward. 'Direct the nūr downwards to intercept the Azadnians, but hold at the middle before spreading it to the flanks. When our main force withdraws, the Azadnians will rush forward, and our overhead archers are at the ready.'

His arms outstretch, as water swirls from the river, like a slice of the great sea in his hands. It climbs as a watery azhdahak, creasing the light of the pale sun. Two thin ribbons of nūr billow toward the centre, and the water collides.

'Direct it to the peripheries,' he orders as he draws forth barriers of water to shield us while I manipulate the last of my nūr through Third-Stratum. It's a jumbled symbiosis, for we are not familiar with each other's affinities. I glean that the Sepāhbad cannot control bodies of water that equate to more than the total amount of Heavenly Energy inside him. By subduing a portion of *a river*... his must be bountiful.

Finally, after I work out the nūr's correct density, steam surges upwards, clouding the valley.

'Fire!' a captain roars from the ridges above our cliff, and the screams begin. Arrows sink in stunning precision; evidence of Za'skar's cruel efficiency. Bodies drop to the ground in a low thunder.

'Fire!' she barks again.

It's long, it's drawn-out, it's sickening. Azadnians crawl like ants from the river toward the tunnels only to be greeted by more archers.

My body begins trembling at their pitched screams. The Sepāhbad glances at me but expresses no reaction. A man who has seen so much mortality in his existence that he has become dulled to death. Bored even, from his skimming glance.

The valley descends into an eerie silence. Above us, the captain orders a retreat to our encampment.

The Sepāhbad scans the surroundings before nodding. 'Rejoin your squadron.'

But a cold fog arises from the cliffs. The mist clings to my skin, so wet I feel caught in the dour of a lake.

'This is not our steam,' the Sepāhbad realises.

A quiver runs across my spine, like fingers scratching lightly. The air tastes foul, not from blood, but rot.

'Can you disperse the fog?' I ask before the cliffs rumble below us. My eyes squint, but the fog makes it difficult to discern anything. Suddenly, a stink of hot breath fans against my back. I've hardly time to think, let alone turn, before an arm wraps around my torso, yanking me out of the way just as something crashes where I stood.

I stumble into the bedrock, the Sepāhbad shoving me behind him. 'Are you well?' he asks, eyes darting down my form.

'What was that?'

'We need to retreat.' He backs me further along the trail while extracting us from the mist. He erects a vertical shield of dense water and clears the fog with a snap. Ahead of us, a spiked, teal-scaled tail slams into the cliff side as a mountain-sized body trawls up the rocky ledges, a forked tongue the size of tall poplars darting where I stood mere seconds ago.

The blood drains from my face. The demonic falak has not been spotted since Prophet Nuh's flood.

What contract did the Azadnian emperor create with the Unseen to force a falak from the Veil into the human world? The serpent before us is mangled, with glimmering red wings, three wide pink mouths, and milky eyes on several bobbing human heads embedded in its scales.

'The bonds from those human souls forced it through the Veil into the human world under Akashun's control.' The Sepāhbad shares in my thoughts before extending his barrier to deflect its ramming tail.

He freezes the water into a thick ice-hewn pick before shooting it right into the third eye of the falak. The creature recoils with a roar and drops off the cliff but its tail wraps around a cluster of pines, saving it from plummeting further. It roars again, undeniably human-sounding. All the more horrifying.

The Sepāhbad skewers it with another ice pick and another. As he does, the valley throbs once again. I watch in shock. Three shadows hurtle from the Heavens, growing in size. Long-tailed creatures half the size of the first falak, swallowing the grasslands. In a mangle of sharp scales, the serpents bellow forward to the retreating auxiliary archers.

The Sepāhbad whirls—

Everything happens in less than a blink.

The auxiliary are suddenly no more. A thousand warriors. Disintegrated in a spray of crimson.

Shreds of skin and wet bones clog the valley. It took one fell swoop of those spiked tails, lashing outward.

There is only a mute silence and the thudding of Sajamistani bodies across the valley – not even the time to cry, to accept and embrace death – that blessing, too, ripped away from the lovers of martyrdom. Everything seems out of reach, out of reality.

I fight a cry blubbering in my throat. These serpents have human – no – have what *were* humans in them. I stare down at my hands; how many souls were sacrificed to make these creatures? What have I done?

The Sepāhbad shuts his eyes, but if he feels the grief, he masks it well as he shoulders forward. Then another realisation: his troops have retreated to the encampment. We cannot take on four serpents alone.

As the falak rages upon the cliffs, the Sepāhbad speaks low. 'The first serpent should be dead from my blows. Which means, according to the theorems of the dark arts, we must slay the creature as many times as the number of souls sacrificed in its creation, and more than one human was used to bond it.' He levels me with a pressing stare. 'I will have to kill the falak a dozen times over, if not more. The Azadnian garrison is prolonging the melee with these Mitra, to summon reinforcements. If we engage, it's a losing battle, with our forces stretched thin.'

'Then we retreat?'

'No.' His hazel eyes darken as he looks upwards. 'I will gamble with Heaven. This will be decisive.'

My gaze narrows. 'What?'

'Heed me carefully.' He faces me. 'Retreat to the encampment, where the flanks await. Be swift. You have minutes, or you die. Do you follow, underling?'

'But—'

'Your life depends on it.'

My protests halt when the serpents scent us. If the vizier wishes to take on four falak, I could not care less, as long as my life is not forfeit. 'Okay, then,' I say after a moment. 'Farewell.'

I begin to stumble along the rocky cliffs. The Sepāhbad raises his palms, flipping them upwards before his eyes shut.

'Third Gate of Heaven,' he recites slowly, and I stiffen at the force of the incantation.

A black blur whizzes above us, and to my astonishment, it's his raven, who perches upon his shoulder. Its unblinking eyes stare forward, but blue pictograms engrave the air in Adamic glyphs around the bird. Mist unfurls from the green carpet of fern and sets upon the decaying birch of the valley like a shock of silver fire.

Aglow, the Sepāhbad's figure cuts a Heavenly aura and I back away. The glyphs encircle his temple like a thin band as golden lines burst forth, spiralling into seventy-seven bonds.

The sky darkens and the clouds split like a river parting around a rock. A bond descends into the Sepāhbad's chest – *a hundredth bond*. As if the cosmos are upended. Impossible. The bonds have manifested into the material world.

His body embraces the glow as the calligraphy burns into his forehead, hammered with a vengeance like a blacksmith gone astray. The largest falak, enthralled, swishes in a blurring lunge on the Sepāhbad. My eyes widen, but a blast of primordial power staves off the serpent's attack, as my leader's mouth chants unfamiliar litanies.

My vision sways, the temporal world threatening to ripple as if the fabric of space and time is being shattered by the Heavens. I do not stop running. Whatever price was paid for that power, the cold truth is, no mortal should have the ability to wield it.

The four falak begin to shriek, the force of their sound making me fall. The Heavens tremble under a weight. Water, as plentiful as the ever-giving seas, pours down.

In the nick of time, I reach the encampment, which is on higher ground sheltered below the mountainous rock, the moans of the wounded carrying all over. But I ignore them, gazing below at the valley, which now looks like a monsoon, the lands flattened except for flood-flung craters. Rain and river weep away the blood, growing more ferocious until they gush over the mountain base.

Bodies, Mitra and filth sweep down the mountainside. The land is excreting its poison as though from a liver, the regurgitation pulled from entombed streams and ancient reservoirs. It does not stop. Above the crashing flood come the wails of dying creatures.

The falak serpents thrash in the waves, drowning one hundred times over, a testament to how many souls were sacrificed to create them. To my ears, their whimpers are exactly that of a babe.

The Unseen is no longer Unseen. The Veil has been lifted and monsters are not nightmares in another microcosm. They walk amongst man.

Around me, Eajīz clutch their heads fruitlessly at the strange power thrumming through the material world, but it is a physical movement against an immaterial force, irrelevant in swaying the command of power. I hear murmurs thrown about. *Eight Gates of Heaven.*

I cannot help but approach Adel, as I point in disbelief at the valley flattened by the Sepāhbad.

'It's conceivable for certain Qabl masters,' he says.

'But this is impossible. I saw one hundred bonds,' I say.

He shrugs. 'In a world where mortals wield powers gifted from the Divine, what is not possible? This is the mastery of the Eight Gates of Heaven. It wrings your affinity dry; it breaks every bond principle, every maxim of human thought, every natural law in Eajīzi. This art form bestows one direct bond from a Heavenly Bird that every warrior who has mastered the Eight Gates can access. Today, the Sepāhbad has only used the Third Gate, not all eight because of its great cost.'

'The monks never taught this.'

He barks a laugh. 'Those monks play fools for the rukhs. What business have rukhs to know the Gates techniques? To summon a bond from one of the three Heavenly Birds?'

I blink twice. I assumed the monks had enlightened me, had shattered the thousands of illusions in the world, righted the contradictions and uplifted the veils between myself and the soul. I am a fool. I had only scratched the surface in the cosmic possibilities of Eajīzi.

Hunger burrows in my stomach. I am nothing. Absolutely powerless – compared to what I *could* be – compared to the paragon of Eajīzi displayed before me.

'Gates of Heaven,' I echo. 'But affinities are already from the realm of the Heavens.'

His thumb and finger pinch together. 'In this, for a window of time, you surpass corporeal restrictions, for the power is not just an extension from the Heavens, it's the gates. The gates are flanked by angels, who guard the souls of the Heavenly Birds and the Divine knows what other creatures.'

'How does one master the gates?' I ask.

Adel's lips twist into a sneer. 'Master? You cannot simply master them. It's unnatural. There are high-ranks paralysed in the monastery for toying with the Gates techniques. You are a low-rank playing with the cosmos where none should. You would be risking your soul, shifting the balance between Brother-Nature, the clay and humankind.'

A part of me cannot help but think the balance of power has already shifted. With Mitra's existence, the order has been eroded. Humans have been seduced into a new era in the struggle between peace and violence, and for the first time in history, it seems humankind has chosen violence willingly. Lines have been crossed; why should we not cross them too?

Beside me, No-Name contemplates this almost eagerly. 'Akashun wields Mitra. If he is pursuing unprecedented power, how can anyone defeat him without a power of symmetrical strength?'

I would be wise to heed Adel's warning, for he is a Seventh-Slash. If it were easy to grasp the gates, then surely Adel would do it.

I ask, 'Can you summon the Eight Gates?'

He seems startled. 'You do not summon the Eight Gates of Heaven. The gates *choose* you. In battle, a steep risk. You could be lost in the psychospiritual world for eons. There are legends of Eajīz who have never returned from their state of meditation. Their souls sucked into an unknown realm on a different plane of time, lost amongst the jinn-folk.' Rather harshly, he adds, 'And if you accomplish it, it's the physical manifestation of greed, the Divine's greatest test to Eajīz – for that's all power can do – *it consumes*.'

34

The nearest Azadnian monasteries are raided to find any bodies left behind in the hasty retreat; we find monastic libraries stacked with copied manuscripts and tablets of the dark arts, waterlogged and ruined.

The Sepāhbad finally appears in our small encampment, ordering the remaining captains: 'If we wait to bury the bodies, we risk inviting the curses of jinn-folk across the local villages.' His cheeks are flushed as if in fever. As he descends past me, he appears paler, his typical grace sluggish as if the Gates of Heaven had leeched his soul completely. But upon a second look, he appears like a warrior who has shaken hands one too many times with war and has come to detest it.

I do not join in sorting the mass graves of Mitra bodies; my squadron is assigned to find any Azadnian soldiers to capture alive.

I walk along the fortification lines through the alpine forest, with the sun waning at eventide. In the trails, at the fantastical hour of sunset, the shadows are thick, the sparrows' tunes imbued with melancholy as if grieving the deaths of today. The sounds of my squadron fade as I trek deeper through bramble, fir carcasses scoring my vision.

Yun. I feel the echo of his presence behind my breastbone. Does my brother approve of Mitra? I suddenly ache for the purpose I possessed in Za'skar, when my anger was pure, and vengeance was a simple game.

My thoughts are cluttered as I sit on a spongy tree that stinks sharply of decay, not unlike the corpses scattering the valley. I think of the Mitra creatures – how can I subdue them? I turn to No-Name, who is silent as ever.

'How can I ever kill Warlord Akashun when he has such power?'

'You cannot,' she says simply.

Unless I can use the Gates of Heaven against him. A raw power that flooded this valley in a matter of minutes. My fingers twitch with flickers of nūr.

A low-pitched cry fractures the melodies of the woodland. I glance at No-Name and she looks baffled too. It sounds like a child. We walk deeper into the conifer trails, my blade clenched between my fingers. As I peek around the trees…

It is a boy. Curled up, sobs wrack his spine, and I tuck my knife into my belt, rushing forward.

'Child,' I breathe. 'You are here? Alone?'

His arm is bent out of shape as he clutches it to his bare chest, back against a stump. He looks up, eyes raking over my pale tunic.

I falter at that. 'I will not hurt you. I can help.'

'Child?' He glances at himself. 'I suppose I am.' His lips curl down. And then he lunges at me, sending me sprawling. 'You killed my brother, you shai'tan!'

Stunned, I freeze as his knife arcs toward my chest and I shut my eyes. It happens fast. My khanjar jerks into his heart, ripping out the other side. He chokes, his features – as young as my students – pinching into agony before he slumps, dead.

'By the Divine,' I recite softly. He is an Azadnian soldier.

I shove him away, refusing to dwell on this as I scan the foliage for more soldiers. He must have run from battle, then become too exhausted to move—

If he was alive, there must be more who had fled the battlefield, wounded. Ahead of me a branch snaps. Bracing my blade, I creep into the clearing until I make out two Azadnians, hidden behind the shrubs, army sashes discarded, bloodied.

My mouth opens to call for my squadron, but they whirl at my presence, raising their hands.

'Please!' one girl begs. 'We were leaving, we defected!'

I ignore the plea, turning to—

Her eyes drop to my quartered sleeves and I realise too late she can see the gold-threading. She drops to her knees. 'I said we defected!'

'I don't care.'

Her body trembles as a feverish cry spills from her lips. 'Have you no mercy? Are we not the same?' She clutches her wounded shoulder.

'The same?'

'The lands of the Camel Road! We were forced into these uniforms and yet, your superiors delight in torturing us,' she hisses. 'Look at the colours you wear.'

My anger rises. 'You defend Mitra—'

'We had no choice!'

'You did have a choice,' I reply scathingly.

'My people do not. My brothers were conscripted from the Dawjad pastures, and more are—'

'Dawjad.' I pause, my blade quivering in my fingers.

'— snatched from our tribes if we refuse!'

My head shakes. These soldiers defended an outpost filled with the sacrifices of our own people. She is lying. She is an enemy. No-Name's voice resounds in my mind. *See them as a bug, a thing to squash.*

I stride forward, but her words tumble out now, no longer so desperate, but instead enraged. 'I assumed you would understand.' She scrambles back as blood gushes out of her wound, likely infected. She will not last. 'I kneel before you begging and you think nothing of it!' Her eyes shine wildly while her injured comrade crawls toward her. My head pounds and a disoriented feeling washes over me, like I am far above, gazing below.

I recall Older Brother and me in the bazaar, watching poets recite odes about the Faceless Dawjad warriors. The reminder of it is cruel.

I cannot. I cannot betray these two to an empire that I do not believe in.

To their surprise, I step back.

'I will not take you,' I start in a low voice, 'but you cannot escape. My squadron has the perimeter secured; they will capture you for torture. Make your choice on how to leave.'

A determination burns in the girl's eyes. She stands, and the other staggers up, graceless in blood, unsheathing their blades. I understand with horrifying clarity what they are to do. And I watch on, helpless, but not opposed to it.

Her eyes study my arms, then my raven mask. 'I have a prayer for those death-worshippers. May we die as free men rather than slaves to humanity. If you live past this, let us meet you in a state of martyrdom.'

It is a curse. A red shame bleeds through me.

'You sound like my uma.'

She smiles, embittered. 'And mine too.' She raises her blade to her neck. 'All hail the Faceless Dawjad clans.'

I know moral disobedience has no place in the Za'skar battalion. But when I meet that girl's eyes, I see – fundamentally – my nomadic brethren.

I let them puncture their own necks with those blades, slitting wide like a red smile, up into their jaw. But in that split second before, I think I see the look of a person who has *finally* won.

My knees sink to the ground; I finally understand the reasoning behind my uma taking her own life. My thoughts shiver and waver, the disturbed surface of a firelotus pond.

If this is true freedom, then freedom must be death. If this is revolution, then revolution, too, is death. Or possibly they were throwing away their one true chance at peace, choosing to spill blood – for that is all they know of freedom. Is this my fate? To die like the rest of them, as nothing, a dead warrior's clan upon my tongue, who also did nothing?

A voice breaks the eerie quiet.

'Suicides, how romantic,' the Sepāhbad begins, and I turn in horror. He examines the corpses in quiet fascination. 'Is that all? What is one's defiance but a quiet protest against an army of thousands. It does nothing.'

And within his grip... a man in Azadnian garb, squirming.

The raven is sat on the Sepāhbad's shoulder as he drags forward the captured soldier, treading on the corpses, seemingly uncaring that he is stepping on the dead.

Vomit flecks the Azadnian's clothes. He stares in disgust, as if sighting an angel before realising it is a demon, but that is the Sepāhbad's allure: a beautiful vision to mask the ugliness.

'The Great Father will avenge us!' the man hisses.

The Sepāhbad's shoulders shake in an empty laugh, but his raven does not move. 'There are worst things than death. I stare it in the face each day; therefore it cannot scare me.' He grips the man's chin between his fingers. 'Let us see how much you fear it.' The Sepāhbad raises a finger my way. 'Hold him by the legs.'

I shakily grab the man's feet. How much had the Sepāhbad heard, and will I be punished next? A sweltering heat radiates from his body. A deep fever. It must be a consequence of the Gates technique. I quickly notice now how his cheeks are red in flush, and his words sound strained.

'Act almighty, but we've all heard the stories of your cruelty,' the Azadnian spits.

The Sepāhbad looks unworried. 'I can be worse.'

Without warning, the Sepāhbad slices off three of the Azadnian's fingers in a smooth arc. It takes everything in me not to wince. The man wails; possibilities must be flitting through his mind – if the Sajamistani cut off his fingers, why not cut apart his limbs?

I hastily suggest, 'We should take him to the encampment.'

'No, underling, we do this now before he succeeds in taking his life. Or will you let him do that too?' Then, facing the Azadnian, he nods at the warm corpses. 'Would you like to follow?'

'Go to—'

'Again, how unnecessary,' the Sepāhbad says calmly. 'I am a pragmatic man. I torture silence, but I am amiable to cooperation. Tell me one thing, and then you may be free in the name of your Great Father. To which outpost was your militia headed with Mitra? You may be a pathetic footman told no intelligence, but it's also the low who do the dirty work. Today, the apprentices transported thousands of Mitra to a different outpost.'

'I know nothing,' he breathes.

The Sepāhbad presses his khanjar against the man's forearm, the squish of skin near my ears making me almost flinch. He slices slowly, back and forth as if sawing the trunk of a tree; every flicker of pain must have been excruciatingly felt. My hand clamps his wet lips as he screams. When the arm is gone, the hand twitches on the clay, dead muscles spasming one final time, blood dripping down black hairs. I stare, almost immune to the grotesqueness of it. A dark thought follows it: this torture could be worse. The Gates technique must mean the Sepāhbad cannot access his affinity until he recovers from the fever.

'You know more, or the other arm will be next.'

Now, words fall out. 'Y-you are too late,' his words slur. 'The melee was a farce. Zayguk has allied with Azadniabad, not Sajamistan as you thought. An invasion is beginning from the eastern front – not Ghaznia – with Zayguk granting passageway into Khor.'

My mind recedes to the last question of the Wadiq tests – it's as if it was prophetic of this moment.

'They crossed today?'

The Azadnian struggles to speak, though he cackles. 'T-this morning.'

'So, the war has begun,' the Sepāhbad says.

My gut curls in. I must find a way to kill Akashun, who must be in Azadniabad's wartime capital.

The Sepāhbad pats the Azadnian's only hand. 'Be free now. You've fallen for charm under your Great Father. Now, die by another.' To my surprise, he circles his fist over his torso in the Azadnian salutation.

The man's heart is carved from his chest, the khanjar sinking like teeth into skin. For a second, I feel that blade sink into *me*, like I am the Azadnian sprawled before a Sajamistani.

The Sepāhbad stands. 'You did not capture them.'

I look into his feverish eyes and make my tone steady, so he has no choice but to hear honesty in my lie. 'Because they took their lives before I could.'

'If you had moved sooner, it would have prevented the suicides. With their feeble loyalty, they'd have confessed information without much prodding, avoiding this man's torture.'

I know he is right. My skin crawls as if I've been flung naked before him – for all my excuses, he saw my trembles on the battlefield; he knows I am sympathetic. The best martial artists must be familiar with pain to inflict it, and mine is a wound bleeding openly for him to study. And his next words confirm it.

'The truth is, in war, no judgement is correct. But the point is not about correctness, it's about compromise. You are an underling, leaving no room for hesitation.'

'I understand,' I say, but I speak too fast because his eyes darken.

'Do you, shepherd girl?' He prods. 'Two soldiers, from the Dawjad nomads, proclaimed allegiance to their brethren. The third seemed loyal to Emperor Akashun. If we spent our time looking at the details of every soldier's philosophy outside the colour of their uniform, well…' His lips curl. 'It wouldn't be a war at all, now, would it? You would fall for false sympathies. In battle, that would kill our warriors. You had sympathy because… an enemy was nostalgic of the vast pastures you hail from?'

'It was a mistake – a foolish, emotional mistake. But,' the words are desperate, clawing to the part of him that perhaps understands; is he not from their tribe, 'they never chose this.'

'Would you like to be a peaceful warrior?' A dark amusement weaves through his question and my disappointment bruises me. 'She is still not certain when the truth is before her eyes. If you saw these soldiers guarding Mitra, would you recite the same defences? These people cling to their history like a ruse of impartiality in war. And now, you sought a charity by letting those soldiers take their own lives. They spoke of freedom, so, naturally, death would become theirs.'

'Because it was.' My throat cinches. I see there is no victory when two empires are at each other's throats fighting over land; no way to be the in-between. The Camel Road is a borderland, the grey amongst the black.

Before the Sepāhbad departs, he brushes one of the corpses with his foot. 'What people forget when they worship their history is that, as beautiful as the idea of a revolution is, all revolutions begin and end with war. All revolution is war. War is what we fight.'

For my disobedience, he informs me my overseer will dole out a punishment on my return to Za'skar. Then he departs, but the raven remains.

It perches on a branch and watches me slowly bury the corpses. For I see myself in them. After I am done, the raven claws its talons across the dirt and I chuckle bitterly. 'Thank you, Rasha,' I whisper as it soars back to its master, who let it stay for the burials.

Like my father, Warlord Akashun is a symbol of strength for a people who've lived in terror of the other empires, people who are weak. Their worship does not make them foolish; it only proves their vulnerability. But heroes are nothing in this world. They fatten by feeding on the helpless because we seek something larger than ourselves. They are illusory symbols, and like all illusions, they can break.

If I must defeat him… I need to remember this. I cannot merely kill him – I must kill the symbol of him, the hope he gives them. Perhaps it would do the world good to have no heroes at all. We like to be ordered. We need fear.

I loved it. Perhaps the world will love it too, I muse to myself.

35

I decide to wait before defecting to Azadniabad's capital. Given its central location in the empire, it's more strategic to maintain my cover as a Za'skar warrior and join Sajamistan's troops moving westward along the Camel Road. Therefore, after the melee, I am sent back to Za'skar to convene with my assigned squadron. Upon journeying there, an unexpected longing swells up my throat. No-Name understands my intent. 'After today, you will never see the pazktab students again.'

'You sound pleased.'

'Because I feel sick when you see them.' She spits as I hasten up the hills toward Little Paradise gardens.

It's predawn, the heavens a dim blue. Trifectas trickle across the sand dunes for training; others stretch on the slanting roofs of the glimmering monastery suspended in the mountainside above the clouds; Qabl sages sweep away dirt from sandstone edifices around jinn-blown glass temples. But a tension wrings the air from the impending war.

I wind up the hills, sighting pazktab students stance training on the grass.

'Master?' Yahya cries.

And the snotty thing throws himself into my arms. The lump in my throat disappears as the weight of him knocks away my breath.

'Yahya,' I say, but it takes a miserable will not to cry out his name. Sohrab comes up grinning and pauses at the sight of me. Yasaman drops her parchments and reed pens, pressing her hands to her face.

Only Arezu watches with a narrow gaze. 'A foolish love.'

'You are the foolish one,' Sohrab snaps. I choke back a dark laugh at the word *love*.

Arezu smiles. 'We know war has broken out across the Camel Road. Za'skar is emptying out its warriors. Our master is leaving, to be chewed apart by enemies.'

'Arezu,' I warn. 'Do not say this before the others.'

She continues as if I am not there at all, eyes as flat as the salt plains surrounding us. 'In war, they will not let our master die slowly. They will mutilate her.'

'Arezu.'

'Master die?' Yahya murmurs.

'I...' My voice trails off. No child – *none* – should have bloodshed as a worldly perspective.

Even if I do not die, by defecting to kill Akashun, I can never return. But how does one explain death to younglings? Was this Uma's duty? To crouch and smooth my cheeks, to look me in the eye and admit that I must learn to kill with a bow and arrow before I may speak, that I must learn to hide before I may roam free in the pastures, I must be old before I am young. How does one tell a child this? But children are no longer children in war; their dreams vanish, and they simply become monsters.

As I stare at them, I conclude it is only a matter of time.

Sohrab reaches out to me but cold habit beats against me. I should find Overseer Yabghu. Why am I here? To inflict more pain?

To be selfish.

'No.' I step away.

Their faces fall. My blood pulses faster behind my ears. With Yahya curled in one arm, tentatively I outstretch the other. Sohrab and Yasaman cling into it, as if I can lift them to safety.

'Swear a Heavenly Oath that you will return?' Yasaman says. *'Please.'*

I cannot look at them. A cry chokes into my words. '*I am a liar.*' And for once, the confession feels absolving. 'I have lied many times and do not dare pretend that I have not. I have used you. But now, I do not wish to lie to you. Not about my intentions. Not about my identity. Not about my duties.'

'Then kill the enemy!'

'Do not say that.' I stiffen, my eyes truly burning. 'Killing cannot be done lightly, most of all by you.'

'But... it is a war. You will have to kill.' Sohrab's words flow too easily, and a part of me wonders what he has seen. 'When you are kicked into a corner and left to scramble, it does not make you a monster. It makes you human.'

Yasaman nods and brushes the necklace of bones at my throat. 'Do that. Be a monster. To live.'

I cannot answer except to pull them closer. Yahya begins crying in his confusion, unable to parse where I will be going.

We remain until the sun crawls up between the mountains like a red creature, swallowing the black-blue into wisps of dawn. Before they break away, I stammer, 'Remember our stances. Continue with a bowl of water, and meditate in the treetops. But please, do not pick a fight with the karkadann to practise. And,' I breathe, my chest caving, 'even if you achieve the stature of Qabl master one day, I want you to always breathe steadily through your pain. I want you to protect each other. I want you to—'

Eajīz are tools. Our purpose is to become terrifying warriors; to be an empire's weapon, the blade in a ruler's grasp. But despite such logic, all I can reason is *no*: I want them safe; they are mine. They are young, and these empires have no damned right to tear them from me. I was wrong to train them. I want to be their protector, to be their master, to be their mother.

But they will continue on their path, and I will walk mine. I hate that fact most of all.

'We know,' Sohrab grins lopsidedly. 'You trained us.'

It's that grin that seizes my spirit and shatters it. *I want you safe, you naïve fools*. And sheer desire seems as good as a millennium of logic, giving me reason to believe that somehow, I could remain at their sides.

But Uma told me of innocent birds in a cage. They must be set free.

I add thickly, 'I am no good and I am sorry for it. Please, on Judgement Day, do not testify against me before the Divine when you learn the truth of who I am.'

They giggle at that, deaf to the urgency. Sohrab clasps a hand to my cheek, kissing it gently. 'You are no good, master. Not at all. But to us,' he smiles, 'your good was enough. And for that, you will survive.'

The grass dances at our feet, the wind echoes my whimper. 'I might survive,' I whisper, 'for you.'

The drum from the pazktab school indicates the start of morning lessons. Sohrab has to rip a crying Yahya from my arms and they depart. But Arezu, who was standing far from the others, does not follow them.

She refuses to meet my gaze. Minutes pass, perhaps longer, before she glances up, her eyes glimmering with unshed tears. 'You do not wish to lie, but lie to me. The way you spoke – you are never like that. Something in you has changed. Whatever is happening, you are never returning, dead or alive.'

'Arezu, I am not worth your tears.'

'I am not crying!' she bursts out before aggressively wiping a stray tear. 'I know you hate me. I know we are pests buzzing at your ears and I know I say I do not like you, but that was never true. I—'

I clasp her shoulders, heart fluttering faster than the wings of a sparrowhawk. 'Never,' I answer carefully. 'I could never hate any of you. You are pests but,' I wipe her tears with the end of my shawl, 'I cannot explain all of my feelings to you.'

Another truth hits me. The idea of her disapproval is the worst. I crave Arezu's regard more than I crave that of my superiors or even my own father. I want Arezu to remember me as anything other than what I am – a selfish creature.

Her eyes slide up. 'Do you love us?'

'I do not understand what love is,' I admit.

She smiles then, a rare expression. 'Neither do I,' she says before embracing me, face buried into my chest.

'I can never understand you,' I blurt. 'You have your family in Khor but you are in the pazktab. Why leave them behind at such a young age?'

'*Age?* Age is irrelevant. I could have waited in Khor for more raids, helpless to them. But no, I will defend my family *here*, and *there*, until my last breath.'

'You fool,' I say as she shivers, and I bunch my cloak around us.

She clenches the bone necklace at my collar, gifted by her, smiling up at it. 'You are the stupid, illogical fool. Not me. I fear for your soul. Will you be like them? Someone who must kill?'

'All warriors kill,' I state carefully. 'Though in the spiritual laws of war, soldiers consent to conflict, and so the gravity of death is not equivalent to cold murder.'

'I mean taking pleasure in it,' she rolls her eyes, 'until the knife that accidentally strikes an innocent is not so damning anymore. Like the raids.' Then her eyes stream with more tears. 'It is so wrong.'

I speak unflinchingly. 'You might be the same. You enlist in less than a year now.'

To my surprise, she shakes her head. 'I decided, after you left, that next year I am returning to Khor. Not even to serve a clanhouse. With my pazktab education, I can be useful. I will teach at the Khorinite monasteries, train their novices even if they are not Eajīz. To help my village. We had great warriors, we can achieve it again.'

'That is good,' I say slowly but her tears keep rolling. 'Why are you upset at this?'

'Because of what you said! You are content to kill more and more!'

'I've already killed,' I speak flatly. 'I come from a clan full of it. It should not matter to you.'

'*It does*,' she snaps before shoving me. 'I care about you and your afterlife. All of it.'

An unexpected warmth billows in my chest, that someone even thinks of my afterlife. 'Then pay alms-taxes for my grave.'

'Dead and you will still be cheating me of money,' she mutters.

This is all I needed, I marvel. If this is how I must depart, I can accept this fate. I decide then, I will lie for her.

'You want the truth? This war is nothing for low-ranks. I will be stationed at the Kin Basin, the northernmost frontier, away from any invasion.'

Arezu pauses. 'So I wasted my tears on you?'

'You know what else?' I kneel, wrapping my shawl tight around her flushed ears, tucking it into her collar. 'When I return, we will buy lamb-stuffed non for Yahya, because that is all I can afford. Then we will go to Overseer Yabghu and borrow his generous stipend and lie about repaying the debt. And we will trade for dates with walnut paste. And we will bribe the pazktab students for favours.'

'Really?' Her eyes gleam wide, almost in relief.

'By the Divine.'

She chuckles and I cannot tell if it's from sorrow or joy. 'Promise me, you will speak another story, around a fire.'

'Yes,' I vow, suppressing my trembling. 'One day I will tell you every folktale, the ones of my Babshah Khatun. You will be the best folkteller in the Camel Road.' I beam at her even as the memory of my girlhood is tight and crooked, like folding my arms into an old tunic whose sleeves no longer fit. 'And your smile... it is like Older Brother. There was not one day he went without it. Even at death when a sword hung above him, he smiled. For he believed in a better world—' I swallow hard.

'Looking at you, the students – I believe him. I believe this world has some good left in it. But not from myself.'

'You have an even prettier smile, master. I wish you smiled more so you can see yourself from my eyes.'

'No one has seen my true smile nor called it pretty, but I think the Divine was saving the blessing to come from you.'

'Then after this war you must smile more.'

I want to weep through the thin joy. 'I will,' I lie, because would I even live long enough to try?

Her eyes shut. 'Thank you.'

Our heads tilt, foreheads together, and her thumbs cup my cheeks. I cradle her in my arms, pretending I can keep her forever. I memorise the sensation of her skin, and the last of her warmth that I cannot keep. The golden horn of the sun finishes its rise, the clouds like white teeth in the bloody mouth of dawn. I have never said farewell well in my entire life. Is a goodbye a simple *peace of death be unto you*, an assurance of the next life? Or are goodbyes like the dawn, a blaze of light that seems to promise something wonderful, but in fact assures nothing at all?

Arezu opens her eyes. She feels like my dawn. Then she smirks through her tears. 'Please get lost, master.'

The dream fades.

36

Stone City, Kin Basin, Sajamistan Empire

I stand in Stone City, carved into the mountains as if it floats by the Divine's will, for that is what the natives claim. The jinn-folk cut into the mountains as if they were clay, arranging them into ridges and quarters. Rose palaces are seamed by strips of bedrock connecting individual townships inside the hallow caverns.

'Do you think it is true, Overseer?' I ask.

'That's "Captain" to you during wartime,' Yabghu reminds me, glancing up from carrying a corpse. 'And is what true?' The dams have broken their bounds and swollen bodies flow downwards, soft scalps bobbing.

'The humans who live here have never touched the ground?' I gesture at the metropolis floating into the mountainsides around us. Stone City, north of Kin Basin, is cool, its interior in enclosed mountains surrounding the steppes. Whatever Heavenly punishment occurred centuries ago against the civilisation, irrevocably changed its geography.

'Perhaps,' he says, as listless as the bodies. Sweat droplets bead down his temple, saturating his ochre tunic. 'Stone City was once a wicked civilisation after Prophet Nuh's time. The Divine commanded the arrogant to be wiped out by angels, who caused a clay-quake.'

A pattern in mankind where eras end in the form of a disaster. To distract myself from the corpses of the reconquered township, I ask, 'What did they do that invoked the Divine's wrath?'

'When revelation was sent to this city, its chieftains ordered the slaughter of any pious worshipper. Stone City was stubborn in their shaman traditions, worshipping jinn-folk of the sky under their deity

Eçe. Its inhabitants were the wealthiest traders, for their harvested agriculture was unique, grown in altitudes this high.' I follow his gaze to gardens, their crops that crawl sideways above us to creep closer to the sun. 'The tribes lived long, long wealthy lives in the arms of the sky and the fingers of the clouds; it was as if they were embraced in the limbs of their deities. The Creator sent angels as a warning of calamity, to stop their magick and their tyranny on the surrounding villages, but none heeded. So, angels squashed the metropolis under their feet and used their wings to send great winds. In one night, Stone City was nearly annihilated. All we have are the engravings of the proto-city on its walls to remind us of humanity's errors.'

Fear grips me. It was their comfort of divinity that made them so arrogant, only for the true divinity to turn against them.

Yabghu continues, 'Now the clans here are superstitious; priests screech to remember their ancestors who paid for their ignorance. They hide above humanity in this city, believing they will be safe from mankind's sins.'

'*Hid*, not hide,' I correct him, glancing in sorrow at the harvest of corpses littering the residential quarters, a warning from Emperor Akashun for refusing to surrender. Each day brings me more westward, and with less time to figure out a way to kill him.

'They have everything to fear now. From their pathetic defences and battle rams, they hadn't been to the ground in centuries.' Yabghu shakes his head. 'Why bother when everything you need is in the sky, closer to the Heavens?'

I wonder how such a thing is possible? For beings to live suspended like flax rope between the ground and open air, stretched taut, neither grounded nor in flight. Would the children born above find the concept of living on the ground as unimaginable as I find living in the air? Or was their refusal to live within the natural order a mistake? Because, looking around us, Stone City is a floating cemetery, like a mirror of its past.

And they are only one of many. Our squadron arrived in early morn, to reconquer Stone City from the Azadnian Kataqul Militia, who were granted passage to it by the bordering qaghanate of Zayguk, on the north-east Camel Road.

In wartime, the Alif warriors are divided amongst the regiments as generals. Alif Adel, the general of our tagmata, crosses through the brass gates of the rose-hued sandstone citadel and nods at our squadron. 'Finish refortifying the southern trails. We've been summoned to Khor as reinforcements. We leave at sundown, using the night as cover,' he orders us.

Captain Yabghu and Lieutenant Negar lead the squadron in sweeping trails through the mountain, re-digging thin moats around the gates and clearing transportation channels that connect to the delta as boats carry rations in and out of Stone City. Beside Katayoun and Cemil, I silently collect corpses along the poisoned streams, stinking with carrion. Above, the Heavens rumble in anger, the moon a forlorn eye fixated on humanity's sins.

Azadniabad aims to conquer Sajamistan's northern territories, including Yalon province, by invading via the Camel Road. Stone City is one township along in the long campaign for Sajamistan to reconquer the central pastures toward Khor. As a strategic wartime capital, the Kin Basin – overlapping Al-Haut province – is a commercial web of silk and steppe-camels. Its trade nodes are not only protectorates for caravans but also exporters to Sajamistan.

As Azadniabad successfully leverages the Mitra trade to the Zayguk Qaghanate, compromising Kin, while simultaneously invading through the Black Mountains to Khor, Sajamistan faces a two-front invasion, forced to stretch a massive commitment of battalions from the homeland. Khor is the buffer for Sajamistan proper's water channels – cutting it off is Azadniabad's fastest way to a conclusive victory.

During our six-week campaign to reconsolidate the protectorates of the Camel Road, Yabghu explained our defensive tactics. Sajamistani soldiers are rotated between tagmatas, to prevent mutiny against their commanders. To offset their numerical inferiority, the Za'skar battalion's squadrons, smaller than in a normal army, but efficient, are dispersed as elite forces in larger troop units, for outflanking manoeuvres in battle and for the greater strategy, a war of movement. The stratagem requires swift communication lines and choosing mountainous positions that are offensive in nature, so the enemy's defences remain off-kilter, pillaging the psychological balance of the battlefield.

Our mobile squadrons had been designated for disruption tactics; we target the enemy's rear, we scorch their supply routes, we bait and trap with the fastest retreats, and we ambush in the night. Strategies birthed by steppe-warriors.

With Azadniabad's new alliances and Mitra's existence, a part of me is impatient, as though our actions are only slowing, rather than stopping, the poison seeping through the red soil.

What war created for Akashun was a push and lever. It was so easy for him to unify the tribe-fractured prefectures into an empire, glued together by the throes of the Camel Road and emboldened by the possibilities of Mitra. Akashun was waiting for war. And any governor who resisted was made an example of. Stone City was merely one of many massacres.

But I've no intention of witnessing a land doomed to subjugation. When an empire's valour is personified by one man, the weakness is obvious: killing their Great Father would leave the children orphaned. Grieving and hopeless, the empire would devolve into unmoored herds retreating into their cavities of prefects and tribes. Only with Akashun's death will Mitra end.

Under the guise of Sajamistan's battalion, each step takes me west – takes me closer to Azadniabad, to find Akashun and kill him.

That night, in the citadel barracks, I awake to shouts. I yank on my uniform, shivering as I make my way into the dry chill. In the middle of the palace courtyards, I see Yabghu rubbing his eyes. The troops are to depart before sunrise for Khor.

A commotion snatches away my exhaustion. Throngs of the city's survivors and priests rush out; others are praying and prostrate in the open. The eerie sight of worship in the dead of night sends confusion through me. Many shout to prepare the mules for departure. Some stand with satchels, trailing towards Stone City's brass gates.

'Where are they fleeing? And why are priests leading prayer so late?' I could understand a few in worship, but before me, I count hundreds.

Katayoun turns and I baulk at the fear in her eyes. 'This place is cursed,' she mutters.

'What happened?'

'Every priest awoke at once. They had the same dream.'

'A dream?'

'Of angels in the Heavens. They warned that believers should seek refuge up and away from these lands.'

'A warning…'

Katayoun faces the worshippers. 'Of corruption. That only Divine guidance would save them. The survivors are abandoning Stone City to climb the Kin Mountains for higher ground, as if Stone City is not high enough.' Her lips twitch up, but her tone is empty. 'We might as well take the leftover war spoils.'

Are the Heavens warning them to flee because of Mitra?

She returns to the barracks but No-Name remains, observing the prayers. 'At least they are taking action, when you do not.'

I flinch. *I don't know what you speak of.*

She smirks. 'Oh, stop playing the fool. You desire to kill Warlord Akashun — but have you really considered the means?'

The dread coalescing in my chest makes me snap. *Of course I have. At Khor, I will defect west through the Black Mountains, to Azadniabad's wartime capital in Navia.*

'Then where is your urgency?' she snaps back. 'You are not strong enough to take on an emperor who has Mitra. Do you know how his power operates?'

From the Qabl monks, I counter, too quickly.

'Exactly,' No-Name says, seething. 'You follow their rules: you inhale rose incense, you meditate on bones, you heed the Qabl maxims, which only help you control your affinity, not exceed its potential. You have knowledge before you, though; you have the texts.'

My gaze narrows. *I have many texts.*

Her hand jostles my leather satchel containing my spare belongings. 'Recall the seals you found in the Mitra rituals. In your first visit to the Keeper, you grabbed a sageism text with those same triangular seals. The Sage Arts. And I told you to pack it in your satchel before you departed Za'skar.'

I shift and face her, the moon casting silver upon us. *I read the text months ago, but it was incomprehensible. Unlike Eajīz, these sages instructed meditating on an energy imbalance. Sages are not Eajīz, they operate under different corporeal laws. They commune with jinn because they are mortals with no Heavenly Energy.*

No-Name's black eyes quiver. 'That principle is reliant on a theological relationship, but what difference does it make? You are losing faith in the Divine, girl. You trained for the Duxzam in strange ways.'

I cast her a dark look.

Her jagged teeth glint. 'You could train more; you could do something useful instead of standing by and letting Warlord Akashun live. You were happy to lick the emperor's hand and you are happy to lick Sajamistan's.'

Shut up, I hiss, but her words are a khanjar's blow.

Her tone lulls. 'You recall the boy you killed – so young, so soft. It was remarkably simple to pierce that blade through his heart. Do not tell me you will become like that boy.'

I will not.

The shadows careen upwards and she inhales like my uncertainty is air for her. 'You don't want to defect to kill Akashun because you are scared… for your Zahr siblings; about betraying your trifecta warriors; of leaving forever. You want to stay.'

Never—

'You are pathetic.' She steps forward and her hand flicks against me. I blink, and suddenly, I'm thrown against the red-clay adobe of a broken temple before crumpling.

Shock resounds through me. She has never touched me against my will until today. She has never autonomously hurt me. Not unless we're sparring.

I expect surprise, but her eyes glimmer in equal parts contentment and guilt. Stunned – almost satisfied – I allow her foot to press down on my neck.

No-Name puzzles over this. 'You do not have the heart of your soul, for the emperor sacrificed it. Without him… you have no conviction. Now I understand. I understand the language you speak. The emperor is gone; who will cause you pain? Provide purpose? Fear not. If that is what it takes. But do not blame me for this. I do this because I care, and I have never cared for anyone before.'

My pulse hammers beneath my breastbone. The satisfaction – the familiarity of this – it's almost comfortable. Do I imagine this?

It matters not. She strokes my cheek before squeezing my jaw, and it hurts.

I let it hurt.

'Sometimes, you hurt the ones you care for, to open their sight.' One blink she is there, and then she elongates, skin morphing into a wrinkly blistered thing; her white hair vanishes, replaced with spiking bramble. We no longer look alike. Her eyes bulge until they droop from the sockets.

Her tongue pulses against four rows of sharp teeth, greeting me with a pointy smile. Her legs morph into hundreds of beetle legs, in *chittering* sounds that screech against my ears. Her face nestles in its oily body.

Terror paralyses me. She's become a dîv.

What the Hells are *you?*

She cocks her head. 'Oh, Khamilla.' Her voice is soothing. 'You wanted this. And I no longer take orders from you.'

She lunges and I dart back, feet slipping on the rocky ground. Then I am sprinting across the mauled quarters of Stone City, past Katayoun who calls after me, past the towering palace gates. I dive against an abandoned hovel.

No-Name crawls upwards on to the reed roofs, scurrying so fast she's a black blur, until she reaches the hut. I barrel forward, stamping my foot until the cracked door bursts open.

'Khamilla,' she calls out, desperate – sounding almost *hurt.*

As her talons scrape my back, I slam shut the door. No-Name hurtles into it, threatening to split the stone apart. I slink into the corner, her accusations turning over in my head.

Is she right? Perhaps my ties to both empires bar me from exploring my Heavenly potential?

You have become bored of your own suffering. The emperor is gone, so No-Name must remind you of the consequences.

Outside, No-Name bangs and shudders the walls. I unclench my aching fingers and peer inside my satchel toward the sageism text, at the triangular seal etched on the red parchment. This jinn-folk's knowledge is a translation, and translations are contingent on civilisations; with the passage of time, languages alter, making the knowledge incomplete.

Outside, No-Name quiets. To my surprise, the shadows around her wisp beneath the door and into the text. The words that challenged me before become clear.

If I want to access the Eight Gates of Heaven, I would need to reform my Heavenly bonds to strengthen them. So I begin reading.

Using the scroll's instructions, I meditate with incense using herbs with cold energy instead of hot. After seven-breath patterns, carefully, I enter a visualisation meditation, beginning with white dahlias before easing into the warm colours of gold, rose and then blood.

With it, the incense wafts into my sensorial experience, dancing on my tongue. Instead of a controlled state, it boils against my soul.

Shadows traverse against the golden light, manifesting into lines. I do not immediately understand what I am seeing, so I cross my legs in the psychospiritual world, simply gazing. But I don't draw near, afraid that if my bonds in this metaphysical realm detect me, they will snap away and disappear. Here, I'm a visiting stranger, watching something wonderful unfold from afar.

The gold dust scatters to reveal gates trailing to different realms, eons away. I distinguish from my Qabl studies the Gates of Time and the Unseen Gates, and then some anomaly into the unknown. There are the gates of the barzakh – the world of souls – where stepping through them guarantees death. I feel in this periscope like a speck, the vista too overwhelming for a mortal.

Eventually, I call on Heaven and my bonds fall into thick seventy-seven bonds. I run my fingers over them, stunned at how they materialised so solidly. They criss-cross my soul like capillaries – like strings attached to my body, as if I am a puppet dangling below Heaven. Each rod hinged in a position so arbitrary, there may not be human logic to its patterning – only Divine reason.

But at second glance, a theorem forms: the bonds are like coded inscriptions of divinity, twisting like a maze.

Based on this finding, instead of focusing on thickening power from the Heavens, I only need to rearrange the twisted bonds and combine the rods together like parts of a machine. If I take one piece of rod and connect it with another, the bond energy doubles.

An instinctive knowledge tells me that these bonds form the vastest, prettiest machine, an engine of unparalleled complexity. It's so dizzying, I can hardly savour its aesthetic pleasures.

The thoughts also evoke a dark suspicion: the reason no monk has spoken of this technique is because it's forbidden, and things are only forbidden if there are terrible consequences. But could I use it to access the Gates of Heaven to defeat Akashun?

Before I latch on to more bonds, the psychospiritual world shimmers. Faces form, and oddly, I see the Keeper of the Great Library. I blink. 'Keeper? Is this real?'

He shrugs. 'Is anything real in the spiritual planes? You opened the sageism text – I am its guardian, as I'm the guardian of many scrolls from the Great Library.'

'Oh.'

He sighs again, the most serious I've seen him. 'You have understood the text. A shame. The meanings derived may seem empirical, but your bias justifies your thoughts and therefore your actions. The book maintains one purpose: simple objective knowledge – until it's bestowed upon you humans. You think yourself better than the jinnfolk? Free will is the most powerful weapon in the world, and it comes from knowledge. But knowledge is a storm changing the terrain, harming its receivers, irrevocably shifting the fabric of existence. I warn you, this technique… what you are to do with that emperor will change this era.'

'For better or worse?'

He shrugs and yawns. 'I do not know.'

I hear it then. There's an undercurrent of rage humming beneath the Keeper's words. In his ancient existence, how long has he witnessed wars being fought for the same reasons but by different civilisations?

As he fades, he says, 'Open your eyes, daughter of the Simorgh.'

But my eyes are open. I have seen the world at the height of greed – this entire war is forged and sustained on damnable greed. But any conflict can reach check, then checkmate – only then will war end. Adel explained it himself: the Gates of Heaven grant the user access to the bond of a Heavenly Bird – it's my only hope to counter Mitra.

I unlock the door and No-Name is sat cross-legged, a little girl now. She beams, crawls forward and sits in the opposite direction from me, with her back against mine, resting her head against my shoulder. 'You need me,' she whispers reassuringly. For an instant, her body wavers, and I see a flash of tangled black lines. I shake away the image.

37

Khor, The Camel Road, Sajamistan Empire

For days, we travel along the blue mountainous trails, wary of Azadnian scouts. If we intercept tribes, Alif Adel orders them gently raided only for supplies to replenish ourselves with warm furs and rations. After a week, we cross into the Tezmi'a delta, uneasiness drifting amongst the troops.

The air blisters with foreboding, each inhale stinking of blood. In our last stop at some obscure township on the western Camel Road, Sajamistani scouts confirm the siege of eastern and western Khor has finally collapsed. The Black Mountain clans conceded passageway through Khor's villages. With no word from our second round of scouts, our tagmata enters the battle with dated intelligence, igniting my nerves.

In the march to the west, we stock up on grain and salted fish. At each village, soldiers man the citadels, and the local governors' expressions are bereft of hope – the soldiers brought war to their doorsteps, and though Sajamistan defends them, she has turned liberated cities into a stockpile of resources to supply her armies.

As we draw closer to Khor's pastures, ahead of me, Yabghu clenches Cemil's shoulder, murmuring fast. My eyes flit down to Cemil's hands, which are shaking.

Khor. This is his homeland, I remember. Once ruled by semi-nomadic Khorinites before those same tribes settled permanently and turned sedentary centuries ago, while still trading or warring with other steppe-tribes like my uma's.

Yabghu catches my eye and gestures Katayoun and me forward. The other warriors split around us as our overseer simply bows his head, honourable as ever. 'I found no joy – *none at all* – being your master,' he scowls, 'but I'd be more saddened at your deaths.' Then, he makes a simple request. 'Live to die in another battle.'

He returns ahead to his lieutenant while my fellow trifecta and I exchange long glances. As I open my mouth to speak to Katayoun, Cemil beats me to it: 'Stay close to my side before you get yourself killed,' he grunts to her.

'Obviously,' she grunts back.

Then to me… I expect anger. For me being Azadnian in a war against them gives him every reason to distrust me, but his stare is uncertain and unreadable.

Steeling myself, I lean in. 'I've no mercy in my soul to forget your attack but…' Quickly, I yank up his sleeve and feel his slight tremble of sorrow not dissimilar to my own, the gold-threading light on his tanned skin. 'I know these markings. *This* is what you have left of them,' I say firmly. 'It will push you onward.'

I move away, but his next quiet words give me pause. 'If I die, let me unburden myself. I regret much. But never have I doubted your will. It reminded me of my own. And Katayoun knows… though I did not want you to win, I gambled on your victory in the Duxzam.' His tone is empty, and I see he is long past this.

'How much?' I test him.

'Thirty idriq.'

'A-an impressive amount,' I say, choking, and there is bittersweet amusement in his eyes as he brushes past me.

From our high elevation, I gaze at the villages, sun reflecting off the glossy grey of the mountainsides bracketing it, cliff plunging into the flatlands below. I think about how the humans are like ants, burrowing and scavenging mechanically in their holes. The world seems so expansive, and we so finite in our miserable hills.

What do the jinn-folk think when they glance down at us? Do they chuckle at our intellect? Or do they shake their heads at our absurdity, wishing to reach their hands into mankind and toy us around like mortal playthings?

We find an abandoned cluster of cattle and stone hovels – not worthy of being called a village – which becomes our final stop. Adel sends scouts ahead to scope the vicinity of Khor's central settlement. But soon, there are shouts, and I hurry over.

The smell of decaying cattle hits my noses, and wet, dark dung buzzing with flies fills the ditches.

'Quickly,' he shouts and I see them.

Yabghu is knee-deep, pulling out humans from the dung. Two villagers are curled up, shivering and filthy in the pool of manure.

Adel barks orders to distribute water and cloaks. By the time they're settled, there are six total and their stories are pieced together.

'It was the creatures,' they say, shivering. *Mitra*. Some fleeing villagers had retreated into the Black Mountains, and others into muck too filthy to be scented by jinn-folk. They were trapped, forced to hear the invasion. A look into the wells shows bodies afloat, for those who jumped to their deaths to flee the creatures.

'A sign of the end times,' a man moans. 'We thought they were humans fleeing, but t-they attacked, like shai'tain. *And the serpents—*'

'Rest now, elder,' Adel says quietly. 'My scout will take you back to our encampment.'

But the woman beside him reaches out her arms and I meet her flat gaze. 'My arms, they are empty,' she says listlessly.

'Of what?' I crouch in front of her, but she looks past me.

'They dragged him away during the last raid.' The implication of it squeezes my chest. Before I can rise, she grips my collar. 'Do you understand how it feels to go through the pain of labour, to have fought death to hold him in my arms, and then to lose him? They took him – *he was pure* – and they took him. I've seen what happens to the ones taken; they will teach him to forget me.'

'I do understand,' I whisper; I have nothing more to offer her.

'Return him, then,' she cries. '*These are your wars, not mine.*'

It's sickeningly familiar. Is it easier to govern a people by enslaving their minds? It is easy, then, to create an army entrenched in your virtues before setting them free to encroach upon their mothers' lands.

The love of violence has nothing to do with it. This is an empire creating weapons to punish people resisting them.

Adel orders a squadron to remain back with the survivors in our encampment. We collect animal bones to leave offerings for the amiable jinn, and say a quick prayer for the dead.

I ready myself as Adel instructs the rest of the squadrons to form a wide-flung position, concentrating our smaller numbers for quick manoeuvring. Khor's central settlement's quarters are arranged in a large oval, cramped between gated entrances, with a three-tiered imperial ziggurat to the west. He decides on a two-pronged barrage: Squadron Two will cover the northern gates beside the Tezmi'a tributaries. Squadrons One and Four will squeeze the Azadnians from the south into the north, where Squadron Two will intercept the enemy from uphill, archers dropping them into the streams below. Squadrons Three and Five are to recover villagers.

We hike up the alluvial path. Dissonant shouts ride the valley breeze between the rocky arches of the Black Mountains. The city itself is a living, wailing creature.

'Is that a chant?' Cemil asks, face hard.

Adel readies a paper kite between his fingers and pauses. 'A prayer.' As if he recognises it. 'You will see soon enough. Your region may not be what you remember. From reports, the Azadnians have besieged every fortress, stripping Khor clean, taking any artisans, siege engineers, healers, farmers, merchants and youth, while using the rest as meat shields in the citadel so we don't fire arrows.'

The squadrons begin rubbing ash and attar into bond points.

We hike down the final trail, in view of the city gates. Clay-rammed houses nestle within the emerald land, some burnt and crumbling in the aftermath of the siege. Smoke billows through dirt roads into a bazaar. The pink-rimmed sky is congested, carrying a miasma of blood.

From our height, we get a full view. Some villagers tend to cattle while others carry out rations for the occupying troops, but the youngest are forced to stand in line around the courtyard of a bone-stone monastery with tarnished raven carvings. Guards stand with long spears, and one by one, each youth pushes up their tunic to their chest or holds out their tongue. Worse is when some are ordered to shut their eyes for the spear to poke against the eyelid, drawing up blood. The three spots of the mortal soul. They line up before a wide clay bowl, letting blood drip into it, chanting in flat tones: *I beseech my soul to the emperor of the Heavenly Crane.*

With it, my bonds quiver weakly.

One Khorinite boy will not cede his blood, hands curled into fists. The spear hilt swings and cracks against his back. Still he stands, so the soldier swings again, aiming at his hands, shattering the bones.

Red sears my vision. 'They use them for Mitra?'

Adel studies me carefully. 'Who knows, underling? They could be punished for dissent, violated, recruited into troops or used for Mitra rituals.' Adel faces the troops, voice eerily calm. 'Watch carefully what they force upon our brethren. To them, Sajamistani tribes are not human, but things to be sacrificed. If the enemy desires sacrifice, we will make an example of them.'

Squadron Two begins the engagement, attacking Azadnian guards at the main citadel fortress beside the Tezmi'a River, while Squadron Three forms a camp to collect survivors. My squadron flocks to the dikes on the west, our offensive focused on clearing the quarters around the smaller citadel, to reach Khor's imperial ziggurat.

Tall copper gates fence off the western entrance, with guards atop bone-stone turrets on this section of the citadel. At our approach, ground-level guards appear. In a blink, my two khanjars erupt with nūr before I flick them through the chests of three of the soldiers like needles bobbing through fabric. Yabghu is approaching another at the other side of the entrance; his Smokeless-Fire affinity rends the air in flashes of undetectable heat energy before guards can shout for reinforcements. The dead bodies' features are no older than mine, and if they are young, they must be new recruits.

'Clear out the citadel,' Yabghu orders my trifecta.

I back away as our squadron pours through the gates and follow Cemil and Katayoun inside the fortress. Strangely, the first limestone staircase plunges into chambers seamed underground toward the ziggurat. By the time I find Cemil in the first corridor, he is crouching near a naked boy who is curled in a corner in a poisoned daze. Worse than the image of him is the blankness in his eyes, which do not register relief at the sight of us.

The boy does not speak, clenching the sable cloak Cemil handed him. His chest is lined in black whorls of soot, marring the flesh.

Cemil turns to me, voice barely a whisper. 'I will take him.'

'Wait.' I piece things together. 'There are more of him because,' I glance again at the boy and his eyes have darkened considerably, 'this is bait—'

The boy lunges. I throw my palm out, a rope of nūr snaring him before he could wrap his hands around Cemil's neck.

'He's possessed!' I cry. The boy snarls, and his mouth froths, a jumble of moans spilling out. Behind us, Katayoun cries out from the barracks as I slam the boy's arms down. He bucks in strength unnatural from the myriad of jinn possessing him.

'Use your olive oil; it isn't too late for him,' I say quickly.

Cemil reaches into his satchel, finding attar and olive oil. We quickly slather it around the boy's neck before Cemil uses the side of his hand to saw against his skin. It's a technique to spiritually behead the jinn's soul. Eventually, the boy's eyes roll back, and he shudders, arms flapping up and down as the jinn escapes, likely, through his fingers. He stills, unconscious but alive.

We rush down the corridor to help Katayoun. We find three more villagers intentionally placed to bait our squadron. Their tongues are bruising blue, eyes bleary, skin slick with a sheen of sweat – unaware of what had been done to them. I see that Mitra has not been seeded within, only the bond of jinn-poisons.

Cemil and I share a look.

'This was an ambush,' I say.

'Will all of the villagers be like this?' His voice is strained.

I gather the first boy and stride away. 'On to the next corridor,' I say.

I emerge from the citadel to find Khor in a chaos of smoke. The villagers are screaming and scattering as our squadrons engage the Azadnian militia. I sprint up toward the western gates, the boy's body jostling in my arms. The clangs and screams of battle carry outside the city gates.

Back at the makeshift encampment, Squadron Three leads away the villagers they recovered. Many unconscious bodies are aligned in rows and as we approach them, the trembling begins.

Yabghu whirls, understanding before I can warn him.

Limbs slacken and mouths yawn open, low sounds stuttering out from the bodies possessed by jinn-folk. I pounce on a woman, but I am too late as her skin stretches, throwing me off. Eyes rolling black, her body merges into another body, and another, until a dozen are swallowed into a slick oily beast with a long black neck.

My head pounds. Another div.

Behind me, Katayoun cries out in horror. 'Do we kill it?'

'Yes,' Yabghu orders. But hesitation flies between our ranks, unsure how much of the creature is man or jinn-folk.

Yabghu crouches and barks at me. 'Return to the fortress and help Cemil; Katayoun and I will hold it here.'

I retreat as warriors wave what little incense they have and wield senna leaves and oils, trying to subdue the jinn-folk through the herbs instead of inflicting mortal damage with their blades. It's useless.

Through the gates, I watch the waves of fleeing villagers. Khorinites run toward our encampment and the grounds tremble from the near-stampede of it all, some carrying the wounded, others simply not caring who they trample with their focus on escape.

The cacophony of cries mingling with the blood and sweat only grows. I try to move forward, but my stomach turns. My head pounds more. I back into a hovel of pens full of waste. I cannot hold it in. I vomit all over the ground, arms trembling from supporting my weight before I face-plant into my sick.

This was us; my tribe and me. But so much worse. The Night of Tezmi'a, they did not stop at fire arrows. They chased after us, even when we fled. They chased us as one languidly pursues a spider weaving up a wall, before being squashed under the heel of a palm merely for existing. They killed us for the rush of crushing the small.

My hands cling to one of the pen's walls. *I cannot save them.* The past intertwines with the present and I cannot tell them apart because time doesn't heal wounds.

My senses slip as I stumble away from the hovel.

'Khamilla?' Cemil bursts out from the small fortress and his eyes narrow on me as he closes the distance. His hand grips my chin, leaning down to my face. '*Hold yourself together.*'

'It's my—' My gasps sputter.

'They need us. You have seen this before, but,' his expression wavers, 'even surrounded by death, *we cannot flinch.*'

I nod and he releases me. One step forward. And then another. Until we are running toward the gates where Alif Adel commands the remaining squadron to form two converging flanks, to cover the northern and southern villages within the township. The air ripples and bends.

'Retreat, it's in the moat!' Adel shouts, and from the northern moat, a long lashing tail snakes out, so tall it obscures the sun.

The air tremors like a plucked string. I blink. The tail crushes the entire left flank into crimson ruin. It lifts again, a great black shadow swallowing us before slamming on to the hovels. With a screech, the falak tears itself free from the moat, dozens of milky white irises flitting left and right: as if the creature is unsure if it wishes to appear more human or jinn. Human heads wave upon its neck before shuddering and rolling out of its skin into scaly figures. One grabs a fleeing villager, biting into the soft flesh of his chest…

'Ghûls inside the falak. They've saved the worst to guard Khor,' Adel says grimly. Though outnumbered, the Alif rotates his hand, funnelling debris into a dense vortex of cosmic currents, creating a wide berth before the falak.

At his signal, we charge toward the serpent. I lunge low, my nūr swathing my khanjar as it pierces a ghûl, red veins pumping through the neck. For a second, something very human wavers in its eyes.

The ghûl does not die. I engage it again, then cut through two more, who scatter at the eruption of blistering nūr before simply knitting back together. I remember the Sepāhbad saying we must kill each creature as many times as the number of souls used to summon it.

Darting back, I summon my shoulder bonds. Instead of attacking me, a dozen ghûls whir past in the opposite direction, toward the ziggurat. Spinning fast, I spot their target. A cluster of robed monks and children shrieking from the stairs of the sandstone structure. I begin to run after the ghûls.

Suddenly, vines sprout from the burnt monastic gardens and tangle around the creatures like a cage before piercing thorns into their eyes.

A Brother-Nature affinity. My feet stumble at it, but I reassure myself. It's a coincidence. Yet, instinct makes my eyes dart around that monastery, where the monks and children escape through a web of flora.

A willowy girl with hair braided into two spheres at the back of her head stands at the entrance of the three-tiered monastery hewed to the ziggurat. Flora brackets form a fortress *exactly* like I taught her. She shields the Khorinites as her power forcibly tears a path of hope for them.

I stare harder, heart plummeting.

No. She is at the pazktab. She's to train in safety—

Unwillingly, a memory squirms through my thoughts. *I will defend my family* here, *and* there, *until my last breath.*

What a fool I am. She meant *Khor*.

And then I am tearing through the dirt, running faster than I ever have. Anything to bring me closer. If only I could reach—

'Arezu!' I cry.

She ushers staggering villagers away, her pazktab tunic in tatters. At my voice, she whirls, loose strands of hair flying like raven feathers. But she does not spot me at that distance. Instead, her eyes bulge in terror at the swarm of ghûls.

She is alone. On that cracked threshold, she is left to their mercy.

'Arezu, run!' I scream.

But the girl has always encompassed a resolve unmatched by anyone other than herself. She places her trembling palm on the monastery steps despite facing the jinn-folk. Her lips move desperately. I *recognise* this; I *told* her this. She begs Heaven for the peak of power in exchange for an oath of martyrdom. Her arms widen. The ground splits, ancient roots bursting in what can only be the Third-Stratum of summoning – impossible for a girl her age. The ghûls, attracted to her purity, pounce.

The air splits. The world glows.

I'm thrown against a hut from the sheer power emanating from her affinity. But I roll to all fours, then I'm running again. Nūr swells, the energy coiling then erupting. My seventy-seven bonds vanquish the first row of ghûls despite the distance, but they reform.

Arezu raises her arms again and again, commanding the roots to stab the creatures, but it's not enough. She is only one girl against dozens. Her shaking limbs slacken. I scream her name. In that split moment, the wind carries a word that will haunt me for eternity: *'Master?'*

Then they are on her. Arezu's head cracks against the stone, dozens of ghûls swallowing her from view.

And then she's gone.

I throw myself at the ghûls, my affinity erupting. 'Kill me! *Kill me instead!*'

I am met only with Arezu's cries as I pass through the horde. They do not die, no matter how much nūr I unleash. But the curse of power, I know, is that when it is needed most, it fails you. My Divine-gifted affinity is cursed, it's wretched, it's an omen disguised as a blessing. It's nothing against forces that usurp natural order.

Desperately, I thrust my khanjar deep into my shoulder before holding out the dripping blood, begging for the ghûls to gorge on me, but it accomplishes *nothing*.

I do not stop fighting, I battle until my arms tremble, I lose all the martial forms and swing wildly. I kill them a hundred times over. I send a true prayer for the first time in months, I beg the Divine to save her until my throat aches.

But war in his cruelty does not care. He taunts me with each tear of her flesh.

At last, when my knife thrusts into the last one and it crumples, my sight latches on the broken thing below me. Her pupils are blown and her scalp is torn apart. A pool of blood streams beneath her body and there is not one wound but *so many* that I do not know where to press my hands and staunch the bleeding.

The wind howls and the clouds sob. Her bloodied lips part as if to whimper words.

I drop to my knees. *'No.'* I try to breathe but pain squeezes my lungs. *'Arezu?'* My voice tears between the pleas.

She cannot see me. Her eyes gaze heavenward, a flower searching for light. But there is no light in this bleak land. And when she is gone, I don't think there will be any left.

'Please, my Creator,' I choke out. '*Save her.*'

Tears roll down her cheeks against the blood flecking her skin. Her hands reach up, clawing fervidly at the air as if aching to hold someone, to feel warmth as death breathes into her, swallowing words into wheezes.

She cannot see me; she cannot hear me. She thinks she is alone. This child is dying. *And she is utterly alone.*

Her trembles cease.

'Arezu!' Frantically, I shake her. 'You cannot die!' I shriek. 'We promised to be warriors, to spit upon our opponents and *fight. We promised,*' I sob.

The regret is blinding. Why hadn't I realised it before; why had I not held her achingly close, tucked her into my shoulder and told her – told all my pupils – that I loved them. That in my time at Za'skar, they were my joy? Why had I not appraised them of this: they were the first people I'd ever loved by choice.

Why was I so selfish?

I gather her marred hands. Tears pearl Arezu's lashes and she stills for good.

No.

'Arezu,' I plead, lifting her to my shoulder.

I cannot save her.

I shake her, once, twice.

I cannot save anyone.

'Arezu!' Again, and again.

Something slams on to my chest, throwing us backwards. A ghûl rises and I crunch my fingers, the nūr splintering it. Though my world has irrevocably changed, the rest of the world has not. I cannot even mourn for the child who only ever knew war – who was never a child, but a weapon.

She's one of millions – the reason why beautiful flowers are picked from a garden but never the weeds. Because humans like destroying beautiful things.

Now I see.

My hands raise to the sky and curl into fists. 'Heavens!' I scream, and the material world shatters like glass and I'm before the light of the immaterial.

My psyche grows into ridges of poisonous blackness, and I feel No-Name at my back.

'She's dead,' I whisper, letting her arms curl into me. 'The creatures I helped create killed her.' I feel hollow. I should not exist. 'Arezu died, not knowing that it is my fault. Her master let her die. Arezu was a child; she had nothing to do with this war. And she is not alone. All of them – the villages, steppes, pastures – they didn't ask for this.'

My hands reach out to grasp my beautiful seventy-seven bonds.

I crush them.

The Heavenly Energy rumbles and shakes before delving into shadows. They are a tide and I'm the shore and I welcome them with open arms.

No-Name gazes in satisfaction. 'When Mitra succeeds, the other kingdoms will fall because of you.' She smiles. Why does winning a war matter when no one good is left? If heroes existed, Arezu would not be dead. If heroes existed, the Camel Road would not be caught between two empires. But heroes do not exist. They never did when I was a child, and they never did for the children here. If heroes don't exist, then one can only be a monster.

No-Name was right. By heeding the warnings of the monks, I thought I could kill Akashun without plunging off course. But to seek power is to resist all ties to natural order.

And so, on my knees within the spiritual world, I raise my bloodied hands, allowing unnatural order to grant me power, to make me their demon so I might destroy another.

Through my fear, rage slams harder. The psychospiritual world pulses as my bonds tangle into each other. From gold, they tinge into black. Some bond lines snap from their Heavenly sources before burrowing down below. The understanding is clear: I am about to do something wrong. Something I cannot return from.

'His Mitra, his war, his greed, *he killed her.*' I tremble. 'Now show me rage.'

Then I'm hurtling from the psychospiritual to the material, the power shattering through the cosmic realms and billowing through my bonds, crackling in spars of light.

At first my vision is a bliss of white: nūr's blazing currents. My body is paralysed to basic commands. I channel the power toward the falak and ghûls and then… Azadnian soldiers. The arches bypass my squadron, who whirl in horror.

'Farewell, siblings,' I hiss.

I want to blast them into oblivion. I know what held me back. It's these bonds, these arbitrary, meaningless gold lines – they are an illusion, compelling Eajīz to think they're safe.

In one swoop, my nūr incinerates hundreds of ghûls and destroys the living quarters of the Azadnian troops. I stare as the sheer brightness blasts them into oblivion, creating smiling skeletons. My arms widen until the light empties out.

This feels good. It's not the gore of it; it's the sheer destruction. It's the asymmetrical power finally within my grasp. The freedom of no constraints to simply erode all in my path in a symphony of destruction. It feels too easy.

I revel in it for a moment, tasting the chaos. This is destruction, but destruction is the force from which I was birthed. *Now it's clear.* I almost grin. The only way for me to rule would be to break the world under the stomp of my feet and glue it back together with their collective fear of me.

My vision tilts and a pair of hands catch my body.

'You complete fool,' Cemil says, but he doesn't sound angry. 'Let's go,' he orders.

I scoop up Arezu's body. We flee to the gates, where the other squadrons have retreated. Corpses block the exit, forcing us to climb over them. On the other side, Alif Adel's eyes blaze black. He points to the southern monastery where the last ghûls have flocked.

'We blow it apart.'

I understand his intention. 'Even if there are survivors.'

'There are none,' he answers. 'Mitra are in the communes. We have no more reinforcements. We kill them *now* before they slaughter the entire township and move into the central Camel Road.' Then he seizes me by the shoulders. 'Our people need us. Use whatever incense remains and meditate.'

We do. Cemil had a marked spot during the battle, and his affinity transmutes pockets of Yabghu's smokeless fire to the southern corners of the township. Meanwhile, I pull from the Heavens, combining my bonds into a colossal mass. Then I tear the nūr into three strips like silver linen. Adel's currents clash into it.

'Widen it into Yabghu's heat!' he snaps.

Digging in my heels, I envision it expanding. Adel commands the currents at each sphere of nūr and smokeless fire, waving them toward the monastery. When the light vortex reaches it, his strength as a Seven-Slash causes several explosions in the southern quarter until nothing but debris and smoke remain. The ghûls die on each impact and any human bodies left are shredded apart.

Then silence.

Adel inclines his face to the sky, grief evident.

'A difficult battle won, warriors.'

38

Reinforcements and supplies arrive from eastern Khor. For hours, warriors and villagers alike sift for bodies through the once fertile valley. The survivors are tended to in a healing tent, and I help distribute rations with Katayoun. Cemil had simply cursed at the carnage of the township, hands shaking, before storming off.

Hours later, after a medic wraps my shoulder, I am granted a short rest. I force myself to address the corpse, laid next to thousands of martyrs, tied with raven-feathered cloth.

When my hands lift the sheet, my sleeve muffles my cry.

Arezu is still dead.

I stand there, frozen. When Alif Adel crosses through the rows of bodies and passes me, I tug at his tunic.

'Tell me that I imagined it.'

'Imagined what?'

My voice veers into something ugly. 'Tell me. I want to forget, I want to be wrong, *please*—'

'Underling.' He pries my hands off.

I point wildly to the body. *'Tell me that's not Arezu.'*

His expression falls. 'Arezu deserted a month ago from the pazktab.'

I fall on to my hands. 'No.'

'It's true.'

Ice claws my chest. 'I had a right to know—'

His face is firmed against remorse. 'Your overseers would never jeopardise this war for personal attachments. Arezu had not yet enlisted. She was simply a brave pazktab girl who fled hastily to defend her township. If word spread of a child running away, it would set a dangerous precedent in the pazktab. What if her peers foolishly followed her? If we had informed you, you would have left your posting. In war, we make difficult decisions, and as your superiors, Yabghu and I decided against informing you.'

All the signs were there. Arezu spoke of her hopes to defend Khor. She begged me to lie about the realities of war – she ached for their comfort so she could believe she had a chance to live. She was a scared girl diving into the throes of battle. When she promised to reunite with me after the war, she was lying to me as much as I was lying to her.

'You knew,' I croak.

'You cannot understand what goes into war until an entire empire's fate rests in your hands.' He pats a hand on my shoulder. I am too numb to recoil. 'Khamilla, no doubt she's a hero. But she is one death out of many. War does that to people; it turns bodies into numbers.'

The frankness of it. The cold condolence is a sharp knife. I stare at other warriors hunched over corpses. The injustice of it cleaves my heart in two. I cannot even protest Adel's logic, because if Arezu was another's comrade, I would not flinch at her death.

'She hoped to be a warrior. To be a Qabl master.'

'A child died saving villagers from the monastery. She's a greater warrior than any of us,' he whispers.

I blink at the burning sensation behind my eyes. 'I wish someone could tell her.'

Adel regards me. Whatever he sees must satisfy him. 'Tell me, in the next battle, what you will do to the enemy?'

I am reminded of the look that engraved his face at the sight of Mitra – the burning, blinding hatred. A people reduced to the simple word *enemy*. At the centre of it, one emperor.

'*The Divine have mercy, I will make them scream.*'

Yabghu approaches me twice to take Arezu's corpse to the gravediggers, but I refuse.

I had thought this war, at the height of its destruction, was true Hells, but this – Arezu's death – flings me to the peak of agony. I prefer screams and cries to this awful stillness. I prefer the hot feel of blood to cold skin, helpless, with a dead body in my arms.

How dare I breathe when the girl below me cannot? She was good. *She was good*. And that goodness murdered her. Goodness is futile.

I do not know what else to do other than to trace my fingers upon Arezu's face, skimming her nose, cheeks, her broken skull. Only once had I held Arezu willingly. And I ache to do it again.

But touching her now is only the echo of what could have been. Her soul is gone. The Angel of Death has led her to the barzakh, and I pray the Divine will bathe her in nūr until the last hour. The certainty embraces me in its own light.

My child has the status of a martyr, a guarantee of Paradise, but...

I will never see her again.

My next breath jolts the air. I only know anger and vengeance, but the thought of snuffing it out terrifies me. Because if vengeance means losing all chance to be good, then what hope do I have to see Arezu in the hereafter?

I wish Eliyas was here; he would speak the beauty of prayers into death. Or Yun, with his harsh but red-warm heart, who would give me a stern talking to and fill me with resolve. I want Babshah to speak a folktale. And Uma with her quiet empathy. But I have nothing but an affection that has rotted, poisonous; it was that that made Mitra. That struck this child dead.

My nails jam into the grassland. But the pain brings a purpose. Fine, then. Though Arezu is dead, this selfish creature will tuck the child in her arms like that midwinter night and speak soothing words. I can do nothing more. Because she is my child. She *was* my child. And in this dark world, I want to bathe my child in light.

But how?

In Azadniabad, we mark the dead with seeds of firelotus, we let nature reclaim their bodies in the cycle of resurrection. But in Sajamistan, they bury their dead with a marker of bone-stone to say this is the realm of the barzakh. However, both empires follow the method of Adam – to bury in the ground facing the first place of worship.

I feel like his accursed son, unworthy of burying the corpse, hiding my sin in the belly of the clay. Still, I prepare Arezu's burial rites in his way. I perform an ablution upon her to cleanse impurities. I place her broken hand on her marred chest and then the right atop.

I prostrate on the dirt and perform a prayer of the martyrs. With her body at my side, I tuck her hair back before raising my palms. I beg the Divine: *please let my words be heard for my child.*

But the request stumbles at the sharp ache inside my chest. '*I-I miss them.*' I wrench the words out. 'Eliyas, I killed him. Babshah I could not save too. Uma, Usur Khan, and now Arezu.' Before I know it, my hands are ablaze in nūr. An old grief that has rotted for years bursts out like an infection and I cannot cleanse it. 'Please – *this pain. Take it away. I cannot bear it.* I would die a thousand deaths to see Arezu's smile one last time. Why had I not *cherished* it?'

A caw above has my head craning. A familiar raven lands lightly, scratching claws against the tired dirt.

'Mourn her,' I gasp to Rasha, 'for I am unworthy.' Then I am pressing my nūr to my mouth. *Swallow it,* a part of me urges. *Forget it all.*

The raven simply stares. *For every martyr, death transcends.* Ravens are vultures, to scavenge and find bounty even in the dead.

'O, Rasha,' I whisper, for this is what the Divine has revealed to me: the pain that I misunderstood my entire life, the pain that I ignored – *it was love.* And it assures me that I'm a true dirt-being of Adam. But the realisation is late.

I sink lower, unable to breathe. 'I'm sorry. To Eliyas for rejecting your love. To Babshah for forgoing my oath and crumbling under the burden of your tales and buzzards. I have run from pain to forget it. I cannot forget you, Arezu. I vow it. I failed in burying Babshah, Eliyas and Uma. But I will not fail you, my child. I honour your burial with this raven to guide it.'

Ravens: my enemies' symbol, but also this girl's honour. I do not fear it.

I begin my true message through the prayer. Tears brim in my eyes and my hands drop to Arezu's face. 'The children of the monastery live because of your martyrdom,' I reassure her. 'You – you perished fighting. Even knowing that if you survived you might be exiled from Za'skar City, you made a Heavenly Oath to earn power for certain death.'

My hand stills.

'You understood the meaning of a true warrior: one who fights not for glory, not for pride, but for justice. You thought you were worthless. But the world knows, *your master knows*, and the ones you saved will always know you are the paragon of a warrior. It was you who made me promise to smile, and even in death, I cannot forgo a promise made to my child.'

My lips clamp but Arezu needs to hear everything: my honesty and my love. I smile then, through my tears, because she deserves more than just my sorrow.

'I know you were afraid – *so afraid* – but the truth is, every mighty warrior feels fear. Because that fear gave you the Third-Stratum – a feat that warriors spend years to accomplish. But the Divine chose *you* for martyrdom.

'I'm sorry for turning you away. For being cold. For never showing you anything but my own cruelty—' I can no longer hold anything in.

'*I'm sorry,*' I suddenly gasp and repeat it. Again and again. I have never felt this. I do not recall a time I wept like this. '*I'm so sorry. For my mistakes that have killed you*. For causing your demise. For being afraid. *For only being a master when I could have been a mother*. Arezu, you and my pupils, you were my first chosen loves, albeit unknowingly. No one ordered me, no one cursed it upon me. *I chose*. I am sorry I never treasured it the way I should have. I was selfish. But you taught me more than any teacher. You were a gift and *I'm sorry I didn't see it.*'

And then I'm sobbing as I think back to the last day in Little Paradise. With the promise of a new dawn, it was the first time my stiffened lips had opened and I was brave enough to tell this child the hopes of my heart. So, I give her one more lie.

'*We promised,*' I cry, 'to spoil ourselves with food. If we cannot in this life, then by the Divine, in Paradise, you and I will reunite. I promised to tell you my folktales. I couldn't do it then, but I could do it before the Heavens. Like how I hold you now: speaking with the tongue of a folkteller, hoping the blessings of an uma find you.'

I bend and kiss her temple and blow my prayer upon her. I repeat that she is safe. By the Divine, she is.

It's said that in my religion – whose mercy I'm unworthy of – that the ones who don't accept the consequences of faith will try to exploit its benefits for worldly gain, and *that* is the measure of a corrupt person, while Believers readily accept consequences in this life, so in the hereafter, they reap the light stretching toward them.

The Believers feel true, eternal peace. They feel nūr.

Nūr is the path to revelation; it's accepting suffering in return for light. But today, it's a light I could never reach.

It reminds me I have always been alone. And I have never tried to change that.

No-Name crouches beside us. 'What will you do?'

Heavenly power is fickle, with as many variables as a complex mathematical equation. Eajīz must have faith in the Divine and, henceforth, the Heavens; we should strive toward morally righteous intentions, then action. But time has run out.

'I will use the Gates technique to summon a Heavenly Bird, even at the cost of my Heavenly Contract,' I whisper.

I can only glare at Heaven. The stars stare down, each chasm between their lights appearing small but, in reality, infinite in scope. Love, I see, is all the withering darkness between the stars, small in appearance but limitless in experience. And if it's so far away, if it's so hard to grasp on to, then love was not for me to begin with.

'With Arezu gone, you need me,' No-Name says. 'I will not leave you.'

It isn't until I hear Rasha's melancholy *caw*, then soft footsteps, that I am roused from my mourning. The Sepāhbad gazes down at Arezu's corpse. To my surprise, there is a darkening from grief, if only for a moment. He arrived with reinforcements following a campaign at the other Khor townships.

Arezu's words return. *A warrior saved me… I do not see the warrior often but sometimes, when they return, they greet me with kahvah and rose faloodeh.*

'It was you.' Another twist of fate, that this child has somehow brought two warriors on opposing sides together in brief respite.

'Arezu?' he simply asks. I manage a nod. He gestures to the path. 'A walk?'

The skies rumble as rain drizzles lightly on to the grasslands.

With Arezu still in my arms, I stand and he places a light finger on my shoulder. I swallow my uneasiness. It's his affinity, to ensure no rain touches us as he steers me in the direction of the gravediggers – slowly – to give us time.

During this, I explain Arezu's death.

When I finish, he nods slowly. 'Our curse as an Eajīz is to bear a world of sorrow. The more pain we suffer, the more Heavenly bonds we gain. Some murder their own loved ones to access more Heavenly Energy – but they fail to realise that true pain is sacrifice. That is why the warriors, on the brink of martyrdom, are able to access large amounts of Heavenly Energy. And Arezu's martyrdom… was accepted.' Then he asks a question. 'Did she tell you about her pazktab recruitment?'

My heart deflates. 'She'd begged a warrior to take her to Za'skar.'

He turns, blocking my view of the gravediggers. 'Nine years ago, a raid was instigated in Khor. In one of the homes I entered, Arezu was surrounded by corpses. Her family had perished but she survived. Her affinity was triggered after her brother and uma were tortured before her.' His lips turn up, bitterly. 'She was eight years old.'

I pause, stunned. 'She said only that her brother died.' Desperation weaves into my words. 'How can her family be dead? She – she told me they are plant-dyers.'

'Were,' he corrects. 'They were those things.'

The clearest answer arrives. This girl, raised by death and scarred by memories, at sixteen years, understood a concept I have spent my life running in circles to grasp: family is not the blood running through your clan or the gnarled roots twisting from beneath a tree in archaic tradition, a cage to be rebuilt generation after generation. It's the people worth every breath, every labour and every act of love to create a home.

My chest tightens. Her home was never limited to a dead clan. Her home was the land left behind.

The Sepāhbad rakes a hand through his hair before gazing at the mounds of dead bodies. 'In the days after, through her grief, she thought I was her brother. She followed me... everywhere. A survival instinct. Orphaned children were taken to the monastery. I forced her there, but in the years I visited Khor's outposts, she recognised me. She had learned about the art of Eajīzi from the monks. She demanded I patron her into Za'skar's pazktab.'

'What did you answer?'

'I said Za'skar is not for children.'

I cradle Arezu tighter. 'And what was her answer?'

His eyes meet mine. 'She said she was no longer a child.'

My eyes water. 'She did?'

He nods and reaches out, his thumb catching my tear.

'Thank you,' I whisper.

We've arrived at the grave site. I pull back the cloth to reveal Arezu's marred features. I touch my bone necklace. There is no peace in this farewell, only deep regrets. I despise them all: myself, emperors, warriors, generals like him for making children think they are heroes.

'They must bury her, to avoid a jinn's curse.' What he does not say: there can be nothing more to remember my pupil by.

'Of course,' I say bitterly. He doesn't respond.

It seems cruel to abandon this child again, to sink her in the cold, barren dirt for eternity, one amongst thousands in graves. She had been alone her entire life, but it seems impossible to let her go now, when she is finally in my arms. The brutality numbs me. I want to protect her. To love her. To pretend she's alive.

But I cannot. Wordlessly, the Sepāhbad holds his hands out.

I pass Arezu to his outstretched arms. For a heartbeat, she is pressed between us, a bridge across a chasm. He looks at her for a long moment. My skin itches and I scratch as he deposits her body on top of the other veiled corpses: a tower of cruelty, as soldiers amass to pray for the dead.

When the Sepāhbad turns back to me, my words tumble out in confession. 'The power I taught Arezu made her haughty. It encouraged her desertion.'

The Sepāhbad nods. 'It's the dilemma any master must face. At some point, no master can control their pupil. You give them the weapons and let them walk on their own.'

At this, I unclasp the bone necklace Arezu gifted me. I press it into his hands. For a second, as he stares at it, something strange flits in his gaze – sorrow, then slow confusion.

He studies me. 'The first loss of any underling is the hardest. But eventually, all of it blurs together.'

I do not want to lose another. If I do, will I become like him, almost immune to it all? 'I never imagined Azadniabad would be capable of this,' I say quietly.

Using the bone necklace, the Sepāhbad gestures to the smear of bodies across the township. 'These enemies are not evil, but drunk on the illusion of free will. They think Akashun is freeing their lives, which ironically chains them more to him. Still, I don't blame them. Sometimes pain is easier to swallow when you fool yourself into thinking the other side deserves it more.'

He looks surprisingly human when he meets my eyes.

'Then the world doesn't deserve that freedom,' I answer. 'If they had something to fear, they wouldn't act out of line at all.'

He picks a fleck of dried blood off my cheek and steps away. He holds it against the backdrop of the graves in the rain. 'Well, they fight for it anyway. So, here is that revolution you spoke of. Is it not beautiful?'

39

I defect that night as the rain falls harder. In the aftermath of Khor, my superiors will be turning to recovery operations before the next battle. With Khor's proximity to the Black Mountain buffer, this is the closest I am going to get to the Azadnian wartime capital. My plan to escape is to use the shadows I summoned with No-Name at the intelligence chambers.

I grab my pack containing khanjars, dried rations and thick wool cloaks for the rain. But I leave behind the Sepāhbad's blade.

'I have to piss,' I tell Katayoun, who nods without caring.

I cross the fortification lines. My gait is assured, as if I'm simply patrolling, until I'm past the streams pouring from the Tezmi'a delta.

'Usur-Khan?' Yabghu calls out.

Then I am sprinting through the trails into the jade-rich mountains. No-Name and I summon the shadows but her teeth clench. 'I cannot maintain it; the shadows are not powerful near your trifecta.'

For hours, we trek along the wet almond trails, following the Tezmi'a River. I retrace three paths to mislead potential pursuers. Eventually, I head north-west at the juncture of the steppe-camel trade. I nibble on measly nuts I pluck from the damp brambles, climbing trees when I hear Azadnian troops through the rain.

After four days, I reach Azadniabad's wartime capital in Navia before sunrise.

A dim blue eats through the rumbling black sky, illuminating the bustling floral capital. I rub frankincense attar before summoning the shadows. They conceal my movements. I trail behind straggling soldiers riding through shell-rock gates in the citadel. Despite my resolve, my chest pangs from hearing barks of dialect, seeing the lotus monasteries, the familiar woodlands with wild goats, the blue poppy gardens within the rainy fog.

The people appear so content. So kind. They are still my kin. Not long ago I was raised here, living their ways.

I wish I could return. My hands fist.

I hate him.

I climb the wet limestone steps of the administrative ziggurat while concealed by the shadows. At the top of the seventh tier, I follow a vizier to a council room. She passes marble and iron doors carved with the Heavenly Crane defeating an eight-headed lion. My heart hammers hard as I pause. The entrance swings open, and advisers pour out.

The chamber preens with lavish crane portraits and stelae. A tall man wearing a gold crane-feathered turban stands at the threshold of a floral balcony, exchanging salutations with an adviser. Shockingly, Warlord Akashun has not changed since I last saw him. He exudes rough charisma. His ebony beard is clipped, brown skin smooth, and he has the corded build of a warlord.

He argues with another man swathed in a pale qaftan with a gold waist-sash, raven hair swept back—

Hyat Uncle?

The shadows flicker and I stumble back. Seeing the man who stood by my father, the very same who'd prompted my path down to Za'skar, is no relief.

Hyat departs with a tight look. Warlord Akashun moves to the lip of the balcony. Outside, a thunderclap booms through the Heavens. The skies tremble as the rain weeps harder on to the balcony.

Akashun backs inside. I will have to trap him by sealing the entrances of the chamber with dense nūr, so no guards can enter.

I glance at No-Name and her hungry eyes. She drops the shadows.

I inhale the torrent of incense swirling in my bonds. My fingers crack, the nūr spitting into the doors. My nūr widens, so compressed that the nearby walls bend inward. The material of the door singes white, welding shut as if under the deft fingers of a blacksmith. There is no time for shocked faces, not even a cry from the guards on the other side. No one will be able to enter the room unless they manage to rampage through sweltering iron and marble.

Akashun, at the commotion, whirls around and spies me across the council room. 'What's this?'

My nūr rises into a gushing wave. He pivots back, hands clasped.

'Nūr,' he recognises, stunned.

A strip like a Veil, as smooth and oily as silk, snaps forward from his hand. I frown at its strange familiarity before it slithers across the kilim rugs and combusts into black needles, shattering the light and throwing me backwards.

I land in third stance and channel a fourteen-breath meditation, my bonds expanding into the Second-Stratum. The flow of time wanes in my vision before I summon a stroke of nūr, holding it like a paintbrush. With two steps, I twist into the air and slam my hands together. Two coils of nūr burst against his Veil in equal force, the blackness dissipating.

When I land, I see not a man, but myself, standing before my clan, bitter years ascending in cruel memory – a violent cycle that never found closure. To end a cycle is to slough it from its roots, even if it means severing the last ties to my people.

Akashun reels back. 'I sense them on you, too. Jinn-poisons. *Who* are you?'

'I am a Zahr,' I answer calmly.

His eyes search me and recognition settles at last. '*You?* You've come willingly to me.'

I step forward. 'No. You killed my Older Brother, my clansmen, then my child, and now my home. So, I have arrived to destroy yours.'

Shoving a khanjar's hilt into my mouth, I lunge toward him.

New-found energy careens through my limbs – the power of grief and anger.

I bound high through the ninth stance, bonds pulsing. My foot uncoils, heel breaking against his chest, but his hands clasp my ankle, wrenching me forward. I drop my weight, swinging around his torso in a low sweep, nūr hissing from my toes. His fingertips smoulder from the dense energy, and he startles back.

I roll to a coiled stance, khanjars between my fingers like talons. When he swings his blade, I follow, my two knives clashing against his shamshir, scattering orange sparks, before my knee thrusts up to break his balance. With an animalistic snarl, my arms encircle his neck, yanking him down. I slam my khanjar into his jaw, but something eclipses from his fingers. A loud *pop*, and my surroundings momentarily blur behind a Veil. Suddenly, his sword slashes my forearms.

Instead of red cuts, my blood ripples like a jinn-poison.

I jump, but he dives into my attack zone, driving into my chest with Veil-fisted hands, over and over again. In rapid succession, I deflect with my forearms, wrist twists, and then a sidestep before spinning again and slashing the nūr-engulfed khanjar across his torso.

Again, *something* converges upwards, blocking me from penetrating skin, like armour – so fast, it cannot have been him. My palm flicks out, projecting compressed energy. The nūr spits three times but that *something* sucks it into its oily walls.

'Fool,' he grits, as we dance faster, bending and parrying before retreating, air whirling around us in rhythm. 'You are connected to the Veils by Mitra; you cannot fight it.'

My form hesitates at this.

When he breaks with his sword, parrying to my chest, my wrists flick out before I cross them, jerking his blade down. I stoop, my foot jamming into his sternum, the blast of nūr sending him flying back to crash against the balcony doors, which fly open into the rain. But another *something* catches him. For a second, eyes wink in Mitra. With no warning, he flies on to my back as if I'm a stepping stone.

My skull knocks to the wet stone, teeth rattling inside my mouth, and I cry out. Pure instinct makes me roll right as his sword thrusts down. With it, something pounds on to my body like stones, pinning me down.

He laughs. 'It feeds off your blood, little bird. Both of us share a bond; you cannot hurt my Veils. It was so easy to convince Eliyas to bring me your blood from your poison training; he thought I would free you from the Mitra ritual. He was a fool.'

My stomach clenches, remembering Farzaneh's explanation. Akashun ingested my resistant blood to replace my father, after he died, and complete the Mitra exchange to become its wielder.

'I've searched for you for years,' Akashun continues. 'Even when your uncle told me you were dead. *Hyat lied.* And now I have the opportunity to siphon your blood.'

'Never,' I hiss. The pain from the force holding me down burns like slow flames. Is this how Arezu felt, dying in agony, feeling every bit of her body gripped and ripped apart?

I cling tight to my anger as if I am hanging off a cliff, rage extending its hands to pull me from the edge. As Akashun leans down, my right hand latches on to his calf. Somehow lifting my left, I drive my blade across his thigh. With another cry, I part my lips, bonds expanding and fluidly ejecting nūr from my tongue. It shoots into his chest enough for me to flex upwards, my palm slamming into his nose.

But it's not enough. Whatever jinn is protecting him from behind the Veil only expands, even as Akashun reels from my blow. Something sharp skewers through my eyes and I scream.

'If you wished to fight me, why even come alone?' he hisses from above. 'But that's how your clan raised you: as their dog, primal and isolated. A job well done, you've made the Zahrs proud.'

The tip of his sword digs into my throat and I gasp, still half blind.

The sheer will in his eyes, the determination of a man who believes he is right, chokes me. 'The only reason you are below is because you've accepted what your father made you. You are content with the meagre bonds fed to you. Monks teach only fragments of information because they're fearful of dipping their toes in the otherworldly. And for that safety, you will die. But Mitra – it's the essence of bondage and sacrifice.'

I can do nothing to change it.

'You can,' No-Name insists. 'Everything about your life was preordained. But now, *you* can usurp it.'

Azadnian soldiers finally burst through the welded doors, eyes flickering between us with the determination of creatures committed to slaughter. My instincts curl as I recognise the path drawn out before me, leading to the end of my desires.

Akashun tilts his head at them. 'It's a shame if you die. But very well. My heirs will do.'

Heirs. They would replace Akashun in a blink.

Repulsion swims through my blood. The devil is not the only one whispering into the ears of mankind. Tyrants may not have chains around our necks, but they control something worse: our ideology.

It was my father and now him. Cutting off one head will not save this continent; it will not save the tribes of the Camel Road.

I could make a choice so the Camel Road would no longer remain torn amongst false choices. Because what choices can the peoples of the borderlands make? To join the army of their enemy or to be pillaged by that same enemy? To sit as smiling mules before armies invade, only to die slowly and miserably, or to resist and die anyway on a path to martyrdom? For them, it is no longer a question of winning a war, but of either accepting Azadnian or Sajamistani suzerainty. Arezu chose it, because she had never lived a life where she had anything else to pick from.

But I accepted that natural order is no match for a person like Akashun who usurps it. I knew in some dark pocket of my being that I did not arrive to kill one man. I came to purge a cycle before it evolves into something worse.

'You are wrong,' I choke to Akashun through the Veil clogging my senses. 'I understand sacrifice. And I understand power.'

Something snaps in my soul. I stare up at the Heavens vomiting rain on the world. The water in its enormity swallows sound into a mute nothingness, except for the shrieks thrown from the high winds.

My eyes shut as I sink into my senses; I revel in the panic thrumming in the lands. I sink further, into the water and sweat moistening the air. I sink more, into the clay stitched by motes of dirt, into a seismic ocean.

I read the design of the world festering below the Heavens.

Why I had not touched its pattern before is due to my selfish will, which attempted to ensconce Heaven into definable planes, when it can never be so. It is a perfect design; no imperfect creature can impose theirs on it. And so, I cannot surrender while encompassing a physical form. I must become immaterial, etching myself into its design.

I release my humanity. I become the world.

The psychospiritual planes embrace me, eliciting a laugh and a sob. Remembering Adel's warnings about drifting, I ground myself in a memory. I imagine the monks beside me.

'Close your eyes.' Sister Umairah's voice careens from the spool of memory. 'The bone-shards are there. You never needed eyes to see them.'

The bone floats behind my eyelids.

'Do you sense death? Do you see with eyes closed?'

Yes, I do. The world floats in a black void of death. I stare as if the blank bone is my consciousness given form. I imagine it taking me to the Heavens.

The laws of the physical realm begin dissolving. A tinge of gold strokes against the white; the shape of bonds kneading through it. I meditate into that bone, wishing I can be there forever, sitting peacefully, scarred fingers resting on bone-stone.

Then I am falling through the past and present, into the Heavens: the buffer between Paradise and Hells. Memories unfurl until I hear my students' farewell.

Be a monster. Until I am no longer in Azadniabad but *somewhere else.*

Around me, shadows of birds graze the backdrop, of gardens and a lake, in golden illuminations. Vak-vak trees curve out, their branches holding thousands of beautiful human heads with fond, upturned smiles, tongues proffering berries. The faces tempt me to take their fruit as if I am Adam.

This must be the genesis where time unravels, worlds merge and realms become one. The cosmos are spread before my eyes, whole worlds on the canvas of the universe appearing as tiny freckles on a cheek.

The truth strikes like spittle in the face. None of us are in control against a higher power. We are the trapped jinni in a lantern knocking endlessly with closed fists against encompassing copper walls.

Eajīzi is one drop of knowledge in a boundless well. Greater worlds are out there, perhaps greater capabilities. So to refuse the Gates of Heaven is absurd. The monks who tell us differently are merely dipping their finger into a pond instead of swimming; they like the illusion of control, because knowing of freedom but not having it is even crueller.

Not me. My face turns upwards. A gentle wind caresses me.

'Foolish servant,' a voice greets me.

I blink and suddenly see the most beautiful entity. It has no features. It simply exists. My mind tells me it is beautiful, though I cannot say why.

It moves, rippling like petals dropping into an oasis. Perhaps my eyes are fooling me that it's more mortal-like than it really appears.

The light of my surroundings crackles about, like Heavenly fire hoping to scathe, but nothing moves – not in the gardens, not in the lake. For all of the surroundings beauty, it's bereft of spirit.

'Where am I?' I ask.

'How very accomplished you feel at your human knowledge, which is nothing more than a grain of sand in a desert. This place is the bond between man and soul, a line so deep it forms the boundaries of the cosmos.'

'We are inside a bond?'

'Yes, neither up nor down, nor earthly. Simply there, inside a bond, below the Heavens.'

Its words trip like a riddle. 'Are you a jinn?'

An iambic laugh flutters from it, and I realise what I first perceived as beauty is, in fact, terrifying. 'Do I look like a fire-being to you? You take, yet you do not know from *whom* you take?'

Only one *creation* is made of nūr. The Creator is pure, but the Creator is no creation.

'You are an angel: a creation of light with no free will.' I lift my hands, every movement ensconced in a blankness, not fast nor slow.

'It seems the human spares some intelligence for herself,' it says. 'I am a Gatekeeper, at the lowest of the Heavens between Paradise and Hells.'

'And I am an ignorant servant,' I confess.

The angel cocks its head. 'You are like the rest – greedy, seeking power, uncaring of its consequences. Is one power not enough?'

'The rest?'

It ignores my question. 'After death, Eajīz will be asked the question of how they used their affinity and what their actions bore. So, tell me why you are here?'

As if compelled, the blunt truth tumbles out of me. 'I was named after a warrior of the Simorgh. I come as her namesake. I seek not a Gate of Heaven but the Eighth Gate. To summon the Simorgh and protect the Camel Road. Please,' I whisper. 'I was told the gates are accessed through the Heavenly Birds.'

It smiles solemnly. 'The test of this life is suffering, greed and love.'

'People will die if nothing is done!'

'The power you seek is far beyond your control. It's a parasite. It will destroy you. But if I am permitted to from the Heavens, it can be given as your test.'

'Then test me!' I beg. 'Old warriors have used the gates. Even the Sepāhbad has the gates! He has so much of power, and he masters it with no consequence. Why may I not have it? *Why am I left to beg at power's feet?*'

'I see,' it murmurs. 'Fighting over this life when the next life should matter instead. This life is a test. Besides, that boy mastered the gates through sacrifice, without breaking his bonds. But *you* – your bonds are broken; you abused your ties to the Divine and are becoming a Corruption. Did you not hear the warning in Stone City? Do you not know what storm is to come?'

My stomach drops. 'It was raining.'

'A flood,' it corrects me, and silhouettes form in the gold mist, showing the Great Flood.

'In every era of corruption, the Divine brings destruction. But there is forgiveness – because life is a blip, it's a test. If mankind was to never sin, they would not exist. But when a civilisation loses all morality and the Divine sees in all cosmic possibilities that they will continue in corruption, *then* He brings destruction to hasten them to the next life. In your case, the Divine gave the pious a dream about the impending storm which will destroy much of this civilisation just as other eras have ended. The Divine warned the believers to flee to higher ground. Many of you did not heed it. You went on to fight your petty war. Many will die and the good will be martyred.'

I begin shaking, not from fear, but relief. 'The ones suffering prayed for a storm to cleanse away their oppressors.'

'A powerful ask,' it agrees. 'This is your test. You are not arbitrary; every action has a reaction that has led to this.'

And I know how to pass this test. 'You want me to use the Eight Gates and summon the Third Heavenly Bird. To save the continent and to not let this era end; I can show that our civilisation is worth saving. People will see the bird stopping the flood; they might change their ways, like the symbolic aftermath of any great punishment.' My head is shaking. 'But I cannot do that.'

'Ah,' the angel tuts. 'This power is your salvation or destruction. So choose.'

My hands fist and my mouth opens. 'The flood is only doing the inevitable. True destruction is a protracted war that kills millions. Slaughter, disease, rape, uprooted nature and famine. But with a flood, our era could end. We can be subdued.'

The angel studies me, unsurprised, for of course the angels have been observing my deeds from the Heavens. 'So, you wish for the Gates of Heaven? Why, when you do not want to protect this entire continent?'

I tremble. 'I will use the Gates technique to save the tribes of the Camel Road. As for the rest of the continent – I will save the *people*, but I will not save the *lands* from the storm. People who have no land have no power. Let the flood ravage the continent. Let the people flee and cower. Let them fear the Simorgh. This flood will remind humanity that we are forsaken before we start anew. People need fear to unite them. Is that not how the people after Nuh survived? A calamity so large, it can only be a holy omen.'

'You despise your enemies for acting like they are god, yet here you are doing the same.'

This is my redemption. 'I choose suffering. I am not worthy of anything else. If I save all of the lands, what of the Camel Road? I would rather live in the aftermath of destruction than in a state of constant violence.'

The soldiers I met who ended their own lives, they understood the concept of sacrifice – they knew people care only when someone is dead. We are naturally reactive beings. We need to see destruction to understand peace.

But the reason peace and freedom throughout the folds of history are so astoundingly rare is because they have never coexisted. You must tear the page of one to bring the other into fruition. And I've witnessed freedom: it's the groundwork laid before me, people tearing each other apart because the only freedom they knew of was violence. If taking away choice means peace, better this than none. True freedom cannot exist in the maelstrom of constant war, coerced by the soldier who holds a sword above you.

Humans are elevated above all animals. Land becomes the measurement of success. They toil over territory as if it's endless gold. But here, above, I see what the universe is: it's vast, it's immense – but humans are feebly confined to that world. What happens when we are done, are other lands next? Are the oceans? Another realm, as we are doing with the jinn-folk? We are so greedy, we are pathetic. Lands will be taken, people will suffer, people will die, but I refuse to watch the cycles repeat.

I look up at the angel. 'I ask again for the Eighth Gate of Heaven to summon the Third Heavenly Bird. Let me save the Camel Road.'

'Be careful,' it muses. 'It comes with a great cost that you will not be able to bear. You were raised on stories of the flood; you were in Stone City, a once prosperous metropolis before a supernatural disaster ended its reign. These destructions that ended civilisations were not merely the Divine wiping tribes from existence – they were done by Eajīz like you, who begged for a solution and used the Gates technique to end entire eras. Stone City, the City of God's Gates, even ancient jinn civilisations that were annihilated – these were by the Heavenly Birds led by Eajīz.'

I see Mitra attacking the Camel Road from both fronts and the world trading on its substance. I see evil normalised. I see the ones controlling its numerical values controlling the world.

The thoughts weave through my morality and empathy, pulverising them to specks of clay. And I let them. It makes me feel human and not human; it's nice. I am far removed. Here, choosing which land to protect from the other is a blink of time.

Is this how emperors feel upon their thrones, commanding war but feeling far from its consequence? I understand the thrill.

'Each action has a consequence, and the repercussions you face are the wages of the past. For that, the test of the gates is bestowed to you.' It pauses. 'Remember, it demands a steep cost.'

Uneasily, I nod. Our surroundings drip into golden tears where the silhouetted gardens and animals melt into nothingness.

'This is a power outside the confines of natural order. I, Keeper of the Gates, have warned you that you – a human – were led by your free will. But hold on to the true purpose of faith. Mercy is everywhere, like grains of sand. I hope with your actions, your people turn to goodness.'

'If I do this, am I damned?' I cannot help but ask.

'Perhaps the Divine will deem that in your cosmic possibilities, you may turn to salvation. Or be damned like your namesake warrior who tried summoning the Simorgh and paid for it.' The angel grips my face between its steepled hands, turning my cheek.

We are above the world in the lowest of the Heavens. The ground glows in stardust which expands into a gold lake flowing below the Mist Mountains, surrounding the vak-vak trees.

Pain coils my belly tight. In the centre of the alcove is a tall tree, its seeds pattering into a gold vortex of life, nourishing lands.

The Simorgh rests at the top of the Tree of Knowledge, floating above the Heavenly Sea, the brilliant creature who was born thrice. She is the Bird King; a peacock with the claws of a lion and the face of an everchanging human. But as I watch, her features morph to show my uma.

'The Third Heavenly Bird burned in the world, watching eras end by human hands. Still, the Simorgh collected knowledge perched upon her tree. She embodied patience. She nourished warriors to protect mankind, collecting wisdom while maintaining peace.' It points to her. 'There she is. The Eight Gates are not offered, they are taken.'

I float down to the Simorgh, understanding I must enslave this creature.

The angel frowns. 'You will hurt it?'

'You said to take the gates.'

'One creature of nūr walked down the path of justice. And now the other walks down the opposite.'

I smile. 'The Simorgh was complacent. She could have conquered mankind and commanded us into obedience, so we would never war again. But she did not. The Simorgh has the luxury of being a peaceful creature. We do not. I reject her. I reject the firebird and her wisdom.'

'Daughter of the Simorgh,' my uma laughs darkly from the Simorgh's countenance. 'Slit my throat; I had done it to myself in the temporal world, so why not in this realm?'

'Yes.' My hands cup her face lovingly. 'We both know only death, don't we?' I murmur.

With my blade, nūr wraps around the neck of the creature and I yank until its neck bleeds. Together, we plummet into the gold sea. It's a strange feeling to be like the devil thrown from the Gates of Heaven, the angel staring down.

The last thing I hear is: *know that though you have been given the power of the Heavens, for eternity you will be alone.*

The rush of power ruptures my thoughts as we fall into a dark world. Here, I seem to exist in a state before consciousness, like a soul suckling in the womb; my vision is muddled, peopled by murmurs and strange languages. Shadows gnash until my bonds bleed from my skin, thinning and combusting. The gold lines wilt like a flower blazing from the dirt only to slump from an early frost.

You abuse us. You cannot use us, the bonds hiss.

I am sorry, I say.

Visions dance around me: I see others before the angel, on their knees, begging. I see Eajīz desperate, unable to save eras. I count many – too many – who decided against saving Stone City, others who caused meteorite showers, ending wars, and yet others who allowed the destruction of the Jazatāh tribes. Then I see a young boy with piercing hazel eyes before the angel, anger sweeping his movements, an anger I've never witnessed in him. But he, too, wisps away into the past.

A long, solid gold bond penetrates my heart. The hundred-bond line loops through my chest, and plunges into every Eajīz I see of the past and present, who used various Gates of Heaven, connecting us.

Suddenly, I understand what the Sepāhbad saw in me.

The truth steals my breath as I stare at the hundredth Heavenly bond extending outward from my heart.

Then my soul returns to my human body below Akashun. As his wet sword sinks into my chest, glyphs arise. The letters sear along my limbs like a hot wick.

'What is this?' Akashun snarls over the pounding rain; his blade cannot penetrate the gold bands formed by the letters.

With the one hundredth bond, my fingers ripple into nūr, a dense precision, sensing every hush of breath, every breath of bond.

My nūr-hands wrap around his throat, carrying us until we are in the sky. My left arm slices inwards. A *crack*, and then clouds split as nūr splinters from the Heavens. It surges into Akashun's body, bursting him like snapped seams, his entrails scattering on the lands below.

Then I am falling, falling down Heaven like a shooting star.

The air suddenly ripples around me, a white void carving into the space. A gold creature thrusts its head out, screeching like a windstorm. Then it swoops down, catching me on its back.

It's immense, with wings speckled in gold and blue, nūr bursting from its peacock feathers. Its long beak curves and pecks at me like a culled fledgling desperate for its orders.

It's the Simorgh: the Bird King.

A metaphysical tide strikes my core. Every Eajīz must feel the way the Third Heavenly Bird threatens to snap all bonds from existence.

And we watch the world as balls of light shoot down from the Heavens, bringing storm winds across the mountains. The trees begin tremoring before standing on their roots and whipping across the city, creatures scurrying after. The clay cracks open like a great egg, swallowing throngs of people. Jinn-folk manifest, flying to the cosmos to escape the great storm.

Below, Azadnians scream at the colossal shift as if the flood is dousing the parchment of the world. Waters rise from the roots, the land spits up its reservoirs, and the blue-black waves engulf the valley, by the angels under the Divine's command.

Shadows from the sky plummet downwards. Birds of every type, dropping as if a poison in the air has struck them. Screams echo from the lands and I begin laughing in disbelief. Had this been how the disbelievers of the Great Flood had felt, as the ark passed in safety while they drowned?

In a panic, I tug at the tufts of the Simorgh. 'We must be quick before the flood destroys us too. Use the nūr to protect the tribes and lands of the Camel Road,' I command it.

The hundred-bond line carves through us, pulling us from the Eighth Gate.

'You are the Bird King,' I urge the Simorgh. 'Send your subjects: cranes, ravens, buzzards, sparrowhawks and ababil to lift and save the people in Sajamistan and Azadniabad. Have the birds carry them so they may see the destruction.'

The Simorgh's wings lift and fall, churning an endless supply of golden cranes and hawks and ababil and ravens that travel at the speed of cosmic light across the continent.

The Heavenly Bird soars us through the grey sky, traversing unnatural distances, travelling faster than the floodwaters, until we soar from the rocky Stone City to above Khor's steppes and its ruined townships to the border of the Zayguk kingdoms, to the valley before the Black Mountains. It opens its beak, huffing its cold light across the pastures like a silver blanket shimmering atop the mountains. We soar to the west and east of the steppe-lands.

The floodwaters press against the nūr, failing to penetrate the barriers as the water spreads across southern Azadniabad and northern Sajamistan. I command the Simorgh's nūr – so pure and unlike my own – like moulding clay in my hands. For a wavering moment, people are the threads and I, as a maker, wind them through my fingers. I demand their submission. I demand their surrender. It is so fitting: the Camel Road is a broken land of revolution; where violence is the seed and anger is the water.

At the tops of the Kin Mountains, crowds of humans huddle in horror – the ones who heeded the warning to move toward higher ground, watching the floodwaters rise.

Another roar overtakes the continent, the flood toppling mountains as they crack and shudder. Villagers' cries follow. Birds swoop and carry the ones who have not drowned.

Many are young on those hills, staring up at the mighty Simorgh's shadow before looking down, watching their homes wash away in the flood – alive but knowing they will have no home to return to in the aftermath. But I think they deserve it. So many of them without their homes, like my own eradicated from their raids.

And when they live with tales about the flood's utter destruction, they will speak of how they thought the nūr was their ark to guide them through the flood, only to have it turn its back on them.

High up, my vision wavers into a kaleidoscopic array of souls, the Veil lifting. The veins of the world criss-cross into sturdy rows, planes of square disks, and the people – the pathetic, puny creatures of the world – appear as no more than specks. And my hand draws from above, pushing and pulling the fabric of the world.

Destroying and creating.

Destroying and creating.

Lands crushed and a girl the subjugator. I smile.

I am a holy mother and the world bows like children at my feet. I stroke shapes on to the canvas of the planet, and I snip the strings of fate. I am no mortal but the extension of a Divine. *I am power.* I hold the book of the world within my grasp, inking fate.

I've saved her, have I not? The Camel Road lives in an island of destruction. She breathes. She exists. And if her salvation is through a brush dipped in blood and swept lovingly across the celestial canvas, I would let the crimson seep into each crevice that carves the land, into every mangled body buried beneath its dirt, to be freed. Better this than the drawn-out invasion of mutilation and indoctrination.

My hand raises to the sky, fisting as if to cup the clouds. My thumb blots the grin of the rising sun as it laughs in glee at all the cruelty. The new dawn breaks into a violent red, bleeding into pink dew. People will see now the promise of the Third Heavenly Bird was a myth.

I always dreamt of a land of peace. But it does not matter what I wanted. I would live with the crushing grief, I would know the enemy is more than just an empty face on the battlefield. This land in Azadniabad was my home as much as the Camel Road. And its people were more than Warlord Akashun.

Questions dart through me that I try to dispel: Had I killed my clansmen? How many Zahrs live? How much of Sajamistan has borne the waters?

But they need to witness the consequences of a flood, high above like me, to realise humanity is nothing against Divine forces. Azadniabad fears now. Sajamistan too. The entire continent does. Finally. And I know well – all fear can turn to love.

What breaks that awful fervour is a slow realisation as the Simorgh sails us north, past Tezmi'a, the pastures of my birthplace in the Camel Road. When we fly across Lake Xasha, the body of water ejects large waves before we can form the last nūr barrier.

'Wait,' I demand. 'Why are you not saving Tezmi'a?' I try to command the bird, but the thought blots like a finger against fresh ink. The creature does not heed me – avoiding Tezmi'a – as icebergs descend to swallow the alpine of my birthplace. 'Wait!'

Somewhere, from an immaterial plane, the angel booms in my mind, *Your power is not an absolute; to take one's home away, your home follows.*

My fists grip the Simorgh's feathers in horrible understanding. 'I don't understand,' I whisper.

The angel corrects me and I hear a smile in its words. *I warned you of the cost. You wished to save the Camel Road from Azadniabad and Sajamistan, but the price was the pastures of your homeland. That is the price of the Gates – an exchange that takes what the warrior values most. For who is Azadnian? Who is Sajamistani? The ones in Tezmi'a call themselves Azadnian, even you yourself. You admit that not one fits a neat definition. Are you a nomad or the daughter of an empire? Where do humanity's borders fall and end? They are from humans. You requested the bird and the power obliged, ungrateful child of Adam's tribe. You were not specific about what you wished to protect. That was the cost of using such a creature. Your true home could not be saved.*

My eyes squeeze shut and my body throbs like the quaking Heavens.

'You wanted this,' No-Name says, sat behind me. 'I thank you for it.'

And she disappears.

The Simorgh was summoned but she did not heal. The dawn of the firebird only destroyed.

40

ERA OF THE SIMORGH, YEAR I

Black Mountains, the Camel Road

Dawn breaks and the nūr peters out, spreading and receding around newly formed lakes as the rain slows on the torn continent. The Simorgh drops me at a crumbled mountain village in the central Camel Road and flies up to the top, curling into mist. My legs buckle and I am giggling, and then I am a sobbing, snotty mess on the ground, unable to understand what I have done. If I think – about the flood, about anything – I will cease to exist.

Not long after, my cries quiet into my belly. No-Name tries to help me stand. As she grabs my arm, a strange feeling stirs between us. I glance up. Something has irrevocably changed.

Her pale hair grazes her chest; thick crimson scars run along her chest and slither to her knuckles as if she's made of broken pieces fused together. Her black eyes, possessing a universe of sorrow, flicker to hope. And her features appear... startlingly similar to mine, more so than ever before.

'No-Name,' I say and her face twists at the title.

'So cruel,' she answers. A fear gnaws at my liver, because I sense it: a *pulse* in her hand. Somehow, *she has a soul*.

I grasp my chest, and it is silent. I feel empty.

'What happened to you?'

She frowns. 'You brought me back to the human realm.'

'Am I imagining this?' I am not sure what is real anymore, not with the flood, not with this war. She leans and punctures her nails into me. 'What are you doing?'

'Watch. The wound will not heal. And you will see that I am indeed real.' There is satisfaction in her gaze.

A terror stampedes over my instincts. I watch the slice of skin, but the wound does not close. 'How is this possible?' My eyes track the cracks in the green cliffs around us, searching for a way out. 'You do not exist—'

'I told you. The heart of your soul was sacrificed,' says No-Name quietly.

'My soul is in me,' I hiss back.

But she steps away and the distance between us makes my body ache, as if we are connected. 'Not entirely. Not until…' Her voice trails off.

Unwillingly, the pieces stitch together like a patchwork quilt. *Until Warlord Akashun's death.*

Memories flip like the pages of a text: No-Name encouraging my training, encouraging my access to the gates, encouraging me to kill Akashun. She had grown so frightening, so large, as if my isolation heightened her strength.

Perhaps I am unwell. I summoned the gates. I do not remember yesterday from today. But – but…

'You have been lying.' My knees buckle.

Akashun had said we are bonded. And in the battle he controlled… the same Veils that are the shadows surrounding No-Name. As if…

Words uttered long ago by Farzaneh fly back to me: *To gain the knowledge of Mitra from an ancient jinn master, the wielder must sacrifice the heart of a soul. A nameless soul. They must sacrifice the heart of the soul of their heir.* She explained, when souls were sold to the Unseen, the bodies became soulless.

A horrible realisation sinks into me.

'Who are you?' I say thickly.

Her voice is low. 'I am no one. I am you. In truth, I was a soul, like you, eons ago, before my heart was sacrificed during the Jazatāh tribes era to access black magick. But in the world of souls, you drift in nothingness,scavenged by jinn, unable to do anything but watch humanity rise and fall with the mind of a babe. And in that realm, I have no body. And what remained of my soul, without its heart, was diminishing. I was starved… starved for the heart of a drifting soul…'

I stumble back. 'My soul. You took the heart from my soul.'

'I saw many nameless souls, sacrificed to the Unseen world to create Mitra. And I… I devoured them. But not one of them,' she exhales harder, in wonder, 'not one of them wanted me.'

My vision blurs. *She is a soul-eater.* 'You devoured the heart of my soul? How?' But it becomes clear. My chest caves in, as I try to breathe. 'It's *you*. You were the jinn master who bartered with my father.'

'I felt a calling.' Her hands are shaking as she speaks. 'I saw it, and I took it.'

'Your words make no sense,' I breathe out.

But that means… No-Name was once a human, before she became what she is now: a creature from the Unseen. 'You created Mitra. You made a jinn contract with my father and devoured me as I was born,' I accuse. Mitra isn't a separate source, Mitra *is controlled by* No-Name. How many souls has she eaten to survive in her long existence?

She glances at her hands. 'It is not only because of your father. You accepted me. A nameless soul is dangerous; it has no roots in this world. Your soul attracted jinn-folk and creatures who wished to claim it. I may have eaten the heart of your soul, but I was only a shadow from the Unseen world, curious about your despair. You were strange… for some reason, you never resisted me, and that allowed me to grow stronger. The human part of your soul that lived in this world desired my company. You let me come to you, many times, when you were in grief.'

'What?' I choke out.

The truth scabs together on a gaping wound. No-Name reflected my thoughts. She was not human. She was an empty canvas; she became whatever I desired. She glutted herself on despair and weakened on my joys because she is a part of my soul. Other memories drift toward me. No-Name despised my students as if their presence hurt her. She was happy when I was alone – she fed on me.

But if she is the jinn master that created Mitra, No-Name was influencing Akashun too.

Mitra works both ways – she was using the bond to send jinn-folk from the Unseen to Akashun.

'You could have stopped Warlord Akashun,' I say in realisation. She does not answer. 'If you were a soul-eater in the Unseen, how are you a human now?' My gaze flits over her.

'To end our Mitra contract, the wielder must die. You killed Akashun.'

Had No-Name wished for Mitra to develop, to eradicate the Veil between jinn-folk and man, to enter the human world and possess a body?

'You used me to kill him,' I whisper. 'You used me to free yourself.'

'That is hypocritical, Khamilla,' she says simply without denying it. 'I was nothing but a soul-eater, with a single-minded desire like a babe: to live. I would do anything to fulfil it. As for Akashun – he wanted Mitra. I cannot plant the seeds of ideas into someone who does not already possess them. I was a thing floating in the Unseen world. No one can instil hatred; they can only stoke it. Your father began the Mitra ritual; he sacrificed your soul to me. Akashun simply replaced him. I never created their ambitions or their monstrosity. That came from your father. So of course I accepted the Mitra exchange as a jinn master. I needed the heart of your soul; I ingested your resistant blood to grow from aimlessness to a human form. Your blood allowed me to send the jinn-folk across the Veil.'

'You wanted Mitra too,' I spit. 'You never stopped them. *You could have*. You could have made Akashun stop this war!'

Her eyes steel, as if to make me understand. 'You know the concept of sacrifice well, Khamilla. You can blame me for the world's brutality, but it's embedded in our blood. Akashun united an empire through his methodologies after the disgrace of *your clan*. Azadnian soldiers followed blindly *by free will*. You chose to save only the Camel Road *by free will*. You accepted my presence in your life *by desire*.'

More questions spill out, to keep my mind from splitting. 'Why would you want something so terrible?'

She looks contemplative. As if *nothing* is at stake. A child given a weapon, one who's learned to walk and whose impulses exceed her control. 'Because the hierarchy of Eajīz no longer matters. The way Akashun wielded Mitra was nothing near its potential. There are many like me. Old souls sacrificed to the Unseen world that will live again. Mortal men and Eajīz aren't strength; we are. I will ensure it, for the Veil between humans and jinn has blurred; the boundary is growing to irrelevance. As it should be.'

'What?' My heart goes cold. It's terrible when darkness is reasonable because it becomes so difficult to resist. Warlord Akashun was never the problem; he was her puppet. How cleverly she spent these years. Now, as a human, all she has to do is demonstrate that she is the embodiment of Mitra, and mortals will flock to her. She hopes to free the Unseen world. She intends to create a new order. 'But why would you want this?' I say, breathless.

She answers simply. 'Because I can.' I begin to scramble back and she inhales sharply. 'Where are you going?'

'Away from you.'

'We are not done,' she snaps. 'Whatever enemy you think I am, you are wrong. You are a defected warrior, your clansmen are gone or dead, your lands are flooded, and Za'skar will hunt you down.'

'Kill me, then.'

She reaches out before pausing. 'That would be foolish. Why do you fear the jinn-folk when the world of humans is an evil, rotting place? You are angry, but eventually you will tire of that, too. It's how we are – lock us up, take away our light, and we morph from intelligent beings to disgusting primitive things crawling on all fours in search of any hope. It's exactly how you were when your parents died. *You need me.* That is why you accepted me and let me grow – why I exist at all.'

My head shakes. But the further I step away, the hollower I feel, anger seeping away. 'I will never need you.'

Her expression is solemn. 'I was imprisoned in the Unseen world for eons, watching humans abuse the magick of jinn out of greed, sacrificing souls. Not anymore. Every soul will be freed. A new era is coming. For now, I will not fight you. Besides…' Her lips play into a coy smile. 'I am hungry.'

'You are not my ally,' I whisper, staring at her features. At how terribly similar we look.

'I learnt much from you. For that, we are tied together. I am the heart of your soul; you cannot be separated from me for long, or else you lose much of yourself – your will, your conviction, your memories, your bonds.' She stands and stretches her arms, eyes darkly amused. 'I will go. *Because I am hungry*. At the very least, this body I have will not last when it is a state shared between you and me. All is well, though. I know just the body to take on my true form.' Her teeth gnash as she backs away. 'I am hungry. Hungry. Hungry. Which food…' Her murmurs fade as she stares at my shadow before an oily Veil wraps around her, and she vanishes.

Epilogue

For hours, I stumble along the cliffs. My skin twitches and my limbs ache.

When night eventually descends like a dark gaping mouth, I collapse before a secluded northern monastery. At this hour, when dusk is nothing more than a thin blanket, I fade to a state close to peace. Perhaps I can imagine it's a time before humans congested the world and nature was alone.

The silence is primal. It's blissful. I do not notice when my skin ripples.

The peace crumbles when a monk cries out at the sight of me, hands wrenching my tunic upwards.

'Prepare the exorcism chambers,' a senior monk barks, but I cannot see; my vision is black and my body writhes. Incense sticks are brought around me and the ifrit – the most ancient of the jinn – controlling my body huffs a dark laugh.

I yield to the blackness.

For days, monks exorcise many jinn from my body. I scarcely remember anything but a blur of pealing creatures using my tongue to howl. Rough female apprentices slather me in blessed olive oil and holy water. From the monks, I catch snippets of the happenings of the outside world. The flood had ravaged southern Azadniabad and northern Sajamistan.

Many civilians had been lifted by thousands upon thousands of Heavenly birds, and carried to watch the Divine punishment.

With the flood, landslides ruptured the fertile valleys, bringing mass famine. Some days, my mind feels empty. Other days, I wonder, what did humanity think as the birds returned them to a ruined homeland?

I giggle at the thought. I do not wish to fight again or take a life. But I giggle at that, too, because I will have to. *Unless you take your life now.* How many of this continent are hungry, diseased and landless because of the flood? How many despise and how many others revere nūr?

But No-Name – she is a living thing. Worse than even Mitra.

No. I cannot think.

When I awaken again, I see the back of a familiar young man perched on the end of my cot, holding a familiar khanjar. The very one he bestowed upon me. The monks must have put together my uniform tunic and reported my presence. I scramble up.

'You will hurt yourself if you move so soon—' The Sepāhbad begins to turn his head.

Even in my weakened state of fever and spasming muscles, I do not wait. I lunge forward, hand wrapping around his throat, sending us crashing to the ground in the small exorcism room.

As my fingers tighten with me over him, our gazes lock. A mistake. I try to cry out but my body is paralysed, his eye bonds flashing outward. My throat twinges as the gold tendrils wrap around my neck, trapping me in place.

'Y-you are here to fulfil your oath,' my voice is thin through the choking bonds, 't-to kill me with your blade for defecting. I welcome it, Jezakicl.'

At his expression, uncertainty shoots up my spine.

His lips tease up with a knowing smirk, eyes twinkling. 'Why would I kill you when you've executed my plan so flawlessly?' Then his next words stop me cold: 'If you assume I did not know the entire time, well… we have your clan to thank. I am here for a simple conversation, Khamilla, eighth child of Emperor Fatih Zahr-zad.'

Glossary

ZA'SKAR INSTITUTE RANKINGS OF QABL MASTERY

Rukh (Initiate level)

- Zero-Slash
- First-Slash
- Second-Slash
- Third-Slash

Trifecta Leader

- Fourth-Slash
- Fifth-Slash
- Sixth-Slash

Qabl Master

- Seventh-Slash

EĀJIZ STRATUMS OF SUMMONING

First Stratum: Basic manifestation through prayer and meditation on death.

Second Stratum: Deeper alignment to soul, allowing dense Heavenly Energy.

Third Stratum: Full summoning capability using a minimum of one-third of Heavenly bonds; enables affinity-specific techniques, or arts passed through clanhouses.

MARTIAL ARTS TECHNIQUES

Attar: Natural perfume oil or incense from flowers and herbs, used in prayer and martial rituals.

Nine Stances: Nine foundational positions for channelling energy in Sajamistani martial arts.

Horse-Stance: Mother of all stances.

Ifrit's Strike of Death: Lethal finger strike that targets Heavenly Bonds in multiples of three.

Seventy-Seven Binding Arts: Bonds wrap around an opponent before releasing dense Heavenly Energy through the affinity.

Iron-bone: A bone-hardening martial technique that culminates in the Iron-Bone limbs.

Iron-whisk: An iron weapon to beat one's self to increase bone density without increasing mass.

Gentle Paths of Dawjad: An Azadnian martial tradition using flow and natural energy, originating from Izur Prefecture.

Eight Gates of Heaven: Highest Eajīzi art; a practitioner opens eight spiritual gates via a shared seventy-eighth bond linked to a heavenly creature to summon pure colossal energy. Each gate risks the soul becoming lost in the psychospiritual realm. Those who survive are seared by a Hellish fever of immaterial flame; misusing it condemns the soul.

HIERARCHY OF CREATION

Creations: Angels – made of nūr, pure heavenly light, with no free will; jinn-folk – made from smokeless fire or other energies, exiled behind the Veil; humans – made from clay, gifted with free will and intellect.

Eājiz (*pl.* Eājizi): A blessed mortal able to channel Heavenly Energy into an affinity, through soul-bound Heavenly Bonds. Trained in Za'skar or monastic orders.

shai'tan (*pl.* shai'tain): Evil jinn who whisper misguidance into human hearts.

Jinn (Smokeless Fire-beings): Sentient beings of smokeless part of the flame. Tribal, moral and capable of forming contracts with mortals.

ifrit: Most powerful but corrupt class of jinn, with various wings and flying abilities.

parī: Mischievous fae exiled from Paradise; gatekeepers in Za'skar.

ghūl: Flesh-feeding entities from the Unseen.

falak: A human-faced colossal serpent last seen during the Great Flood, linked to divine judgement.

Heavenly Simorgh: Bird of radiant heavenly light. Symbol of wisdom, resurrection and kingship.

Heavenly Crane: White bird of grace and healing; brought salvation during the Great Flood.

Heavenly Raven: Three-headed bird of death and prophecy; known for guiding martyrs.

quqnoos: A phoenix made of fire, unlike the light-born Simorgh.

azi / azhadak: Flying serpentine beasts from the Unseen realm.

dîv: A soul-devouring fiend from the Unseen realm. Often black-scaled with claws, fangs and several heads, existing to corrupt and destroy what the Heavens have made to increase its life force.

ganj: Scaled serpents guarding the gates of royal treasuries.

ababil: Paradise birds that drop stones from the heavens to protect the righteous.

zār: A wind demon from the Unseen realm that possesses the weak and demands sacrifice; also found in the Great Library of Za'skar.

karkadann: A massive, blue-skinned bull with a spiralled horn, found in the hinterlands where the Veil is thin. Nearly impossible to tame, its horn holds powerful healing properties

MARTIAL TERMS

Alif Warrior: An odd-numbered circle of Sixth- and Seventh-Slash warriors in Za'skar tasked under the Sepāhbad.

Sepāhbad-vizier: In Sajamistan, the head of the left-hand martial viziers; the general of generals. Oversees Za'skar affairs as the most powerful Eājiz.

Sepāhbad-vizier of the Jinn: In Za'skar, the jinn equivalent of a general of generals, also called the Keeper of the Great Library.

Left-hand / Right-hand Viziers: Court-appointed officials. Left-hand viziers handle martial and economic matters; right-hand viziers handle jurisprudence and social affairs.

Trifecta: A unit of three warriors trained together under an overseer in Sajamistan martial arts. Formed for the trinity raven for balance and unity.

Marka Tournament: An ancient winter solstice tournament of strategy, spanning from jinn tradition, where any Za'skar squadron competes for territory banners to rise in martial rank.

MAJOR REGIONS AND CLANS

Azadniabad: Empire of the Heavenly Crane, governed by eight great courtly clans and warlords across eight prefectures.

Sajamistan: Empire of the Heavenly Raven, ruled by a Sultana and governed by bird clanhouses across provinces.

Izur: A northern prefecture under a mysterious young warlord, ruling both the steppe peoples and Prefecture Izur.

Za'skar: The oldest metropolitan city in the world, located in Sajamistan. A gated city within a city, where jinn and mortals coexist and the Veil is thin.

Yalon: Former winter capital of Azadniabad, under the Zahr clan.

Navia: Spring capital and indigenous home of the Zahr clan.

Stone City: A sky-bound, zealot city in the Kin Mountains along the Camel Road. Inhabitants believe their ancestors were punished by a clay quake and must never return to the sinful ground.

The Camel Road: A vast east-west trade route traversing the continent, contested by empires and home to many nomadic or former nomadic tribes.

Zahr Clan: One of the eight great courtly clans of Azadniabad. Known for poison specialisation.

Clanhouses: Bird-named factions within the Sajamistan court that sponsor and patronise low-ranking warriors, influencing martial and political affairs.

BIRDS OF HEAVEN TERMINOLOGY

Adam: The first human, moulded from clay.

Affinities: Seventy-Seven Divine-granted affinities linked to virtues, received through feathers of the Heavenly Crane and Raven; non-hereditary in nature.

Heavenly Energy: Spiritual essence flowing from the Heavens through the bonds into the human soul (ruh).

Ruh: The soul within humans and jinn.

Heavenly Bonds: Seventy-Seven immaterial golden bonds on the soul, used to channel Heavenly Energy. Most warriors can access only one-third in their lifetime.

Eye Bonds: Bonds located and activated through the eye, paralysing the opponent to guarantee a hit of the affinity.

Mitra: A powerful blood contract, often at great costs.

Heavenly Contract: A sacred pact with the Heavens to receive and use an affinity; breaking it results in Corruption.

A Corruption: A cursed being afflicted by jinn possession, illness and severed affinity due to a broken Heavenly Contract or using black magick.

Black Magick: Forbidden power requiring blood, sacrifice and jinn worship. Originated during the Jazatāh Era, when two angels taught magick to humanity as a Divine test.

Jazatāh Era: An ancient era when tribes from eastern Sajamistan learned black magick, worshipped jinn kings, and conquered the continent before the Heavenly Birds and the first Eājiz rose to free it

Duxzam: In Sajamistan, a duel sworn under a Heavenly Oath where anything may be wagered, convened by a witness from the Unseen Realm.

Qabl Order: Founded under the Heavenly Raven. Teaches meditation on death, corpses and martyrdom, but with balance through nature.

1000 Wings of Crane Monastic School: Founded under the Heavenly Crane. Teaches meditation and harmony with Brother-Nature.

Brother-Nature: Embodiment of Clay and nature: flora, fauna, minerals, poisons and medicines.

Martyrdom: A Heavenly Oath to unlock full Heavenly Energy at the cost of one's life.

Sage Arts (Sageism): Techniques allowing non-Eājiz monks to commune through the Veil for knowledge. Once abused by the Jazatāh tribes.

Heart of the Soul: A mysterious core of one's essence.

The Veil: The boundary between the Seen and Unseen worlds.

Seen World: The physical, human world.

Unseen Realm: Realm of jinn-folk and Veiled forces.

Heavens: A psychospiritual realm between Paradise and the Hells and other realms.

barzakh: The world of souls, a realm where souls dwell before judgement and afterlife.

Jinn Wars: Ancient wars between jinn tribes before the Divine sent angels to sweep them into the hinterlands behind the Unseen realm.

Spring of Heavens: A nourishing affinity tied to the world's nourishment.

nūr: Pure, cosmic light from the Heavens. It is the essence from which angels are made and a source of truth and clarity.

kahvah: A traditional hot tea beverage without milk.

halva: A sweet dessert made from sesame or semolina flour and sugar.

non: A flatbread baked in stone ovens, with region-specific quill inscriptions.

threading: An ink tradition using plants and milk to dye regional motifs. Gold represents the Camel Road tribes; black, blue and red the outer empires and courtly titles.

Flood Festival: Commemoration of the day Nuh departed the ark after the Great Flood.

saktab: A strategic game played on a sand-grain-divided board where players capture territory.

bone-stone: A dense, pale material forged from crushed animal bone and stone, used in Sajamistan for buildings, jewellery and ceremonial objects.

Acknowledgements

First, I am grateful to the Most High, the Most Generous. Truly I do not deserve the privilege of being a writer; who am I to even dare put words to paper. I hope I can live up to a fraction of that burden.

To Paige who plucked this from the slush pile, gave me hope, and stood by me amongst everything. I am truly blessed to have a badass advocate like you. You've literally changed my life.

Vicky Leech Mateos, you gave this book its home, its chance; amongst some noise from people who didn't mean well, I was scared. But what I valued most was your unwavering support in my character, principles, steadfast belief in my honesty, and most importantly this book. Thank you for your empathy and courage. I am blessed to work with your genius; you transformed Khamilla's story! To Katy Follain, who was so enthusiastic giving this book a home at Bloomsbury UK. To Aine Feeney, and Fabrice Wilmann your editorial support was so monumental. Sharona Selby, you copy-editor extraordinaire, I love our coffees. Charlotte Phillips, Holly Minter, Abigail Walton, Ben Chisnall, Joe Roche, Lucie Moody, Mariafrancesca Ierace, and the entire Bloomsbury UK team, I am so fortunate to work with you. Mikaela Roasa, Eden Railsback, Jennifer Lambert, Lauren Ridgewell, Neil Wadhwa, Dori Carlson, Natalie Meditsky, and the rest of Harper Collins Canada and Hanover Press in the US, thank you for being amazing teams.

Emily Varga, I get emotional thinking about how you've stood by me from the first day I decided to take my writing more seriously. From debuting, to running a whole podcast together – you are not a friend, but a sister. The same way Khamilla found family, I found a family with the people who became more than just online writing friends. Thank you for inspiring me, for being loyal, even at times when I am scared, and can't find it in me to speak, you become my voice against all of the noise.

Brighton, you are equally to blame for the people I unalived in part 1 of this book. Thank you for helping me kill off more characters!

June Hur, you are a remarkable friend, supporter, and critique partner; I love our history sessions. Umairah, my first reader, you were always Khamilla's fan from day one. Hanna, my Oxbridge sis, Paris feels like my second home because of our shenanigans, sharing academic theories, coffee shop hopping, and doing everything in between. To Chinelo, you are my sister, always; I love you. Vaishnavi, your kindness has powered me through every hurdle. I am forever grateful that you slid into my DMs because we were the only brown writers. Gigi, Michelle, Tanvi, Birukti, Tigest, Arushi, Maha, Ehigbor, Sarah Underwood, Deborah, thank you for your constant support.

Sami, Chandra, Gigi, Angel, Kate Dylan, Maiga, Kat, Victor, Hugh, Anna, Avione, Bri, Amanda, Cate Baumer, Lindsay, and the entire PitchForks slack, my rocks from day 1. George too, you are a saving grace; thanks for being my hustle partner.

Vaneezeh, Fatima, Amna, Dania: you taught me what a Muslim community is. Sidrah and Asmaa, you unhinged sisters. Alhamdulillah for selfless sisters like you. And Sidrah for literally being my twin. To baby Zak, I am blessed to be your khala; your presence changed my life.

To my Oxford Union squad, thanks for wasting my time but giving me five books worth of plot and characterisation, you crazy machiavellian politicians. My professor at Oxford, Dr. Michael Rochlitz, our nerding out on Russian, Chinese, Caucasus and Central Asian history, politics; and of course books, and chess is so fascinating! It was truly a student and supervisor match meant to be. To Dr. Dylan Clark, you probably don't know that I'm an author, but your courses to this day shaped my values: to never abuse knowledge, to seek it but to understand its responsibility, and use it in a way that can help the world, one small change at a time. To St Antony's College and the Bodleian libraries for being a second home whilst I edited this chonker.

To my mama and dada, you taught me hard work, unconditional love, laughter, and FOOD. Alhamdullilah. Though you cannot understand my books, you always support me! Even my goat farm.

Finally, to any reader who picked up this book: hate it or love it, it's a privilege. You don't know how much it means to a writer to have someone read their work. It's the biggest honour. May we have a world free from oppression: free Palestine, Kashmir, Sudan, the Uyghurs. Ameen.

A Note on the Author

Sarah Mughal Rana is a Muslim author of stories with touches of magic including being the acclaimed author of *Hope Ablaze*. Outside of writing, she is an MPhil student at the University of Oxford, exploring the intersection of economic policy and human rights. Beyond the page, Sarah co-hosts *On The Write Track* podcast, where she spills the tea with bestselling authors. Her short fiction has appeared in a number of fantasy and contemporary romance anthologies. When she's not writing, you can find her diving into historical rabbit holes or honing her skills in traditional martial arts.